Hope from Acorn Hill

Hope from Acorn Hill

MELODY CARLSON

Guideposts

New York, New York

Hope from Acorn Hill

ISBN: 987-0-8249-4915-0

Published by Guideposts
16 East 34th Street
New York, New York 10016
www.guideposts.org

Hidden History by Melody Carlson © 2003 by Guideposts.
Winter Wonders by Melody Carlson © 2004 by Guideposts.

Distributed by Ideals Publications, a Guideposts company
2630 Elm Hill Pike, Suite 100
Nashville, TN 37214

Cover Illustration by Deborah Chabrian
Interior Design by Marisa Jackson
Typeset by Müllerhaus Publishing Group | www.mullerhaus.net

Printed and bound in the United States of America
10 9 8 7 6 5 4 3 2 1

GRACE CHAPEL INN

A place where one can be
refreshed and encouraged,
a place of hope and healing,
a place where God is at home.

Hidden History

Chapter One

*T*he day was clear and sunny, and a crisp breeze rustled the leaves of the big maple tree in front of the large Victorian house. Alice Howard breathed deeply as she strolled up the walkway, pausing to admire her sister Jane's terra-cotta pots, now spilling over with chrysanthemums in a rich array of russets, reds and golds. Alice could feel autumn in the air, and she was ready for this long hot summer to come to an end. It was still a bit early, but she looked forward to things like leaves crunching underfoot and steaming mugs of hot cider and orange pumpkins piled by the front door. She sighed with sweet contentment as she walked up the front steps to their wide and welcoming front porch.

"Hello there," called her older sister from the shadows.

"Oh!" Alice jumped in surprise. "Goodness, I didn't even see you there, Louise."

Louise chuckled. "I *thought* you were daydreaming." She patted the swing. "Come sit with me and chat."

Alice had barely set her bag down and joined Louise on the swing before Wendell sprang from the corner and landed on her lap. "Hey, big boy," she crooned. "How are you doing?" She was answered with a contented purring sound as the heavy cat settled himself comfortably in her lap.

"Silly old cat," said Louise as she reached over and scratched his head. "You would think that he would want a cooler place to sleep on a warm afternoon."

"Oh, Wendell's always been a snuggler."

"Care for some lemonade?" asked Louise as she reached for the pitcher and an empty glass.

"That sounds lovely."

Louise handed her the cool glass. "How was work?"

"Pretty busy for the middle of the week," said Alice. "I guess everyone was out trying to enjoy the last of their summer vacations. We had a car wreck involving a family of five, a girl who'd been thrown from a horse, as well as several cases of food poisoning from the Pine Grove youth camp."

"Good grief!" exclaimed Louise. "Were they all right?"

"Yes, thankfully, by the end of the day not one of our patients was in anything worse than fair condition and all appear to be headed toward full recovery."

"Thank goodness for that. Your job is really exciting at times."

Alice smiled. "At times, but mostly it's routine. I'm grateful for that. I can do without days like today."

Louise patted her on the knee. "Well, you should be relieved to know that we will not have any guests until tomorrow. We will all enjoy a nice quiet evening tonight."

"Oh, that sounds good. Where's Jane?" asked Alice. "In her garden?"

"The last I saw she was in the kitchen about knee-deep in lemons."

"Just to make lemonade?"

"Actually, Aunt Ethel dropped off two boxes of lemons this morning. According to her, Lloyd's brother from California showed up with about a 'truckload' of them. Lloyd has been sharing them with everyone in town. Jane started out with lemonade, but that barely made a dent in them." Louise chuckled. "I will say this, the house smells delicious."

"Well, it's a good way to bring summer to an end," said Alice.

"It does feel as if fall is creeping up on us."

Alice leaned her head against the back of the swing and sighed. "Can you believe it's been nearly a year since Father passed away?"

"It does not seem possible."

"It's exactly one year on Friday," Alice said.

"Yes, that is one date I will not forget, but I have never been as good as you with dates."

"Somehow remembering dates has always been easy for me." Alice set down her empty glass. "Even as a little girl I knew everyone's birthday and Mother and Father's anniversary and all sorts of little things. In the last few years Father often relied on me to be his walking calendar." She chuckled. "In fact, I just reminded Pastor Thompson that next Sunday is Grandparents Day. I hope he didn't think I was trying to interfere. Father always liked to give the grandmothers a carnation on that day."

Louise adjusted her glasses as she counted the stitches on her latest knitting project. "Well, I will probably never be the lucky recipient of a Grandparents Day carnation."

Just then the youngest sister stepped out with a plate of lemon squares. "What's this you're complaining about, Louise?" she asked as she set the china plate on the nearby wicker table, nodding an invitation.

"Not being a grandmother," Alice answered for Louise as she reached for a sticky yellow bar. "Oh, Jane, these look lovely."

"I am not complaining," said Louise as she set aside her knitting in exchange for a lemon square. "I just doubt that Cynthia will ever make me a grandmother. Goodness knows I would be thrilled just to see her married and settled down. But, of course, she is a busy career woman, and I think she is waiting for Mr. Right to come along."

"What's wrong with that?" said Jane as she refilled their glasses. "I was older than Cynthia when I married, and sometimes I wish I'd waited a little longer myself."

Alice reached over and patted Jane's hand. "How were you to know things would turn out that way with Justin back then, Jane?"

"That's true enough," said Jane. "But being nearly forty and never married, well, I think maybe I just panicked."

"Panicked?" said Louise with raised brows. "It is hard to imagine your panicking about anything, Jane."

Jane tossed her oldest sister an indulgent smile. "Oh, sure, I probably come across as in control most of the time, especially if I have a lot of confidence in an area, cooking or gardening, for instance."

"Or decorating or art," added Alice.

"But when it comes to romance..." Jane sadly shook her head. "Well, I'm just not too savvy about things of the heart."

"Maybe it's a family trait," suggested Alice. "It's never been my strongest suit either."

"Well, speak for yourself," said Louise. "I think I

fared quite well in the love and romance arena. Eliot and I came close to celebrating forty years of blissful marriage before he was called to his eternal reward."

"Blissful?" Jane's brow furrowed slightly. "I can remember a couple of times when you and Eliot weren't even speaking to each other. How about that Christmas back in 1978 when you showed up here by yourself, and Father had to—"

"Oh, we don't need to go back there, Jane." Alice smoothed her hand over Wendell's furry coat. "Perhaps Louise's memories have grown sweeter with the passing of time."

Louise nodded. "Yes, Alice is absolutely right. I probably have forgotten a few unhappy things over the past few years, but for the most part, Eliot and I were quite content together."

"Isn't it interesting that of the three Howard women, only one of us had a happy marriage?" Jane asked.

"Father and Mother had a very happy marriage," said Alice.

"Yes," agreed Louise. "I never saw any other couple more in love than those two."

Jane reached for a second lemon square. "Well, I guess I'll have to take your word for that."

Alice nodded. "It's true, Jane. They were completely

devoted to each other. How Father grieved for Mother after she died. It was no surprise that he never married again."

"And, goodness knows, he had his chances," said Louise.

"That's right," said Alice. "There was a time when it seemed like every widow in Acorn Hill was chasing him."

"Not to mention the divorcées." Louise started to laugh. "Do you remember Mrs. Paulson, Alice?"

"Phoebe Paulson!" Alice slapped her hand over her mouth to suppress her giggles. A frightened Wendell leaped from her lap to the porch. "Oh my, I'd nearly forgotten about her."

"What happened?" asked Jane with eager curiosity.

Both Alice and Louise were laughing so hard that neither of them could speak.

Jane frowned. "Come on, you guys, tell me the story of Mrs. Paulson."

"You tell her," sputtered Alice.

"Where do I start?" Louise pulled out a lace-trimmed handkerchief.

"Was that the lady who worked at the pet shop when I was little?" persisted Jane. "I remember I got a hamster there once, and it died the next day, but she wouldn't give me my money back."

"Yes." Louise nodded as she dabbed her nose with her

handkerchief. "That was probably after the incident with Father. She never did like us much after that."

"It wasn't long after that little incident that she moved away," said Alice.

"What happened?" demanded Jane.

"Well, it was summertime," began Louise. "As I recall, I had recently come home from my first year at college. Alice must have been about sixteen. Apparently Phoebe Paulson had moved into town a few months earlier, and as you said, Jane, she worked at the pet shop."

"The pet shop went out of business later on that year," said Alice.

"Just a coincidence, I am sure," said Louise.

"On with the story," said Jane with increasing impatience.

"Right. Mrs. Paulson had started attending Grace Chapel services in the spring."

"After she noticed what a good-looking widower the pastor was," injected Alice.

"Yes. I am sure that must have influenced her considerably." Louise cleared her throat. "Well, I could tell right from the start that this woman was trouble. She was going for the Marilyn Monroe look. Her hair was bleached platinum blond, and her dresses were so tight that I thought she was going to burst right through the seams."

"She was a bit plump," injected Alice.

"She wore far too much makeup, and her perfume could knock you over if you were downwind from her."

"She drove a brand-new red convertible," said Alice. "I think it was a Pontiac, and I must admit that, at sixteen, I thought it was rather nice."

"Yes, and she liked to park that flashy automobile right in front of our house when she came over for church services," continued Louise.

"She only lived a few blocks away."

"She would slowly get out of her car, making a huge production of it. Then she would strut past our house and toward the church as if she were a famous movie star. I am sure she was hoping to catch Father's eye."

Jane laughed. "And did she?"

"Well, to be honest, I think most of the males in Acorn Hill were aware of her. She was not beautiful—certainly not in the way that Mother had been, but I suppose she was attractive in a flashy way."

"In those days divorce was still a bit of a scandal," added Alice. "But Father, as usual, was gracious and kind to her, and for the most part the congregation followed his example."

"Actually that might have helped to give her the wrong idea," said Louise. "It did not take long for her to start playing the damsel in distress. First it was a flat tire right in front of our house."

"Convenient," said Jane.

"Yes." Louise rolled her eyes. "It was a *puncture*. Even in the summer's heat, Father got down on his knees, still wearing his Sunday suit, and fixed it for her."

"She thanked him by making a coconut cream pie," said Alice, making a face. "Worst pie we'd ever tasted. Crust just like cardboard."

Jane chuckled. "Then what happened?"

"Well, it seemed that Phoebe decided to give a dinner party—to get better acquainted with people from town, she said," continued Louise. "Naturally, she invited Father."

"And?" said Jane.

"Father went." Louise shook her head.

"What was wrong with that?" asked Jane, leaning forward.

"Well, when Father got to Phoebe's there were no other guests."

"Phoebe had this romantic-looking table set for two," said Louise. "Father said she had candles and flowers everywhere."

Jane shook her head in astonishment. "Wow, this woman didn't beat around the bush, did she?"

"Not a bit. Well, Father was back home again within

minutes. The look on his face was absolutely priceless. His hair was all mussed up and his bowtie was crooked." Louise began laughing.

"Did he tell you what had happened?" asked Jane.

Louise stifled her laughter. "Actually, the first thing he said was to get him an ice pack."

"An ice pack?" Jane looked confused.

"Apparently, he had been making some sort of excuse to Phoebe about why he could not stay for dinner after all. Knowing Father's sense of integrity, he was probably trying to come up with something that was actually true. Well, as he was backing up, he ran up against an ottoman and toppled backward, thumping his head on a coffee table. He had a nice little lump too."

Jane was giggling now. "Oh, I can just imagine that. Poor Father."

"So I fixed him an ice pack and insisted that he tell me the whole story." Louise's face grew stern with the memory. "After hearing what had happened, I was completely out-raged at that silly woman. While Father was out of earshot, I telephoned her and gave her a serious piece of my mind."

"You didn't!" said Jane.

"I most certainly did." Louise firmly nodded her head.

Now Jane glanced over to where Alice was quietly listening. "Where were you when all this took place?"

"I'd gone out with friends that night," said Alice.

"Where was I?" asked Jane.

"You were so little that we'd already put you to bed."

"Always missing out on the good stuff." Jane sighed and then continued her questioning. "How did Father feel about everything? I mean he was such a dignified gentleman, not to mention a respected pastor...why, I'm sure he must've felt silly."

Louise nodded. "At first, he seemed confused, and I thought perhaps it was a result of the blow to his head. But later on that evening, I found him sitting in his den looking so dejected."

"Poor Father," said Jane.

"I went in and talked to him about it some more. He felt guilty, as if he had somehow led that brazen woman on. I assured him that some women were just like that and that he must not blame himself one little bit." Louise smiled. "It turned out to be one of our best father-daughter chats ever. I hugged him and told him that I was proud to have him as my father. Then I confessed what I had said over the phone. I felt certain he would be disappointed with me. I knew it was not a very Christian way to behave. And, goodness gracious, I was a minister's daughter."

"So, how did he react?"

"Well, he just threw back his head and laughed.

Honestly, I do not think I had ever heard him laugh so hard. Then he grew sober and thanked me, but he also made me promise to forgive her, as well as not repeat the events of the evening to anyone."

"But it was too late," said Alice. "I had just come home and heard Father laughing in the den. So I popped my head in and insisted upon hearing what was so funny. We sat in the kitchen until fairly late that night, enjoying a good laugh over ice cream and berries."

"And I slept through the whole thing?" Jane looked dismayed.

"Oh, Jane, you were only about four or five—too young to understand something like that. If it makes you feel any better, you are now the only other one, besides us, who knows the whole silly story," said Louise with a firm nod. "Even Aunt Ethel never heard about this."

"That's right," agreed Alice. "I suppose we should keep it that way."

Jane grinned, then winked. "Don't worry. The family's scandalous secret is perfectly safe with me."

Louise waved her hand. "Phooey, Jane, the Howard family does not have any scandalous secrets."

Jane's eyebrows lifted mysteriously. "Oh, every family has its secrets, Louise. They just don't realize it until they stumble over them."

Chapter Two

$\mathcal{M}$ ore than ever before, Alice looked forward to her days off from the hospital. While she loved her work and was devoted to her job, having her sisters at home and an inn to run had made her time off much more interesting than it had been.

Guests would be arriving by noon and there was much to be done before then. To Louise's pleased surprise, all four guest rooms were booked throughout the weekend. Alice thought perhaps it was a blessing that Vera, afraid that she was coming down with the flu, had called early in the morning to cancel their usual walk.

"Goodness, I hope it's not that horrible end-of-summer flu that's been going around," Alice had told her best friend. "Make sure to drink lots of fluids and get plenty of rest."

"Shall I take two aspirins and call you in the morning too?"

"This is the morning," Alice had reminded her, laughing, and then hung up the phone.

Jane came down the stairs wearing her running shoes and sweats, her hair pulled back in a neat ponytail. Alice thought, not for the first time, how her fifty-year-old sister could almost pass for a college coed, if one did not look too closely at the tiny sets of crow's-feet that crinkled the edges of her clear blue eyes.

"I feel guilty," said Alice. "You're going running, and I didn't even walk this morning."

"That's too bad." Jane grinned. "You could always go with me."

Alice firmly shook her head. "It's one thing for me to walk several times a week, but I'm afraid jogging would play havoc with these joints of mine. Besides, I thought I might use this extra time to get an early start on things this morning. How about if I begin gathering some blooms for your floral arrangements?"

"That'd be wonderful, Alice." Jane leaned over to stretch her calves on the stairs. "Aren't the roses looking spectacular these days?"

Alice nodded. "I've never seen them so magnificent. Don't worry, Jane, I'll be careful to put them straight into water just as quickly as I cut them so they don't wilt."

"Oh, I know you will, Alice. You've become a real expert at cutting blooms."

"Thanks to your helpful instructions." Alice bent

down to straighten the hallway runner. "Want me to start a pot of coffee too?"

"Oh, you're an angel." Jane was jogging in place now and Alice could tell she was eager to begin her morning workout.

"Enjoy!" called Alice with a wave of her hand. Then she went off in search of the flower bucket and cutting shears.

The yard and garden truly did look splendid—better than it had since Alice's childhood, when her mother lovingly tended the garden. Even so, Alice realized it was only a matter of time before the first autumnal frost would change everything, and not long after they would be entrenched in winter. In the meantime, she was thankful simply to enjoy the end of summer. Taking time to actually smell the fragrant roses as she cut, Alice recalled how different this all had looked before Jane took charge. Alice had not paid much attention to the yard back then as there were too many other things that demanded her attention—her full-time job, taking care of her father, church-related responsibilities and just the everyday chores of living.

Alice vividly remembered the way she had seen the garden exactly a year before, the day her father had died. Although bright and sunny, the day had seemed gloomy. After attending to the details of her father's funeral, she had walked through this same garden and looked sadly at the beds overgrown with weeds and the brown patches of lawn, scorched by summer's heat and lack of water. She had felt guilty and depressed as she had observed its neglect.

But now to witness firsthand the amazing results of Jane's restoration efforts, to gaze upon the greenery and the colorful blooms and the fresh garden produce, well, it seemed nothing short of a miracle—as did their life together at Grace Chapel Inn. Indeed, Alice had much to be thankful for.

Wendell sashayed up to her with his tail held high as he rubbed himself against her legs, back and forth, before he contentedly settled down in a sunny spot and stretched himself out to take full advantage of the warmth and enjoy a sunbath.

Alice smiled at the silly cat and, despite the anniversary the day marked, she resolved to be happy. She would rejoice over a life well lived. She truly believed that death was merely a transition into the next stage and that it was nothing to fear. So, as she cut the full blooms and quickly slipped them into the cutting bucket of cool water, Alice expressed her sincere thanks to God.

"Dear heavenly Father, You are the blessed Redeemer of all things," she prayed. "And I thank You for how You have breathed Your life and love into this old house and garden. I also thank You for my dear sisters, and I pray Your blessing on the guests who will be arriving here today. I ask that You will refresh them during their visit with us. Amen."

Soon her bucket was overflowing with flowers. Alice took them into the kitchen and set them on the maple counter by the deep soapstone sink. She knew that Jane was the true artist when it came to floral arrangements, or anything artistic for that matter, but Alice felt the roses looked perfectly lovely just as they were, hither and thither, in the rusty old bucket.

She washed her hands and began making coffee. Being a dyed-in-the-wool tea drinker, Alice had not developed a taste for coffee, but her sisters both enjoyed a cup or two in the morning. Naturally Jane bought only the best whole beans to be ground daily. Alice had to admit that she appreciated the aroma of the freshly ground coffee and even sampled the dark bitter stuff from time to time, when she was feeling adventuresome, but it simply was not her "cup of tea."

"Ah," said Louise from behind her, "that smells lovely, Alice."

"Good morning," said Alice brightly. "Isn't it a beautiful day?"

Louise looked curiously at Alice. "Have you forgotten what day it is?"

Alice smiled. "You mean Father?"

Louise's brow lifted slightly. "Yes. Are you all right?"

Alice nodded. "I was just thinking about him. I know I was broken up last year about losing him, but now when I think of him it's only with happy memories and thankfulness."

Louise looked relieved. "Oh, I am so glad. I did not want this to be a day of grief." She poured herself a cup of steaming coffee. "You know, on the one-year anniversary of Eliot's death, I was not nearly as composed as you are today. To be perfectly honest I was a bit of a wreck that day."

"Well, that was different." Alice poured hot water from the teakettle into her favorite porcelain teapot and replaced the lid. "Eliot was younger than Father, and you two had hoped to enjoy your golden years together."

"Yes, that is true. Even though Eliot was quite a bit older than I, I had expected him to live to be an old man. I felt cheated to lose him so soon."

Alice poured tea into her cup and joined Louise at the table. "I'm sure it was difficult for you, Louise, but you seemed so strong. I guess I had no idea it hit you so hard. I'm sorry."

Louise smiled. "Oh, I wanted people to think I was strong. I wanted my sorrow to be private. In retrospect I realize that I made a mistake trying to appear so in control." Louise sighed, then smiled and asked, "Now, what shall we fix for breakfast?"

They had just sat down to hearty bowls of oatmeal with cinnamon and currants when Jane came in the back door. She was still puffing and red-cheeked from her run. "Anything left?" she asked, slightly breathlessly as she refilled her water bottle from the sink faucet, wiped her brow and enjoyed a long swig.

"Yes, we made plenty," said Louise. "We felt like celebrating September with a pot of oatmeal. We used your special recipe."

"Good for you," said Jane. "I think I'll grab a quick shower first and reheat it when I'm done."

"I'll freshen the linens in the bathrooms upstairs," offered Alice. "Louise said the beds are already made up."

"I've got a fresh batch of chocolates in the pantry," said Jane, "if you want to take some of them up while you're at it."

After breakfast was finished, Alice went from room to room, happily arranging fresh towels as she admired the welcoming look of the four unique rooms. Who would not be comfortable here? She carefully set one of Jane's homemade chocolates wrapped in gold foil in the center of each downy soft pillow. The small gesture was something their guests really appreciated. She and her sisters had decided early on that Grace Chapel Inn would be known for small, loving details, like fresh flowers in every room, sheets of the finest percale (line-dried in the summer) and the crystal bowl in the dining room that was always filled with fresh fruit for the guests to enjoy. Then, of course, there were Louise's impromptu piano concerts, the occasional special tea and Jane's fabulous breakfasts. The sisters believed that it would only be a matter of time before they had a waiting list a year in advance.

Alice plumped the tapestry pillow in the easy chair as she gave the last room, her parents' old room, a final inspection. As usual, everything looked absolutely perfect. Sometimes she wondered if her parents could look down from heaven and see what their three daughters had accomplished together in their family home. Did they like what had been done to their old bedroom? Surely her mother would appreciate the garden theme, and her father had always been fond of green. She hoped that it made them as happy as it had made their daughters. She adjusted a slightly crooked picture on the wall, and then, satisfied that all was in order, Alice left to go back downstairs.

"We just had a cancellation," announced Louise from the little office tucked beneath the staircase.

"That's too bad. Did they say why?"

"It was the Mosleys from Lancaster. Mrs. Mosley explained to me that their oldest daughter just went into labor this morning. She is three weeks early and they feel they cannot possibly leave now."

"Well, that's understandable. Will we refund their deposit?"

Louise frowned. "You know our policy, Alice."

"But isn't this a medical emergency?" protested Alice. "Don't we have an exception for that?"

"Well, it is not their own medical emergency." Louise turned back to the computer with straight shoulders.

"But it's their daughter, Louise. Imagine if it were Cynthia."

Louise shook her head, then turned back around. "Yes, I suppose you are right." A slightly exasperated smile crossed her lips. "Oh, you are so much like Father, Alice Christine."

"Well, I'll take that as a compliment."

"All done upstairs?"

"Everything is set."

Louise glanced at her watch. "And with time to spare. What do you plan to do today?"

Alice shrugged. "Actually, I don't have any firm plans. Is there anything I could help with around here?"

"Well, Jane did say that we need to clear out the laundry room. We have been using those shelves in there as a catchall, and it is starting to look rather shabby."

"Shall I begin sorting through it?"

"Oh, would you mind?"

"It's not my favorite kind of chore, but it does need doing."

"And you are so good at organizing, Alice."

Alice laughed. "That's because I'm the only one of the three of us who doesn't mind throwing things away."

"Indeed!" Louise's eyebrows shot up.

"Don't worry. I promise to set aside anything that I'm uncertain about so that you and Jane can both check it out. Okay?"

"That's perfect. Now I need to get back to these e-mails. It is so handy the way Jane has got us hooked up to that bed-and-breakfast website now, but I keep forgetting to check the messages, and they can pile up fairly quickly. I am sure that it has been at least three days since I last looked."

Alice went out to the laundry room. It was a small,

enclosed space that had once been part of the back porch, but it had been used as a laundry for as long as Alice could remember. She even remembered the original washing machine—well, original to her. It was a big white and aqua tub with an agitator and a wringer consisting of what resembled a pair of giant wooden rolling pins. When the clothing had been washed and rinsed, her mother would carefully load the clothing, piece by piece, into the jaws of the wringer.

"Never put your fingers in here," her mother had warned Alice on more than one occasion as she had stood by to watch the fascinating process. "Your fingers would get squashed flatter than pancakes." Then Alice would beg to hear, once again, about the time her mother had gotten her long brown braid caught in a diaper that was going through this intimidating machine.

"Well, it was shortly after Louise was born," her mother would tell her. "I was still quite new at being a mommy and a housewife. One morning I realized that all of Louise's diapers were dirty, so I ran downstairs in my nightgown thinking I would quickly wash a load of diapers before the baby woke up." This is where Alice would laugh: How funny it was to think of her big sister, Louise, wearing diapers. Then she would quiet down and wait for the rest of the story.

"Naturally I had not had a chance to put my hair up, and as I was putting the clean diapers through the wringer, I somehow got the tip of my long braid mixed in with the diapers. I suppose I was putting them through rather fast. Well..." Her big eyes would always grow bigger at this part. "The next thing I knew my hair was being pulled right into that ornery wringer. I cried out for help but knew there was no time to waste. I could not reach the off switch and my head was getting closer and closer to the wringer. And it just kept pulling. So, holding onto my braid, I stretched as far as I could with my right foot" —at this point, she would pause to illustrate how this could actually be done— "and I kicked wildly, trying to knock that cord out of the wall. I am sure that I was praying too. I had no desire to be scalped by this stubborn washing machine, not to mention being discovered down here in my nightgown. Thankfully I was able to get the electrical cord loose and I managed to escape with my hair intact. Father and I had a good laugh about it afterwards. And from that day on, I have always made certain that my hair is safely pinned up and I am fully dressed before I attempt to do the laundry."

Alice smiled at the memory. The wringer washer was long gone, and in its place were a modern washer and dryer. But as Alice looked around the room she could see Jane's point. The room was overdue for some serious organization. So she gathered boxes and trash bags and began to dig in.

"What's going on in here?" demanded a shrill voice that Alice knew belonged to Ethel.

"Hi, Aunt Ethel," she said as she peered up from behind a stack of boxes.

"*Tsk-tsk*. What an awful mess," said Ethel. "What on earth are you trying to do here?"

Alice looked around the chaos she had created and sighed. "Well, sometimes you have to make a mess before you can bring something back to order."

"Yes, that's true, but it looks perfectly awful now."

"I was just thinking about how Mother would be out here using the old wringer," Alice said, changing the subject.

"Yes, when you and Louise were little ones, that wringer got a lot of use," said Ethel. "I can still remember I was visiting when Daniel enclosed the laundry for Madeleine. I was only a girl, but I thought it was a bit pretentious to have an *enclosed* laundry room." She laughed. "I thought my brother was probably turning into a snob."

"Really?" said Alice.

"Naturally, I was wrong. Dear Daniel didn't have a snooty bone in his body. But having grown up without

such luxuries as enclosed laundry rooms or electric refrig-
erators on our little farm in Englishtown, I wasn't too
sure about these highfalutin ways. Of course, I knew that
Madeleine had been raised in a well-to-do family and I
guessed that she expected Daniel to continue along that
same line."

"Are you saying my mother was pretentious?" asked
Alice with a slight arch to her brows. It was not often
that Alice felt defensive, but she could bristle if anyone
criticized her parents.

Ethel looked up at the ceiling. She seemed to be carefully considering her answer—a very unusual act for the
older woman. Finally she spoke. "I would never say that
Madeleine was pretentious," she said slowly. "She was a
generous and kindhearted woman." She paused, somewhat dramatically, before she continued. "But, she did
have a certain way about her that could have easily been
mistaken for, well, how should I say it? Perhaps *putting on
airs* would best describe it."

Alice felt her jaw tighten. "I only had the privilege of
knowing Mother for twelve years, Aunt Ethel, but I never
saw her do anything that slightly resembled 'putting on
airs.'" Alice forced a smile. "But maybe I understand what
you're talking about. Mother had a certain panache. She
was a beautiful woman with the kind of style that turned

heads. Even as a girl I could see that. In fact, I think Jane has the same thing, but I would never in a million years call that sort of style 'putting on airs' any more than I would call a beautiful rose proud or pretentious."

Ethel seemed to consider this. "Perhaps you're right, Alice." She ran her finger over the dusty windowsill and frowned. "And perhaps you're right about this room needing a thorough cleaning too. I suppose I simply hadn't noticed. Now, don't let me keep you. I only stopped by to see if Jane would sell me a box of her wonderful bonbons. Lloyd was just saying how much he adores them. And Wilhelm's shop was completely out this morning."

"She just made a fresh batch of chocolate truffles yesterday," said Alice.

"Oh, goody." Ethel clapped her hands together like a little girl, and Alice turned back to her sorting. Alice suspected that Lloyd Tynan would not be the only one to be enjoying Jane's chocolate truffles before the day was over.

By noon Alice had managed to clear out the shelves and fill a number of boxes, some for the trash and others for the attic. One box she set aside for further investigation. It was an old hatbox that Fred Humbert had discovered while renovating the rectory several months earlier. The work had been done to make a home for their new pastor, but Pastor Thompson had surprised everyone by offering it to the assistant pastor, Henry Ley, and his wife Patsy, after they lost their own home in a storm. Alice still smiled to herself every time she thought of it. That was probably the first day when she fully accepted the pastor as the man who might one day fill her father's shoes. Certainly he was young and did things differently from the way her father would have done them, but she sensed that the two men had the same sort of heart.

Finally, she wiped down the painted shelves and removed the last of the cobwebs and stood back to admire her work. The room really did look rather nice in an old-fashioned way.

"Want any lunch, Alice?" called Jane from the kitchen door.

"Sounds good." Alice pushed a stray strand of hair from her eyes as she set the broom back into the broom closet.

"Whoa, Alice!" cried Jane as she stepped onto the porch and looked into the small space. "What have you done?"

"Oh, I hope it's okay. Louise said—"

"It's not okay, Alice." Jane gave her a funny look. "It's *fantastic*." Jane studied the room. "Maybe I'll paint those shelves a nice sage green." She fingered the old curtains. "And I think these could stand to be replaced."

Alice glanced around. "You know it could be rather sweet out here with the right touches."

"It's going to look great. I can see it now." Jane nodded with enthusiasm. "But, honestly, Alice, I never would've felt inspired to fix it up if you hadn't cleared it out first."

"Then we're a good team. Now what's this I hear about lunch?"

"Nothing special, just a turkey and apple salad and some potato rolls..."

"That sounds special to me. Just let me wash up."

"What's that?" asked Jane as she pointed to the hatbox.

"It's something Fred found in the rectory. We were so busy at the time that I just stuck it back here and forgot all about it. I took a peek just now and it looks like some papers of Father's. I didn't want to throw them out. I thought I might go through them more carefully later."

Alice picked up the box. "Who knows, they might even contain some of those old family secrets you were warning us about."

Jane laughed. "Yes, I'm sure it's just full of them. Maybe Father even wrote his own account of that silly incident with that old Phoebe Paulson. Now, there's a story I'd like to read in his own words."

Chapter Three

*I*t was not until later that evening that Alice had time to open the box of her father's old papers. The day had been extremely busy with the arrival of three couples and one single. Louise had even managed to fill the room left empty by the cancellation. A couple who had e-mailed earlier that week about staying at the inn to celebrate their thirtieth anniversary was thrilled to learn of the cancellation. Jane had made a special chocolate torte for the occasion, and the couple, several of the other guests and the three sisters had gathered in the parlor to enjoy an impromptu celebration that evening. Alice thought it was sweet when the husband, Dirk Winston, made a little speech about the summer he and his wife had become engaged.

"It was toward the end of the Vietnam era, but the war machinery was still going strong. I'd just been drafted into the army," he said. "I was only nineteen and feeling pretty scared at the time. Of course, I don't think I admitted this to anyone back then. Guys just didn't talk like that in those days. It wasn't macho. Still, I felt it was my duty to go." He turned and smiled at his wife. "Anyway, all through high school I'd had a secret crush on this cute redheaded girl, but I was such a shy guy that I could never ask her out. Then one day I was working at the counter at my dad's appliance store, and Marsha walked in and came straight up to the counter. When I asked if I could help her, she asked if it was true that I had been drafted. I told her yes."

Marsha laughed now. "So I looked him straight in the eye and said, 'Dirk Winston, you cannot possibly go off to that horrible war without taking me out on a date first.'"

He smiled. "Of course, I agreed, but I told her that I only had three weeks before I had to leave for boot camp in the Midwest."

"Well, we made the most of those three weeks," she continued for him. "Dirk actually got up the nerve to propose to me the night before he left."

He grinned shyly as he took her hand in his. "And, well, the rest is history."

They all visited some more. Alice felt certain that the Winstons were enjoying their anniversary, but she also sensed they were ready for some alone time. She helped to wind down the party by excusing herself to go to bed. The others followed suit. Still weary from her cleaning spree, Alice slipped upstairs and took a quick shower, then put on her pink-and-white-striped cotton pajamas before she flopped down on her bed and stared at the hatbox that was waiting on her night table. Wendell made himself comfortable next to her and purred loudly as she gently scratched his belly.

It was late, but she was eager to see the contents of the box. Gently nudging Wendell aside, she reached for it and set it in the center of her bed, then removed the lid. She began to carefully examine the contents piece by piece. She sorted through a pile of college papers and a stack of old sermons. Although other people might think these papers worthless, Alice did not. They were windows to her father's early life. When she reached the bottom of the box, she breathed in sharply. There lay a very old-looking journal with an old black silk tie wrapped around it. She reverently removed it from the box, undid the tie and examined the burgundy cover. The heavy cardboard was tattered and bent around the edges. Written across the cover in neat penmanship that she recognized as a youthful version of her father's was the title *The Private Journal of Daniel Joseph Howard, 1925–1927*. Alice figured that her father must have been about fifteen at the beginning of the journal, and around seventeen by the time he finished it—three precious years of his adolescent life. She could not imagine what her father might have been like as a boy. He had seldom spoken of his youth. To her, he had always been a fully grown man, dignified and mannerly, but quick to smile or laugh at a joke. Mostly she had simply thought of him as her father, as well as the respected pastor of Grace Chapel.

Excited, she put on her reading glasses and opened the slightly musty journal. Flipping through it, she saw that both sides of the pages were filled with even lines of both pen and pencil writing. There were even a few drawings—nature sketches and some sort of mechanical diagrams here and there.

She turned to the first page and started to read.

> *Growing up in Englishtown, Pennsylvania, could influence a young man to do one of two things. It could make him want to settle down and make his home here for good, or it could make him want to turn his back and simply walk away. As for me, I plan to leave this place and never look back—*

Alice was startled by a quiet knock on her door. Setting the book aside she got up to answer it and found Jane standing out in the hallway in her long nightgown.

"Are you okay?" asked Jane.

"Yes, I'm fine. Why?" asked Alice.

"You just looked weird, like you'd seen a ghost or something."

Alice put her hand on her chest and gave a little laugh. "Well, maybe I have. I found Father's boyhood journal in that box from the laundry room, and I was just reading it. Your knock startled me, but I'm perfectly fine."

"I'm sorry. I saw your light on and wondered if I could borrow a nail file. I just snapped a nail off and I can't find my file anywhere."

"Of course. Come in."

Jane followed Alice into the room, leaving the door open behind her. Then Alice began looking through her top bureau drawer for her small, leather manicure kit.

"Is this Father's journal?" asked Jane as she picked up the worn old book.

Louise poked her head in the door. "Sorry to interrupt, but did Jane say something about Father's journal?"

"That's right," said Alice as she handed Jane the manicure kit.

"I didn't know Father had a journal." Louise's expression looked as if she had been banned from some special party.

Alice motioned for her older sister to come in. "I rescued this box from the laundry room today, and I was just going through it now to see if it held anything of interest."

"Have you read it yet?" asked Jane.

"I barely started the first entry." She frowned slightly.

"What's wrong?" asked Jane.

"Oh, I don't know. I guess the beginning caught me a bit off guard."

"Why?" asked Louise with interest. "What did it say?"

Alice looked at her two sisters, obviously ready for bed themselves. Louise had on her pale blue robe. Streaks of cold cream still showed on her cheeks. "Well, I could read it to you, if you like. Although it is getting late...."

"Not too late for me," said Jane. "I was going to start a new mystery tonight, but now you've got me curious about this mystery."

"I am not ready to go to sleep either," said Louise.

Alice motioned to her bed and easy chair. "Go ahead and get comfortable."

Her two sisters sat down, Louise in the chair and Jane Indian-style on the bed. Alice put on her reading glasses and began to reread the opening paragraph aloud. When she came to the statement about leaving Englishtown for good, she paused. "Doesn't that sound a bit odd?" She glanced at her sisters from over the top of her reading glasses and waited for them to respond.

Louise nodded. "Yes, it does not sound like Father. It sounds as if he wanted to run away from something."

"He was only fifteen at the time," Jane pointed out. "Perhaps he'd gotten into some sort of scrape."

"Maybe," said Alice doubtfully. "It's hard to imagine Father doing anything that would get him into any kind of serious trouble."

"Well, read on," insisted Louise. "Do not just leave us hanging here."

So Alice continued.

Now some folks might think that sounds a bit harsh or ungrateful, but many people in my town are quick to judge me by my family, or by my name, or even by my appearance. This is a heavy burden for a young man to bear.

"Goodness," said Louise. "That sounds very sad. I had no idea that Father had sorrow like that in his life."

"Do you really know anything about his life?" asked Alice. "I mean prior to his going to college and seminary and marrying Mother?"

Louise frowned. "I do not. Father never talked much about his family. Oh, I knew he grew up in Englishtown and that his parents had died young. But other than that..."

"Go on, Alice," urged Jane. "This is interesting. Please, read some more."

My ninth grade English teacher, Mr. Dolton, has encouraged me to keep a journal as a way of understanding some of the hardships life has dealt me. I am not sure that it will help much or change anything, but I respect Mr. Dolton and am willing to try.

"I do remember Father's mentioning Mr. Dolton," said Louise suddenly.

"Yes," said Alice. "Father always spoke highly of him. I think they remained friends right up until the time Mr. Dolton passed on."

Alice adjusted her reading glasses.

I have also come to believe that I may have a true affinity for words, and Mr. Dolton heartily agrees with me on this. I like the way words appear on a clean white sheet of paper and I love the way they sound when spoken by someone with correct pronunciation. I have a dictionary, given to me by Mr. Dolton, and I enjoy looking up and practicing new words. Unfortunately, this irritates my father. He has little respect for words or for education for that matter. He firmly believes that eight years of school should be "plenty good 'nough for any Howard boy."

"Oh my," Louise said, "I never knew that Grandfather Howard was like *that*. Father never said a word—"

"Maybe that's why," Jane interjected. "Maybe his father embarrassed him."

My father never finished the fourth grade himself and is quite proud of it. Of course, he does not see any correlation (my new word for the day) between his lack of education and his financial, not to mention social, standing within our community. In fact, his response to a disparaging comment or reproachful glance is to simply insult whoever dispenses it. It is not that our community is so terribly mean-spirited or disapproving. My father invites much of the harsh criticism he receives by letting his small farm get more and more run-down and by not seeing to the most basic needs of his family. I am also sure it is of little help that he remains quite friendly with the local ne'er-do-wells and imbibes bootlegged libations upon occasion, although I am not certain that this latter habit is common knowledge throughout our small community—

"My goodness!" said Louise, slapping her hand over her mouth.

"This is rich," said Jane, suppressing laughter. "Our grandfather hung out with bootleggers."

"No," corrected Louise, "it only says that he imbibed bootlegged libations occasionally."

"Well, isn't that something?"

"Indeed." Louise sadly shook her head.

"Oh," said Alice, closing the journal, "perhaps we shouldn't be reading this."

"I don't see why not," Jane said. "It is part of our family history. If Father wanted it kept top secret, he would've destroyed the journal long ago."

"Perhaps." Alice considered this. "I do not know...." Louise frowned. "I am not sure what I think about this."

"What *can* you think?" asked Jane. "It's not as if we have any choice about who our ancestors are or what they may or may not have done, Louise. Look at it this way: We got lucky on the Berry side. As far as we know, they were outstanding and accomplished citizens. So maybe the Howard side does have a few skeletons, or embarrassing secrets. Maybe that's just how life balances out sometimes."

"Besides," added Alice, "it certainly didn't harm Father. He grew up to be a wonderful man, loved and respected by all who knew him." She shook her head in astonishment. "Not a bit like his father...apparently."

"I find this all rather, well, shocking," said Louise.

Jane gently poked her in the arm. "Oh, Louie, does it embarrass you to learn that your heritage isn't quite as genteel as you'd thought?"

"It is not that, Jane." Louise stood up, folding her arms across her chest.

"Well, I can understand how you both feel," said Alice soothingly. "While I do think it's rather interesting to find out that our grandfather was, shall we say, less than a wholesome character, it is a little disturbing too."

"Well, maybe that is enough reading for tonight," said Louise as she went toward the door.

"But it was just getting so interesting," said Jane stubbornly. "Do you mind if Alice and I continue to read without you?"

Louise stopped and turned. "Well...I would really like to hear more too."

"I have an idea," said Alice. "It is late tonight, and we should keep it quiet up here for the sake of our guests down below. How about we make a date for tomorrow evening, say seven thirty. We can meet in Father's library and read from his journal for an hour. How does that sound?"

Louise nodded. "That sounds quite nice. Despite this discovery about the questionable character of our grandfather, well, I am curious to see how it affected Father's life. Not only that, but Father was quite a good writer, don't you think? His love of words was rather sweet."

"Yes," said Jane. "And to think he was only fifteen."

"Okay," said Alice. "It's settled then."

"And no cheating," said Jane, waving her finger under Alice's nose.

"Cheating?" Alice blinked at her younger sister.

"Yes, no peeking ahead to see what's in the journal. We all get to hear it for the first time together."

Alice nodded. "Fine. No reading ahead."

"If anyone can be trusted," said Louise with a tired yawn, "it is Alice."

"Yes, *Alice* certainly doesn't take after Grandpa Howard," said Jane, as she gave Louise a sharp glance. "I wonder who does."

"Do not look at me," said Louise. "I firmly believe in the benefits of a good education, and everyone knows that I am a teetotaler."

"Maybe it's Aunt Ethel," Jane said with a giggle.

"Now, Jane," said Alice, "that's not fair."

"I know," said Jane. "I was just being mean. The truth is, I'm probably the most like our ornery old grandpa."

Naturally, Alice and Louise protested. Then they all laughed, hugged and said good night.

Alice tried to imagine her paternal grandfather after she finished her bedtime Bible reading and prayer time. Certainly, he had been nothing like her father, in disposition or in spirit. There must have been some reason that he had been such a cantankerous man. Perhaps life had been hard on him or he had been severely disappointed somehow. Whatever the cause, she was eager to find out more about her father's family during his boyhood years. Good or bad, it was, after all, the Howard family history.

Chapter Four

*H*ave you heard the news?" asked Ethel before she was barely through the swinging door that connected the dining room and the kitchen. Alice turned to see her aunt bedecked in a purple and pink flowered dress that provided a vivid contrast to her dyed-red hair.

"Hi, Aunt Ethel," said Alice as she hung one of Jane's pots above the stove.

"What news?" asked Jane as she emerged from the pantry.

"Are these left over from breakfast?" asked Ethel hopefully as she eyed a plate of freshly made raisin scones.

"Help yourself," said Jane. "We're just finishing cleaning up."

Within seconds, Ethel had a cup of tea and a scone and was seated at the kitchen table. "Did you hear about Clara Horn's baby?" she asked between bites.

"Clara Horn's *baby*?" repeated Jane. "Good grief, that woman must be at least seventy years old."

"Do you mean a new grandchild?" asked Alice as she hung up the dishtowel and poured herself a cup of tea. "Although her daughter is probably old enough to be a grandmother herself."

"Audrey Horn, a grandmother?" asked Jane. "Why, she's a year younger than I am."

Alice laughed. "That's still old enough to be a grandmother."

Jane frowned. "Thanks a lot."

"It's nothing personal, but if you do the math, you can see—"

"Excuse me," interrupted Ethel. "I was trying to tell you about Clara Horn's *baby*."

"Clara Horn's baby?" echoed Louise as she came into the kitchen. "What on earth are you talking about, Auntie? Clara is almost as old as you—"

"Older," snapped Ethel. "I'm *trying* to tell you girls the latest news and I can hardly get a word in edgewise."

"Excuse me," said Jane as she hung up her apron. "Louise, did you give the Winstons directions to the local antique shops? They had mentioned wanting to find something special to commemorate their anniversary."

Louise nodded as she poured herself a cup of coffee. "I did. And I told Mrs. Miller about Sylvia Songer's shop since she is an avid quilter. And I told Mrs. Bauch-man about Time for Tea after she complimented us on the tea."

"Well, the Chamber should give you a special award, Louise." Jane poured the last of the coffee into her brightly colored mug and finally sat down at the table. "All right, Auntie, go ahead and spill the beans. You've got a captive audience now."

Ethel looked slightly miffed. "I've got a mind just to leave without saying another word."

Jane laughed. "I'd have to see it to believe it."

"Jane," said Louise in a slightly scolding tone.

"Go ahead," encouraged Alice. "Tell us about Clara Horn's mysterious baby."

"Yes," agreed Jane. "Did Clara find a basket on her porch? Or perhaps it was hidden under a cabbage leaf in her garden?"

Ethel smiled slyly. "Well, I suppose her baby would enjoy a cabbage leaf in her garden. For that matter, you better watch out for your own garden, Jane."

"What kind of baby are we talking about?" asked Louise.

"A *pig!*" exclaimed Ethel. "Clara Horn has gone out and gotten herself a pig."

"A pig?" Louise blinked. "What could Clara Horn

possibly want with a pig? Why, her backyard is no bigger than a postage stamp."

"Exactly," said Ethel, tapping the side of her head with her index finger. "We're beginning to think that Clara may need to get her head examined by a professional."

"Do you mean a pet pig?" asked Alice.

"Like a potbellied pig?" added Jane.

"I think she called it something like that," said Ethel. "But, good grief, what pig doesn't have a potbelly? Your uncle Bob raised pigs on our farm for a few years, and that's the whole point: You fatten them up for slaughter in the fall. They all have potbellies."

"But she probably got a Vietnamese potbellied pig," said Jane.

"Who cares where she got it," said Ethel. "The problem is, it's a pig. And Clara does *not* live on a farm."

"Lots of people in California got potbellied pigs for pets during the nineties," said Jane. "It was quite the fad."

"Well, maybe in California," said Ethel. "Everyone knows that those people out there are all half-crazy anyway."

Jane just rolled her eyes.

"Where does Clara intend to keep her pet?" asked Louise.

"That's just it," declared Ethel. "She keeps the nasty thing in her house. I've heard that it actually sleeps in her bed." She shook her head in utter disgust. "The woman is clearly losing her marbles."

"Oh, come on," said Alice. "Maybe she's just lonely. It hasn't been that long since she lost her husband."

"Well, I remember what it's like to bury a husband," said Ethel. "And you didn't find me sleeping with a dirty old pig."

This pronouncement sent the three sisters into side-splitting laughter. Ethel just sat there, staring at them as if they were no saner than Clara Horn. "Well," she finally said as she reached for her oversized purse, "I never."

Alice was the first to recover. "Sorry, Aunt Ethel. We're not laughing at you. It's just so funny—about the pig and all."

"Yes," agreed Louise, placing her hand on Ethel's arm as she used her lace-trimmed handkerchief to wipe tears of laughter from her eyes. "I must agree with you, dear, I never would have considered sleeping with a pig after I buried my husband either—"

Jane lost it all over again, and Alice was not far behind her. Louise, still stifling her own giggles, kindly took Ethel by the arm and walked with her out the back door.

"I don't know what's wrong with me," said Jane, wiping her wet eyes with a tissue. "That was just so funny."

Alice nodded. "Yes, and you know how laughter's

contagious. As soon as you got started, I just couldn't help myself."

Jane rose from her chair and went to the back door. "Well, it's also good medicine. I needed a laugh."

"I just hope we didn't offend Aunt Ethel."

"Not to worry, it looks like Louise is smoothing it all over." Jane pointed out to the garden where the two older women stood talking amidst the roses.

"So, do you think it's really true about Clara?" asked Alice as she rinsed her teacup and set it in the dishwasher.

"You mean that she sleeps with a pig?"

"Please," begged Alice. "Don't get me going again."

"Why not?" said Jane as she walked to the cupboard and reached for her big mixing bowl. "I've heard they make nice pets. Very intelligent. Only one problem."

"What's that?"

"They start out cute and small, but they can grow up to be enormous. They can weigh hundreds of pounds."

"Goodness. I can't imagine Clara Horn caring for something like that."

Jane was sifting flour into the bowl. "I thought I'd whip up some sugar cookies. They're not fancy, but I just got a yen for them this morning. Maybe it's all this down-home talk about pigs." Jane laughed.

"Sugar cookies sound delicious to me," said Alice. "Are

you using Mother's old recipe? She used to make the best ones. Bigger than my hand with the fingers widespread. Of course, my hands were a lot smaller then."

"I probably won't make them that big. They might not look very dainty for our guests."

"Perhaps I could take a few to Vera," said Alice. "She wasn't feeling well yesterday."

"That's a great idea," said Jane. "I'll set aside a special plate for her and Fred."

Alice took Vera her cookies later in the afternoon, but on her way, she saw Clara Horn wheeling an old-fashioned baby buggy down the street toward her. Alice paused to say hello. "And who's in the baby carriage?" asked Alice, but she was afraid she already knew.

"Why, this is my baby," said Clara with a twinkle in her eye. "Her name is Daisy." Then she held her forefinger over her lips. "I think she's still asleep."

Alice peeked into the baby buggy to see a pair of dark beady eyes and a black snout poking out of a white baby bonnet. "Well, hello there, Daisy," said Alice.

"Oh, Daisy," said Clara, bending over to see. "Did you wake up already? I thought you were still taking your afternoon nap."

Alice was not sure what to say next. It would feel disingenuous to say, "What a pretty baby."

"How old is she?" she finally asked. "She seems quite small."

"Daisy just turned seven weeks," said Clara proudly. "Barely old enough to be weaned from her mother. She still drinks from a bottle sometimes. Really, isn't she just the sweetest thing you ever saw?"

"I've never seen anything like her," said Alice honestly. She studied the dark face and began to think that the pig was rather cute, in a piggy sort of way. Then she reached out and patted the small animal on the head. The pig gave a soft grunt and Alice smiled. "She's really quite nice," said Alice.

Clara nodded. "Yes, she's a darling."

"Have a good day," said Alice and continued her walk toward Vera's house. Alice smiled to herself. Not only did she have freshly made sugar cookies for Vera, but she also had an interesting story to share.

The two friends sat on the sofa in Vera's living room and laughed over Daisy.

"A real live pig?" asked Vera.

"Yes. I saw it with my own eyes," said Alice. "Her name

is Daisy and she's actually sort of cute. She's much smaller than I expected. Although Jane says they can grow to be hundreds of pounds."

"My word." Vera laughed again and shook her head. "Well, your visit is making me feel better, Alice. I was feeling pretty blue before you got here."

"Oh, don't worry, Vera. People often get a little depressed when they're ill. Believe me, I see it every day at the hospital. I'm sure you'll be back to yourself in no time."

"I hope so. I've already missed three days of school. That's more than I've missed in the last three years. And here we are only starting the term." Vera shook her head. "It's hard on the kids having a substitute this soon."

"Well, there's nothing you can do about that. Try not to think about it and just take it easy."

"That's about all I can do," said Vera. She held up a book. "Fred brought me this new novel that I've been wanting to read, but I barely make it through a single page before I fall asleep again."

Alice patted Vera's hand. "Resting may be your best medicine right now. And for that reason, I'm going to leave you to it. May I get you anything first?"

"You already got me juice and tea, Alice. I think I'll be perfectly fine until Fred gets home."

"I'll be praying for you, Vera," promised Alice.

"Thanks." Vera looked up with sad eyes. "I appreciate it."

Walking toward home, Alice prayed for her dear friend. She asked God to comfort her and give her rest and help her to get well. When she got home, she found her sisters and several of the guests gathered on the front porch, enjoying tea or lemonade and sugar cookies.

"Come join us," called Jane.

"I met Clara Horn's baby," announced Alice as Jane poured her a cup of tea.

Jane began giggling, and Louise quickly explained to the guests what was so amusing about this little bit of news.

"Tell us about it," urged Mrs. Miller.

"Well, the piglet's name is Daisy. She's about seven weeks old, drinks from a baby bottle and wears a baby bonnet. Oh, yes, and she was being transported in a baby carriage. It was really rather sweet."

"It will not be so sweet when the piglet grows up into a great big hog," said Louise.

"I saw a special about those pigs on TV once," said Mrs. Miller. "They were having a hard time finding homes for them when they grew too big to be house pets."

"Poor Clara," said Alice. "She really seems to love Daisy."

"I hope she does not get too attached," said Louise.

"According to Aunt Ethel, Mayor Tynan will be looking into the town ordinances before long."

"Oh, you people and your small-town politics," said Mr. Miller. "Something like this wouldn't cause anyone to even bat an eyelash where we live."

"Don't be so sure," said Mrs. Miller. "How would you like it if our neighbors had a three-hundred-pound pig? I'll bet you wouldn't waste a minute before you'd be calling the authorities and complaining."

"Only if it became a nuisance," he defended himself. "I say, live and let live."

Jane chuckled. "That's not how it works in a small town. People really get involved in other people's business here. You should've seen what we went through just to renovate our family home into this inn."

"Really?" Mrs. Miller looked surprised. "This is such a lovely place. I can't imagine how anyone could've protested."

Jane launched into stories of some of the crazy battles that the sisters had to fight just to get the townspeople on board.

"But the town came through for us in the end," Alice said. "When it looked impossible to get our roof fixed, everyone in town pitched in and helped out. We wouldn't be open today if they hadn't. You see, the people here are really very generous and good-hearted. It's just that they can be a hard sell sometimes, but when they're convinced, then you couldn't ask for better neighbors."

"Well, we can't always say that about where we live," said Mr. Miller. "Fact of the matter is we don't even know most of our neighbors."

"We used to," said Mrs. Miller sadly. "Then old friends started moving out and new folks moved in. Well, it just got hard to keep track."

"I suppose we quit trying," added her husband.

"Maybe we should give it another shot," said Mrs. Miller. "I noticed that the new folks on the right have a new baby. And the woman was hanging what looked like a handmade quilt on the clothesline."

"You said how you love to quilt," said Louise, pointing to the bag of fabric that Mrs. Miller had purchased at Sylvia's Buttons that day.

"Yes, mentioning the quilt would be a perfect way to start a conversation," said Mrs. Miller. She smiled and nodded her head. "Yes, I think that's just what I'll do when I get back home. You ladies and your friendly little community have inspired me."

Alice smiled. "That's one of my prayers for each of our guests."

Then Mr. Miller pointed toward the plaque that hung by the front door. "We liked what your sign says."

Then he proceeded to read it aloud. "'A place where one can be refreshed and encouraged. A place of hope and healing. A place where God is at home.'"

"That's nice," said Mrs. Miller. "By the way, we noticed that the little church over there has the same name as your inn. Why is that?"

Louise told them a bit about their father and the church, and Alice invited them to join them for the next day's worship service.

"We haven't been to church since the children were small," admitted Mrs. Miller. "I'd like to go tomorrow." She glanced at her husband and he was nodding.

Chapter Five

*A*ll was quiet at the inn when Louise, Jane and Alice met in the library to continue reading from their father's journal. Alice had brewed a pot of orange pekoe tea and had arranged pot and cups on a large silver tray on their father's old mahogany desk.

"Do you want me to continue reading?" asked Alice. "Just because I found the journal doesn't mean that I should be the only one to read. We could take turns."

"I think you have a fine reading voice," said Louise. "If Jane has no objections, I would like you to be the official reader."

"So would I," said Jane. "That is, if you don't mind, Alice."

"Oh, I don't mind at all. I love reading Father's words."

Jane pulled out the big leather chair and smiled. "Well, if you're doing the honors, it seems only fitting that you sit in his chair."

Alice was self-conscious about being the center of

attention. A faint blush colored her cheeks as she sat down and put on her reading glasses. "Okay, I think this is where we left off, right after the part about occasionally imbibing bootleg liquor." She cleared her throat and began to read.

...Although I am not certain that this latter habit is common knowledge throughout our small community. For if it were, I am sure my father would be fined for breaking the laws of prohibition, or more likely, thrown in jail since he has no money to pay fines. Would I feel bad if my father were locked up in jail? I am not sure how to answer that question honestly. I realize that my father does provide for us in what I would describe as a random manner. He does put in his crops and, weather permitting, harvests them, but if it were not for my mother's gardening and canning abilities, my fishing skills and the kindness of neighbors, I know we would go hungry more than we do. I should not complain about eating since it is really much better now that all my older siblings have moved on, although I know my father misses the extra farmhands. I miss them too, but not so much for their sturdy backs as for their companionship. I wish they would come back home to visit occasionally, although I know they probably will not, since they have not done so yet. I think I miss my sister Alice most of—

"I had almost forgotten about Aunt Alice," said Louise as she poured each of them a cup of hot tea. "Do you remember meeting her, Alice, back when we were little girls? She and her husband came to visit for a few days one summer."

Alice nodded. "Yes. She seemed quite old at the time, but I think it was only because she'd had a hard life. If memory serves, she was only a few years older than Father."

"That is right." Louise handed Alice a cup of tea. "There were four others who were older than Aunt Alice."

"I know that Father came from a large farm family," said Jane. "But I never really thought much about his siblings, since I never met any of them—except for Aunt Ethel."

"Aunt Alice, Father and Aunt Ethel were the youngest," said Alice. "There were three other brothers and one sister. Of course, all but Aunt Ethel passed on long ago. Let's see, as I recall, John was the oldest, and I think he lived in Michigan. Then came Martha, who died of typhoid as a child. Then there was Charles. He moved somewhere down south where his wife's family lived—South Carolina, I think. And, of course, there was Dad's favorite brother, Adam."

"Was he the one who died in World War I?" asked Jane. "I remember Father mentioning him in sermons a few times." Alice nodded. "Yes, that was Adam, the brother who taught Father to fish. Father loved him dearly."

"Alice, I officially nominate you to be family historian," said Louise. "I cannot believe you got all those names and the birth order straight. Will you write that down somewhere so we can keep track of it?"

"Of course. I better do it before my memory begins to fade."

"That is a good idea, but I want to hear more of the journal. Please keep on reading," urged Jane.

Alice picked up where she had left off.

...I miss my sister Alice most of all, but I wish her well with her new husband Asher. He seems like a good man and he holds down a steady job. I just wish they did not live so far away, but maybe it is for the best. Alice and my father never got along well. I am sure that was only because she spoke her mind to him. She did not appreciate his treatment of our mother, nor do I, and she was always quick to stand up for me when it came to my education. Every time my father decided it was time for me to quit school and work on the farm, it was Alice who opposed the idea. I suppose that is why this year has been so much harder. With Alice gone, I am forced to fight my own battles with my father. My mother is a good woman, but she is intimidated by my father. I have only seen

her stand up to him once, when I was a small boy, and that did not go well. I believe she is worn down and weary from living with such a cantankerous man. The light in her eyes seems to be mostly snuffed out now. Although I see it flicker ever so slightly when she sees me come into the room or when she is reading her Bible. Other than those two things, I cannot see even the tiniest bit of joy in her life.

"That poor woman," said Jane. "To think of what she had to put up with after having all those children, and losing two."

"Very sad." Louise shook her head.

Sometimes I dream of leaving this place and taking Mother with me. Other than hurt pride, I do not think my father would miss us very much. In my dream we wait until he goes off with friends since we know that means he may not be back for hours or even days. Then we pack everything we can fit into my mother's big garden cart and we slip away without even leaving him a note. We walk and camp until we reach another town where I go to work and earn enough money to support us. I am certain that we could live together quite happily. I think, in time, the light would come back into Mother's eyes. To support this dream, I am saving as much money as I can from my job at the newspaper. I have worked my way up from delivery boy to janitor, but only being able to work for a few hours after school each day does not pay very much. I suppose I will have to give up school entirely after Mother and I run away from here. Perhaps that will make my father happy.

"Do you think he really does it?" asked Jane. "Did he actually run away from home with his mother?"

"Not that I know of," said Louise. "But I am sure that we will find out."

Alice paused to sip some tea. "That's the end of the first entry. Do you think we should save the next one for tomorrow?"

"Is it very long?" asked Jane. "I feel as if that wasn't enough."

Alice thumbed through the next entry. "It's only a couple of pages."

"Do you want to read it?" asked Louise.

Alice nodded, then continued.

November 5, 1925.

"This is nearly a month later."

Today is a happy day for this Englishtown farm boy. Unbeknownst to me, Mr. Dolton entered an essay I had written for English class in a statewide contest. It was only an essay on fishing and not very special. If I had known it was to be entered in a statewide contest I might have chosen a more impressive subject, but Mr. Dolton assured me that it was a perfectly fine paper. So fine, in fact, that this afternoon, Mr. Dolton announced to the entire school that my essay had won. For a prize, I will receive twenty dollars. I have never had that much money in my entire life. Mr. Dolton had already notified the newspaper where I work part-time, and they came over to the school and took a photo of me and will compose a short article about my good fortune. They will even print a copy of my essay in the newspaper after the contest people return it to me. This is all very good news, and I am most thankful to Mr. Dolton, but I wish there was some way to keep my father from learning about the prize money. Twenty dollars would go a long way in helping Mother and me to get away from here, but I am afraid that my father will find out about my windfall and insist that I contribute it to the farm. Harvest has not been good this year, partially because of him and partially because of the inconsistency of the elements, not to mention the falling price of corn. I suppose I should be willing to share, and perhaps I will. But I wish I could save it. I feel quite optimistic to think that my essay was good enough to win. Mr. Dolton says that if I keep up this kind of work, I may even win a scholarship to college, but in order to do so, he reminds me that I must stay in school

and keep my marks up. I am not sure what lies ahead, but today
I feel hopeful. I think I shall go fishing to celebrate.

"Ah," said Louise. "Good for him."

"Thank God for Mr. Dolton," cheered Jane.

Alice closed the book. "It reminds me of how impor-tant it is to encourage young people," she said.

"Like the girls in your ANGELs group?" said Jane.

"Yes, and Louise's piano students," added Alice.

"And Jane's work with Josie," said Louise, referring to a lonesome little girl whom Jane had befriended.

Alice smiled. "I think Father would approve."

"I wonder if there's anything more we should be doing," said Jane.

Alice considered that for a moment. "You know, one of the most impressive things that Father used to do was simply talk with kids. He'd ask them questions about their lives or about what they were thinking or feeling."

"And did they actually tell him?" asked Louise.

"Oh, you'd be surprised at how much they opened up." Alice used a napkin to blot a spot of tea from the surface of the desk. "Kids really responded well to Father. I think it's because he never talked down to them. And he never seemed to judge them either. I think they sensed this and respected him for it."

"Well, it's something to aim for." Jane stood up and began gathering the teacups.

"And to pray about," added Louise.

Alice nodded. "Yes, we should be praying for these kids. I'm sure there were people praying for Father when he was growing up."

"God only knows what kind of difference that made," said Louise as they turned off the lights and closed the library door.

Chapter Six

Sunday was such a busy day that the three sisters opted not to read from their father's journal in the evening. The next day Alice found herself thinking about her father's boyhood days as she made her rounds in the hospital. She was on her way down to the lab to pick up some blood test results when she saw Vera sitting in the waiting area.

"Vera," said Alice. "What are you doing here?"

Vera gave her a weak wave. "Waiting."

Alice sat down beside her. "How are you feeling?"

Vera just shook her head. "Not so good."

"Is Fred here?"

"No, I didn't want to bother him. I went to the doctor again this morning and insisted he find out what's wrong with me. I didn't know he was going to send me over here. I hated to make Fred leave work, and I figured I could at least drive myself." She sighed. "But now I'm exhausted."

Alice studied her friend's pale face and the dark

circles under her eyes. "You look exhausted. How long have you been waiting?"

Vera checked her watch. "About thirty minutes."

"When did you last eat?"

Vera shrugged. "Breakfast."

"Okay." Alice stood up. "You stay right here."

Vera made a half smile. "Where do you think I'd go?"

Alice patted her shoulder. "I'm going to find out what the holdup is."

Alice spoke to the lab nurse and managed to speed things up a little. Then, after delivering the blood test results upstairs, she set off to the cafeteria to get Vera something to eat. It was not long before the lab tests were completed and Vera was munching on a bran muffin and drinking some orange juice that Alice had brought her.

"I wonder if you should have a nap before you try to drive home," said Alice. "Or maybe I should call Fred."

"Oh, I'll be fine."

Alice studied her friend and shook her head. "You don't look fine, Vera. You should lie down for a bit." After Vera finished her snack, Alice took her to an empty room and made her rest.

"I feel like a preschooler," said Vera as Alice covered her with a blanket.

"That's just fine," said Alice. "Better a preschooler

than a wreck on the highway. I don't want you to leave until I see you again. I'll try to get the results from your lab tests by then."

Vera sleepily thanked her, and Alice set off to finish her shift, wondering if she should take Vera home herself. As she checked on patients and gave meds, she prayed for Vera, asking God to give the doctor and lab workers real clarity about what was ailing her dear friend. But when she went back to the lab, they didn't seem to know any more than they had before.

"Her doctor may come up with something more," the technician said. "But from what I've seen everything looks pretty normal."

"Well, I guess that's good," said Alice. "If nothing else, it should reassure Vera to know that nothing terrible is wrong."

Vera was not reassured. "I know you think that's good news," she said as Alice walked her to her car. "But we still don't know what's wrong. And if we don't know what's wrong, then how do we fix it?"

She paused in front of her car, fiddling with her keys. "You know that my mom and my aunt both died from cancer when they were about my age."

Alice nodded. "You've told me that before. But that doesn't mean you—"

"It runs in families."

"The lab tests didn't show anything abnormal."

"They missed it in my mom and my aunt too," said Vera.

"Medicine wasn't nearly as evolved then," Alice reassured her. "They missed a lot of things."

"It still happens," said Vera. "I've read stories in the paper."

Alice hugged her friend. "Well, it's not going to happen to you. We're going to get you through this, Vera. Now, remember what you're always telling me. Instead of worrying, go to God. Ask Him to lead you through this and to make you well. That's what I'm doing."

Vera nodded and opened her car door. "You're a good friend, Alice."

"Now, you're sure you can drive home?"

"Yes, you did a good job of taking care of me. I'm sure I'll be perfectly fine." She smiled. "In fact, I feel better than I've felt all day. Maybe the doctors are right. Maybe nothing is wrong."

Alice was not completely convinced as she walked back toward the hospital. Still, she would take her own advice and keep praying. "Dear heavenly Father," she prayed, "please take care of Vera and encourage her heart. Touch her with Your healing hands and show the doctors how best to help her get well. And show me how to be the best kind of friend to her. Amen."

Finally it was five o'clock. Alice was relieved to go home. For some reason, Mondays always felt like the longest workday to her. She knew the house would be quiet again since all the guests had checked out, and they were not expecting any more until the middle of the week. Alice and her sisters had learned to appreciate having their house to themselves for a few days at the beginning of the week. But it was never long before they would look forward to sharing their home again, to meeting new friends and to busying themselves with the happy chores that came with running a bed-and-breakfast.

When Alice got home, she saw a strange car parked in front. Slightly disappointed to think that they had guests, she decided to go in through the back door.

"Who's here?" she asked Jane as she set down her handbag and peeked into the pot that Jane was stirring. It looked like vegetable soup and smelled deliciously of basil and garlic.

"Unexpected guest." Jane replaced the lid and turned the gas down. "She just called this morning. Seems she was in need of a quiet break and found us on the website and drove on down. She just got here. Louise is showing her to the Sunrise Room."

Alice smiled. "My room?"

Jane nodded. "Yes, we think that's the most peaceful room."

Each sister had chosen the décor for one of the guest bedrooms. Jane had decorated the fourth guest room, the Garden Room, as she imagined her mother would have done it.

Alice reached for one of Jane's homemade breadsticks. "I must admit I was looking forward to no guests today."

"Me too." Jane was now shredding lettuce for a salad. "But she seems nice. Her name is Susan Newby. Apparently her husband's out of the country on business and her job was making her crazy, plus she has a grown daughter and grandbaby living with her, and she just needed to get away."

"Poor woman." Alice finished off the breadstick. "Well, I hope she enjoys her stay."

"I invited her to have dinner with us."

"Good. May I help you with anything?"

"No, you go on and change. Put your feet up for a bit. Louise promised to set the table."

"Thanks, I'm feeling a little tired."

Jane's brows lifted. "Too tired to read from Father's journal tonight?"

Alice smiled. "Actually, that's one thing I have been looking forward to all day."

"Oh, good. So have I."

Alice not only put her feet up but also managed to take a little snooze before dinner. When she went downstairs she was feeling refreshed, and she was eager to meet their unexpected guest.

"Where are you from?" she asked Susan after grace had been said.

"Philadelphia," said Susan.

"It turns out that Susan grew up in the same neighborhood where Eliot lived as a boy," explained Louise.

Jane passed the salad to Alice.

"Of course, with a common name like Smith, it is hard to know if her parents would have known Eliot's folks anyway," continued Louise. "It is funny, I always thought that when I married it would be to someone with a more exotic name. Something more interesting than Howard— not that I dislike the name Howard." Louise shook her head. "Then I went and married a man named Smith."

Jane laughed. "What were you thinking?"

Louise smiled. "That I was in love."

"It was worth the name?" Jane asked teasingly.

"Very much so." Louise turned her attention back to Susan. "Not that it matters, since most of Eliot's family have passed on now, but what was your family's name?"

"Graves," said Susan.

Alice felt a ripple of interest go through her. "Graves?" she repeated.

"Yes," said Susan as she helped herself to another breadstick. "These are delicious, Jane. Do you give out recipes?"

Jane grinned. "I'm in the process of putting together a Grace Chapel Inn cookbook."

"What a good idea." Susan sighed. "I think you women have it all figured out just perfectly." She glanced around the elegant pale green dining room and at the pretty bouquet on the table. "What a wonderful way to live. I've dreamed of running a bed-and-breakfast someday—after Tom and I retire." She paused and rolled her eyes. "Believe me, a bed-and-breakfast sounds especially blissful right now. My daughter Katy is staying with us until her husband comes home from the military and, let me tell you, her little Jamie is really a handful."

"How old is your grandson?" asked Jane.

"Two and a half." Susan groaned. "The terrible twos—he's into absolutely everything. And, naturally, Katy and I don't agree about how to raise children at all. It's not that I want her to spank him or anything, but if she could just contain him. When he broke a crystal vase that Tom and I received as a wedding present, it was the last straw. I had put it up high too. I still can't believe that vase survived my own three children and thirty-three years of marriage, but in a matter of seconds was destroyed by my only grandson."

"Oh, that is too bad," said Louise. "But it will not be long before your grandson grows up. I would give anything to have grandchildren."

"I'd be happy to share him with you." Susan made a face. "Oh, I'm sure I must sound like a horrible grandmother, but I have just reached my limit. It helps when Tom's home. He balances things out. He's been gone nearly two weeks, and I just didn't think I could survive another one. Thankfully, I have lots of vacation time stored up. I decided it was time to use some. During my break at work this morning, I searched through a bed-and-breakfast site and saw Grace Chapel Inn listed. Something about the name just sounded peaceful and quiet and soothing. Also, the name Acorn Hill seemed familiar. I'm not even sure why. Maybe I lived here in an earlier life." She laughed.

Alice had been trying hard to follow the conversation at the table, but the mention of the name Graves had distracted her. Finally, she said, "You mentioned that your maiden name is Graves. You don't happen to have a brother by the name of Mark, do you?"

Susan's eyes opened wide. "Yes, I most certainly do."

"Is he a vet?"

"You know my brother?"

"Oh, it's been years," said Alice. "I thought I recalled that he had a younger sister. I just couldn't remember your name."

"Well, it really is a small world," said Susan. "Now, what was your name again? I know Louise introduced us before dinner, but I must admit that I've been so stressed out lately that I seem to be forgetting things. I'm surprised I could even remember my maiden name."

Alice smiled. "It's Alice. Alice Howard."

Susan grew thoughtful. "Weren't you Mark's girlfriend?"

Alice felt her cheeks grow warm. "We dated when I was in nursing school."

"How's your brother doing?" asked Jane, as if she knew him personally, but Alice suspected she was just trying to extract information that Alice would be too shy to inquire about.

"He's doing well—awfully busy though. Even though we live in the same city, I hardly ever get to see him. He's a vet for the zoo. Actually, he's the head of all the vets."

"How nice," said Louise.

"Does he have a family?" asked Jane.

Susan shook her head. "He never married. Of course, he says it's because he's married to his work. I suppose that's not far from the truth. Tom and I used to try to match him up with some of our women friends, but Mark was forever forgetting to show up or canceling at the last minute. Not too many women can handle being stood up for a sick gorilla."

They all laughed at this, and Jane continued her line of questioning. "So does he do anything for fun?"

"Mark's idea of fun is traveling to strange places to treat strange animals."

"Sounds like he hasn't changed," said Alice.

Susan turned and looked at Alice. "Is that what broke you two up?"

Alice shrugged. "It was so long ago. It's hard to remember exactly what happened."

"Well, that probably wasn't it," said Jane. "Alice loves animals. She'll stop on an eight-lane freeway to help an injured squirrel."

Alice tossed Jane a glance.

"Okay, but you *would* for a dog."

Alice smiled. She could not deny Jane's statement.

"Isn't that how you got Waffles?" asked Jane.

"Waffles?" said Susan.

"That's a dog I had years ago. Just a mutt someone had lost—"

"You mean abandoned," Louise corrected her. "And

anyone who saw the animal could clearly see why. I do not think God ever made an uglier dog."

"He was a *good* dog," protested Alice. "Best dog I ever had."

"Stupid as a stone," added Louise. "Why, that dog used to chase parked cars."

"He'd had a head injury," said Alice.

"One among many," quipped Louise.

They all laughed again.

"Well, you ladies have been good medicine for me," said Susan as she blotted her mouth with her napkin. "Just what I needed. And to think one of Mark's old girlfriends lives here." Susan stood, thanked them for the delicious meal and excused herself for a walk in the garden.

After the kitchen was cleaned up and evening chores done, the three sisters met for tea in the library. Once settled comfortably, Alice began to read.

November 19, 1925.

My father insisted that I contribute my essay contest money to the farm. He said it will be used to "buy seed for next year's crops," but then he took off and we have not seen hide nor hair of him for two and a half days. Mother is very sorry about the whole thing, but there is nothing she can do about it, and I certainly do not blame her for our unfortunate situation. Just the same, I am very angry with my father. The honest truth is I wish he would leave us for good and never come back. If I believed in God, I would pray for this to happen. I quit praying to God when Adam was killed in the war across the Atlantic. Oh, I may have been only eight at the time, but I knew exactly what I was doing. I had prayed almost daily before that, sometimes twice a day. I mostly prayed that God would keep my favorite brother safe from the Kaiser's bullets and make my father a good man, but when God failed to protect my brother, I decided it was useless to pray for my father, and so I quit praying altogether. I am sure it would be the final blow for my mother to discover that I no longer believe in God.

I heard Mr. Dolton speaking to the science teacher once. Mr. Benson is supposedly an atheist, in other words, someone who does not believe in God. I think that would adequately describe me, although I have yet to announce to anyone, "I am an atheist." Mr. Dolton said, "You have to be awfully brave to be an atheist." Mr. Benson said, "Why is that?" and Mr. Dolton answered, "Because it is so risky if you are wrong." The other teacher just laughed. The problem is I like and respect Mr. Dolton much more than I do the science teacher. I would feel better if Mr. Dolton were an atheist too.

"Oh, dear," said Louise as she refilled her teacup. "That poor misguided young man."

"Not so much misguided as searching for the truth, don't you think?" Jane asked.

"I suppose. But what a harsh early life he had."

"God promises to use all things to our good," said Alice, "when we love and serve Him. Obviously, that's what He did with all of Father's hardships."

"It certainly seems that way," agreed Louise. "Our dear father was one of the best men that I have ever known."

"To think he once considered himself an atheist," said Jane. "That is so amazing."

Alice sipped her tea before she began reading again, continuing with the same entry.

I must admit that Mother and I have enjoyed the peace and quiet while Father has been away. In the evening after I have tended to the livestock and chopped firewood, I can read and study for as long as I can keep my eyes open, and Mother sits happily by the fire as she knits a blue woolen scarf. She thinks that I do not know it is for me, but last week she asked me my favorite color, then traded eggs for the blue yarn. My essay appeared in the newspaper this week, and the editor asked if I would consider writing for the paper. Of course,

I said, "Yes," and then he told me I could be in charge of the obituaries. Now, I realize I should not complain and this is only a place to start, but our town is so small that sometimes months can go by before anyone dies. I hate to sound as if I would be glad to see someone die. Honestly, I would not, but I would like a chance to write something that I could get paid for and have printed in the paper. So, I have taken to creating fictional obituaries, just for the practice. Here is the one I wrote tonight.

Horst Clarence Bartholomew died on Wednesday of this week. His lifeless body was discovered in the barn next to the milking stool and overturned bucket. It is suspected that he expired while milking his cow, Bessie. The exact time of Horst's passing is unknown for the only witness was the cow, and she is not talking. It is unclear whether or not Bessie had anything to do with Horst's untimely demise, but Leonard Barnes, the town's undertaker, has revealed that Horst's large balding forehead did bear the undeniable shape of a cow's hoof print. Horst's funeral is planned for Friday at the Christian Church on Brown Street and all friends are invited to attend, but please leave your cows at home. Horst is survived by his widow Marybeth Bartholomew who is currently trying to find a new home for her cow Bessie.

The sisters chuckled over their father's boyish sense of humor.

"At least he did not let life get him down," said Louise.

"It's the sign of a true survivor," said Jane, "the ability to find humor in everyday life. Good for Father."

Alice closed the journal. "You know it bothered me, at first, to think of Father having such a hard childhood and youth. But the more we read this, the more I think that God really used all the sadness in his life to make him into the kind of man who could do the sorts of things he did."

"Like reaching out to those who were suffering," said Louise.

"Or helping people in need," added Jane. "I remember clearly how Father always helped out whenever he heard of people in need. It didn't matter if they went to our church or not."

"That's right," said Alice. "Helping Hands ministry was his idea. It was the first outreach for needy people no matter where they go to church—or even if they don't go at all."

"You know, Father may not have talked about his past much, but it is clear that it affected the way he served God and his fellow man." Louise sighed. "I guess I do not feel quite so uncomfortable knowing that the Howard family history had its dark moments."

"So, it doesn't bother you to think that we may have some skeletons in the closet?" asked Jane.

Louise puckered up her mouth. "Goodness, Jane, it is not as if anyone committed murder."

"Not that we know of," said Jane with a mischievous grin.

"Oh, Jane."

Chapter Seven

*A*lice was relieved to learn that Vera had been able to return to school, but she could tell that her friend was exhausted when she telephoned her after work.

"The doctor can't seem to tell me much of anything," said Vera. "None of the tests came back conclusive about cancer, but since it does run in my family, he wants me to have some more tests done later this week."

"Well, they'll figure this out," said Alice. "How is Fred doing?"

"He's worried. I try not to talk to him about it too much. I don't like upsetting him. I'm glad I have you to talk to, Alice. It really helps."

"I just want you to get better, Vera. You let me know if there's anything I can do, okay?"

Vera agreed, and Alice hung up the office phone, saying aloud, "Poor Vera."

"Something wrong?" asked a voice from behind her.

Alice turned to see Susan. She nodded her head. "My

best friend is ill, and they can't seem to figure out what it is. She's really frustrated."

Susan nodded. "That's hard. In this day and age, we expect the medical experts to have all the answers. We forget that they don't know everything."

"Isn't that the truth," said Alice.

Susan looked at Alice's uniform. "Did you and Mark meet through medicine?" she asked.

"In a way. He'd just started practicing veterinary medicine, and I had found a cat that had been hit by a car...."

"And you felt sorry for it and took it to the vet clinic?"

Alice smiled. "All right, I suppose it's true what they say about me being such a softy toward animals. Especially those that have been hurt."

"I think it's sweet." Susan put her hand on Alice's arm. "And I can see why Mark liked you so well. You never married either?"

"No, I didn't. My nursing career took a lot of my time, and I've always done a lot of church work. When I began to care for my father, as he grew more elderly, somehow marriage just never quite fit in for me. I guess I believe that God just calls some of us to be single for a purpose. I'm perfectly happy with my life."

"Oh, I'm sure you are," agreed Susan.

"So, are you feeling a bit more rested today?"

"Definitely. But even so, I plan to stay into the weekend. My husband doesn't get home until Sunday evening, and I don't intend to leave until I know he's on the plane and flying over the ocean."

"Good for you," said Alice. "It'll be nice having you around. Now if you'll excuse me, I think I'll go change."

After her shower, Alice considered her little speech to Susan. It was not untrue, but Alice sensed that she had been trying too hard. But why? Why should she feel any need to convince Susan that being single was nothing less than perfect for her? Oh, yes, she sometimes wished that she had married and had had children, even grandchildren, but usually those moments were brief. She knew that she had a family within the church, and more recently, with her two beloved sisters. Still, there was a little something that nagged at her. Maybe it was that old "what if" question.

Alice went over to her bookshelf and pulled out a scrapbook. It was something that her father had given her while she was still in high school. He had pasted her first perfect report card in it, along with a red ribbon she had won at a track meet in junior high. "The rest is up to you," he told her.

"But what shall I put in it?" she asked. "I don't have any more ribbons."

"Put in things that mean something to you," he suggested. "It's just a keepsake for you to enjoy when you are older."

So Alice had begun sticking this and that on the sturdy gray pages—photos of friends, her graduation announcement and her honor roll tassel. She set it aside after she started nursing school in Philadelphia, too busy with a full load of classes and her part-time job at the pharmacy to keep up with such things. Of course, that changed at the end of her sophomore year when she rescued the wounded cat and began to date the handsome young veterinarian, Mark Graves. After that she started taping in movie stubs, birthday cards, theater tickets, pressed flowers and even the few love notes that he had sent her during the more than two years that they had seen each other exclusively. Alice flipped past these faded bits of memorabilia now, going to the later pages of her scrapbook. These pages held recent newspaper clippings sent to her by an old college friend, Virginia Herman, who still lived in Philadelphia and stayed in touch. Several of them were about Mark's career.

Alice studied the most recent photo of Mark. He had kindness in his dark eyes. She liked that he sported a full beard. It was hard to tell by the grainy newspaper photo, but his hair looked fairly gray. He looked dignified, like someone Alice would enjoy knowing. And yet they lived in completely different worlds—only an hour away, but a lifetime apart. She closed the book and sighed. How odd to think that Mark's sister was downstairs right now. Wasn't life funny?

Susan joined them for dinner again, along with Ethel. Jane did not mind extra mouths at the table. She often said it was easier for her to cook for a group. This was fortunate, since the more people heard about Jane's fine culinary skills, the more they seemed to show up at mealtimes.

"Are you ready to go to the meeting, Alice?" asked Ethel after they finished a dessert of chocolate mousse.

"Meeting?" Alice frowned. "Oh, I totally forgot."

Ethel smiled. "Good thing I stopped by. Better go get a sweater, it is starting to get cool. I'll wait."

Alice thanked Jane for the lovely dinner and then excused herself. Her steps felt heavy as she went upstairs. While she was committed to the church and the board meetings, she would have preferred her sisters' company tonight.

"I guess we'll have to wait until tomorrow for our reading," said Louise as Alice and Ethel headed for the door.

Alice nodded. "Sorry, I completely forgot about this meeting."

"What reading?" asked Ethel as they walked over to the church.

Alice considered this. She would not mind if Ethel read the journal later, but this time with her sisters had been special, and she did not want anything to spoil it. "Oh, we just decided to have reading nights."

"You mean like a book club?" asked Ethel as Alice held the door open for her.

"Something like that."

"Well, I think that's a complete waste of time," said Ethel. "If you're going to read a book, just read it. You don't need to belong to a group. I think it's just something that Orpha woman invented to sell more books."

"You mean Oprah Winfrey?" Alice stifled a giggle.

"Yes, that woman on TV. I heard she got rich selling all those books for reading groups."

"Actually, I don't think she gets money from selling books. She just promotes good books because she loves to read."

"*Humph.* That's what she'd like you to believe."

"Hello," called Lloyd from down the hall. "You girls are running a little late tonight."

"Blame it on Jane's chocolate mousse," said Ethel as she patted her hair.

As usual, the board meeting was not terribly exciting,

and that was fine with Alice. She did not enjoy those times when members felt the need to light off fireworks. Tonight they discussed the budget and the church's part in the upcoming, first annual Fall Festival. To the community's great surprise the idea of a Fall Festival had originated with Mayor Lloyd Tynan during a Chamber meeting only a few weeks earlier.

"I think it's important for Grace Chapel to be involved in the Fall Festival," said Lloyd. "It shows that we're an interested and active part of our community."

Florence Simpson frowned. "Since when did you become a cheerleader for civic celebrations in our town, Lloyd Tynan? Haven't you always said that we should keep things the same in Acorn Hill?"

He nodded. "Yes, but sometimes change is good. We all saw how much the town enjoyed our summer celebration and how it brought people together. Nothing wrong with that."

"Besides," said Sylvia Songer, "the purpose of the Fall Festival is to support community services. I'm all for that."

"I don't know," said Florence with her usual skepticism. "Too much change can make a mess of things too. I suppose we'll start having a Winter Festival and then a Spring Festival. Maybe we can have one every month. We can change our name from Acorn Hill to Festival Hill."

Lloyd cleared his throat and stood up. "Actually, whether or not Acorn Hill has a festival is not this board's decision. The town has already decided that it will happen. What we are discussing tonight is whether or not Grace Chapel would care to participate in it."

"That's right," said Ethel. "And I think that the Fall Festival is important. Besides, all of the proceeds will be going to good causes. Right, Lloyd?"

"Exactly," he smiled. "Local businesses and philanthropic organizations will choose a charity to receive the profits from their various booths or activities. It'll be good for Acorn Hill commerce as well as for the community."

"I'd like to suggest that all proceeds from anything our church participates in should be donated to the Helping Hands ministry," said June Carter, owner of The Coffee Shop.

"Is that a motion?" asked Fred.

June confirmed that it was, and Alice gladly seconded it.

"May we open it to discussion?" asked Florence.

"Of course," said Fred. "That's what we've been doing."

"Well..." Florence stood up and cleared her throat, "as Lloyd has pointed out, there are already a number of philanthropic groups involved in this—this celebration. I don't see any reason for Grace Chapel to go jumping onto a bandwagon that may or may not be heading for a disaster."

"What sort of disaster?" asked Ethel.

"Who knows," said Florence. "It might rain that day. Or what if someone from out of town fell and got hurt and decided to sue?"

"And the sky might fall too," said Lloyd Tynan. "Really, Florence, you must know that the town has insurance to cover such things."

"But we must be prudent," she continued. "It's our job as board members to protect our church."

"That's true," said Alice. "But the church's job is to serve the community."

Fred nodded in agreement. "I think it's time to put this to a vote."

There was only one vote cast against the church's participation in the festival. They also agreed—*almost* unanimously—to donate all church proceeds to the Helping Hands ministry. And finally, at half past eight, Fred called the meeting to an end.

"How's Vera doing?" asked Lloyd as they began to stand up.

"Not so well," said Fred. "She'll have more tests on Friday."

"Maybe we should, uh, pray for Vera to get b–better,"

suggested the assistant pastor, Henry Ley. "Before everyone leaves."

So they paused with bowed heads on Vera's behalf. Then Patsy Ley invited everyone to enjoy the brownies that she had baked. "It's a new recipe," she explained. "With coconut and pecans."

"Have you seen Clara's *baby* yet?" Ethel asked Florence Simpson as the two older women made their way to the dessert table.

"No, have you?" said Florence.

"The brownies look lovely, but I better pass," Alice told Patsy. "I already had one dessert tonight."

"Not me," said Sylvia Songer. "These are much too tempting to pass up."

"I think I'll hurry on home," said Fred. "I need to check on Vera."

"Here," said Patsy as she loaded some brownies on a paper plate. "Take some with you."

"Well, it's simply the ugliest thing you ever saw," continued Ethel in a voice loud enough for everyone to overhear. "It's got this awful black snout and bristly hair. *Ugh.*" She shuddered dramatically. "Can you imagine keeping that smelly thing in your house?"

"Not in *my* house," said Florence. "I think Clara Horn has completely lost her senses."

"I've heard those potbellied pigs can grow to be hundreds of pounds," continued Ethel. She poked Lloyd Tynan now. "What do you think of that, Mr. Mayor?"

He shrugged as he picked up a brownie. "Well, I spoke to the town manager today, and it seems we don't have anything in the ordinances that prohibits it."

"You must be joking," said Florence. "You mean people can have farm animals right here in town?"

"Well, it seems our laws are a little outdated. In fact, did you know that according to our ordinances, you aren't allowed to smoke or chew tobacco in town?"

"Now that just figures," said Florence. "I better tell my husband to leave his pipe at home next time he takes a stroll through town and to watch his step if Clara's filthy pig has been out for a walk."

"Clara's pig isn't filthy," said Alice. "She is actually rather sweet."

"*Harrumph*. It just figures you would side with her, Alice. You're always for the underdog," Florence said.

"Under*pig*," Sylvia whispered to Alice.

Alice giggled, then said, "I don't see how Clara's pig is hurting anyone or disturbing the peace. Daisy seems to be a sweet little thing."

"Daisy?" Florence shook her head. "She actually calls it Daisy?"

"Or 'baby,'" said Ethel. "She wheels it around town in a baby carriage, you know. Just wait until that animal grows into a big fat hog. She won't be so cute then."

"Well, she's sure cute now," said Sylvia. "She brought Daisy into my shop the other day, and she's just about the cutest thing I've ever seen."

"Oh my," said Florence. "I think you need to get your eyes checked, Sylvia."

Alice decided it was time to make a break. "If you'll all excuse me, I'd like to call it a night. I have to get up early for work tomorrow."

"You and me both," said Sylvia as she linked arms with Alice. "Let's walk together."

"I'm sure that Lloyd will be happy to see you home, Aunt Ethel," said Alice.

"No problem," said Lloyd.

Alice sighed as soon as they were out the door.

"You and me both," said Sylvia.

They both laughed as they walked toward the exit.

"I don't know why they love controversy so much," said Alice. "It just wears me out."

"It's because there's not much else going on in their lives," said Sylvia as they left the church. "Haven't you noticed that the ones who love to gab and criticize are the ones that don't have much of a life?"

"But what about Cyril Overstreet?" asked Alice. "He doesn't have too much going on in his life, yet I've never heard him say a mean word about anyone."

"Yes, you're right. I guess it's not fair to generalize about people."

"Do you really think Clara's pig is the cutest thing you've ever seen?" asked Alice as they paused to part ways on the sidewalk.

Sylvia chuckled. "Oh, you know me. I'm sometimes given to exaggeration. But it's true that I thought Daisy was cute. I can't believe she'll grow up to be a 'big fat hog,' as Ethel likes to put it."

"Well, as long as she doesn't bother anyone, I don't see why it should matter."

"Nor do I." Sylvia smiled. "Good evening, Alice."

Alice went up the front porch steps and jumped when she heard a creaking sound to her right. "Who's there?" she called.

"I'm sorry, Alice," said Susan. "Wendell and I were just out here enjoying the quiet and the crickets and the moonlight. I didn't mean to startle you."

"Oh, I'm sorry to disturb your peace." Alice's eyes adjusted to the darkness until she finally spied Susan in the wicker rocker with Wendell curled up comfortably in her lap as she stroked his fur. "Louise usually leaves the porch light on."

"That's my fault," said Susan. "I saw the moon just starting to come up over that hill, so I slipped in and turned off the light."

Alice looked up at the nearly full moon. "Oh, isn't that pretty."

"You want to join us?" asked Susan. Then she laughed. "It sounds silly for me to invite you to sit on your own porch."

"I'd love to join you," admitted Alice. "Especially after that meeting I just escaped from." She sat down in the porch swing and leaned back her head.

"Board meetings can be pretty awful," said Susan. "Believe me, I know."

"What is it you do, Susan?" asked Alice. "I don't know if I've heard you mention it."

"I'm the curator for a corporate art collection."

"Oh, that must be interesting."

"It is. But board meetings can get pretty tedious."

"I'll bet they don't waste all their time arguing about potbellied pigs," said Alice.

Susan laughed. "Well, no, that particular subject hasn't come up yet. But you'd be surprised at the silly things that can consume some people."

They chatted amicably for a while and then grew quiet.

"Do you mind if I ask you something?" said Susan.

"No, of course not."

"It's really none of my business, but now that you have had time to think about it, do you remember why you and my brother broke up?"

"You know, it was so long ago that it is a bit muddled in my mind. We were both young and had definite visions for the future. I had commitments that I felt I had to honor, and Mark had things he felt he needed to do. Life just pulled us in two completely different directions. We wrote letters and called for a while, but we slowly drifted away." Alice knew that was not the complete story, but it was the best she could do at the moment.

"That makes sense. Mark's life and routine have never seemed very conducive to a long-term relationship. Every time I turn around, he seems to be hopping off to some strange locale to treat an exotic animal. Did you know that he spent two months in Antarctica last year treating penguins for some kind of fungus?"

Alice laughed. "I'll bet he had the time of his life too."

"Yes, I'm sure you're right about that."

"The next time you see your brother, please give him my best."

"Of course. I'm sure he'll be interested to hear about my visit and the way of life here in Acorn Hill."

"I'm sure he'll think it is quite tame compared to the lifestyle he's accustomed to."

"Sometimes tame is very welcome. I'm falling in love with your little town. Just this morning, the owner of that darling little fabric shop was encouraging me to take up quilting."

"That's Sylvia Songer," said Alice.

"Right. Sylvia's Buttons. Then there's that woman in the bookstore with all the cats. What a hoot. She was trying to get me interested in some seventeenth-century biography—not exactly my thing."

"That would be Viola Reed. She's quite a character. Believe it or not, she and Louise have the same taste in literature."

"I guess I better not let Louise catch me saying anything negative about Viola's books."

Alice smiled as she stood. "It's been nice talking with you, Susan, but I've got to get up early tomorrow. I'm glad you're enjoying your visit."

"Yes, I think I'll have to make Grace Chapel Inn a regular event. Maybe I'll bring Tom next time." She chuckled. "Or not. He might not appreciate it the same way that I do."

"Acorn Hill is an acquired taste," said Alice. Then she told Susan good night and went inside.

Other than the night lights that they always left on

for guests, the house was dark and still. Alice tiptoed up the stairs, assuming that both her sisters had already turned in for the evening.

"Alice?"

She turned to see Jane coming up the stairs behind her. "Oh, Jane. I thought you'd gone to bed."

"I was just finishing up a batch of muffins for breakfast tomorrow."

"I thought I smelled something delicious coming from the kitchen."

"Cranberry-orange muffins. Go get yourself one before bed if you like. They're nice and warm right now."

"Tempting, but I better pass."

"Did the board meeting run this late?" asked Jane when they had reached the third floor.

"No, I was just out on the porch, watching the moon and getting better acquainted with Susan."

"Did she mention Mark?"

Alice laughed quietly. "Oh, Jane, you make too much of that."

"He was your beau, Alice. Sometimes I think that there's a story that you're holding back—a story that a sister should share with her sister."

"Oh, the old guilting-the-sister trick, Jane. Really, I thought you were above that sort of emotional blackmail."

Jane chuckled. "Well, it was worth a shot."

"Nice try. Now, if you'll excuse me I really am exhausted. Six o'clock seems to be coming earlier than ever these days."

After Alice finished her prayers and nightly Scripture reading, she was unable to go to sleep. It felt as if thoughts and memories of Mark Graves were haunting her. She tossed and turned and tried not to look at the clock. Even when she did finally fall asleep, her old beau intruded on her dreams, and not in a pleasant way. The dreams were confused and backwards and nothing made a bit of sense.

Chapter Eight

Alice was happy to see her workweek come to an end as she signed out on Thursday at noon. It was nice to know she had three and a half days to do just as she pleased—to an extent. She buttoned her sweater against the chilly breeze and hurried across the hospital parking lot to her little blue Toyota. She planned to swing by Vera's on her way home. Fred had called from the hardware store to let her know that Vera had not felt well enough to go to school that morning.

"I'm sorry, Fred," she had told him from the phone at the nurses' station. "Is there anything I can do?"

"Well, I hate to bother you at work, Alice, but I'm really worried about her."

"What can I do?"

"That's the problem. I don't have the slightest clue. I just thought I'd let you know that she's home and not feeling so hot."

"I'll pop in and see her as soon as my shift ends, Fred. Today is my half day."

"Thanks, Alice. You have no idea how much I appreciate that."

Alice found Vera resting on the couch. She looked pale and weak. Alice could see why Fred was so worried. She encouraged Vera to have some herbal tea and a piece of toast.

"You've got to keep your strength up, Vera."

"I don't know how. It seems all I can keep down these days is a little lukewarm tea and dry toast."

Alice sat down on the chair beside the couch.

"Oh, Alice, why can't the doctors figure out what I'm dealing with? I feel so certain that it is cancer."

Alice reached for Vera's hand. "None of the tests show any signs of cancer, Vera. You need to think more positively."

"I know. I know. But it's hard to feel positive about anything right now. I can't believe I'm stuck here on this stupid couch while a substitute teacher is probably winning over my fifth graders during their first month back at school."

"Oh, Vera. No one can possibly win over your fifth graders. You know how much they always love you. They always cry about having to leave at the end of the year."

Vera waved her hand, dismissing the idea.

"I think we should pray," said Alice as she bowed her head. "Dear heavenly Father, You made Vera and You know exactly what's wrong with her. I pray that You will help her to get well and help the doctors to figure this thing out. In the meantime, I pray that You will give her the patience to endure this trial. Amen."

"Thanks, Alice. I can see why you're such a good nurse. I always feel better after you've been here." She smiled. "Maybe I could go to work tomorrow."

"Don't count on it, dear. Besides, we've got those tests tomorrow."

"Yes, well, maybe by Monday."

"Finish your tea, Vera. I'll be by to pick you up tomorrow at nine to go to the hospital."

"I feel bad making you go to the hospital on your day off, Alice."

"Nonsense. I love the hospital, and taking you isn't the same as working anyway. If you're feeling well enough we might even stop for a bowl of soup on our way home. Remember not to eat or drink anything after ten o'clock tonight."

"Thanks, Dr. Alice."

Alice smiled and squeezed her hand. "You're going to be just fine."

Alice did believe that Vera would be just fine and that whatever was plaguing her would soon disappear. Still she prayed as she drove home and parked her car next to the house.

Two new guests were just registering at the front desk when she walked in.

"This is my other sister Alice," said Louise. "Meet the Parkers, Alice. They drove all the way up from Charleston, South Carolina."

"Goodness, that's quite a distance," said Alice. "What brings you up here?"

"My wife thought we were going to see some fall foliage," said Mr. Parker in a sharp voice. "Seems she was wrong."

"It is a bit early for a lot of color," said Alice. "But I've noticed some things are beginning to turn."

Mrs. Parker looked a bit embarrassed. "I guess I got my facts mixed up. I thought this area would be at its peak by now."

"Every year is a bit different," said Alice. "There have been times when the colors are looking quite beautiful by now, but we've had a late summer this year."

"I told you that you should've asked," said Mr. Parker. "But you were so certain that you were right."

"I just thought—"

"Just thought," said her husband. "That's the trouble. You need to do more than think."

Louise and Alice exchanged looks, and Louise cleared her throat. "It is possible that the color is better up north," she said in a firm voice.

"I'm sick of driving," said Mr. Parker. "The only thing I want to be driving is a golf ball. Do you have any good courses around here?"

Louise took some brochures from the front desk and handed them to him. "There are several advertised in these."

"It's nice to meet you," said Alice, wanting to escape this couple and fix herself some lunch. "I hope you two will enjoy your stay."

"Thank you," said Mrs. Parker. "It seems to be a lovely place."

"Is there a bathroom in our room?" barked Mr. Parker.

"Yes," Louise assured him as Alice ducked down the back hall that led to the kitchen.

Alice found Jane chopping celery. "Did you meet the Parkers?" she asked in a soft voice.

Jane chuckled. "Yes, I had the pleasure of their acquaintance."

"Mrs. Parker seems sweet."

"That man makes me want to scream."

Alice nodded as she looked in the refrigerator. "He's the kind who makes you thankful to be single."

"If he snipes at his wife one more time, I might have to slap him."

"I can just see the headlines in the *Acorn Nutshell*," said

Alice as she took some leftover pasta salad from the refrig-erator. "Renowned Chef of Grace Chapel Inn Assaults Guest." She held the bowl up. "Mind if I finish this?"

"That's what it's for."

Alice told Jane about her visit with Vera as she ate her lunch.

"I thought perhaps I'd make something to take over to them for dinner tonight," said Alice as she rinsed her bowl.

"Oh, you don't have to," said Jane. "I'll just make enough of this chicken soup for them and we can put in that extra loaf of bread and—"

"*Yoo-hoo*," called Ethel from the back porch, "come see what I brought you."

Jane and Alice went out to the back porch to see Ethel setting down a box of apples. "Lloyd and I took a lovely drive out in the country this morning and we discovered the best little produce stand. Can you believe these apples were picked just this morning?" She leaned over and smelled them.

"They look beautiful, Aunt Ethel," said Jane. "Thank you."

"I got a box for me and one for you girls. I think I'll make applesauce with mine. I haven't made applesauce in years."

Jane picked up an apple to examine it closer. "I think

I'll bake up a couple of pies. We can send one over to Fred and Vera."

"How is poor Vera?" asked Ethel.

"Not too well," said Alice, giving her aunt the details while Jane filled a colander with apples to take into the kitchen.

"That's too bad," said Ethel. She looked into the laundry room. "Goodness sakes, it looks different in here. What's changed?"

"Well, for starters, Alice cleaned it up," said Jane.

"Oh, I know that."

"Then I painted these shelves," said Jane as she ran her hand across the smooth sage-green surface. "And I made some new curtains too." She pointed at the home-spun plaid fabric in shades of green, rust and gold.

"Well, it looks right pretty in here," said Ethel. "Who would've thought you could make a laundry look so pretty."

"What is going on out here?" called Louise from the kitchen. "Are you ladies doing the laundry?"

"Auntie brought us some apples," said Jane as she carried the colander into the kitchen and set it on the maple counter.

"Very nice," said Louise as she glanced at the rosy-cheeked apples. "But I am in serious need of a cup of tea right now."

"I just put the kettle on," said Alice. "It should be ready any minute."

"Jane, do you have any of those ginger biscotti left?" asked Louise.

"I most certainly do." She reached for the jar. "Aunt Ethel, would you care to join us?"

"Oh, maybe for just a bit. You know it's Bingo night tonight, and I promised Lloyd that I'd come early to help."

"That man is about to drive me crazy," said Louise as she sat down at the kitchen table.

"What can you possibly mean?" sputtered Ethel. "What on earth has Lloyd done?"

Louise waved her hand. "Not Lloyd, Aunt Ethel. I mean one of our guests. I suppose I should watch my tongue, but he is the sort of man who gives a bad name to his gender."

Ethel laughed. "Then you couldn't possibly be speaking of Lloyd." Then she leaned forward with fresh interest. "Who is this guest, Louise, and what has he done to ruffle your feathers so?"

"He is just a big, loud-mouthed brute," said Louise as she reached for a piece of biscotti. "The man is rude and picks on his poor wife. Quite frankly, I wish he would go back to where he came from, or perhaps just fall into a deep hole somewhere."

"Louise," said Alice in a quiet voice. "Don't forget we're called *Grace* Chapel Inn. We can't exactly go around throwing our guests out on the street."

"Unfortunately, you are right." Louise took a sip of tea.

"Especially at times like this when we're not fully booked," warned Jane. "And don't forget that we've still got one room that's vacant this weekend. We need every paying guest we can find."

"I think I would rather live on beans and rice than put up with obnoxious boors like that Mr. Parker," said Louise in a hushed voice, as if he might have been listening at the door.

Ethel frowned and shook her head. "Well, I suppose that even the obnoxious boors need to be loved."

Everyone paused to look at her. It was such an un-Ethel-like thing to say. "You're absolutely right, Auntie," Alice finally said as she patted her aunt's soft arm. "That sounds just like something that Father would say."

Ethel smiled. "It does, doesn't it?"

For the first time, Alice tried to consider how it must have been for Ethel as a child, having a father like the one described in Daniel's journal. It could not have been easy. No wonder Ethel could come across as prickly sometimes. She had probably learned those ways as a small child.

Chapter Nine

The sisters were happy to find themselves gathered in the library once again, eager to read more poignant memories from their father's journal. Jane had made a lovely apple pie with a lattice top that smelled of cinnamon and brown sugar. An identical pie, along with hot soup and homemade bread, had long since been delivered to the Humbert household.

Louise carried a pot of Earl Grey tea into the room, complete with a flowery tea cozy to keep it hot. "Do not worry," she assured them. "It is decaffeinated." She set the porcelain pot on the tray and sat down in an easy chair. "That way it will not keep us awake until dawn."

"I missed our little session the last two nights," said Jane as she flopped down into the other easy chair.

"Yes," agreed Louise. "I have been wondering if Father ever got to write an actual obituary."

"Well, let's find out." Alice put on her reading glasses and leaned back into the desk chair as she opened the precious book.

December 12, 1925.

Mother is very sick. It started out as an ordinary cold, but now she has a bad cough that seems to get worse with each passing day. She is so weakened by it that she could not get out of bed today. I asked my father if I could go for the doctor, but he said we do not have money to pay for such luxuries. I think I will go to town tomorrow morning to see if I can trade some labor for a doctor's visit and some medicine. I noticed the clouds were thick and gray as I walked home from school today. I think it will snow tonight. I am usually happy to see the snow come, but this year is different. Perhaps I am growing up. This year, I feel worried about Mother's health as well as all the extra chores that come with the harsh winter weather. I do not enjoy getting out of bed while it is still dark out, and I do not enjoy going out into the freezing cold to crack the ice on the water troughs. However, I know better than to complain, for then I would give my father excuse to tell me that I should quit going to school. He thinks that is the answer to every problem. Somehow I know that he is wrong, and sometimes I try to imagine how his life might have been different if he had gone on to school. He is not a stupid man by any means. He can fix a harness or wagon wheel better than anyone, when he has a mind to anyway. Unfortunately he has no respect for books or learning, and I believe this has contributed greatly to his general dissatisfaction with life.

Alice paused and reached for her teacup. "That's the end of that entry."

Louise sighed. "It is simply amazing the way that Father, even at such a young age, was attempting to understand his father better."

"It is," agreed Jane. "Most teenagers these days wouldn't give a parent like that the time of day. If anyone had an excuse to rebel against his parents, it was our father."

"Shall I continue?" asked Alice, and both sisters nodded eagerly. "Look at this," said Alice as she turned the next page. She held it up so they could see the lovely sketch of a rose. "Look." Alice pointed to a detail in the drawing. "He even included the thorns."

"What does it say there?" asked Jane. Alice read.

To Mother, December 21, 1925.

"How sweet. Do you suppose he gave it to her?" asked Louise.

Alice shook her head as the realization hit her. "No. Let me continue." She adjusted her glasses and read. *"Mother died today—"*

"Oh dear," said Louise.

"Poor Father," said Jane.

The doctor was here two times in the last week, but it was no use and his medicine was of little help. He said that Mother had pneumonia and our only hope was to keep her warm and comfortable and to pray. I did not tell him that I had given up praying a few years ago. I did not think that he would have understood. Although I actually tried to pray last night, I felt dishonest. It is not that I was unwilling to become a hypocrite for the sake of Mother, but I was afraid my prayers might do her more harm than good. I figured if there really was a God, he would not be pleased with me for not believing in him until I became desperately in need. And I figured if there was no God, why should I waste my breath? The neighbors have been in and out of our house all day. I am amazed at how death draws people together, and I wonder why these women did not come to my mother's assistance sooner. Perhaps it would have helped her to live. I do not know how to describe the sadness I feel. It is like a heavy cloak that is encasing me. It is hard to think clearly and it is difficult to breathe. I have not cried. Indeed, I wonder if I am too old to cry now. Or perhaps I am just afraid that if I begin to cry I shall never be able to stop. My chest and throat ache from holding this pain inside of me. I think I shall go out into the fields and walk far enough away so that I can scream my pain into the darkness of the night.

"Oh my," said Alice as she looked at her sisters. Both were wiping their eyes, and she now realized that she, too, had tears running down both cheeks. "Poor Father."

"Keep reading," gasped Jane. "Please, Alice."

December 24, 1925.

My sister Alice and her husband Asher were the only other family members to attend Mother's funeral yesterday. My other two brothers both live too far away to make this trip in the winter. My father was surprisingly civilized during the funeral service, quite sober too. He even invited Alice and Asher to stay with us through the Christmas holidays. Not that we will have much of a Christmas without Mother. Alice went through some of Mother's things this morning and found the blue woolen scarf that was nearly finished. I told her that Mother was making it for me, and Alice sat right down and finished knitting it. Then she gently wrapped it around my neck and said "Merry Christmas." She is a good soul. Father slipped out tonight after supper. We all knew where he was headed, and I do not think any of us cared. It is not that he has been terribly mean or awful lately. In fact, he has been quite subdued and perhaps even a bit sad. Even so, he is a difficult person to be around at best, and I think we were all relieved when he left. Alice turned the radio on to Christmas music and made a big rice pudding complete with fat raisins. All in all, it has not been such a horrible day. I am still very sad and I miss Mother more than I can say, but it did help me to go out into the snowy fields and cry. There is a big hole in my chest now. An emptiness that I fear shall never be filled again. Oh, how I miss my mother. Now, I shall write my first authentic obituary.

Rose Mary Bergstrom Howard came into the world on June 5, 1879, and passed on to her eternal reward on December 21, 1925. The beloved mother of six children, Mrs. Howard is survived by sons John, Charles and Daniel, as well as her daughter Alice. Preceding her in death were her other two children, Martha and Adam. Mrs. Howard enjoyed the rural life of agriculture and was quite skilled at cooking, sewing, knitting, preserving and gardening. Her delectable raspberry jam often won first place at the Crawford County Fair, and her tea roses were surpassed by none. A good-hearted and generous woman, she will be greatly missed by her family and friends.

"That poor woman was only forty-six years old," said Jane. "What a short and sad life."

"What a sweet obituary," said Louise. "Do you think it was printed in the newspaper?"

"I don't know," said Alice. "The next entry isn't until after the New Year. Shall we save it for next time?"

"Yes," said Louise. "I am ready to call it a night."

"I like our grandmother," said Jane. "I think, despite her inability to stand up to her husband, she was a good woman."

"Father surely seemed to love her," said Alice as she placed a bookmark in the journal.

"It was hard for a lot of women back in the old days," continued Jane. "I'm sure if our grandmother lived today, her life would've turned out quite differently."

They sat quietly in thought, and then jumped at the sound of someone's knocking at the door to the library. Louise got up to open it.

"Is this where you keep the books?" asked Mr. Parker. He had on a dark blue velour bathrobe and matching bedroom slippers.

"Why, yes." Louise blinked. "This is the library. We were, uh, just leaving."

"Well, I need something to help get me to sleep," he said in a grumpy voice. "Don't know why you folks don't have any TV in the rooms. What kind of a place you running here anyway? Trying to haul us all back into the nineteenth century whether we like it or not?"

"I hope you can find something you like," said Louise in a stiff voice as the three sisters gathered their things and filed past him and into the hallway.

"Don't you have any westerns in here?" he called as they slipped away.

"*That man*," said Louise in a hushed voice.

"Take a deep breath," whispered Jane. "Count to ten if you need to."

Alice giggled as she, not for the first time, considered how fortunate she was to be a single woman. "You might want to count your blessings while you're at it."

Alice did thank God later on that night. She sincerely offered thanks for being blissfully unmarried as she took her time to prepare for bed. First she slathered herself in a new rich moisturizer that a friend from the hospital had introduced her to. Then she took the time to file her nails, getting each one just so. She loved the sweet simplicity of her single life, her ability to come and go mostly as she pleased, to read late into the night if she liked, or to sleep in occasionally when she did not have to work. She liked the luxury of not sharing her closet or her bathroom or even her private thoughts if she did not want to. Yes, it was definitely a very good life—preferable to that poor woman's downstairs. How could she endure such endless harassment? Alice felt that she herself had much to be thankful for as she turned on her reading light and picked up the latest mystery book that Jane had lent to her.

She looked down at the floor where Wendell, as usual, seemed to be waiting for her to finish her bedtime preparations. He patiently sat on her braided rug, his tail switching back and forth as if counting down the seconds until she would finally retire. Then, in the same instant that she got into bed, Wendell hopped up. He circled around on her fluffy quilt a couple of times until he found the perfect spot and curled into a pudgy ball right beside her. He closed his eyes and happily purred as she scratched the top of his head.

"You're the perfect companion, Wendell," she told the fat tabby. "You never talk too much and you never ask nosy questions. You're not rude or touchy or bossy. Okay, you're a little bit bossy sometimes. But really, you are much nicer than a lot of people."

Then she opened her book and sighed, and, completely content with her quiet little life, she began to read.

Chapter Ten

"We were so busy yesterday that I forgot to ask how Vera's tests went," Louise said to Alice as they tidied up the front hall.

"The results won't be back until next week. But at least Vera was feeling a little better. We stopped at a new lunch spot in Potterston, and she was able to eat almost a whole bowl of soup."

"Well, that is good news," said Louise. "Maybe she just had a bad case of one of those foreign flu viruses that are always going around. Probably caught it from one of her students at school."

"Maybe."

"Hey, Alice," said Susan as she came down the stairs.

"Hi, Susan. How are you?"

"Great, actually. I was just thinking about taking a little walk to town."

"It's a nice day for it."

"Do you want to join me?"

"As a matter of fact, I wanted to run into Sylvia's Buttons and look at fabric. I was trying to talk my friend Vera into making a braided rug. She is the one who has been ill. I thought it might help her to get her mind off of her troubles."

"Maybe I should do the same thing myself when I get back home. It might distract me from my daughter and grandson."

The two women walked toward town. "Tell me if I go too fast for you," said Alice. "I usually walk with Vera and we can really get going."

"No, I like a quick pace," said Susan. "Makes me feel younger."

Just as they turned the corner to go down Hill Street they nearly ran into Clara Horn pushing her baby carriage at near-breakneck speed.

"Goodness, Clara," said Alice. "Where are you going in such a hurry?"

"It's Daisy," said Clara. "She's sick and I wanted Dr. Bentley to see her, but he refused. He said that he could not treat animals and that I should take her to the veterinarian in Potterston, but you know I haven't driven a car since my Oscar died." She bent over her carriage and stared at the piglet as she wrung her hands.

"May I see her?" asked Susan.

Clara stood up straight and smiled. "Yes, but do bear in mind, she's not looking her best today. I think she may have eaten something that upset her little tummy. I'm so worried I don't know what to do."

Susan leaned over to peer at the little pig. "She doesn't seem very perky, does she?" She smiled at Clara now. "Well, I have a car. Would you like me to drive you to the vet?"

"Oh, would you? Could you? I can pay for your gas."

Alice also leaned over to get a better look at Daisy. "She does look a little under the weather," she agreed. "But you're on vacation, Susan. I can drive Clara and Daisy to the vet. Besides, I know exactly where it is. That way you can go ahead and do your shopping and whatnot in town."

"And miss out on this?" whispered Susan. "Not on your life."

Alice grinned at her. "Well, okay then. I suppose we better head back up to the inn. Do you mind walking some more, Clara?"

"Not at all. Anything to get help for my baby."

When they got to the inn, they left Daisy in her carriage under a shade tree while they called ahead to be sure that the veterinary hospital was open. And to everyone's dismay, it was not.

"I have an idea," said Susan suddenly. "My brother is a vet. I'll call him and see if he has any advice."

So Susan dialed a number and then waited for her brother to get on the line. Alice felt slightly apprehensive as she listened to Susan explaining the situation with Daisy. At the same time, she told herself not to be silly, this was a case of a pig in need. Then Susan asked Clara a few questions—prompted by her brother—about what and when the pig had eaten and whether she was running a fever and a few other things before she finally hung up.

"Okay, it could be a number of things," said Susan. "Daisy may have ingested something toxic, like a plant or cleaning solvent. Do you think that's possible, Clara?"

"I don't see how. I don't have any poison plants that I know of, and I haven't been doing any cleaning." The old woman put her hand over her mouth. "Oh my goodness, do you think that someone may have intentionally tried to poison her? I know that some people don't think much of my little Daisy Waisy."

Susan and Alice exchanged glances. Then Alice said, "I honestly don't think anyone in Acorn Hill would try to poison an animal. No matter how much they might complain about Daisy, people aren't really that mean."

"Another possibility is that Daisy may have

accidentally eaten an object like a coin or a marble," Susan suggested. "It could be upsetting her tummy, but unless it's a large object, it should pass through her with no problem."

"I suppose that's a possibility. I do sometimes drop things on the floor and it's hard for me to bend down to pick them up. And, of course, my eyesight's not what it used to be." She brightened now. "Maybe that's it. Perhaps Daisy has simply swallowed a penny."

Susan nodded. "Yes, that's probably it."

"I just love Daisy so much," said Clara. "I can't bear the idea of losing her. You know I lost my Oscar last year, and I've been so alone since then. Having Daisy for company has been a real godsend for me."

Alice patted the older woman's hand. She remembered the time that Florence Simpson and Clara Horn had assumed mean things about her father, but that had been last Christmas, and Alice had long since forgiven both women. Besides, after Clara's husband had died, everyone had noticed that she seemed to change dramatically. Many of her friends assumed she was becoming senile, but listening to the old woman today, Alice suspected that Clara was mentally sound but just lonely.

"Would you like a ride home?" offered Alice.

"Oh, that would be lovely, dear. I am a bit worn out."

She smiled. "You're such a dear girl, Alice. I've always felt that you were such a fine Christian. I used to tell your father as much."

Alice laughed. "Well, thank you, Clara."

When Alice got to Clara's house, she took the folded carriage out of the trunk and carried it into the house, while Clara carried little Daisy.

"Would you mind taking a look around, dear?" said Clara. "To see if I've dropped anything on the floor that Daisy might accidentally eat?"

"Sure." Alice found the small, tidy house to be in order. "I don't see a thing, Clara. It's all neat and clean."

Clara smiled proudly. "You know, Oscar always said I was the best housekeeper. Come into the kitchen, dear. I'd like to send something home with you. Do you like homemade pickles?"

Alice told her she did, and Clara filled a small box with several jars of bread-and-butter pickles. "I always put up far too many," she explained. "But I hate letting those cucumbers go to waste. Oh, how about some plums. The tree in my backyard was just loaded this year. May I send a bag of plums with you too?"

"Oh, Jane will be thrilled with pickles and plums," Alice assured her. "And if there's anything we can do to help with Daisy, just feel free to call."

"Thank you, dear. I appreciate that."

Alice decided to go ahead and stop by Sylvia's Buttons on her way home. She hoped that Susan had proceeded with her own plans despite their interruption. Perhaps she would even run into her.

"Alice," called Sylvia as the bell tinkled on the door, "what brings you in here?"

"I told Vera that she should try making a braided rug to get her mind off her troubles."

"She's still sick?"

Alice nodded. "They did more tests yesterday, but she won't hear anything about them for a while."

"Well, I've got a lot of nice scraps in that big basket there. What colors do you think she'd like?"

"She really likes red, white and blue," said Alice. "She's got a lot of Americana accents."

"Oh, that would make a nice braided rug. Let's see what we can find."

It took about an hour, but the two women finally managed to fill a plastic bag with an interesting mix of red, white and blue fabrics. Not only that, but Alice found an apron pattern that looked fairly simple.

"How long do you think it would take to whip up one of these aprons?" she asked Sylvia. "I thought maybe I could make a few to sell at the Fall Festival."

"Oh, that's such an easy pattern, Alice, I'll bet you could easily finish one within an hour, maybe less."

"Okay, then, I guess I'll get enough fabric to make several. I think these fall patterns might be fun."

"What a great idea. How about this one with pump-kins and squash?" asked Sylvia. "And there's the one with the squirrels and nuts."

Soon Alice had chosen fabric for six different aprons. "This is going to be fun," she said as she stacked the bolts on the cutting table.

"I'm giving you a fifty-percent discount on Vera's rug pieces," said Sylvia as she rang it up on the cash register.

"Oh, you don't have to—"

"Just tell Vera that's my get-well wish for her."

Alice smiled. "I know she'll appreciate that."

Alice decided to drop off her treasure. She knew it was too early for Fred to be home from the hardware store, especially on a Saturday. Vera was in the kitchen when Alice went in.

"You're up," said Alice happily.

"Yes. I'm feeling much better. I thought I'd get an early start on dinner and surprise Fred."

Alice hugged her friend. "Oh, I'm so glad you're feel-ing better." She held out the bag. "Maybe you won't be needing this after all."

"The rug scraps?" Vera peeked into the bag. "Oh, those are beautiful. Of course, I'd still love to make a rug. Let me pay you—"

"No. It's a get-well gift from Sylvia and me."

"Well, you'll still have to give me lessons and get me started."

"You bet. Let's start it next week." Alice patted Vera on the back. "Just remember not to overdo it. Take it easy and give yourself time to feel better."

"Thank you, Dr. Alice."

Alice said good-bye and hurried home to see if she could give Jane a hand with dinner. Carrying her box of pickles through the back door, Alice found Jane creating a pretty flower arrangement.

"That's gorgeous," said Alice.

"Thanks, I'm trying."

"Clara Horn sent us some nice juicy plums as well as some homemade bread-and-butter pickles."

"That was nice of her. By the way, we filled one of our vacant rooms for tonight. The Fisks, from New York City, were driving through town and saw the inn."

"That's good news." Alice paused to admire Jane's creation. Her ability to make flowers look like a work of art was really amazing. "You certainly are making the most of the last of the summer blooms."

"Yes." Jane had a twinkle in her eye. "I thought we could use a special bouquet for dinner tonight."

"Are you making a special dinner?"

"Maybe," said Jane mysteriously.

"Who's coming?"

"I'm not sure."

Alice was confused, but if Jane wanted to play games she might have to play alone. "Well, do you need any help?"

Jane turned and faced Alice, looking at her as if she was assessing her before she firmly said, "No, I don't need any help."

Alice just shrugged. "Fine."

"But there is something you can do for me."

Alice brightened. "Sure. What?"

"Go up and take a shower and put on a nice outfit and really try to look sharp. Okay?"

"Well..."

Jane seemed to be thinking. "What if I had someone from the city coming, from the art world, you know, here to see my work—"

"Your paintings?" asked Alice. "Someone is coming to—"

"I'm just saying, 'what if,'" continued Jane. "Would you try to look a bit more, well, cosmopolitan?"

Alice laughed. "I'm sure I wouldn't even know where to begin."

"Okay, how about this. You go get your shower and then I'll come up and help you. Would that be okay?"

"Well, I guess so, if it's that important to—"

"Oh, it is. Thank you so much. Take your time. I'll be up in about half an hour, okay?"

"You're sure you want to waste your time on me—"

"Oh, I do, Alice. I really do."

"Okay then..." Alice just shook her head as she walked through the kitchen. Jane was definitely acting crazy tonight. Alice paused by the mirror in the dining room to look at herself. Maybe she did not look fashionable, but her hair was neatly cut and her chambray shirt was clean and pressed. But apparently this would not impress Jane's big-city friends. Well, if this was going to help Jane get a toehold into the art world, Alice would do whatever it took to help.

Apparently it would take a lot, thought Alice a short time later, as she patiently stood waiting while Jane applied a bit of blush and lipstick and even a little eye shadow. Alice had not worn eye shadow for decades.

"Is this really necessa—"

"Yes," snapped Jane. "Just trust me, okay."

Alice took in a deep breath and waited. Already Jane

had used a combination of clothing that Alice would never in a million years have picked out—especially if she was trying to impress someone. Jane had selected a denim skirt that Alice had bought on sale a few years before and had meant to hem but never got to it. It hung nearly to her ankles, but Jane seemed to think that was perfect. Then she had made Alice try on a loose orange silk sweater of Jane's that was a little wider at the neckline than Alice was used to.

"I don't know," said Alice.

"You have beautiful shoulders, Alice," said Jane. "And besides, we're going to use a scarf and some jewelry. Just wait until I'm finished. You're still a work in progress."

Jane did something with Alice's hair, liberally squirted her with perfume and then spun her around to look at the full-length mirror attached to her closet door.

"Oh my!" Alice's hand went up to her mouth.

"What do you think?" asked Jane proudly.

"I don't know. I don't look like me."

"Yes, you do. Only better."

Alice was not so sure. "I feel sort of silly."

"Just hold your head up and remember that you are beautiful." Jane smiled. "You really are, Alice. I mean, everyone knows you're beautiful in spirit, but you're so pretty too. You just don't do anything to show it off."

Alice frowned. "No, I've never been into showing off."

"Sorry," said Jane. "Bad choice of words. You've just never optimized the good looks God has given you."

"Hmm..."

"Okay, now this is the deal. I want you and Louise to stay up here until dinnertime."

"Whatever for?"

"Oh, I just thought it would seem more elegant for my two sisters to come down the stairs at dinnertime. Don't you think?"

Alice shrugged. "I think my baby sister is losing it."

"Promise you won't come down until it's time."

"How will I know—"

"I'll ring a bell."

"A bell?" Alice's brows lifted. This was just getting more and more bizarre, but she decided to humor Jane. It was her party and her guests.

"Okay, maybe I'll use this time to cut out some of these aprons."

"That's perfect," said Jane. "Now I better get busy."

Four aprons later, and what seemed like only a few minutes, Alice heard a bell ringing downstairs. Jane had not been kidding. Pausing to glance in the mirror once more, Alice tried to do what Jane had said, holding her head high and shoulders back, as she exited her room.

"Alice," said Louise, "you look lovely."

"Thanks, but don't you think Jane is taking this a little far? Did she dress you too?" Alice studied Louise's outfit of pale blue sweater set, beige skirt and pearls, but could find nothing out of the ordinary.

"I am perfectly capable of dressing myself," said Louise. "You, on the other hand, could sometimes use a hand."

"Thanks a lot."

Candles were lit downstairs and jazz music played softly. Alice could hear happy conversation coming from the living room. "Did they start the party without us?" she whispered to Louise.

Louise just smiled.

"Here are Alice and Louise now," said Jane as she greeted her sisters with both hands outstretched. "We have a surprise visitor tonight, ladies. Susan invited her brother Mark to come down for a little visit."

Alice felt her eyes widen and her throat went tight. Mark Graves was here? In Acorn Hill? In her own home? Why had she not been warned?

"Well, I actually invited him to come out here to check on that sick little pig," explained Susan. "I felt sorry for that poor old woman, and as it turned out Mark wasn't busy this weekend...."

Alice felt as if everything were in a blur. She could see

the tall man in the tweed jacket, a dignified stranger with charcoal-colored hair that was light gray at the temples, and a salt-and-pepper beard. He reminded her of a character in a movie, a sea captain perhaps.

"Louise," he said as he shook her sister's hand. Then he stepped toward her and took her hand in his. "Alice, it's so good to see you again."

"Mark," she somehow managed to say. "It's been years."

He nodded and she felt as if she were sinking as she looked into his eyes.

He smiled broadly, as if he was truly glad to see her, and said, "You're looking well."

She tried to form an answer but felt tongue-tied and stupid, as if she were sixteen again. Goodness, she hoped she was not about to do something really ridiculous, like faint. *Dear God*, she prayed silently, *please help me to hold myself together tonight.*

Chapter Eleven

*H*er prayer was answered. Somehow, and she felt it nothing short of miraculous, she was able to converse and laugh and ask appropriate questions as they all gathered around the large mahogany table in the dining room.

"Jane, you've really outdone yourself tonight," said Alice as Jane finally presented her special dessert with dramatic flair.

"I haven't had baked Alaska in ages," Mark commented.

"Speaking of the cold part of the world," said Louise, "I heard that you were treating penguins down in Antarctica not long ago."

That was all it took for Mark to launch into another interesting story, complete with a humorous account of how he had to go around wearing a fisherman's smelly jacket after his expensive Gortex parka mysteriously disappeared one night. "The truth is that I grew to truly appreciate that greasy oilskin coat. I think it kept me warmer than the one I'd brought. So much for today's new technology in outerwear."

"You should write these stories down," said Jane. "They'd make an interesting book."

"Actually, it's already been done," he told her. "Ever heard of the book called *Zoo Doctor*?"

"And then, of course, there is the old James Herriott series," said Alice. "I so enjoyed reading those books years ago. In fact, all this talk of animals makes me want to read them over again."

"Yes, Eliot and I used to watch the stories on public television," said Louise. "One of the few times we ever turned on the TV. But, oh my, we would just laugh and laugh over it."

Finally, dinner came to an end, and Jane suggested that Mark might enjoy a tour of the house.

"Yes," he said, "I do remember being here long ago, but it seems different to me now."

"We have done a lot of renovations," Louise explained.

"Jane is our decorator," said Alice.

"Alice helped me quite a bit with the painting," said Jane. "Why don't you show Mark around, Alice?"

"I'll help you clean up, Jane," said Louise.

"So will I," offered Susan. "Anything to get another

look at that kitchen. You've got to see her kitchen, Mark. It is just darling."

"Not until it's cleaned up a bit," warned Jane. "We normally don't allow the guests in there, but Susan is becoming more like family since she's been with us all week."

Susan grinned. "Hey, maybe you could adopt me."

Alice knew this was a setup, but what could she do other than cooperate? "Well, you've obviously seen the living room and the dining room, and I assume the foyer."

"That's about it. And I must say the rooms look splendid. Jane really has a touch."

"Yes, she's an artist, you know." She led him back into the hall.

"I recall your saying how artistic she was, but she must have been quite young...back then."

Alice smiled. "Yes, Jane would've still been in grade school"—she followed his choice in words— "back then."

"This was my father's den. But, as you can see from the plaque, we call it the library now, although I usually forget."

"This is a handsome room," said Mark as he perused the bookshelves. "Your father was quite a reader."

"Yes." Then she chuckled. "Although we have a guest right now who doesn't think much of this library."

"Why?"

"No westerns," she said with a smile.

Mark nodded. "No, your father didn't strike me as the western type."

Alice turned and studied Mark. He had only met her father a couple of times. "What type did he strike you as?"

Mark's face grew serious and he seemed to be considering his answer. "Actually, as I was young and immature at the time, I'm not sure that my opinion of your father was accurate."

She nodded. "Yes, I can understand that, but I'm curious about how you perceived him."

"Do you mind?" Mark nodded to the desk chair as if he wanted to sit down.

"Of course, have a seat."

"Thank you." He sat in the chair and ran his hands over the smooth surface of the desk. "Very nice."

Alice sat down in an easy chair across from him. This evening felt very odd. She felt almost as if she were an actor in a movie, as if none of this were really happening.

Mark was looking at Alice as if perhaps he, too, thought it was all a bit strange.

"In answer to your question about your father, Alice,

I suppose…well, I may have thought your father was a bit stuffy."

Alice blinked. "Stuffy?"

Mark's brow furrowed with what appeared to be regret. "I know, I know. I probably read him completely wrong. I'm sorry."

"No, I appreciate your honesty. Really, it's rather interesting. Anything else?"

"Well, I could tell that you and your father were quite close. I suspected you were his favorite—"

"His favorite?" Alice shook her head. "Oh no, I don't think Father ever had a favorite."

"I wouldn't be so sure. You two seemed to have quite a connection. I suppose I might've been a bit jealous."

"Jealous?"

He nodded. "It sounds silly now."

She smiled. "I suppose so. That was so very long ago."

He sighed. "Yes, it seems like another lifetime. I think I am a completely different person now."

"As am I."

"Yes. We've both changed considerably."

She sighed. She was not sure if it was a sigh of relief or perhaps disappointment, but she suspected that they had just confessed that what had happened so long ago was really and truly over.

"Would you like to see the rest of the house?"

He said that he would, and Alice, playing tour guide, showed him through the parlor and the sunroom, pausing at the staircase. "I'd show you the guest rooms upstairs, but they're all taken. Well, except for one."

"Actually, I think I will be staying in that one."

She nodded. "Of course."

"I'm sorry if my unexpected visit took you by surprise, Alice," said Mark as he ran his hand over the smooth banister. "Susan didn't mention you or even tell me she was staying at your family's home. She did pique my curiosity when she said it was in Acorn Hill, and I thought it would be fun to see this town again. I knew there was a possibility that you might still live here."

"Well, I'm glad you came." She could hear laughter drifting out from the kitchen, and part of her longed to be there, out of this uncomfortable situation.

"Really?" His eyes lit up slightly. "I wasn't sure."

She looked down at the floor. As usual, the carpet in the foyer had a wrinkle in it. She controlled herself from bending down to straighten it. She looked back up at him. It seemed the least she could be was honest. "I have to admit that it was a bit of a shock but, yes, it's good to see you again."

"Do you ever think—"

"There you two are," said Susan as the three women emerged from the kitchen. "Well, did you get the full tour, Mark? What do you think?"

"This is a beautiful home," he told her. "These ladies have done an incredible job restoring the place."

Susan came up and linked arms with her brother. "I thought you'd like it. I'm so glad you could get away. I feel as if I haven't seen you in ages."

Alice could feel Jane's eyes on her, and she suspected she would be fully interrogated before she was allowed to go to bed tonight.

"You must see this kitchen," said Susan as she led Mark toward the back of the house. "It is so charming."

"How's it going?" Jane asked as soon as Mark and Susan were safely out of earshot.

Alice could see that her sisters were eager for a report on Mark. It was one of the few times in her life when she was certain that she had the undivided attention of both of them. "All right."

"Come on," said Jane. "That's not an answer."

Alice looked from Jane to Louise and just shook her head. "I can't believe you two. I assume you were in on this too, Louise?"

Louise's lips curled into what looked more like a smirk than a smile.

"My own sisters." Alice tried her best to appear betrayed.

Jane took Alice by the arm. "How else could we have gotten you to cooperate?"

"Cooperate?"

"Yes. Think about it, Alice. What do you think you would've done if I had announced that Mark Graves was joining us for dinner?"

Alice shrugged.

"Oh, come on. You would've been a bundle of nerves. You might've even made up some lame excuse not to join us. I just figured this way would be easier for everyone."

"But, Jane, you lied to me."

Jane shook her head. "No, I did not lie. Believe me, I was very careful not to lie."

"But you told me you had some art people coming to—"

"No, Alice, I said *what if* I had some art people coming to dinner."

"Oh, Jane, this is so—"

Just then the phone on the reception desk rang. "Goodness," said Alice, slightly startled. She picked it up and said, "Hello, Grace Chapel Inn."

"Alice?" cried a shrill voice. "Is that you? Oh, mercy

me, I need help for my Daisy. She's not doing well and I..." The old woman broke into sobs.

"Clara. Now calm down. Tell me what's wrong."

"I think she's dying," she sobbed.

"Hold on, Clara. I'll be right over." Alice hung up the phone and ran to the kitchen, where Susan was just showing her brother the handmade tiles that Jane had put up.

"I have to excuse myself. Clara's pig is in distress. I'm going over right now to see if I can help her to—"

"I'll drive," said Mark. "I have a medical bag in my car."

The two of them took off in his SUV, speeding toward Clara's house on the other side of town.

"I'm sorry to have involved you in this—" began Alice.

"Are you kidding? This is what I do for a living, Alice. I love saving animals."

Alice smiled to herself. Mark was a good man. She had always known that.

"This is it," she told him.

"Now, it's possible that we may need to operate. Are you okay to assist me? I know that you used to be a nurse."

"I am still a nurse," she told him as he grabbed his bag and they both jogged toward the house.

Mark was right; Daisy did require surgery. Alice quickly sterilized Clara's kitchen table and told the old woman to wait in the living room until they were done. Fortunately, the surgery went perfectly. Mark quickly located the source of Daisy's digestive problems. "I think it's some sort of pit," said Mark as he pointed to the dark object.

"I'll bet it's a plum pit," said Alice. "Clara's tree was loaded this year."

"*Uh-huh*," said Mark as he began to stitch Daisy back up.

Soon he was finished and Alice went out to the living room to tell Clara the good news.

"Oh, you really are an angel, Alice. But where did you find the pig doctor?"

Alice laughed. "Actually, he's a famous veterinarian who has treated exotic animals all over the world."

Clara blinked. "And he came all the way here just to help my Daisy."

Alice nodded.

"Glory be."

Alice returned to the kitchen to clean up. Mark was still keeping an eye on the piglet's recovery. Alice knew that recovery time was just as important as the actual surgery. Things like heart rate, blood pressure and breathing needed careful monitoring.

"She's a cute little thing," said Mark as he set aside his stethoscope.

Alice laughed as she gave the kitchen table one final wipe down. "Not everyone in this town would agree with you on that account."

"That's too bad. These little guys really do make excellent pets. They're very intelligent and can be trained to do just about anything."

"But don't they grow up to be enormous? Jane said they could weigh up to three hundred pounds as adults."

"Not these little ones. This is a miniature Vietnamese potbellied pig."

"A miniature?"

"Yes. See how tiny she is now? If she were a regular one she would already be weighing in at twenty-five pounds. But as a miniature, that's about all Daisy will ever weigh when she's full-grown. And she'll only be about twelve to fifteen inches tall."

"Really?" Alice paused with the sponge still in her hand. "Only twenty-five pounds. Why, lots of dogs are bigger than that. I'll bet that Harry is even bigger than that."

"Harry?"

"Viola Reed's cat. He helps to manage the Nine Lives Bookstore."

"Wow, that's a good-sized cat."

"But anyway, this means that people shouldn't be picking on her."

"Viola?"

Alice laughed. "No, Clara. Some folks in town have been giving her a hard time. Some even thought she was getting senile."

"Because of her pig?"

"Because they didn't like the idea of a giant hog walking down the streets of Acorn Hill."

"Most towns have ordinances against farm animals within the town limits."

"According to the mayor, who is also my aunt Ethel's beau, we apparently do not."

Mark started laughing now. "This town sounds more and more like something out of an old TV sitcom. Like *Mayberry RFD*, or maybe it was *Green Acres*. Didn't they have a pig on that show?"

"I don't know. I've never been much into TV."

"Why should you? You've got enough entertainment in this town to keep you going for years."

She smiled. "So, maybe now you can see why I wanted to come back here."

He checked Daisy's pulse again. "I can now. It wasn't quite so obvious forty years ago."

"*Forty years?*" Alice shook her head. "That doesn't even seem possible."

He looked up at her. "You sure don't look forty years older."

She laughed and felt herself blushing. "Well, thank you, Doctor. You don't either, but I suspect we're both suffering from diminishing eyesight."

"And your sense of humor has only improved over the years."

"I suppose I used to be fairly serious."

"And, as long as I'm handing out compliments, you were an excellent assistant in that surgery. You ever consider taking up animal medicine?"

She chuckled. "Now, wouldn't that be something."

Soon they were both satisfied that Daisy was making a perfectly good recovery. Mark wrote down some very specific instructions for Clara and promised to check on Daisy the following morning.

"Thank you for coming, Dr. Graves," said Clara. "You're a real answer to prayer."

They did not speak much as he drove back to the inn, but Clara's words played over and over in Alice's mind—"*a real answer to prayer,*" "*a real answer to prayer.*" *Whose prayer?*

Chapter Twelve

"Good morning," said Mark as Alice came downstairs to help Jane set up breakfast. "I've already been out to check on our patient, and she's looking fit as a fiddle."

"Oh, that's such good news. I'm sure Clara is feeling relieved."

"Yes, she insisted I take home some of her pickles."

Alice smiled as they walked into the dining room together. "They're really quite good."

"I felt just like James Herriot."

Suddenly Alice realized that Mark was probably used to collecting some considerable sums for his medical expertise. "Uh, instead of billing Clara, since she lives on a very tight income, do you think you could just bill me instead?"

He firmly shook his head. "Are you kidding? Do you think I'd actually let you pay me for the fun we had last night?"

"That doesn't sound very good," said Mr. Parker as he closed the *Philadelphia Inquirer* with a loud snap. He scowled up at the two of them as if they were teenagers caught sneaking a kiss on the front porch.

"Good morning, Mr. and Mrs. Parker," said Alice in a formal voice.

"Good morning," said Mrs. Parker with a smile. "We took your sister's advice and drove up north yesterday and—"

"Wasted another perfectly good day, not to mention a full tank of gas," said Mr. Parker. He looked toward the kitchen. "What does a guy have to do to get another cup of coffee around this place?"

Alice felt Mark's eyes on her as she hurried toward the sideboard and picked up the nearly full carafe sitting on the hotplate just a few feet away from Mr. Parker. "Here you go," she said as she refilled his cup.

"Oh," said Mrs. Parker, "I didn't even notice that sitting there. Anyway, as I was saying, we saw some nice fall color."

"Ha," grunted Mr. Parker. "We saw a couple of trees that were barely turning."

"They came up here from South Carolina," Alice explained to Mark, "in hopes of seeing some fall foliage." Then she turned back to the Parkers. "I'm sorry, this is

Dr. Mark Graves. He is a well-known veterinarian of exotic animals."

"How interesting," said Mrs. Parker.

"I think I'll go give Jane a hand in the kitchen," said Alice, eager to escape the Parkers.

Mark looked at her hopefully. "Mind if I join you?"

She smiled down at Mrs. Parker, then spoke in a conspiratorial tone. "Normally, we don't allow guests in the kitchen, but Mark is like family." Then she led him through the swinging doors, suppressing her laughter.

"Thank you," he said quietly. "I don't think I could've taken another word from that guy."

Jane nodded as she rinsed a mixing bowl. "He's been making me crazy all morning. First of all, they were already up when I came down here, just sitting in the dining room waiting to be fed." She shook her head. "Good grief, it was six o'clock in the morning, and we make it clear that we begin serving breakfast at seven."

Alice laughed. "Well, maybe they have big plans for the day."

"I hope the plans are to leave and never come back." Jane smiled at Mark. "So what's the prognosis on Clara Horn's pig?"

"She's going to be just fine," said Alice. "Mark had to operate last night and he did a brilliant job."

"I figured it must've been something big," Jane glanced curiously at Alice and turned back to her omelet, carefully laying in sliced vegetables, "since you guys got home so late."

"Daisy had ingested a plum pit," said Mark as he pointed to a plate of freshly made scones. "You mind?"

"Not at all. That's what they're for," said Jane.

"Would you like some coffee or tea?" asked Alice.

"Coffee would be grand. Black."

Alice poured him a big mug out of the fresh pot that Jane had just brewed and set it in front of him, along with a pot of homemade raspberry jam.

"*Mmm*, a guy could get used to this."

Jane glanced at Alice, lifting her brows.

"What can I do to help?" asked Alice.

"How about flipping those pancakes," said Jane. "I think they're ready."

Soon Louise joined them, and, with the kitchen now crowded and breakfast in full swing, Mark made himself scarce—to Alice's relief. Her respite was short-lived, however, since his exit signaled the start of Jane's inquisition.

"So, tell us," said Jane. "How did it go last night?"

"The surgery went perfectly." Alice turned the last pancake over. "Mark is a great animal doctor."

"I don't mean *that*," said Jane.

"So Clara's pig is all right then?" asked Louise as she sliced up a cantaloupe.

"Yes. She was plugged up with a plum pit, poor thing."

"Enough with the pig talk," said Jane, clearly exasperated now. "I want to hear the *good* stuff."

Alice looked at her younger sister with wide innocent eyes. "*The good stuff?* Whatever do you mean?"

Jane glared at her and then turned back to the omelet to layer in shredded cheese. "You know what I mean, Alice. How did it go with Mark?"

Alice pretended to look confused but at the same time knew she was not much of an actress and would not be able to hold off her persistent sister for long. "It went fine with Mark."

"Did you guys *talk?*"

"Of course we talked. Did you think I would just sit there like a dummy?"

Louise laughed. "That thought did cross *my* mind."

"Thanks for the vote of confidence." Alice began removing the pancakes from the griddle, carefully stacking them on the heavy platter that Jane had already warmed. "Shall I take these out now, Jane?" she asked.

"Yes, I'm done with the omelet. Looks like everything's ready."

The Fisks came down for breakfast, and the dining

room was filled with cheerful chitchat. Clara Horn's pig was the hot topic of the morning, although Mr. Parker thought it was all a bunch of nonsense. But he would.

"We always let our guests know that they are welcome to join us at church," announced Louise. "The service starts at ten and lasts about an hour."

"Casual dress is perfectly acceptable," added Alice, since she had come to notice that many of their guests did not bring outfits that they felt were suitable for church.

As it turned out, the Parkers and the Fisks checked out, and only Susan and Mark joined them for church, sitting with Alice and her sisters. Alice felt vaguely surprised by their attendance and found herself distracted from the message as she wondered what they would think about Pastor Kenneth's sermon. She knew that Mark had not grown up in a religious family. In fact, she remembered how he had described his parents as "free thinkers who embraced scientific theories more readily than religion." Indeed, the topic of religion was one of the major areas about which Mark and Alice could not find common ground.

"Did you like the sermon?" Louise asked no one in particular as they walked back to the inn.

"It was sort of interesting," said Susan. "I've heard that Bible story before—I think when I was a child and went to church with my grandparents—but I guess I never really gave it much serious thought. Or else I thought it was really about seeds and growing things."

"I know the parable is supposed to be about faith," said Mark, "but I think it could also be applied to things like truth or knowledge. Those things won't grow unless they are planted in fertile soil."

"I never thought of that," said Jane. "But that does make sense."

"It does," agreed Alice. "Although I think Jesus wanted us to consider it in regard to faith. If you think about it, faith is a much harder concept to understand than knowledge or truth."

"You're right about that," said Mark as they reached the house. "It took me years to figure that out."

Alice turned and looked at him in astonishment. "You mean you finally figured it out?"

He laughed. "Well, to be honest I'm not sure that I'll ever *completely* figure it out. Let's just say that I accept it as a part of my life now."

"Yes," said Susan in what seemed to be a mock-serious voice. "Mark became *religious* a few years back."

"I don't like to think of it as religious," he said as they walked up the steps to the porch, "as much as having a relationship with God."

Alice was amazed. "How did this happen?"

"Would anyone like some lemonade or tea?" offered Jane. "It's so nice out here that I thought we might like to sit on the porch for a bit." Orders were taken and Alice offered to help, but Louise told her to stay put.

"You can keep Susan and Mark company," she said.

"So tell me how this happened," said Alice after they were seated.

Mark leaned back in the wicker rocker, and in the same instant, Wendell hopped into his lap.

"That's Wendell," said Alice. "Do you mind?"

Mark smiled as he petted the purring cat. "Of course not. Did you forget that these guys are my buddies?"

Alice laughed. "Wendell must not know that about you yet. He can't stand the veterinarian."

"That's probably because he experiences pain with each visit. That trains a lot of animals to hate going to the vet. It's different in my work since I usually make house calls—or zoo calls."

"But back to what you were saying," said Alice, still bursting with curiosity. "What brought about this change in you, Mark? I remember back when we were...uh, friends...that you didn't want to have anything to do with religion or church."

"That's true. As I'm sure you recall, I thought it was

a ridiculous waste of time, not to mention a sure way to kill brain cells. I was convinced that Christianity was an antiquated cultural oddity and only suitable for people who needed a crutch to lean on." He smiled. "Problem was, there came a time in my own life when I needed a crutch myself."

"Was that when you had your heart attack?" asked Susan.

He nodded. "Yes. At the time I really thought I was going to die, and I must admit it scared me. I had no idea what would come afterward. A good friend from the zoo helped get me to the hospital, and he prayed for me as he drove what felt like about eighty miles an hour through heavy traffic. I thought the drive alone was enough to kill us both. Yet there was something strangely soothing about his prayer. Chuck stayed with me during my entire ordeal, and then he came back to visit the next day. Well, I knew he was a Christian—he'd never made any secret of that—and I decided that I wanted to hear more about his faith. Naturally, he was happy to share. He brought me a couple of books to read during my recovery. When I was released from the hospital, he took me home and presented me with a Bible before he left. 'Investigate this for yourself,' he challenged me. 'God will never be intimidated by your questions.'"

"That's true enough," said Alice.

Jane and Louise came back, depositing a tray with drinks as well as a nice selection of chocolates and biscotti.

"Don't let us interrupt you," said Jane as she sat down next to Alice.

"I was almost done," said Mark. "So I started reading that Bible and it was the strangest thing, but it started making sense to me. I suppose that was God planting a seed of faith in my heart, like the one your pastor described today. Then I began attending church with Chuck, and finally about a month after my heart attack I gave my faulty heart to God."

"That is wonderful," said Louise.

"It really is," agreed Alice.

"He never even told me about his conversion for a year or so," said Susan.

Mark shrugged. "I guess I wanted to make sure it was absolutely for real."

"And you really think it is?" Susan looked skeptical.

"It's been nearly five years," said Mark. "It's been real the whole time."

She just shook her head.

Mark continued. "Susie and I were raised in a somewhat atheistic home. Oh, our parents never used that word exactly, but they were quick to put down religion as some sort of weakness. They felt that anyone involved in church must have a serious defect or a character flaw."

"Goodness," said Louise, "how sad."

"They didn't like it when our grandparents tried to take us to church," admitted Susan. "I thought that was kind of weird. I would never do that to my children. As a matter of fact, Katy has just started going to church. Did you know that, Mark?"

He smiled. "Actually, she started going to my church."

Susan shook her head. "Yeah, it figures. Oh well, to each his own."

The group began breaking up, but before Alice could leave, Mark asked her if she would give him a tour of the town.

"Sure, if you'd like. I warn you that there's not much to see, and a lot of things are closed on Sundays."

"That's okay. I'm just curious about the town," he said.

They strolled through the streets of Acorn Hill, and Alice told him who lived in each house and who ran what business, pointing out anything of interest that happened to cross their path. Mark showed genuine interest, and slowly Alice found herself becoming more and more relaxed with him. She began to remember why it was she had liked him so well nearly forty years before. But these thoughts she kept strictly to herself. Finally they found themselves back at the inn.

"I've had such a great time," he told her as he glanced at his wristwatch. "But I'd better start heading back to the city now." He grinned. "Believe it or not, I'm an usher for the Sunday night services at my church."

"Hey, bro," called Susan as she came down the stairs lugging her bags, "give me a hand here."

"You checking out too?" he asked.

"Yeah, Tom is supposed to be home around five. I better get there ahead of him so I can do some damage control."

"You mean that sweet little grandson of yours—"

"Please," she said. "Don't get me going. I've had such a nice, restful week, I don't want to send my blood pressure soaring again."

He laughed as he carried her bags to the front door. "Well, I guess this is good-bye," he said. "I've already loaded my bags into my car, and I settled my bill with Louise yesterday."

"Are you leaving already?" asked Jane as she came down the stairs.

"Yes, we both need to get back to the city," said Mark. "It's been a pleasure meeting you and staying at your delightful inn." He turned to Alice. "Be sure and tell Louise good-bye for us too."

"I certainly will."

He smiled and glanced around the room. "I honestly feel as though I have traveled back in time here. I can see why you ladies love this little town."

"It's home," said Alice almost apologetically.

He nodded. "Lucky for you. Now you ladies take care."

"You too," said Alice.

"Drive carefully," called Jane as Susan and Mark walked to their cars.

To her complete surprise, Alice suddenly felt a lump growing in her throat. She turned and looked at Jane with wide eyes.

"What's wrong?" asked Jane. "Are you okay?"

Alice nodded. "I think I'm just tired."

Jane rubbed Alice's back in a gentle circle. "Poor Alice. You've had a long, tiring weekend. Maybe you should go take a nap. I feel bad to think that your workweek will be starting tomorrow. I'm afraid your time off hasn't been terribly restful."

Alice thought Jane was exactly right about that. With weary legs, she climbed the two flights of stairs and collapsed on her bed and sighed and just waited.

No, she thought, she was not going to cry this time. That would be silly and childish and totally uncalled for. At the same time she did feel strangely disturbed and unsettled. She was not exactly sure why. Finally, she decided that she was simply overreacting to everything that had happened during the last few days. She reminded herself of Mark's wonderful conversion story. She decided it was time to thank God for yet another answered prayer. Indeed, it was a prayer she had been diligently praying for forty years. It had been a long time coming, but Mark Graves had finally made it out of the wilderness.

Glory be to God!

Chapter Thirteen

*V*era's recovery from her mystery illness turned out to be short-lived. By Wednesday she was sick again, had missed another day of school and was more depressed than ever. All the results of her tests were negative.

"That's the good news," she told Alice that evening when Alice dropped by with a casserole, compliments of Jane. "The bad news is I'm right back where I started. I'm only able to hold down a bit of tea and a slice of dry toast now and then. The rest of the time I feel rotten. I'm so sick of this, Alice." Tears flooded Vera's eyes.

"Oh, Vera, I'm so sorry." Alice patted her arm.

Vera ran her hand through her limp hair. "I almost think it'd be better to just find out that I had cancer and get it over with. Do the treatment or whatever. I know that must sound pitiful, but that's how I'm starting to feel."

"I wish there was something I could do," said Alice.

Vera smiled wearily. "Keep praying."

Alice nodded. "Speaking of praying, I have a wonderful story to tell you, but I'll have to save it for another time. I've got ANGELs tonight." She reached over and squeezed Vera's hand. "I'll remind the ANGELs to pray for you especially hard this week."

The ANGELs all promised to keep Vera Humbert in their prayers. Naturally they knew her, since they had had her as their fifth grade teacher. And it came as no surprise to Alice that they still loved her dearly and were eager to pray for her speedy and full recovery.

"Can we give our quilt to her?" asked Ashley Moore as she traced a diamond pattern onto some moss-green fabric.

"That would be nice," said Alice as she showed Sarah Roberts how to use the cutting wheel. "But remember, we all agreed to raffle it off at the Fall Festival." She crossed her two forefingers, their secret code for "don't tell," then said, "The proceeds are supposed to go to the Helping Hands ministry, remember?"

"That's right." Sarah nodded, and as if reciting a Scripture verse, she said, "It's going to go for people who need help with food and clothing and paying their electric bills."

"Yes. What Mrs. Humbert really needs most of all right now is our prayers," said Alice.

"But all we have here is a pile of pretty scraps," said Ashley. "I can't believe that we'll really be able to get this quilt done in time for the Fall Festival."

"I guess it's a matter of faith," said Alice, "and hard work. Besides, Ms. Songer has promised help if we need it."

"I think we're going to need it," said Jenny Snyder as she cut a pumpkin-colored rectangle. "This is taking forever."

"But it's going to be so beautiful," said Ashley. "I'll bet we make a thousand dollars."

"No way," said Jenny. "No one would pay a thousand dollars for a quilt."

"If they were rich, they would," Ashley insisted.

"And generous," said Alice with a smile. "But Jenny's probably right. A thousand dollars is a bit much for a quilt."

"Too bad," said Ashley. "That would probably buy a whole lot of food for a needy family."

By the end of the night they were nearly finished with their cutting, and Alice told the girls she would finish up at home what little was left.

"And we get to start sewing next week?" said Jenny. "I've always wanted to learn to sew."

Alice nodded. "Yes, Ms. Songer is going to get us going on it. But before we go, let's pray."

Alice was touched that every single ANGEL prayed for Vera. When they were done, each promised, once again, to keep praying for her until she got completely well.

"Now, that's what I call real faith," Alice told them as the meeting ended.

Alice wondered where her workweek had gone when she finished her half-day on Thursday. She had been so worn out from the week's flurry of activities that the past few days had been a bit of a blur. And then, to Alice's disappointment, she and her sisters had been unable to coordinate their schedules and get together to read from her father's journal. First, Jane had gone out with Sylvia Songer on Monday night. Then on Tuesday, Louise had driven into Philadelphia to play piano accompaniment for a former student who was auditioning on the violin. At least Alice had been able to sew some aprons during those two nights. Then, of course, Alice had been busy with ANGELs the night before.

"It's about time," said Jane as the three of them finally gathered in the library. "I was about to give up."

Louise poured tea for the three of them while Alice

found the place she had marked a week ago. "Here we are. Grandma Howard had just died and Father had written her obituary."

"Oh, please read it again, Alice," begged Jane.

"Yes," agreed Louise. "It was so sweet."

And so Alice read the obituary again, then moved on to the next journal entry, written about a week later.

January 4, 1926.

Alice and Asher went home before the New Year and I was saddened to see them go. However, I did feel encouraged when Alice told me that I might come live with them if things ever become too difficult for me at home. Naturally, she did not say this in front of my father, and she said it very politely, but I knew exactly what she meant. She meant if my father became impossible to live with. I watched Asher's face as she made this kind offer to me, and I was not entirely convinced that he was in complete agreement. However, he said nothing. Still, it creates a small doubt in my mind. For the truth is, I would rather be unhappy in my father's house than to disrupt my sister's happy home with the added responsibility of my presence. I know that they are struggling to make ends meet just now. Asher makes very little working at a shoe store, but he is also studying to be an accountant. "To better himself" is how Alice puts it. Still,

I promised my dear sister that I would keep her generous offer in mind.

What surprises me is that my father has been quite easy to get along with of late. I am not sure if this is because he feels saddened by my mother's death, or perhaps a bit guilty that he did not do more to save her, or maybe he is relieved that she is gone. I cannot bear to think it might be the latter and have determined that I must push such negative thoughts from my mind. In the meantime, I shall try to make the most of this quiet on the home front. I shall try not to aggravate my father and to do my chores quickly and without complaint. My goal is to maintain my high marks in school and somehow secure my escape from here in the furtherance of my education. Mr. Dolton says "education is the key to a brighter future." In fact, he has this statement posted right above the blackboard. I am sure he must know what he is talking about, too, since his life seems bright and rewarding to me. Mr. Dolton has a pretty wife who is also a teacher. They have no children and when I asked him about this once, he just laughed and said, "Look at how many children God has blessed us with at this school." Sometimes I wish that Mr. and Mrs. Dolton could adopt me, but I know this is nothing more than a silly dream. For one thing, I am probably too old, but beyond that I am fairly certain that children cannot be adopted if their parents are living. And although my father has not much of a life, he is still alive.

But oh how I miss my mother. If I knew how to pray or if I believed in God I would demand to know why he took her away from me. I would shake my fist in his face and ask him, why? Why? Why?

"Poor Father," said Jane.

"What a lonely life." Louise set her knitting aside.

Alice reached for her teacup. "But do you see something? I think he's changing. I think he's beginning to search for God."

"I suppose," said Louise. "But he does not sound very hopeful about it."

"But that's the perfect place to start," insisted Alice. "When you're in despair, the only place to look is up."

"That is the reassuring part," said Louise. "We know that Father does figure things out, ultimately. I just never realized he had to pass through such darkness and tragedy to get there."

"You know I thought of something the other day," said Jane. "I suppose it's obvious, but I'd never considered it before."

"What's that?" asked Alice.

"Well, obviously Aunt Ethel and Father were only half sister and brother."

Alice nodded with realization. "I hadn't thought

about that either, but you're right. Ethel wasn't born when Father's mother died."

"Interesting," said Louise. "I do not recall ever hearing either Father or Aunt Ethel mentioning that. Do you think she knows?"

"Oh, she must," said Alice. "But we should agree to keep quiet about this. Especially since Father never mentioned anything."

"Do we have time to read another one?" asked Jane.

"I don't see why not," said Alice as she reopened the book and adjusted her reading glasses.

February 20, 1926.

I turned sixteen yesterday. It feels like a big step from fifteen and I suspect I should begin to act more like a man. Of course, no one acknowledged this milestone. My father has never kept track of such insignificant things as birthdays. It was always my mother who would commemorate such events. She would usually make me a small cake and present me with a homemade gift like socks or a shirt, and for that reason the day would feel special. Mostly I tried not to think of such things yesterday. Fortunately, for me, today was much brighter. Mr. Dolton asked me to stay after school. Naturally, I was worried. I did not recall doing anything wrong. I have found after years of being picked on for being "different" it is best to keep a low profile at school. I try to mind my own business and stay out of trouble. It seems to help that I have been growing like a weed lately. I am taller than my father as well as most of the boys in my class. Unfortunately, my trousers are unable to keep up, or perhaps I should say down. They have been let down as far as they can go and they still only hit just above my ankles. But back to Mr. Dolton. I walked down the quiet halls to his classroom feeling nervous and afraid that something was wrong. Was it possible that my father had paid the school a visit and threatened to make trouble? I have not seen my father for a couple of days and I feel certain he is up to no good. But Mr. Dolton was smiling when I walked in. He reached out and shook my hand and asked me to have a seat. "Your high marks and fine schoolwork have come to the attention of Mr. Brant, Daniel," he told me. "As a result he is recommending you for the Thornton Scholarship." I have heard of that scholarship before, but I did not know it was a complete four-year scholarship. "But it is a little early," I said. "I still have two more years of high school left." As it turns out this is exactly what Mr. Dolton wanted to speak to me about. "I know that your father is resistant to your continued schooling," he told me. "And you are far advanced for your class. We could easily move you into the junior class, Daniel. Of course, you would need to pass a few tests, but we have no doubts that this will pose any problem for you. What *do you think?" I told him I thought it was a grand idea. "The only problem is that we need your father to agree to this," he finally said. "Do you think he can be persuaded?" I considered this, and then promised Mr. Dolton that I would give it my best try. "I will be praying for you," said Mr. Dolton as he shook my hand again. I wanted to ask him if he really believed his prayers would make any difference, but at the same time did not want to offend the good man.*

I think I was relieved to find that my father was still gone when I got home this evening. I took care of the chores, cleaned the house, cooked some supper and did my homework. Still, my father did not come home. I paced back and forth across the wooden floor in front of the fireplace, trying to come up with an ingenious way to present this new idea to my father, but came up with nothing. I noticed my mother's old worn Bible sitting by her favorite chair next to the fireplace, and I actually bent down to pick it up. I stood there for a long time just staring at it as I considered reading it. Yet I resisted this unexplainable urge. My only question now is where did that urge come from?

"See," said Alice triumphantly as she closed the journal. "He is getting closer and closer to calling out to God."

"It's interesting," said Jane. "I never thought that Father and I were much alike or had much in common.

Oh, I always knew he loved me dearly, and of course I loved him too. But I had always assumed that Father was born a godly man." She smiled. "There is something so reassuring about hearing that he, too, had to struggle to find his faith."

"I wonder why he never shared this with us," said Louise.

"I've been thinking about that too," said Alice. "And I think I've come up with a reason."

"What?" said Louise and Jane simultaneously.

"I think he may have been trying to protect us."

"From what?" asked Jane.

"Well, we lost our mother when we were at the age when he might have started explaining a bit more about his sad past and family history. Since we were trying to recover from our own tragedy, perhaps he felt it would have been too much for us."

Louise nodded. "Yes, that makes sense. I do recall his using illustrations in his sermons that I now realize probably came from his own life."

"I'm so glad you unearthed that journal," said Jane. "It gives us a view of Father that we would never have had without it."

Chapter Fourteen

There's something in the mail for you, Alice," said Jane as she came back into the kitchen. She waved a small envelope as though it were a flag.

Alice dried her hands on a dishtowel and reached for the letter. "It's not such a big deal, Jane, I do get mail occasionally."

"Not like this one." Jane smiled mysteriously.

Alice looked at the return address and saw that it was from Mark Graves, but said nothing and just tucked it into the pocket of her sweater.

"Aren't you going to open it?" asked Jane.

"Yes." Alice smiled at her and then returned to loading the dishwasher.

Jane rolled her eyes, then went back to her baking project. "Don't you want to know what he said, Alice?"

"Yes," said Alice as she loaded the last plate.

"Well?" Jane dumped another cup of flour into the bowl.

"Anything else you need help with in here?" asked Alice.

"Yes, I need help getting a certain sister to open up to me."

Alice patted Jane on the back. "If I had anything to say, you know that I would say it, Jane. It's just that you're blowing this all out of proportion."

"But he's your old beau, Alice. He shows up out of the blue and you two seem to get along and now he's writing you letters—"

"*Letter*," Alice corrected. "And it feels quite thin. It's probably the vet bill for Clara Horn's pig."

"Oh, Alice."

"Now, if there's nothing more I can do for you, I promised to pay Vera a visit today."

"How is she?" asked Jane.

"It's off and on. One day she is well enough to go to school and the next day she's down."

"And they still don't know what it is?"

Alice shook her head. "Vera feels certain it's cancer."

"Oh no. Didn't her mother die of cancer?" asked Jane.

"Yes. And an aunt."

"Well, it does run in families. I read an article the other day about a very rare cancer that is easily missed in tests." She paused to think. "I may still have the magazine. Do you want me to go look for it?"

"Yes, when you have a moment. It may be a shot in

the dark, but I'll read it to see if the symptoms sound like hers."

"Yes, that's a good idea. Would you like to give her some of that ginger marmalade that I made yesterday?"

"That's a great idea, Jane. Ginger is good for digestion, and that seems to be one of Vera's biggest problems lately. She's lost about ten pounds since this started."

"Not a fun way to lose weight."

When Alice arrived at Vera's, she found her friend despondent. Vera had no interest in Jane's ginger marmalade or much else for that matter. Alice tried to get her to work on the braided rug with her, but Vera declined.

"It's your day off, Alice," Vera finally said after Alice unsuccessfully attempted to engage her in conversation. "Don't stick around here with me. I know I'm depressing."

"You're not depressing, Vera," said Alice as she set a fresh cup of herbal tea next to Vera. "But I do think you're depressed."

"Who wouldn't be?" said Vera in a flat voice.

"I know it's hard." Alice bustled around the living room, picking up old newspapers and folding the afghan and plumping the pillows. "I hate sounding like Pollyanna, but you've got to look at the bright side."

"*The bright side?*" Vera frowned. "And what, pray tell, is the bright side?"

"Well, your tests are negative. You have the whole community praying for you. That has to be some consolation."

Vera's eyes filled with tears. "Oh, Alice, everyone has been so kind, but this is weighing me down. Sometimes I wish that I could just close my eyes and not wake up."

"Oh, Vera, you don't mean that."

"Maybe I do. We all have to die sometime."

"But think about your daughters. Don't you want to be around for their weddings...and then for grandchildren? Can you imagine what fun it will be to have little ones running around your house at Christmastime?"

Vera closed her eyes, leaned back on her pillow and smiled ever so slightly. Then, looking at Alice, she said, "You are a Pollyanna, Alice, but you're sweet and I love you." She waved her hand in a dismissive gesture. "Now, do me a favor and skedaddle. I need to take a nap."

Alice straightened up Vera's kitchen and bathroom and then, discovering Vera fast asleep or doing a good imitation of sleeping, Alice quietly exited. Outside it was overcast and chilly, which probably had not helped Vera's spirits much. Alice prayed for her as she buttoned up her sweater and headed back toward home. As she walked by the park, she slipped her hands into her pockets and discovered her still unread letter from Mark Graves. Despite the nip in the air, she decided to take a moment in the park to read it. It was not that she wanted to hide anything from Jane, but her younger sister's curiosity about Mark Graves was unsettling. Alice sat on a bench and opened the envelope. A small handwritten note was inside.

Dear Alice,

I cannot begin to describe how wonderful it was to see you again. I chuckle to myself when I remember how we performed late-night surgery on Daisy the pit-eating pig. I must say you are a most capable assistant. Of course, your training and experience is probably superior to that of others I have worked with (since you work on humans).

I realize it has been many, many years since we dated, Alice, and perhaps I am out of line for even asking, but could I see you again? I will understand if you're not interested. After all, it has been almost forty years. Even as I write this, I cannot say what I am actually suggesting or where I think this might go, but I thought I should at least pose the question.

Sincerely and with admiration,

Mark Graves

Alice reread the note and then read it a third time. Finally, she folded it and slipped it back into her pocket, thankful that she had chosen to read it in private. She could not begin to imagine what Jane would say. Of course, her sister would probably encourage her to write back immediately and nag her until she did so. Alice did not know what she would do. Certainly, she liked Mark and was glad that he had given his heart to God. Still, she was not sure of much else.

She stood up and stretched, glancing up to the trees overhead. She was surprised to see that they were finally beginning to turn color. The green leaves tinged with russet and gold contrasted prettily with the dull gray sky. It would be only a matter of days before they would be ablaze with color. Too bad the Parkers had not planned their fall foliage tour just a week or two later. On the other hand, Alice was relieved that they had already come and gone, and she hoped they would not decide to come again. But if they did, she would do her best to be hospitable. Perhaps she would even stock the inn's library with a few western titles.

As Alice walked home, she tried not to think about the letter in her sweater pocket. Part of her wanted to simply pretend that it had never come. She imagined herself tucking it deep into a drawer and forgetting about it. Yet another part of her felt a sense of nervous excitement. She felt almost giddy. Alice smiled to herself. Now, that would be something—sixty-two-year-old Alice Howard, spinster, nurse and church board member, acting giddy. No, she thought, giddiness would definitely not become her.

"Did you read the letter?" asked Jane before Alice even had a chance to hang her sweater on the hook by the back door.

Alice nodded. "Do I smell ginger cookies?"

"Yes. It's almost time for the first batch to come out." Jane tossed her sister a mischievous grin. "Wanna trade? Cookies for information?"

Alice decided to play. "I'll have to see the cookies first."

"Right this way," said Jane. With a flourish, she slipped on a black and white gingham oven mitt and opened the oven door. "Voilà!" She held out a sheet full of generous-sized, red-brown cookies that smelled heavenly. She waved the tray in front of Alice in a tantalizing way.

Alice caved in. "All right, all right, you win."

"Win what?" asked Louise as she came into the kitchen. "*Hmm*, those look good, Jane."

"Come join us," offered Jane. "And you can hear the latest about Dr. Graves."

Louise's brow lifted with interest. "Dr. Graves? What is there to hear?"

"Alice got a letter." Jane put the cookies onto a cooling rack.

Alice pretended not to listen as she filled the teakettle.

"From Mark Graves?" asked Louise.

"Uh-huh." Jane went for another cookie sheet.

"Is it serious?" asked Louise.

Alice turned on the gas under the kettle, still not answering.

"That's what I want to find out," said Jane. "I've bribed Alice with cookies."

"Yes." Alice turned around and faced them both. "You can be sure that I would never tell you without the cookies."

Jane smiled. "Oh, I knew you'd give in, Alice. I just thought they would sweeten the deal."

Louise sat down at the kitchen table. "Why is Mark Graves writing you letters, Alice?"

Alice put three cups and saucers on the table and then sat down. "Just being friendly."

"Just friendly?" Jane turned from where she was putting tea leaves into the pot.

"Yes, it was simply a friendly letter, saying that he enjoyed his visit and would like to come again sometime." Alice thought that was mostly the truth.

Louise nodded. "Sort of a thank-you note then?"

"Yes," said Alice as she fingered the fringe of the red and white placemats on the table. Had he not expressed appreciation over her help with the surgery? Besides, why did she have to tell her sisters everything? After all, this was something she did not completely understand herself.

"That was all?" Jane set a plate of cookies on the table with a look of disappointment.

"What more did you want?" asked Alice.

Jane shrugged. "Oh, I just thought maybe..."

"Maybe Dr. Graves had notions of romance?" Louise asked.

"I don't know." Jane returned to the stove for the teakettle.

"Despite what Jane says sometimes," said Louise in a slightly lowered voice, but loud enough for Jane to hear, "she is a hopeless romantic."

"So what if I am?" Jane set the teapot on the table and pulled up a chair for herself. "I think that Mark Graves is a nice man." She winked at Alice. "If I didn't think Alice was interested, I might even go for him myself."

"Jane!" scolded Louise.

"I'm just kidding. Besides, he's way too old for me."

"Yoo-hoo," called Ethel from the back porch.

"Come join us, Auntie," said Jane. "You're just in time for cookies and tea."

Ethel grinned. "So nice living next door to one of the best cooks in Acorn Hill."

"One of the best?" said Alice. "I thought Jane was the best."

"Oh, we don't want to go getting the big head now," said Ethel as she sat down.

"Jane's head will never get big," said Alice. "She does everything beautifully and yet she never even seems to notice."

"Oh, stop it," said Jane as she poured her aunt a cup of tea.

"So what are you girls gossiping about today?" asked Ethel.

"Gossiping?" said Louise, raising her brows. "We were simply discussing Alice's friend."

"Alice's friend?" repeated Ethel with interest. "Are you referring to that nice veterinarian who was here last week?"

"That would be the one," said Jane.

"Well, let me tell you, Clara Horn thinks that young man is the next best thing to sliced bread."

"Young man?" said Alice. "Mark Graves is sixty-five years old."

"It's all about perspective," said Ethel. "So why exactly are we discussing Mark?"

"We're not discussing him," said Alice. "We're simply having cookies and tea."

"He's a fine-looking man," said Ethel with a slight nod of her chin.

"And distinguished in his field," added Jane.

"Yes," said Ethel. "According to Clara, he's the best vet in the country."

"One of the best," said Alice.

"The word around town is that Clara's pig would be bacon by now if not for that valiant rescue last week," said Ethel.

Jane nudged Alice with her elbow. "See, he's even a hero."

"Not necessarily, Jane." Ethel set her teacup down with a clink. "*Tsk, tsk*. The truth of the matter is most folks would've been relieved to have seen the last of that little porker."

"Oh, Aunt Ethel," said Jane. "That's not very nice."

"It's the truth." Ethel nodded vigorously now, causing her chins to tremble with the motion. "Like it or not, your hero has only managed to prolong the inevitable."

"How so?" asked Alice.

"Lloyd is already working with the town council to get something on the books forbidding farm animals within the town limits."

"That won't necessarily apply to Daisy," said Jane. "She was here before the law was enacted. I'm sure Clara Horn could get some sort of grandfather clause to exclude her."

"She shouldn't need to," said Alice suddenly. "I'd almost forgotten that Mark said Daisy will only grow to the size of a mid-sized dog. She's a *miniature* potbellied pig. Surely the town should have no problem with a pet of that size."

"She's still a pig," said Ethel.

"She'll only be this tall," said Alice as she held her hands about a foot apart. "And Mark says they make excellent pets. Better than cats and dogs."

"*Mark says...*" Ethel sighed dramatically. "Well, the fact is your Dr. Mark Graves doesn't have to live in our little town. If he did, he might be singing another tune."

What kind of a tune he would be singing was a complete mystery to Alice. She glanced at her sweater still hanging by the back door and thought of the letter tucked safely in the pocket. Would she read it again? Or answer it? Or would she simply hide it away and forget all about it? She still was not sure.

Chapter Fifteen

Saturday had been hectic, even though Mr. and Mrs. Hanley were the only guests. By evening, life had finally slowed down enough for the sisters to meet in the library to continue the reading of the journal.

"I thought the Hanleys would never stop talking," said Jane as she flopped down in an easy chair. "They're really nice, but that woman can go on and on."

"No time to waste," said Louise as she glanced at the clock on the bookshelf. "Go ahead and get started, Alice." Alice turned on the desk light and opened the journal to where they had left off.

March 10, 1926.

I am still amazed that my father agreed to let me take the test to skip a year of high school, but I suspect his pride played into it somewhat. When Mr. Dolton and the other school officials met with my father and me, they managed to convince my father that I was an exceptionally bright student and that this was a great opportunity for me to advance myself. I could see my father sitting a bit straighter in his chair as he absorbed this information, and he even had the audacity to say that intelligence runs on his side of the family. I had to bite my tongue. The important thing remains that he signed the paper and for the time being I feel assured that I will be able to continue my schooling until graduation. Of course, I know that, at any given moment and for any reason, my father could change his mind. I only hope that he does not. I passed my exams with flying colors. Mr. Dolton gave me a new writing pen for the occasion and said he was proud of me. These were his exact words: "Daniel, if I had a son, I would want him to be just like you." I do not think the man could have said anything to make me feel better. More than ever I want to do my best and succeed at this challenge. I must put away any distractions like fishing or dawdling or sleeping too late in order to accomplish this task and make Mr. Dolton and the others proud.

"That is wonderful," said Louise.

"It's kind of sad too," said Jane. "To think that he was only sixteen and taking on such responsibilities."

"Maybe," said Alice. "But I think it made him happy."

"I suppose." Jane shook her head a bit doubtfully. "But to give up fishing."

Alice laughed. "He only had to give it up for a short while to improve his life greatly. We all remember how much he enjoyed it while we were growing up."

"Read more, Alice," said Jane.

April 8, 1926.

I am experiencing a mix of feelings tonight. I am not even sure how to describe them. My father came home from working in the field just before sunset. I noticed right off that he was whistling. I cannot remember hearing him whistle ever before. He smiled, actually smiled, at me when he came through the door and hung up his hat. As usual, I had supper ready. It was only a pot of stew, warmed over from last night, but my father complimented my cooking. Then he said, "But you will not have to be cooking much longer, boy." I considered asking him why, but thought better of it since he seemed in a hurry to eat. Then he quickly cleaned up, changed his shirt and told me he was going to town.

This all seems to confirm a rumor that I heard while working at the newspaper this week. It seems that my father is courting Gladys Mulligan, a young seamstress who rents a room above the newspaper. I do not know what to think about this new development. On one hand, I feel relieved to see my father in good spirits. On the other hand, I feel this is a betrayal of my dear mother. At times like this I wish there

*were someone I could talk to. I walked past the spot where
my mother used to sit by the fireplace, and I noticed that
her shawl and Bible were missing. I am afraid my father has
disposed of them. I would ask him where they went, but I
do not want to risk angering him. I understand now what
the expression walking on eggshells means. I feel this is how
I must live my life.*

"That must be Aunt Ethel's mother," said Jane.

Louise nodded. "Would you like to read some more,
Alice?"

"Yes, I'd love to. I must admit I'm curious," said Alice.

May 26, 1926.

*I have been so busy with preparing for my final exams
that I have neglected to write in my journal lately, but I cannot neglect to write tonight. My father married Gladys Mulligan yesterday.*

*I thought something was odd when he came into the
house right after morning chores, showered and shaved and
put on a clean shirt.*

*"Are you going somewhere special?" I asked when I
heard him whistling.*

*"Getting myself hitched," he said in a matter-of-fact way,
as if he went off and got married every day. I was shocked*

but told him "congratulations" and shook his hand. Then he said, "Take care of things, son," and took off. I was not very surprised when he did not return home last night, but I still could not convince myself that he had actually gotten married. Today when I came home from school and my work at the newspaper, however, I found Gladys Mulligan making a cherry pie in my mother's kitchen. She smiled at me as if this were a perfectly normal occurrence, and then proceeded to tell me she was my new mother. I cannot even remember what I said to her, but I did excuse myself to the barn. I went into the hayloft and sat for an hour or so. It is not that I expected my father to invite me to witness his marriage, but nevertheless it does hurt to be shoved off to the side. Somehow I managed to soothe my wounded feelings and come into the house when my father called me for supper, and I did congratulate them both on their marriage, but as soon as I finished my supper of overdone meat and underdone biscuits, I excused myself to my room, saying I needed to study. "You'll have more time for the books now," my father said to me. Then he turned to his young bride and said, "Daniel is the smart one in the family. He takes after me." I know I should have been happy to receive a compliment from my father, but it set my teeth on edge like when I take a bite of a bitter green apple.

"Oh my." Louise shook her head.

"That was short," said Alice. "Shall I read one more?"

"Please do," said Jane.

June 8, 1926.

Today was a very good day, although I am sad that it is the last day of school. Mr. Dolton took me aside during lunchtime to tell me that I had finished at the top of the junior class. "I know you have been working hard, Daniel," he told me. "I thought you should know that your efforts are paying off." I thanked him and told him that I plan to work even harder next year. Then he inquired about my home life. I had confided to him about my father's marriage and how unsettling it had been for me. Fortunately, Mr. Dolton has been a great source of encouragement. So today I told him that I seem to be adjusting to my new circumstances. "Well, it looks as if your new stepmother has made improvements to your wardrobe," he told me with a smile. This is true enough, for Gladys, as she allows me to call her, did sew me a fine new pair of brown corduroy trousers that reach all the way to the tops of my shoes, for which I am grateful. Now, here is what I found the most amazing about my day today. As I was leaving the school grounds, Adele Brooks called out to me. I have known Adele for years. To be truthful, I have admired her for years. She is a short and pretty girl with long blond curls and sparkling blue eyes. Adele is not only pretty, she is very kindhearted and smart too. She may be the only student who has never once made fun of or laughed at me over the years. "It does not seem fair that you get to be a senior next year, Daniel," she said as she walked along with me to the newspaper. "We have been in the same class forever, and now you are leaving me behind." I tried to act nonchalant, as if it were not such a big deal that I had skipped a year, not to mention that I was now walking down the street in her company, but the whole time my heart was pounding like a drum and my palms were sweating. I could not believe that I was actually strolling down Main Street with the lovely Adele Brooks—

"That is so sweet," said Jane.

"Jane," said Louise.

"Oh, sorry," said Jane.

Alice chuckled and then continued.

As we walked through town, I glanced around to see if anyone was watching the two of us together. Although I still do not know for the life of me if that would have been good or bad. The truth is I have never before felt the way I felt today. I am not sure how to begin to describe it, but I think it was akin to being lightheaded and smitten and dumbstruck all at once. I suppose it could be what I have heard the girls call spring fever, or maybe I am pixilated, but the trouble is I *cannot get Adele Brooks out of my mind. Still, it is not such a bad problem, not really.*

Alice closed the book and smiled.

"How perfectly adorable," said Jane.

"It is such a relief to know that Father's life was not completely gloomy," said Louise.

"That little Adele sounds like a real heartthrob," said Jane.

"Imagine Father smitten like that," said Louise.

"Oh, everyone should be smitten once in a while," said Jane. "Or at least once in a lifetime. Father was lucky. It seems he was smitten twice."

Alice wondered about that as she prepared for bed. She did not fully appreciate being "smitten." Not that she could remember it so very well, but what she did remember were feelings of uncertainty and insecurity and that constant nagging concern and wondering if he would ever call or write or whatever. She remembered feeling as if she were hanging by a thread and worrying if he loved her as much as she loved him. And in the end, she had never really known.

She glanced at the drawer on her bedside table, the place where she had put the letter from Mark Graves beneath a stack of handkerchiefs. She thought about how she would answer his letter. She would tell him politely that she, too, had enjoyed seeing him again and that she was so very glad that he had finally discovered God. But she was not sure what to say after that.

She took out her stationery and began to write. As she expected, the first two lines were easy, but then.... She sat and stared at the pale lavender paper trying to find a way to express her feelings. Finally she set the letter aside and went to bed. Perhaps she would find the words in the morning.

Chapter Sixteen

After church, Alice invited several of the ANGELs to gather at Sylvia's Buttons to work on the quilting project. "I'm afraid it's the only way we'll ever get this finished in time for the Fall Festival," she told Ashley and Sarah. "Ms. Songer has promised to help us finish the piecing today."

"Do you want us to call the other girls?" asked Ashley.

"That would be wonderful," said Alice.

As it turned out, all but a couple of the ANGELs showed up, and by five o'clock they were nearly finished piecing the quilt together.

"You girls are amazing," said Sylvia. "I've seen grown women who don't work as quickly."

The girls all beamed at her praise.

"It's for a good cause," said Linda Farr. "It's going to be auctioned for Helping Hands."

"I know." Sylvia made the secret sign. "Alice has made me an honorary ANGEL and I promise not to reveal the creators of this splendid quilt."

"It's so pretty," said Kate Waller as she ran her hand over the rich fall colors. "I think Jenny was right, and it should sell for thousands of dollars."

Alice laughed. "Well, I hope we can get it done in time for the Fall Festival. We have two Wednesdays left to get it quilted."

"May I help?" asked Sylvia.

"Of course. We'd love it," said Alice.

Alice stopped by to check on Vera on her way home. She had noticed that the Humberts had not been in church and it worried her.

Fred met her at the door. "Vera's under the weather again, Alice," he told her in a hushed voice. "She's asleep right now."

Alice could see the frustration on his face, as well as the messy house behind him. "What can I do to help, Fred?"

Fred ran his hand through his thinning hair and sighed. "I just wish she'd get well. I don't get it. Vera has always been the healthiest person I know."

"I know, Fred. None of the tests have been a bit helpful. I realize how frustrating this is for her, and you too. If there's anything I can do—"

"You've been doing plenty, Alice. We really appreciate it, but don't wear yourself out. You've got a lot on your plate with your job and the inn."

"But I love Vera, Fred. I want to be here for her."

He nodded. "She appreciates it. We both do. Thanks for checking on her, Alice. I'll tell her you were here."

"And I'll call later."

Once again, Alice prayed for Vera as she drove the short distance home. Even as she prayed, she wondered why the doctors had not been able to discover the cause of Vera's illness. "Please, give us patience," she finally prayed. "Help us to trust Your will, heavenly Father. Help us to trust that You're holding Vera and all her troubles in Your hand. And comfort her now. Show her that You are taking care of her no matter how dark it may seem. Amen."

Sunday evening, with the weekend guests checked out, Alice and her sisters looked forward to some quiet time together. After a light dinner, they gathered in the library, and Alice began to read from their father's journal again.

July 29, 1926.

I try to write in my journal at least once a month, but it has become more challenging during the summertime. I assumed I would have more free time with school out. I imagined myself reading books for pleasure, fishing and writing in my journal, but between farm chores and my job at the newspaper, I often fall into bed exhausted before ten o'clock.

Naturally, my father takes full advantage of my "strong back" as he likes to put it. I am fairly certain that this is the only way my father values me, as a farm hand, a strong back, a pair of willing hands, a virtual slave. He has said numerous times that I should quit school altogether and work the farm "like a man." He has even hinted that all this—sorry little farm that it is—might one day be mine, but I feel certain that I do not want it. Other than the river and the fish, I would not give a hill of beans for it. Of course, I would never dream of saying such a thing to him. I am not daft. Besides, my father's wife (I am still unable to call her my stepmother) has been hinting that she is "with child." This has made me realize that my father will soon be having a new family, perhaps a new son who will want to farm with his father. Perhaps they will enjoy a good relationship. My father does seem to be mellowing of late, but it is hard to tell how long his mood will last. I could not help but hear him and Gladys arguing last night as I was drifting off to sleep. That is why I have moved my bedroom from the house to the barn, taking up residence in the hayloft. Other than mice and other varmints, it is much more peaceful out here. But before I cease my writing for the night, blow out the lantern and drift off to sleep, I must say my summer has not been all hard work and disappointment. No, there have been some very nice highlights along the way. (1) Having an occasional soda with Adele. (2) Writing a

couple of articles—not obituaries—for the newspaper. (3)
Visiting with Mr. Dolton and asking him how and why he
is so certain there is a God. I have discovered he is not a bit
intimidated by my questioning and lets me speak my mind.
I appreciate this greatly. (4) I am also looking forward to a
dance to be held in two weeks. Adele told me that she plans to
attend with some of her girlfriends. I doubt that I shall have
the nerve to ask her to dance, but at least I shall go and hope
that she does not dance with anyone else.

Alice paused and looked at her sisters. They nodded
their unspoken agreement that she should go on.

August 12, 1926.

I went to the dance last night. It was held in the town
square with oriental lanterns strung all around. The girls
wore pretty dresses in pastel colors and the fellows were
scrubbed clean with straw hats and bowties. My plan was to
remain on the edge of this affair, a safe distance for an out-
cast. Oh, I do not really think of myself as an outcast, but
I know that I do not fit in. People know that I am one of
those Howard kids from that rundown little farm on Farley
Road. I suspect some even feel sorry for me. I suppose that
might hurt as much as anything. So my plan was to remain
as invisible as possible, to blend into the trunk of the tree

that was supporting my tired back. I managed to do this for about an hour. During this time, I kept my eye on Adele, and I know she was watching me too. So it came as a surprise when she accepted invitations to dance from a couple of our classmates. Most surprising was that she willingly danced with Leon Stevens, especially since we both agree that Leon is not the nicest person. The truth is that Leon is a bully. I speak from experience. More disheartening was that Adele did not dance with Leon once, but three times. I was so exasperated that I was preparing to leave when the bandleader announced that the next song would be a ladies' choice. Out of curiosity, I stuck around, and the next thing I knew Adele was tapping me on the shoulder. Embarrassed, I admitted to her that I do not know how to dance. She said she would help me. I only stepped on her toes a couple of times, and she did not complain, although she did admit to being vexed at me for not asking her to dance. "But I will forgive you if you can assure me that it is only because you are shy and not much of a dancer." I told her that was exactly right and she absolved me of all offenses. Then I asked her why on earth she wanted to dance with someone like Leon. "I thought that might make you jealous," she retorted. I did not tell her that it had worked, but I did manage to ask her to dance a few more times before the evening ended. I noticed some of the boys offering to walk various girls home, but this would take more nerve *than I could summon. I hope Adele understood. As I walked home by myself, in the light of the half moon, I felt incredibly lighthearted and happy and unexplainably hopeful. At one point I paused and looked up at the star-studded sky and thought, maybe, just maybe I have been completely wrong. Maybe there is a God after all. So, standing there on Farley Road, I said something that resembled a prayer. I said, "God, if you are truly there, and truly real, please show yourself to me. I do not actually want to be an atheist. It just seemed my only recourse a few years ago when I was so disappointed by life in general." That was about all I said, and I am not sure anyone would regard that as an actual prayer. I am still not sure about it myself, but I figure if God is real, he ought to be willing to show himself to me. Time will tell.*

"That is so wonderful," said Jane. "I just love the way Father dealt with his faith journey in such a no-nonsense way."

"It's no wonder that God called him to be a pastor," said Alice.

Later that evening, Alice decided to finish her letter to Mark. If her father could muster the courage to ask Adele to dance, not to mention asking God to reveal Himself, surely Alice could manage to write a simple letter. After throwing away several feeble attempts, Alice forced herself to finish one and actually seal it in the envelope. At the same time she felt as if she were sealing her fate.

She feared that her letter seemed stiff and formal, but she knew no other way to write it. She had tried to be honest as she explained to Mark that she was not sure why he wanted to see her again, but if it was important to him, she would be willing to meet. She knew that the message was not inviting, and she was not positive that she would mail it. She decided to pray about it.

"Dear heavenly Father, this whole thing with Mark is confusing and disconcerting to me. My life has been peaceful and fulfilling without him in it, and I see no reason to invite the possibility of frustration and even heartache now. I want to place this in Your hands. I ask that Your will be done. Amen."

Content that her future was safe in God's hands, Alice drifted off to sleep.

The next day, Alice had just put the letter to Mark in the hospital's outgoing mail when she saw Pastor Kenneth waving to her as he left the pediatrics ward. "Alice," he called with a smile. "How are you doing today?"

"I'm well, Pastor. Are you visiting someone?"

"Yes. Bobby Dawson."

"I didn't know Bobby was in here. What for?"

"He broke his collarbone playing touch football yesterday afternoon."

"Poor Bobby. How's he doing?"

"Not too badly, and his spirits picked up as I was leaving."

Alice frowned. "Why's that? Surely he wasn't happy to see you go?"

Pastor Kenneth laughed. "Not exactly. He was glad to see some new visitors coming—a group of giggling teenage girls bearing balloons and ice cream."

Alice nodded. "That ought to make him feel better."

"Or encourage him to play up the pity factor."

"He might as well enjoy his convalescence."

"Speaking of convalescing, I noticed the Humberts were not in church yesterday. How is Vera doing?"

"Not very well. In fact, I was thinking of giving you a call today. I've been visiting when I can and helping out, and my sisters and I have been taking food over, though not every night. Vera is having a pretty hard time, and I'm wondering if the church might be able to do—"

"Of course," said Pastor Kenneth. "You don't need to say another word. I feel bad that I didn't think of offering help."

"You've got so much going on. I could've called, but I kept thinking she'd be feeling well soon."

"But she's not." He shook his head. "Have they discovered anything yet?"

"No. Vera is almost convinced that it's cancer, but so far all the tests have been negative."

"Poor Vera. She needs the support of her church family more than ever right now. I'll call Ellen Moore. She's heading up Helping Hands now. I'm sure she'll have some ideas."

Alice sighed. "Thank you."

He patted her on the arm. "Never hesitate to ask for help, Alice. There are a lot of people in our church who aren't so busy as you, and they're just waiting to be needed."

"Yes, I forget that. My father used to say that when we try to do everything ourselves, we rob others of the blessing of giving and helping."

"Your father was a very wise man."

Alice's week felt a little less busy, knowing that Vera now had additional help. Ellen Moore helped out with food and cleaning on Tuesday, and Florence Simpson took the following day. Alice wondered how Vera felt about that, because she and Florence did not always get along well. Of course, very few people, other than Ethel, seemed to get along with Florence.

"I balked at getting this extra help at first," admitted

Vera during Alice's visit on Friday afternoon. "But I can see that it's taken a load off Fred."

Alice set the freshly made pot of Vera's favorite herbal tea on the kitchen table. "Are you sure you feel well enough to be up, Vera?"

"I try to move around as much as I can, and I've actually been feeling a bit better today." She eased herself down into the chair with a tired sigh. "Did I tell you that Clara Horn was my helper today? She even brought her pig with her."

Alice smiled. "How's little Daisy doing?"

"Clara says she's been as right as rain since your miracle doctor fixed her up. I'm thinking maybe I should have this Dr. Graves come take a look at me."

Alice laughed. "He's an animal doctor, Vera."

"Maybe that's what I need."

"Well, I'm glad to see you're getting your sense of humor back. Maybe you are on the mend after all."

"I've been trying to take your advice," said Vera. "I've been reading my Bible a lot and thanking God for the good things in my life. Did I tell you that Polly has a boyfriend?"

"No, is it serious?"

Vera nodded as she sipped her tea. "I think so. She called last night and said that if she ever gets married, she would like to have the reception at the inn."

Alice shook her head. "Your little tomboy Polly talking about getting married, now isn't that something."

"I hope she'll take her time about it."

They chatted for about an hour, but Alice could see that Vera was getting tired. "I think you should go lie down, Vera. You don't want to be all worn out when Fred gets home."

Vera sighed. "It seems hard to believe that I'm actually ten years younger than you, Alice. I feel like I'm about a hundred and two these days."

As usual, Alice prayed for Vera as she walked home. Once again she wondered what this mystery ailment could possibly be. She had already hunted through her own medical books, but like the doctors she came away without an answer. Still, there had to be one—even if God was the only One who knew it. "Dear heavenly Father," she fervently prayed as she neared the house, "please, please, show us what's wrong with Vera and how to treat it. I know You have all the answers to all our questions, and I believe You can show us what is making Vera sick. Thank You. Amen."

The phone began to ring as soon as Alice stepped into the house. She picked up the one in the hallway and was surprised to hear Mark Graves on the other end.

"I got your letter," he told her, and then he laughed

lightly. "Believe me, Alice, I can understand how you might feel a little skittish."

"*Skittish?*" She pondered his choice of words. It sounded like something someone would say about a horse, perhaps even a flighty young mare. But then Mark was a vet, and it was likely such animal descriptions came easily to him.

"Listen, I can understand your hesitation, Alice. To be honest, I thought you might just tell me to go take a leap."

She had to laugh at this. "That seems a bit harsh, not to mention rude."

"Well, I appreciate your graciousness toward me, Alice, as well as your willingness to get together. I hoped we could just talk, but I don't want you to feel any pressure. I just see this as two old friends spending some time together. Does that sound okay to you?"

She felt relieved. "Yes, that sounds fine."

"So, how about dinner tomorrow night?" he asked.

Suddenly her sense of relief vanished. "Oh, I don't know about that—"

"Look, Alice, everyone has to eat." His tone was persuasive. "And it's no big deal to share a meal together. It's not like this is a date or anything. Okay?"

She hesitated. "Okay."

"I could pick you up around six."

"That would be fine."

They said good-bye and Alice hung up the phone and took in a deep breath. What had she gotten herself into?

"Who was that?" asked Jane as she popped her head around the corner from the office beneath the stairs, making Alice jump.

"I didn't know anyone was here," said Alice.

"Obviously," said Jane. "I'm guessing that was Mark Graves."

"How could you tell?" asked Alice, certain she had said nothing to give it away.

"The tone of your voice." Jane offered Alice a chocolate. "I just made these today, a new recipe."

Alice took a bite. "*Mmm*, good. How can you tell from the tone of my voice?"

"It's just that you sounded so, so guarded. So what does Dr. Mark want?"

"Just to talk. We're going to dinner tomorrow."

Jane's brows lifted. "Dinner?"

"It's no big deal," said Alice, repeating Mark's words. "Everyone's got to eat. It's not an actual date."

"Oh no." Jane shook her head slowly, indicating that she did not believe a word that Alice was saying. "I'm sure it's not an actual date."

"Well, it's not." Suddenly Alice felt very unsure. "Is it?"

Jane wrapped her arms around Alice. "Hey, don't worry, sweetie. It'll be fun for you. Now what'll we dress you up in?"

"*We?*"

Jane grinned. "Hey, this is what sisters are for."

Chapter Seventeen

On Saturday, no matter how much Alice protested, Jane refused to back down from her "offer" to help her select an outfit. "Come on, Alice," urged Jane. "When was the last time you went out on a date anyway?"

"I told you this is *not* a date," said Alice.

Louise frowned from her post by Alice's doorway. "Mark Graves called you, invited you to dinner, plans to pick you up here tonight, right?"

Alice nodded.

"So, what about that is *not* a date?" asked Jane as she examined a brown pantsuit. "How old is this little number?"

Alice attempted a feeble smile. "Probably from the seventies."

"Going for the retro look, are we?" Jane hung the suit back in the closet and shook her head. "We need to take you shopping."

"But—"

"No buts, Alice." Jane looked at her watch. "We could

even grab some lunch in town. Do you want to come, Louise? We could probably invite Aunt Ethel over here to keep an eye on things for an hour or two."

Louise shook her head. "I agree that Alice needs help with her wardrobe, but I am afraid I would only muddy the waters, Jane. I would be trying to force her into cashmere, and you would be trying to get her into something from Bangladesh or Timbuktu. I think I had better just stick around here and mind the fort."

"So should I," said Alice.

Jane narrowed her eyes. "No more arguing from you, Alice Christine Howard. Your closet is so dated that you could probably sell your clothes as collectibles."

"I thought you liked vintage clothing," said Alice.

Jane rolled her eyes. "Yes, when it has style. Unfortunately, that doesn't describe your closet."

Louise chuckled. "I am afraid I must agree with Jane on that account, Alice."

"Betrayed by my own flesh and blood," said Alice as Jane shoved her cardigan at her.

"Come on, let's get going, sis. Nellie's had some new fall clothes come in last week. Maybe we'll get lucky there. Otherwise we'll have to head over to Potterston." Jane was literally pushing Alice out the door now. "Anyway, there's no time to waste."

"Have fun," said Louise.

To Alice's surprise, it was not nearly as painful as she had imagined. First they stopped at the Coffee Shop where she and Jane each ordered the special of the day, BLTs with a cup of vegetable soup. Then they headed over to Nellie's. In no time, Jane had an armload of items and was gently leading Alice toward the dressing room.

"She's not much of a shopper," Jane explained to an amused Nellie.

"I've noticed," said Nellie.

Alice waited for Jane to hang the clothing items on the brass hooks.

"That's good for starters," said Jane.

"Are you going to stay in here and dress me too?" asked Alice.

"No, I'm going to go look for a few other things." Jane pulled the curtain closed. "But holler if you need a different size. And don't you dare take anything off before you let me see it."

"What if I hate it?" asked Alice.

"I'll be the judge of that," retorted Jane, only half joking.

Alice could hear Jane and Nellie laughing, and despite her pretense of chagrin, she found herself giggling too. Really, this was not so bad. And Alice admitted to herself that she probably could use something new for church.

The first outfit was hideous. "I look like an over-grown ANGEL," said Alice as she stepped out for Jane to see the top and skirt.

Jane nodded. "Yes, that is a bit young, but it was worth a try."

The next one was better, a long-sleeved dress in a becoming shade of blue. "How about this?" asked Alice hopefully.

Jane added a scarf and belt but still just frowned. "Too boring," she finally said. "What was I thinking?"

Finally, after about a dozen outfits, or so it seemed to Alice, they both agreed on one. "I'm sure this jacket is much too expensive," said Alice as she fingered the buttery suede. "And it's not very practical."

"Forget practical," insisted Jane. "Don't even look at the price. It's going to be my gift."

"But you can't—"

"It's an early birthday present," said Jane. "You can't refuse a gift, Alice."

"But—"

"No buts." Jane smiled. "That butterscotch color looks so perfect with your hair and complexion, Alice. That jacket is just screaming for you to take it home."

Alice turned and admired the jacket in the mirror again. "It is very pretty."

"And it's so nice with that tweed skirt," said Nellie with approval. "I never thought of putting the two together, but honestly they look like they were made for each other."

"I really don't need to get this sweater," protested Alice as she opened the jacket to reveal a moss-green turtleneck. "I have a perfectly good brown turtleneck at home that I could wear—"

"No way," said Jane. "That color is perfect on you."

Alice studied her reflection in the mirror then frowned. "What sort of shoes do you wear with an outfit like this, Jane? Are my loafers okay?"

Jane looked down at her feet. "Good question. No, your loafers are not okay." She glanced over at Nellie. "I think this outfit calls for boots, don't you agree, Nellie?"

Nellie grinned. "And I just happen to have some that would be perfect."

"Boots?" Alice made a face. "I only wear boots when it snows."

"I'm not talking about snow boots," said Jane.

Before Alice knew what had happened, Nellie was helping her into a pair of smart russet-colored boots. "How do they feel?" asked Nellie.

"Actually, they're comfortable." Alice walked around a bit. "I don't know why I've never considered boots before."

"You look wonderful, Alice," said Nellie as she went to assist a customer who had just entered the store.

"Go look in the mirror," Jane said.

Alice did not know what to think when she saw her reflection this time—the stylish jacket, the flowing skirt and boots. Maybe it was just too much. "Oh, I don't know, Jane. This really isn't me."

"Just who are you, Alice Howard?" demanded Jane as she crossed her arms in defiance. "You wear your nurse's uniform to work every day. Then you come home and put on jeans and a shirt. For Sundays you wear skirts and dresses straight out of the seventies. Is that the kind of fashion statement you really want to make?"

Alice laughed. "I'm not sure I want to make any sort of fashion statement."

"Do you like the outfit?" asked Jane.

"Of course," said Alice. "It's beautiful, but for someone else."

"Why for someone else?" asked Jane. "Are you saying you're not good enough to wear an outfit like this?"

"Oh, I don't know...." Alice considered Jane's challenge. Perhaps it was true.

"That's it, isn't it?" Jane stepped closer now, peering into Alice's eyes. "You don't think you're good enough to dress like this, do you? Sure, it's okay for Louise to wear pearls and cashmere, and you like seeing me in my vintage clothes and funky jewelry. But, you think that you're some kind of Cinderella."

"And that would make you…"

"*Alice*! I'm serious. For some reason you don't think that you're worthy of wearing nice clothes. I don't agree. Your clothes should express what a truly wonderful person you are inside."

Alice could not think of a word to say in her own defense. Perhaps she had no defense. Maybe Jane was right.

"Now, please, take off those new clothes," insisted Jane. "Hand them over to me, and Nellie can start ringing them up."

Alice smiled at Jane's bossiness. Her little sister could really take over if Alice let her. Fortunately, Alice did not mind letting her, at least not this time.

"Don't look at the total." Jane winked at Alice as she emerged from the dressing room. "I've checked the bill and it's right." She handed Alice the bag that contained the boots. "I added another skirt. It's a green A-line that goes with that sweater. It'll look great with the jacket, and I think Louise will want to give it to you for your birthday."

"Jane!"

"Trust me, Alice." Jane smiled and gave her sister a squeeze.

"It's a good thing you had me drive," said Alice as they heaped the packages into the back of her car.

"Are you angry with me?" asked Jane as Alice drove toward home. "I know I was being really bossy."

Alice started laughing. "No, of course I'm not angry with you. I should thank you, Jane. This is probably something I should've done years ago. I just never knew how."

Jane sighed and leaned back into the seat. "As I've told you before, that's what sisters are for."

Louise heartily approved of their choices and insisted that Jane was exactly right in picking out the skirt for an early birthday present. "It is perfect," said Louise as they showed her their purchases.

"Believe me, it wasn't easy," said Jane.

"I can imagine," said Louise. "Did she kick and scream much?"

"*Yoo-hoo*," called Ethel from the back door. "Anyone home?"

"Come in, Auntie," said Alice.

"Looks like someone's been shopping," said Ethel. "Jane out spending money again?"

"I know you think I'm the clotheshorse of the family," said Jane, "but these are actually for Alice."

Ethel blinked. "For Alice?"

"Yes," said Jane. "You know it's okay for Alice to look nice too."

"Well, of course. It's just that Alice has never been one to put much into her appearance."

"I had no idea everyone thought that I was such a mess," said Alice as she went to the sink to fill the teakettle.

"Not a mess, dear," said Ethel. "But not exactly a fashion plate either."

"Well, you should see her in this," said Jane as she held up the suede jacket. "We're talking chic."

It was only a matter of minutes before Ethel heard the news that Alice had a date with Mark Graves.

"Not a date," protested Alice.

"Call it what you like," said Jane, winking at Ethel. "Mark is picking her up at six to take her to dinner."

"Sounds like a date to me," said Ethel. "That reminds me, I have a date with Lloyd tonight." She poked Alice in the arm. "See, you don't hear me going around and acting as if it's not a date. Call a spade a spade, Alice."

Alice just shook her head.

"So, if you girls will excuse me." Ethel stood. "I thank you for the tea, but I need to get home and get started on my primping routine." She turned to Alice with a slight scowl. "It wouldn't be a moment too soon for you to start on your own primping, Alice Christine." Then she left.

Alice frowned and Jane giggled. "Oh, don't take our comments to heart, Alice."

"That is right," said Louise. "You are a very nice-looking woman who could look even nicer if you put your mind to it."

Alice shrugged. "Beauty is only skin-deep, you know."

"And, believe me, the older I get the better I know it," said Jane.

"I just never wanted to be superficial," said Alice. "I never wanted to be one of those women who think that her outer appearance is more important than what's on the inside."

"Yes," said Louise. "That is an admirable trait, Alice. We could learn from you."

Alice sighed. "And *I* could learn from you two as well. But I'm not ready to spend two hours primping."

Jane laughed. "Maybe if you looked like Aunt Ethel, you would."

"Jane!" scolded Louise. "Shame on you!"

Instead of primping, Alice took a quick shower, then settled down in her easy chair with a book, but it was not long before she fell asleep. She jumped to hear someone tapping on her door.

"Alice," called Jane as she opened the door and peeked

in. "I thought it sounded awfully quiet in here." She came into Alice's room. "And here I find you snoozing away when Mark Graves will be here in less than fifteen minutes."

Alice yawned sleepily. "Fifteen minutes? No problem, I usually get ready for work in less than ten."

Jane grabbed her by the hand and pulled her up. "But that's work, this is a—" She stopped herself. "Uh, this is dinner with an old friend. Besides, Louise wants to see you in your new duds before Mark gets here."

Jane flopped down in the easy chair and flipped through a magazine while Alice dressed. Then Jane handed Alice a gold chain with a large, moss-green agate pendant attached. "Try this, Alice. I think it'll look great against that sweater."

"Thanks, Jane," said Alice as she admired the necklace in the mirror. "That looks really pretty."

Then Jane started going through Alice's scant selection of makeup until she found a tube of coral lipstick. "I think you should wear this shade," she told her.

It was nearly six when Jane gave her final approval to Alice. "Come and see her," she called to Louise.

Louise smiled and nodded and indicated for Alice to turn around. "Very nice, Alice," she finally said. "I do not think I have ever seen you looking so well."

"Thank you," said Jane with a mock bow.

Louise patted Jane's back. "Jane, you do excellent work."

"Good grief," said Alice. "You two make me feel like I'm about six years old."

"I'm sorry, Alice," said Jane as she brushed a piece of lint from her jacket. "You just look so gorgeous that I can't help taking some of the credit."

"I think I hear someone at the door," said Louise.

Alice felt the fluttering of butterflies in her stomach, but she took a deep breath and reminded herself that she was sixty-two years old and simply going to dinner with an old friend.

"You'll be fine," Jane whispered to her as the three sisters walked downstairs together.

Alice took another deep breath and prepared herself for what she hoped would be a pleasant and blessedly uneventful evening.

Chapter Eighteen

*A*lice and Mark chatted amicably as he drove to a new Italian restaurant in Potterston. Then, after the initial awkwardness of sitting across the candle-lit table from one another disappeared, Alice found it relaxing to visit with him. He told numerous entertaining stories of veterinary trips along with humorous animal anecdotes. Then he asked her questions about herself and her job at the hospital, as well as her life in Acorn Hill. To her surprise, he seemed sincerely interested in her slower-paced lifestyle in rural Acorn Hill.

"Acorn Hill seems a lovely place to live, maybe even to retire," he told her over coffee and dessert. "Although I'm not sure that I'm ready to retire yet myself. After I turned sixty, I promised to hang on for another a year or two. But here I am at sixty-five and still going strong."

Alice smiled. "You obviously take good care of yourself, Mark. And sixty-five no longer seems so terribly old to me. I think our generation thinks of itself as younger than the generations that went before."

"I agree wholeheartedly. I feel that as long as I am fit and able, there's no reason to quit practicing. Sure, I might need to slow down a bit, perhaps not travel so much, but I think I need my work to keep me going and feeling young."

"That's exactly how I feel," said Alice. "I did go to part-time last year, but that had to do with helping out at the inn. That's a job too."

"Still, there's no denying that we are getting older, Alice." He chuckled. "I realize that I'm not up to wrestling orangutans at this stage of life. Consequently, I have considered the idea of taking up practice in a small town someday." He smiled. "Maybe that day isn't as far off as I'd thought."

"You certainly did a wonderful job on Daisy. Clara Horn has been telling everyone in town what an absolute marvel you are."

"It almost seems like fate, Alice." He set down his coffee cup. "The way our lives have come together again after all these years."

"It is interesting, isn't it?"

"It makes me wonder if God is trying to show me that I should consider setting up a practice in Acorn Hill."

"God does work in mysterious ways," said Alice. She felt uneasy at the idea of Mark Graves's living in Acorn Hill but was determined not to show it.

"I know that you don't have a vet in your town," he continued.

"The closest vet is in Potterston." Alice picked up her teacup.

"How would you feel about it?" he asked.

"About getting a local veterinarian?" She knew she sounded coy, but she just could not bring herself to believe that he really wanted to know how she, Alice Howard, felt about him, Mark Graves, relocating to her hometown.

He grinned. "So tell me, what would you think if *I* took up a small-animal practice in Acorn Hill, Alice?"

She did not quite know how to answer this. "Well, Mark, if you truly believed that Acorn Hill was where you were supposed to be, I would happily welcome you into our community."

He frowned slightly. "That sounds a little impersonal, Alice. Do you mean you would welcome me like the Chamber of Commerce, drop by with a welcome basket?"

She laughed. "Did you have something more in mind?"

He shrugged. "I guess I'd like to think we could continue getting reacquainted."

She considered this. "Of course, Mark. I appreciate

that you used the word *reacquainted*, because I don't feel that we know each other very well. I feel certain that once you get to know me better, you'll see what an uninteresting person I am."

He reached over and took her hand. "I don't think so, Alice."

She took in a quick breath, thankful for the dimly lit restaurant, for she knew she must be blushing. "I lead a frightfully boring life, Mark, compared to yours. Although, I must admit that I like it just fine."

"Alice, are you ever going to forgive me?" he asked, still holding her hand.

"Forgive you?" She blinked. "Whatever for?"

"For being stupid and shallow and letting you slip away."

She felt her lips curling into a smile. "Oh, Mark, I've long since forgiven you for that. And, quite honestly, I've had to forgive myself too. Perhaps I should even ask you to forgive me."

His brow furrowed. "Why would I need to forgive you?"

"I was young and foolish and had unrealistic expectations for our relationship."

"Well, I suppose we both made mistakes. Let's forget about them and move on."

She nodded. "I think that would be wise."

"So, you're not opposed to the idea then?"

"Of your relocating to Acorn Hill?"

"Yes. You don't think my presence would crowd you?"

She smiled. "Acorn Hill is small, but there's always room for one more."

"I wouldn't want you to think I was trying to pressure you into a relationship, Alice. Although I would like to continue our friendship."

"And so would I, Mark."

"That's all I wanted to know."

Alice felt a confusing mixture of feelings as Mark drove her home. She maintained her end of the conversation, chatting lightly about some of the challenges of running a bed-and-breakfast, but the whole time she was wondering exactly where this thing with Mark could be heading. Was he really only looking for a friendship with her? Or was this meant to be the beginning of something more? She remembered how she had assumed that he wanted to marry her forty years before and how she had been hurt when he stopped calling. Oh, she knew it had to do with a number of circumstances, including their disagreements about religion and her commitment to staying in Acorn Hill and wanting to be near her father. She also knew that most of those conditions had changed since then. So what did all this mean?

Mark walked her to the door and thanked her for

joining him for dinner, then politely told her good night. For some reason she had almost expected him to take her hand or even attempt to kiss her in the same way he had done back when they were still in college. But he did not. She felt silly for even considering such a thing. What had come over her?

"How did it go?" asked Jane before Alice even had a chance to slip upstairs to her room to ponder these things further.

"I'm not sure," said Alice.

"Come in the kitchen and tell me about it," said Jane. "Louise has already gone to bed, but I was just finishing up a batch of biscotti, and I put on the teakettle when I heard Mark's car out front."

Alice was not sure that she wanted to tell Jane about it. But somehow, seeing her sister in her pink bunny slippers and plaid bathrobe, looking so hopeful, Alice decided to give in.

She removed her pretty suede jacket, carefully hung it on the back of the chair and sat down. "Mark is considering setting up a small-animal practice in Acorn Hill."

The kettle was whistling, and Jane scurried across the checkerboard tiles to retrieve the teapot and fill it with the boiling water. She set it on the table and looked at Alice with wide eyes. "Are you serious? He wants to move *here*?"

"You left the bright lights of San Francisco to move back here."

"Well, that's different." Jane set their teacups on the table, then sat down to pour. "I have you and Louise here, and this is home for me."

"Mark's parents are dead, and although Philadelphia is his hometown, I don't get the impression he feels much at home there. He's longing to retire in a small town."

"A small town where you live?"

Alice shrugged. "I'm not convinced that it's because of me, Jane."

"What if it was?"

"I don't know."

"How do you feel about Mark, Alice?"

She shrugged again. "I'm not sure. I'm not saying that to be evasive, Jane. The honest truth is I don't know how I feel. Mostly I feel confused by the whole thing. Part of me wishes that Mark Graves were still just a piece of my past."

"But the other part of you?"

"I guess I'm curious. I can't deny that I like Mark. He's a nice man, but I don't really know him. He has changed a lot."

"For the better, it seems."

"That's true, but that probably just makes it harder."

"Because it's more tempting to get involved?"

"Maybe."

"Well, what's the harm in trying?" asked Jane. "I realize that it didn't work for you way back when, but there's no reason you two couldn't try it again."

"I'm not even sure that Mark wants to 'try it again,' as you put it."

"Maybe he does. Maybe he doesn't. Why not just keep your options open, Alice? No one's asking you to commit for a lifetime. Just get to know him again. What could it hurt?"

"Nothing, I guess." Alice sighed.

Jane blew over the surface of her tea. "You know, Alice, despite how upsetting it was to go through everything with Justin, I'm not sorry that I married him."

"You're not?"

"I know I act like it was the worst decision of my life. But sometimes I think that if I hadn't married him, well, I might've spent the rest of my life regretting it."

"So you're saying it was better to have loved and lost—"

"'Than never to have loved at all.'"

Alice nodded. "Yes, but don't forget that I did love, and I lost. It may have been forty years ago, but sometimes it feels like just yesterday."

Jane patted Alice's hand. "That's because you have such a tender heart."

"Have you forgotten about Justin yet?"

"No, no, I haven't." Jane frowned, then brightened. "I will tell you this, though, if the day comes when the right man comes along, I wouldn't be afraid to take the risk of getting to know him better."

"The right man?" Alice smiled. "Do you mean someone like Pastor Kenneth?"

"Oh, you sound just like Aunt Ethel now. Simply because Pastor Ken and I are good friends doesn't mean I want to marry the poor man. I just happen to enjoy his company, plus I admire him a lot."

"Well, I'm with you there, Jane. He's a good man. In some ways he reminds me of Father."

"Alice, do you think it's possible that you never married because you could never find anyone who could measure up to Father?"

Alice considered this. "Oh, I don't know. I have never thought about that possibility. But don't forget what the Bible says about some of us being called to be single. The honest truth is that I've been perfectly happy living as a single woman. There's a lot of freedom in the single life, you know."

Jane smiled. "I suppose that's sort of what I thought, but I'd always wanted to ask you. Thanks for letting me."

"I don't have any secrets, Jane. I suppose I might

seem like a private person sometimes, at least to you, but that's probably because you're so comfortable with yourself and you seem to be open and up front about almost everything. I hope you never feel that you can't ask me about something."

Jane's eyes twinkled. "Okay, then, did Mark kiss you?"

"Oh, Jane!" Alice shook her head, then started to giggle. "Well, if you must know, he didn't. And to be honest, I'm still not sure whether I feel disappointed or relieved."

Jane laughed. "Oh, I know exactly what you mean, Alice. Sometimes life stays a whole lot simpler without the fateful kiss."

Chapter Nineteen

*B*ecause of meetings, last-minute preparations for the Fall Festival and Alice's "date" the night before, it was not until Sunday night that the three sisters were finally able to meet again to read from their father's journal.

"It feels like it's been ages since we did this," said Jane as she dropped generous dollops of whipped cream on the three dishes of still steaming apple cobbler.

Louise set their desserts along with forks and napkins on a big tray. "Are you ready, Alice?"

"Coming." Alice picked up the teapot and the three of them proceeded to the Daniel Howard Library.

"As nice as all our guests were this past weekend, it's lovely to have the house back to ourselves," Jane commented.

"I wonder how we'll feel if this place ever starts getting booked throughout the week," said Alice. "I mean we had a couple of fully booked weeks during the summer, but I can't imagine keeping up that kind of frantic pace seven days a week, week after week."

"Nor could I," said Louise with a sigh. "I am sure you both noticed that I sneaked off for a long nap after chapel today."

"That's the beauty of running our own business," said Jane as she handed them each a dish of cobbler. "We set the rules. We never have to accept reservations for the beginning of the week if we don't want to."

Alice smiled as she lifted her fork. "You're absolutely right, Jane, and that is a comforting reminder."

Louise took her cobbler and leaned back in the easy chair, putting her feet up on the little needlepoint footstool that their mother had stitched more than fifty years before. "It is not such a bad life, is it, girls?"

Jane laughed. "Not at all."

"This cobbler is scrumptious, Jane," said Alice after a couple of bites. Then she opened her father's journal and began to read.

September 11, 1926.

I am extremely thankful for two things tonight. Make that three. First of all, I am thankful that the bulk of summer farm work is finished. We got the crop in last month and now we have just finished tilling our fields to prepare them for a winter crop. It seems that my father's marriage has made him a lot more industrious. As a result, I have never worked so hard in my life. Next I am thankful that school has begun. More than ever I feel I am more interested in academics than in farming. Still, I know to keep these opinions to myself. The third thing is now that school has begun I am able to see Adele Brooks on a regular basis. On the first day of school she walked with me to the newspaper office. Of course, we stopped for a soda first. We were having quite a nice visit until a couple of her girlfriends asked to sit with us. I am sure my face turned the color of a ripe tomato, and although I tried to be polite, I fear that my social skills were sadly lacking. The next day I searched for help in the form of a book in the library. I found one, which is titled Manners, Etiquette, and Proper Protocol for Youth. It promises to help make me into a "courteous young man capable of performing with comfort and ease in any social setting." We shall see.

Alice set down the book and shook her head. "Father was the politest gentleman I've ever known."

"Yes," said Louise, "and now we may know how he got that way."

Alice continued.

September 28, 1926.

Gladys has been out of sorts lately. I am sure this has to do with her "delicate condition," but I have learned to lay low. Consequently, I try to spend as little time in the house as possible. I have done my best to construct what I hope will be a cold-proof space in the hayloft. I have made myself an igloo out of stacks of hay bales and old blankets and quilts. My new abode is complete with a board wedged into the bales to provide a shelf for my schoolbooks and a kerosene lamp to read by. I have put my mother's Bible there as well. I came across a box of Mother's things while hunting for extra blankets in the attic. The Bible was right on top. I feel that she would want me to have it and to read it. Since I am rethinking my previous commitment to atheism, I have decided it can do me no harm to read from the book occasionally. So far my little room has been comfortable, albeit slightly itchy, but the cold weather is still a ways off yet, and I may eventually be forced back into the house for warmth. My father seems not to notice my absence and, in fact, has been staying away a bit more himself of late. I try not to think about where it is he may be going or with whom. We ran a front-page article in the newspaper this week about some bootleggers up north who were accused of shooting a revenuer. Their stills and goods were confiscated and destroyed, and three men were arrested. I made sure to leave a copy of this newspaper on the table where my father eats his meals. He's not much of a reader, but I think he could tell from the photos and headlines that it was not good news. I doubt that he knows any of those men, but it might be a good reminder to him that there are prohibition laws being enforced in the Commonwealth of Pennsylvania. Adele has continued to be kind to me, often sharing her generous-sized lunch with me. I suspect that she packs it especially for this purpose for I rarely see her eat much. Some of our classmates now refer to us as a couple, but I am not convinced that Adele thinks of us in that way for she still enjoys chatting with other boys occasionally, especially the more outgoing ones who are involved in sports. Football is big now. I have been invited to play, probably because of my height—I measured six feet tall during the health scans at the beginning of school. My job at the newspaper makes football impossible, but I am not sure that I would want to play anyway. The idea of running around a soggy field and knocking heads together does not appeal to me much. However, I am sure I would make a brave attempt if I could afford the time and thought it would impress Adele. As it is, I try not to let her see how I feel when she is friendly with the football players. She and her girlfriends wave banners bearing our school colors as they watch the games. They say it is quite exciting, but so far I have had no opportunity to witness this firsthand. I think I shall attempt to keep it that way.

"I wonder how it was that Father grew to love football," said Jane. "I remember his taking us to lots of the high school games."

"I think it was his way of connecting with the youth and the community," suggested Alice. "He even attended a few games the year before he died."

"I never understood the game myself," said Louise. "In fact, I concur completely with Father's opinion when he was in high school. I, too, have no desire to witness the sport firsthand."

"Oh, I enjoy taking in a game or two each year," said Alice. "In fact, I may go to the next home game."

"May I join you?" asked Jane.

"Of course," said Alice. "We'll take some warm blankets and a thermos of hot cocoa, and it'll be great fun. How about you, Louise?"

"*Humph.*" Louise looked unconvinced. "I would rather be warm and dry and drink my cocoa in the comfort of my own home, thank you very much." Wendell hopped onto her lap and made himself comfortable.

"Oh, Louise," said Jane. "It wouldn't be fall without football. It is fun in a mindless sort of way."

Louise petted the cat and shook her head. "No, Jane, if I want to have some mindless sort of fun, I can spend an evening with old Wendell here."

"Hey, don't insult our cat," said Jane. "I happen to think he's quite intelligent, for a feline anyway."

Alice laughed. "Father used to say the same thing."

That night before Alice went to bed, she prayed specifically for Vera again. She knew that her friend was scheduled to go in for more extensive tests during the week, in Philadelphia this time. Once again, Alice asked God to give someone in the medical community the specific answers needed to diagnose Vera and to help her get well. Then, to bolster her faith, she read a familiar Bible verse: "Ask and it will be given to you; seek, and you will find; knock and the door will be opened to you. For everyone who asks receives; he who seeks finds; and to him who knocks, the door will be opened" (Matthew 7:7–8).

When Alice started the car the next morning, the car radio came on. It wasn't her habit to listen to the radio on her way to work, but when she recognized the voice of Dr. Bob Boshaw, she decided to listen. He was discussing the dangers of herbal medicines.

"I know that everybody thinks these herbs are perfectly safe," he said in his laid-back Southern drawl, "just because they grow out of the earth and look leafy and pretty. The truth of the matter is a few of them can be quite dangerous, and when used in combination with a prescribed drug or medical procedure, can even be lethal.

That's right, I said *lethal*. Okay, I'll admit the occurrence of death isn't common, but it can happen. So, maybe you're looking at that herbal dietary supplement or even a harmless cup of herbal tea in a new way. Good. Go ahead and read the label."

Alice turned the volume up when he said "harmless cup of herbal tea" and listened intently as he read through the list of dangerous herbs. Most of the names sounded unfamiliar, until he mentioned comfrey.

"Some folks drink comfrey tea to soothe their digestion, and I've heard that it tastes pretty good too. But, it's poisonous, folks. Comfrey tea can make you sick as a dog."

Alice tried to listen to the rest of his show, but all she could think of was how Vera had been practically living on comfrey tea during the past couple of months. Vera's daughter Jeanie, always experimenting with herbal treatments, had introduced her mother to it the previous summer when Vera had suffered from some mild indigestion. Vera had felt that the tea helped. She had even offered it to Alice, but Alice had never cared for the taste of herbal teas. Even so, she had faithfully made it for Vera often enough. Goodness gracious! How many times had Alice actually encouraged Vera to drink a cup of comfrey tea? Alice had been enticing her best friend to drink poison.

For the first time in her life, Alice wished for a cellular phone. Tempted to speed the remaining distance to Potterston in order to use a phone, she decided to calm herself by praying.

"Dear heavenly Father, please help me to get this news to Vera. I'm so sorry that I ever encouraged Vera to drink that awful stuff, but I didn't know. Please, take care of Vera. Don't let this harm her."

Alice had tears streaming down her cheeks as she parked her car and hurried into the hospital. She stopped at the front desk and asked to use the phone.

"Is something wrong?" asked the receptionist.

"I hope not anymore," said Alice as she dialed Vera's number.

"Hello?"

Alice could tell she had awakened her friend, but she did not care. "Vera, we need to get you back into the hospital for some new tests today," she told her.

"Alice? What are you talking about?"

"It's the tea, Vera. It's making you sick. Whatever you do, do not drink another drop of that comfrey tea."

"Alice, are you okay? You don't sound like yourself. What's going on?"

Alice tried to explain calmly to Vera what she had heard on the radio. "Now, I'm going to hang up and call your doctor and tell him what I've found out. Then we'll see if we can get you scheduled for some new lab work today."

"Are you sure, Alice? I just don't see how herbal tea—"

"Vera, promise me that you won't drink another drop of it. And don't throw it out, we should probably have it tested for toxicity."

"Okay, Alice. You sound a little crazy, but I'll trust you on this."

"Good. Now just take it easy. I'll see you before long."

Chapter Twenty

By the end of the day, everyone concurred that Vera Humbert's good health had indeed been impaired by her regular consumption of the seemingly innocent comfrey tea. The good news was that it appeared that no permanent damage to her liver had occurred. By simply removing the tea from her daily diet, she would be her old self in no time.

After it had become clear that Vera was in no immediate danger, Alice had sent Fred back to work, telling him she would drive Vera home at the end of her shift.

"I am so thankful that you heard that radio show," Vera told Alice as they walked out to the parking lot together. "Although I do feel foolish to think that I was poisoning myself."

"How could you have known?" Alice shook her head as she unlocked her car door for Vera and waited for her to get in. "I feel so awful to think that I was encouraging you to drink the horrid stuff. I'm sure I must've brewed you a pot every time I came over."

"You just thought you were helping." Vera sighed as she fastened her seatbelt. "I'm the one who thought it was so good for me. It seemed to help my stomach upsets last summer."

"According to Dr. Bob, dangerous effects are associated with very few herbal remedies, but I guess it's a good reminder to read up on things before we try something new."

"I'll say."

"But what about Jeanie?" said Alice as she started the car. "Doesn't she drink comfrey tea too?"

"I already called her from the hospital," said Vera. Then she laughed. "I managed to catch her on her cell phone. She told me she gave up herbal teas as soon as she went back to school. Apparently she's into coffee now, but she was extremely sorry for introducing me to that nasty stuff."

Alice reached over and squeezed Vera's hand. "Well, at least we know now."

"Yes, it's such a relief."

"You know, I prayed that God would show us what was wrong with you," said Alice as she turned onto the highway. "Just last night, I got out my Bible and read the verses in Matthew about asking and knocking, and then I specifically asked God to reveal an answer for you."

Vera began to cry, dabbing her eyes with a tissue. "And

He did, Alice. He used you to show us the answer. I've learned something through all this. I've learned to trust God despite my circumstances. I know that I whined and complained a lot at first, but more recently I began reading my Bible and praying and basically trusting God for the outcome of all this. I actually think this experience has helped me to deal with my fear of cancer and dying." Vera sighed. "And I think it was good for me to allow the ladies from church to help me out too." She made a little face. "It wasn't easy having Florence Simpson in my house, but I do think it was good for me. She's not quite as bad as I thought. Believe me, I've never seen laundry done so precisely in my life."

Alice laughed. "Good for Florence."

"I think this whole thing has humbled me," Vera admitted. "I suppose I needed that."

"I guess we all need that from time to time," said Alice. "It's a good way to be reminded that God is still on the throne and in control of things."

"Amen to that."

"Now, won't your fifth graders be glad to have you back," said Alice.

"I can't wait," said Vera. "The doctor said I can return to work as soon as I feel strong enough. I feel so much better already."

"You don't need to rush things, Vera. Give yourself a chance to build up your reserves. The doctor said that your body would need some time to flush the toxins out of your system."

"Yes, believe me, I plan to do everything he recommended."

News of Vera's near poisoning spread around town quickly. Carlene Moss from the *Acorn Nutshell* printed a feature story about it, including how Alice Howard had prayed for an answer and then heard the Dr. Bob show the following morning. She also included a list of the more dangerous herbs and their various side effects.

"That was really something about Vera Humbert," said their waitress, Hope Collins, when Alice and Jane met at the Coffee Shop on Thursday afternoon. "I had no idea that herbal teas were dangerous."

"Most of them aren't," said Jane.

"Apparently there are a few people who can tolerate comfrey tea," added Alice, "but I would recommend that people avoid it altogether. The hospital contacted state health officials. I hope they'll come out with a warning."

Hope refilled Jane's coffee cup. "Well, June took it pretty seriously after reading that article in the paper. She's already gone through our herbal tea selection to make sure we're not poisoning any of our customers. We don't want to read 'Tragedy at June Carter's Shop' in the *Acorn Nutshell*."

"I'm sure you don't. I did the same thing at the inn," admitted Jane.

"How's business over there?" asked Hope as she wiped down the counter.

"Just getting busy again," said Jane. "Our first guests for the weekend just checked in this afternoon. We'll be full up by tomorrow until Sunday."

"Remember how some folks said it would never fly?" Hope grinned. "Guess it was just a matter of faith, eh?"

"That's exactly right," agreed Alice. It was hard to believe that only a year ago Hope was not too sure about where she stood in the area of her own personal faith. But over the course of the past year, she had begun coming regularly to church, and was even attending the women's Bible study group now. Alice knew this had a lot to do with her own father's influence with Hope. He had engaged in many inspiring conversations with this waitress during the last couple of years of his life.

"Earth to Alice," Jane said for the second time.

"Sorry," said Alice.

"Daydreaming?"

"Sort of."

"Does it have anything to do with a certain veterinarian who's thinking about moving to a small town?"

Alice shook her head. "No, not at all."

"Oh, come on, Alice. You can be honest with me."

"Really, Jane." Alice lowered her voice. "If you must know, I was just thinking of what a great influence Father had on Hope before he died."

Jane nodded. "Sorry."

Then Alice grinned. "Not that I haven't thought about Mark this week, but it's been so busy that I haven't had much time to obsess over anything."

"That's good. I don't think I would've believed you if you tried to tell me that you haven't even given him a second thought."

"Second and third."

Jane sighed. "Good to know that you're human, Alice. Sometimes I think you're too saintly to be real."

"Oh, Jane."

"It's true," said Jane. "And that article in the *Nutshell* only raised you to a new level."

"Good grief," said Alice. "I hope that's not really true."

"What's wrong with that?" teased Jane. "After all, you're the head of the ANGELs. It only makes sense that you of all people would've already arrived at sainthood."

Alice made a face.

"Speaking of the ANGELs, how's the quilt progressing?"

"We finished it last night," said Alice. "Thanks to Sylvia. It's really beautiful. I've a mind to bid on it myself. How are your chocolates coming along?"

"I never thought I'd see the day when the smell of chocolate would make me feel nauseated," said Jane. "But I almost hit that place this morning. Thank goodness for Louise and Aunt Ethel. They offered to package up the last of them for me this afternoon."

"I'm sure they'll all be sold before noon," said Alice. "And it won't be long before you're ready to concoct more."

"I hope you're right. We figured they should raise at least a couple of hundred dollars for Helping Hands."

"Hello there, ladies," said Craig Tracy, the local florist. He sat down at the counter across from them.

"Hi Craig," said Jane. "Did you get in those ornamental cabbages yet?"

"I sure did." He waved to Hope. "I dropped them by your house just a few minutes ago."

"Thanks," said Jane. "But you didn't need to do that."

"Hey, it was worth the trip. Louise rewarded me with a couple of your chocolate truffles." He grinned. "And I got to see your front porch."

"So what'd you think?"

"It looks super, Jane. If you don't mind, I think I'll stop by with my camera and take some photos."

"Feel free."

Alice was confused. Why would Craig want to take photos of their house? "What's so special about our porch?" she asked Jane in a lowered voice.

Jane just shrugged mysteriously. They visited with Craig and Hope for a bit longer. Then Jane, who had walked from the house, rode the short distance home with Alice.

"Oh, look what you've done here," exclaimed Alice as the two of them strolled up the front walk toward the pumpkin-lined steps of the front porch. "How delightful." She stopped to admire the cornstalks that leaned against the columns. "This is so clever, Jane."

"I thought it was time to spruce up for fall," said Jane. "I drove out to the farmer's market this morning and loaded as much stuff as I could into the back of Louise's car. Which reminds me, I still need to clean it out."

"And the scarecrow!" exclaimed Alice. "He's adorable. Did you make him?"

"I did. Don't you recognize the overalls?"

"Are those yours?"

Jane laughed. "It's a temporary loan. He has to give them back to me when he's done with them."

"And look how you've painted his pumpkin face." Alice shook her head in wonder. "You are a marvel, Jane."

Jane opened the front door and held it for Alice. "Gee thanks, sis. I never knew that painting a pumpkin face equates with being a marvel."

"Well, it's just like listening to a radio medical show adds up to being a saint."

"Okay, Alice. I guess we're even."

"Hello girls," called Louise as they entered the kitchen. "Oh, Alice, did you see what Jane did to our front porch?"

Alice was not sure how Louise meant that. "It's wonderful. Don't you love it?"

"Well," Louise frowned slightly, "I suppose the children will like it for trick or treating on Halloween, but do you agree that it is a little over the top?"

"Not at all," said Alice. "I'm sure our guests will enjoy it."

Jane patted Alice on the back. "Thanks, sis." Then she pretended to scowl at Louise. "As for you, if you hadn't been so sweet and generous as to finish wrapping up my chocolates today, well, I might just take serious umbrage to your comments about my harvest decorating."

Louise attempted a weak smile. "I am sorry, Jane. At least you did not put up any of those creepy spider webs that people are so fond of draping about their homes this time of year. I still cannot figure out what that is all about."

"It's about fun," said Jane. "Now that you mention it, I think I might have to look into those too."

"Oh dear." Louise just shook her head. "By the way, Jane, I put your cabbages out on the back porch." She chuckled. "Aunt Ethel was quite perplexed about those. She thought they were for eating but did not think they looked very appetizing."

"Didn't you tell her they were just for looks?"

"Goodness, no," said Louise. "She already thinks we are a bit nutty for—as she says—'buying all those pumpkins just to decorate the front porch.' Can you imagine how she would react to using cabbages as decoration for your flower boxes?"

"Well, I did buy a couple of pumpkins for pies and some pumpkin custard."

Alice turned to Louise. "Is Cynthia still planning to arrive tomorrow evening?"

"Yes." Louise smiled. "Since we are fully booked, she will be staying in my room with me."

"Are we still on to read tonight?" asked Jane hopefully.

"I am," said Alice.

"Count me in," said Louise.

"Maybe I'll have time to whip us up some pumpkin custard before then," offered Jane. "I've been thinking about it all day."

Later that evening, when the three of them gathered in their father's den to read, they also enjoyed warm pumpkin custard and cinnamon spice tea.

October 31, 1926.

The grange hosted a Halloween party tonight. I had no intention of attending since it's a long walk there and back, plus I had studies to attend to. But I changed my mind when my father and Gladys announced they were going and invited me to ride along in the Model T my father recently got in trade for one of our cows. Now I wish that I had not—although, perhaps it is for the best. The party was in full swing when we arrived and Gladys and my father seemed in good spirits as they joined the others already on the dance floor. I lurked in the shadows unsure of how to occupy myself, until I noticed Adele and a couple of her girlfriends at the refreshment table. Now this was a surprise to me, for Adele had made no mention of coming to this event. Of course, I had not either. I started to walk over to say hello, but before I got there and before she saw me, Leon Stevens approached her. The next thing I knew the two of them were out on the dance floor. I told myself that Adele was only being polite and retreated to the shadows, but as the night wore on she and Leon danced every number together. I never bothered to say hello, but found my father and informed him that I was tired and planned to walk home. My thoughts, as I walked down the lonely road, were as cold and black as the night and I was feeling quite sorry for myself. Then an amazing thing happened. I began thinking about something that I had read in my mother's Bible just the night before. It's a story that my mother often told me as a child, about the two men who built houses, one on the sand and one on the rock. Of course, it makes sense to build a house on a firm foundation. Who would want to build a house on the sand? As I walked down the dark road, it occurred to me that I was like the foolish man. I was building my house on the sand. Suddenly, I wanted the stability of believing in a real God, a living God. I knew that I wanted to build my house on a rock, and so I prayed, actually prayed, that God would show me how to do such a thing. Then just as I came up the hill before our farm, I saw a great light coming at me. It was only the moon, but what a beautiful full, yellow moon it was. I just stood there and stared at it. Then I thanked God as I walked home in such light. Of course, I am saddened at Adele's false-ness toward me, but I have decided that if I truly build my house on the rock, such small storms shall not matter. I will

not be nearly so disturbed by them. I cannot wait to tell Mr.
Dolton about what I have done.

Alice's voice was quavering as she finished that line. "Oh, isn't that beautiful?"

"Wonderful," breathed Louise.

"Amazing," said Jane. "I'm so relieved for him," said Alice. "And so glad we didn't have to wait any longer for him to find God."

"Amen," said Louise.

The sisters sat in companionable silence as each thought about the passage Alice had just read. Then Louise sighed and began to put away her knitting, a small pink wool item.

"That looks like it's for a baby," said Alice.

Louise nodded without answering.

"Who had a baby?" asked Jane with curiosity.

"Someone," said Louise mysteriously.

"Who?" demanded Jane.

Louise just lifted her brows and tucked her knitting project back into her bag. "Lots of people, I am sure. Babies are born every day."

"Louise," said Jane impatiently. "Who had a baby? It's obviously a girl, although I'm not sure that strong shade of pink would look good on a baby."

"On this girl it will."

"So, you have already seen her?" said Alice, unwilling to give up.

"As a matter of fact, yes."

"You are obviously not about to tell us about this mysterious baby girl."

"Oh, all right." Louise looked embarrassed. "It's for Daisy."

"Daisy?" Jane gasped. "Daisy the pig?"

Louise nodded. "I ran into Clara at the store yesterday and she mentioned that Daisy had a bit of a chill from the cool weather and I thought—"

Jane threw back her head and laughed. "My prim and proper sister is knitting a sweater for a *pig*."

"Oh, Jane."

"Don't 'Oh, Jane' me, Louie. This is too funny."

Jane's laughter was contagious and Alice soon joined in. "It's really sweet of you, Louise," she managed to sputter.

"Thank you." Louise wore her stern music teacher expression now. "It is just that I had finished all my knitting projects for the Fall Festival, mostly scarves since Sylvia felt they would sell the best. And, well, I still felt like knitting, and, goodness knows, I'll probably never get the chance to make any baby things for Cynthia...."

Jane stood up and patted Louise on the shoulder. "Oh, it's okay, Louie. I have to agree with Alice. It is sweet of you, but it's also incredibly funny."

Louise smiled, and then suddenly her expression turned stern again. "All right, you two do not have to tell anyone about this little project, especially Aunt Ethel."

With Alice and Jane sworn to secrecy, they said good night and went off to bed.

Chapter Twenty-One

$\mathcal{F}$riday, as usual, was busy with new guests arriving, and there was added activity generated by the Fall Festival. "Jane," said Alice, "Sylvia called while you were out jogging this morning. She wants to know if you're going to drop off the jewelry that you are donating for the Grace Chapel booth today."

"Oh, that's right," said Jane, smacking her forehead with the palm of her hand. "I almost forgot. I have the pieces upstairs, all ready to go, but I've got so much going on that—"

"Why don't I drop them off when I deliver the quilt and my aprons?"

"Did you finish all your aprons?" asked Jane.

"Yes. The last one before I went to bed last night. I'm going upstairs to get them now."

"I really want to buy the one with the squash and pumpkins on it," said Jane.

"Oh, Jane, I can give it to you."

"No." Jane shook her head. "This is for charity. Besides, it will make a more impressive display if all the aprons are laid out together."

Alice laughed. "Always the artist."

"But," Jane held up one finger, "can you put a 'sold' sticker on that one for me? Then I'll stop by the booth and pay for it tomorrow."

"It's a deal."

"Thanks, sweetie."

Alice found Louise in the kitchen. "Do you want me to take your knitting with me to Sylvia's booth?" asked Alice. "I'm on my way now."

"Thank you, Alice, that would save me a trip. It is all in a box on my dresser upstairs." She lowered her voice. "Just do not put Daisy's sweater in by mistake. It's up there too."

"Don't worry, Louise." Alice winked. Alice went up to Louise's room and could not hold back a chuckle when she saw the dainty pig sweater complete with a matching bonnet.

Alice finished her errands in town before noon, then hurried home to see if she could be of help to her sisters.

"You should see how great the town is looking already,"

she told Jane as she started unloading the breakfast dishes from the dishwasher. "Craig followed your example and decorated the exterior of Wild Things with pumpkins and cornstalks. And outside Sylvia's store is a cute scarecrow lady wearing a patchwork skirt that Sylvia plans to auction off. And a lot of the booths are going up and—"

"Alice," Louise called from the reception desk. "Telephone."

Thinking it was Vera, Alice went into the hall and took the receiver from Louise. "Hello."

"Hi, Alice, this is Mark."

Alice blinked. "Mark? Hello, how are you?"

"I'm doing well. I just wanted to let you know that I plan to go to the Fall Festival tomorrow."

"How on earth did you hear about that?" she asked, hoping she did not sound rude. "I mean, certainly there isn't any promotion going on in Philadelphia."

He laughed. "No. I just happened to look at the *Acorn Nutshell* this week."

"You get the *Nutshell* in Phil—"

"No, no. I looked it up online."

"The *Nutshell* is online?"

"Actually, it was a surprise to me too. I was doing a little research about Acorn Hill, looking into things like population and growth and community clubs and activities, you know, in case I should actually decide to make the big move someday. And there was the newspaper. For kicks, I decided to read it. By the way, congratulations on helping your friend to figure out what was making her ill. That was remarkable."

"Well, thank you."

"Anyway, Susan and Tom plan to join me, and I just thought I'd let you know that I was going to be in town. I thought perhaps, if you're not too busy, we could all four go to dinner later on. This is just a day trip for us, since Susan already discovered that your lovely inn is booked up."

"We are booked up," said Alice. "I'm sorry."

"So how about it?"

"Dinner?" She considered this, unsure of what she really wanted to do.

"I know it's last-minute," he said quickly. "And I'll understand if you—"

"Dinner would be lovely, Mark. I'd like to meet Susan's husband."

"Great." Mark sounded truly relieved. "So, shall we plan to meet somewhere, or do you suppose we'll just run into each other in town."

"I'm sure we'll run into each other," she told him. "If not, just drop by the inn. I'm sure we'll connect before evening."

"Sounds good."

"See you tomorrow then," said Alice, still wondering what had made her agree to this unexpected dinner date. She hung up the phone and returned to the kitchen, where Jane and Louise were just starting to fix some lunch.

"What's up?" asked Jane.

"Mark and his sister and brother-in-law are coming to the Fall Festival tomorrow."

"That's nice," said Jane. "The more the merrier."

"He just called to tell you that?" Louise looked doubtful.

"Actually, he invited me to join the three of them for dinner."

"And?" Jane paused with her large knife in midair.

"I agreed to go." Alice shook her head. "Although I'm not quite sure why."

"Why not?" Jane turned back to where she was chopping up pumpkin and tossing it into a pot with melted butter and what looked like onions and herbs.

"What are you making?" asked Alice as she peered into the big pot.

"Pumpkin soup," said Jane.

"Back to Mark," said Louise. "You said you do not know why you agreed to go out with him, Alice?"

She shrugged. "Oh, I don't know why I said that.

I guess Jane's right, there's no reason not to go out with him. Besides, I'd like to see Susan again and meet her husband."

"Well, if you really want to..." Louise still looked unconvinced.

"Oh, Louie, Louie," said Jane. "Don't make this into something it's not. Alice isn't eloping. She's simply going out with some friends to have a bit of fun."

Louise scowled. "Does Alice *think* it is fun? I am not sure that she actually does."

"I probably do seem as if I'm dragging my heels," said Alice. "Mark's invitation just caught me off guard, but Jane's right. I do think it'll be fun. Don't worry."

"All right," said Louise. "If you really want to do this."

Jane rolled her eyes, but she was standing where Louise could not see her. "Want to hand me that chicken stock, Alice?"

Alice brought her the chicken stock and watched as she poured it in. "Is this like your squash soup?"

"Similar, but I use a few different spices."

"Hello?" called a female voice from the dining room.

"That sounds like Cynthia," said Louise with excitement. She opened the swinging doors to the dining room. "Oh, it is so good to see you, honey."

"Hi, Mom." Cynthia came into the kitchen, set down

her bag and gave her mother a big hug. "I decided to leave work early and bring my project with me."

"Welcome," said Jane with a warm smile.

"Hey, Aunt Jane," said Cynthia, giving her aunt a hug.

"Hi, Cynthia," said Alice. "Did you have a good trip?"

"Not bad, Aunt Alice." She now gave Alice a hug. "I feel like I've come home."

Louise smiled. "That is what we wanted to hear, honey. Let me help you get your things to my room. Jane is just starting some pumpkin soup."

"Ooh, sounds lovely."

"I don't know why Louise seems so resistant to the idea of your dating Mark," Jane said to Alice when Louise and Cynthia were out of earshot.

"We're not dating, Jane." Alice watched as her sister stirred the just simmering pot.

"Okay, whatever you want to call it." Jane replaced the lid on the pot and turned the flame a bit lower. "I just don't know why she keeps insisting upon throwing a wet blanket on everything."

Alice considered this. "I think she's just trying to protect me."

"Protect you?" Jane frowned as she removed a loaf of pumpernickel bread from the bread drawer.

"I haven't thought about it for ages, but Louise was

quite indignant when Mark dumped me almost forty years ago. Maybe she's afraid it will happen again."

"*He dumped you?*"

"Well, it probably was more of a mutual parting of ways, but I didn't see it like that at the time. We had a disagreement over religion, and then he and Father didn't hit it off. Plus he couldn't accept my need to live in Acorn Hill. We had a lot of differences."

Jane nodded.

"I'll bet that Louise remembers how hurt I was and just wants to make sure it doesn't happen again."

"You're probably right, Alice." Jane looked truly repentant. "There I go, assuming the worst about my dear sister again. When will I ever learn?"

"You were just protecting me too." Alice smiled. "How sweet to have two sisters looking out for my best interests."

"It's because we love you."

"Thanks," said Alice as she gave Jane a hug. "Now what can I do to help?"

"The soup's going to take a half hour more. I thought we'd make a green salad and slice up that bread and—"

"*Yoo-hoo,*" called Ethel from the back porch, "anybody home?"

"Come in," called Alice.

"Did I see Cynthia arrive a little while ago?"

"You did," said Jane. "She and Louise went upstairs to get her settled."

"What is that lovely smell?" asked Ethel, peering curiously at the big soup pot.

"That's pumpkin soup," said Alice.

"Would you like to join us for lunch?" asked Jane. "It might be a bit crowded, eating in the kitchen, but if you don't mind getting cozy—"

"I don't understand why you think you must eat in the kitchen when you have guests staying at the inn," said Ethel.

"Sometimes we do eat in the dining room, but we try to avoid doing so, particularly at lunchtime," explained Alice, not for the first time. "Our guests use the living room and would notice us taking a meal in there. It would be awkward for everyone."

"That's right," said Jane. "Already we've been asked 'what's cooking?' more times than I care to recall."

Ethel lifted the lid and took a peek at the soup. "Pumpkin soup? I don't believe I've ever had that."

"It's a bit like squash soup," said Jane. "It won't be ready for another thirty minutes or so."

"That's fine by me," said Ethel. "I had a late breakfast anyway. I met Lloyd and gave him a hand with the Chamber booth. Oh, you girls should see it. It looks grand."

"I did see it, Auntie," said Alice as she washed a big red tomato. "It's impressive."

"Are you girls coming to the Chamber's chili feed tonight?" she asked.

"The Chamber's proceeds are going toward the Kitchen Project, correct?" asked Jane.

Ethel nodded, causing her chins to jiggle. "That's right. Remember, Grace Chapel helps out with the Kitchen Project, too, mostly during the holidays. Lloyd said this year might be even harder than usual for some folks. Last year there were only about a dozen families who asked for assistance with groceries, but he expects that to double or triple this year, what with the layoffs at the factory in Potterston."

"Oh my," said Alice. "I hope we can raise a lot of money with the festival."

"I'm praying that we'll have lots of out-of-towners come," said Jane as she sliced mushrooms.

"With deep pockets and generous hearts," added Alice as she washed a green pepper.

"Alice's—uh—friend is coming," said Jane. "Remember the veterinarian?"

"The one that Clara thinks walks on water?" said Ethel. "Of course." She narrowed her eyes slightly as she studied Alice. "Are you getting involved with him, Alice?"

"Involved?" Alice cut the green pepper in half and began cleaning out the seeds. "He's just a friend who's interested in possibly relocating his practice in Acorn Hill."

"I thought that he treated elephants and penguins and such," said Ethel.

"That's been his focus, but he's considering a practice with small animals as a way of moving into retirement."

"Oh." Ethel eyed the pumpernickel loaf. "Would you like me to slice that for you, Jane?"

"Sure. I thought nice hearty slices would be good. About an inch. Then we'll warm it in the oven."

"Hello, Aunt Ethel," said Cynthia. "I thought I heard your voice."

"Well, Cynthia," said Ethel as she set down the knife and opened her arms wide, "I'm so glad you're here."

Cynthia hugged her great-aunt and looked around the kitchen. "Oh, it's so good to be here."

"Been working hard?" asked Jane as she handed her niece a carrot stick.

Cynthia nodded and took a bite. "I'm getting ready to go to the international book convention again, but there's so much to get done first."

"Tough work," said Jane with a friendly tone of sarcasm, "jetting off to Frankfurt every fall."

"Yes, and just in time for Oktoberfest too."

"Do you get to do any sightseeing?" asked Alice.

"Last year we took a day trip down the Rhine. It was very pretty."

"*Humph*," said Ethel. "There are plenty of places in the good old USA to see. Besides, I've heard that international travel is getting more and more dangerous."

"Oh, Aunt Ethel," said Jane. "I'm sure more people get killed driving on our freeways than flying overseas these days."

"That's statistically true," said Alice. "I've heard that flying has never been safer."

Soon the five women sat down at the kitchen table, and elbow-to-elbow they bowed their heads and thanked God, not only for the good food, but also for their loving family. "And bless all the booths and activities of the Fall Festival this weekend," said Alice. "And help us to raise enough money to help anyone in need and to make Acorn Hill a better place for everyone to live. Amen."

"Amen," echoed Ethel as she rubbed her hands together. "Now, let's see what on earth this pumpkin soup tastes like."

Chapter Twenty-Two

Cynthia convinced her mother and her aunts to allow her to join them for their journal reading session that evening after the chili feed.

"Only if you promise not to breathe a word of this to Aunt Ethel," said Jane.

"It's not that we're trying to exclude her," said Alice. "But there are some things in here that aren't terribly flattering to her father."

"I know," said Cynthia. "Mom told me a little about it."

Alice opened the journal and filled in Cynthia on how Daniel had given his life to God in the last entry. "It was really beautiful about how the full moon rose and lit his way home afterward," she said. Then she began to read.

November 30, 1926.

I officially joined Mr. Dolton's church last Sunday. I

had visited three times before I made the commitment, but it seems the right thing to do. Naturally, Mr. Dolton was pleased and he gave me a book to read called Being a Servant in God's Kingdom. Naturally Gladys and my father do not know what to make of me. "Why do you want to go traipsing off to church, boy," my father asked last Sunday, "if no one's making you?" I told him that God makes me want to go, but he just scratched his head and told me I was starting to act like my mother. I continue to stay in my bale room above the barn. So far I have not been too cold at night, but I pile on the blankets. I actually think it may be warmer than my old room upstairs where I often found ice on the inside of my window during winter. I must say I do enjoy my privacy and I feel certain that my father and Gladys do not miss my presence in the house. Gladys seems to have settled down some and does not complain so much about her "delicate condition." However, she does not appear to like housework much and likes cooking even less. I try to help out when I can, but sometimes I think it is better simply to stay out of her way. I do pray for my father and Gladys now. I am not sure that it is doing them any good, but it does make me feel better.

"That is the truth," said Louise. "I think that the only reason I pray sometimes is to make myself feel better."

"But look what happened when Alice prayed last

week," Jane reminded them. "God helped her to figure out Vera's mystery illness."

"Mom told me about that," said Cynthia. "That was amazing, Aunt Alice."

Alice smiled and looked back at the journal. "Shall I read another? It looks like the next one wraps up the year." She flipped through the remaining pages. "And the entries are less frequent after that."

They all agreed to finish up Daniel's 1926.

December 25, 1926.

Christmas Day. For the first time in my life I appreciate this holiday for what it is truly meant to be. Even though I am home alone, since Gladys talked my father into taking her to her parents' home to visit, I do not feel the least bit lonely. They did invite me to go, but I could tell from Gladys's description that her parents have a very small home and my presence would only contribute to the overcrowding there. This was perfectly fine with me, as I wanted to attend the candlelight service at church last night anyway. I must say that it was the most glorious event I have ever participated in. Indeed, I tried not to let anyone see that it brought tears to my eyes. I thought of how much my mother would have appreciated a service like that, and then I felt the strongest sensation that she was looking down from heaven and watching me. It was as if I could even feel the warmth of her smile. This was a wonderful Christmas present to me. Afterward, Mr. Dolton asked me what my family was doing for Christmas and when I told him, he insisted upon taking me home with him and his wife that very evening. I thanked him for his kindness but explained that I needed to return to the farm to tend to the animals. Then Mrs. Dolton insisted that I must join them for Christmas dinner. I plan to do this at two o'clock this afternoon and I am sure I will enjoy a fine time with them, but I have also relished this quiet day of simply reading the Bible, praying and meditating, and being on my own in the house. Still, I suspect that it is not good to spend too much time on one's own. I do not want to become a hermit. I even decided to give my father and Gladys a Christmas present of sorts. I got up early and after tending to the livestock, I spent a good part of the morning cleaning and scrubbing the house. I filled the wood box and even washed the window above the sink. I am not sure if they will notice or even appreciate my efforts, but it did fill my heart with joy. I finished reading the book that Mr. Dolton gave me. I am learning how important it is to have a servant's heart, although I feel certain it will take me my lifetime to figure that out.

"That sounds just like Grandfather," said Cynthia. "So wise and humble. It's hard to believe he was only sixteen at the time."

"I think some people are just more naturally that way," said Jane. "Take our own Alice here."

Alice waved her hand as if to brush away the compliment. "If I appear humble, it's probably only because I make more mistakes than the rest of you. And as far as wisdom goes...well, I hope we all get a little wiser with each passing year."

"That is right," said Louise. "There must be some benefit to the gray hair and the aching joints." She stood and stretched. "If you will excuse me, dears, I think I will take my weary old self to bed."

The next morning, the house was abuzz with guests making plans for the day. The sun was out and the air was crisp and everyone was enthusiastic about the Fall Festival.

"It's such a wonderful idea to have a fair like this in the autumn," said Mrs. Anderson. She and her sister had driven down from Meadville to enjoy the weekend. "We plan to shop until we drop today."

"Good for you," said Louise. "You know all the proceeds from the festival will be going to local charities."

"All the better," said Mrs. Anderson. "Do you think it's too soon to head out?"

"Not really," said Alice. "The booths are supposed to start opening up at nine."

By ten o'clock all the guests had departed, as had Louise and Cynthia. Jane and Alice were finishing cleaning up the kitchen.

"Is that what you're wearing today?" Jane asked Alice as she closed the dishwasher.

"I thought so." Alice looked down at her off-duty uniform of blue jeans, sweatshirt and tennis shoes. "Is it bad?"

"It's okay for cleaning the kitchen or maybe walking with Vera." One of Jane's eyebrows was arched, her way of saying that all was not well.

"Well, I suppose I could change my sweatshirt, maybe put on a sweater. Would that make you happy?"

Jane dried her hands, hung up her dishtowel and took Alice by the hand. "Come on, sister. You need to do some serious sprucing up and I'm here to help."

As they walked up the stairs, Alice noticed how pretty her younger sister looked in her long denim skirt and paisley silk vest. But Jane had always had style. Like Mother, she seemed to be born with it. Alice, on the other hand, definitely had not.

Within minutes, Jane had changed Alice's entire look—quite painlessly, too, since Alice still got to wear her jeans.

"I never would've thought to wear this suede jacket with jeans," said Alice as she stood before the mirror and allowed Jane to play with her hair.

"And that scarf really sets off your eyes," said Jane. "And see how something as simple as exchanging those chunky white walking shoes for nice brown loafers really pulls your look together. It actually makes your jeans look nice."

Alice nodded. "And I don't even feel like someone else. Well, not quite. Thanks, Jane. When you're not busy cooking, making chocolates, decorating houses, gardening or making jewelry, perhaps you could teach a 'how to dress' seminar for old ladies."

"You forgot painting," said Jane as she set down the hairbrush and grinned.

Alice laughed. "It's just not fair, Jane. You got all the creative talent in the family."

Jane gave Alice a squeeze. "You've got something that's a lot more important, Alice." She nodded. "Remember what Father said in his journal. You've got the servant's heart, and that is no small thing, sister."

The two sisters walked to town together but parted ways since Jane had promised to help Sylvia with her booth and shop today. Alice had barely said good-bye when a couple of ANGELs ran up and grabbed Alice by the arm.

"Wow, you look nice, Miss Howard," said Sarah.

"The bidding on the quilt has already started," Ashley told Alice in a hushed voice as if it were all top secret.

"It's already up to fifty dollars," said Sarah eagerly. "And it's only eleven now. At this rate, it might go up to a thousand dollars by five o'clock."

Alice smiled at their enthusiasm. "Wouldn't that be something?"

"Are you going to bid on it, Miss Howard?" asked Ashley.

"As a matter of fact, I had planned to."

"Right this way," said Sarah as the two girls escorted her directly to the silent auction section set up under an awning near the hardware store.

"You sign up there for a number," explained Sarah as she pointed to a table with a rust-and-gold plaid tablecloth. "That way no one but you and Mr. Humbert knows what you're bidding on or how much you bid. He said that's so no one gets angry with anyone else for outbidding them on something."

Alice chuckled. "I suppose that makes sense." She waved at Fred. "Hey, are you managing the silent auction?"

"Only for a couple of hours. Then I have to go mind the store. Vera plans to take over for me at noon."

"How's she feeling today?"

"According to her, she's never felt better."

"We were all praying for Mrs. Humbert," said Sarah.

Fred reached over and patted her head. "I thank you, Sarah, and all you ANGELs. God was listening."

"So was Miss Howard," said Ashley. "To the radio, I mean."

They laughed, and then Fred assigned Alice a secret number.

"Tell Vera I'll be by to help her later," said Alice. She went over to where their beautiful autumn quilt was displayed and moved the top-bidding price up five dollars.

"That's your bid," said Sarah triumphantly. "We know what your number is now, Miss Howard."

She placed her crossed fingers over her lips and the girls did likewise.

"We know," said Ashley. "We won't say a word."

"Thanks," said Alice.

The two girls then escorted Alice around to see their favorite spots, a bead booth and a candle-making booth, and finally they talked her into having a cotton candy with them. She pulled at the sticky pink confection and laughed. "Goodness, I haven't had cotton candy in years."

"Why not?" asked Ashley.

"I guess I just never thought to."

"I'll never give up cotton candy," said Sarah with all

the conviction of a preadolescent. "Even when I'm an old, old lady, I'll still be eating it."

Alice gently poked her little friend with her elbow. "Hey, watch it."

"Not that you're an old lady, Miss Howard," said Sarah quickly.

Alice smiled as she pulled another sticky strand from the paper cone. They walked around some more, pausing to watch the puppet show being put on by the fire department. It was about fire safety and a bit silly, but the puppets were cute.

"Hello there," said a deep voice.

Alice turned to see Mark Graves standing beside her. "Mark, how are you?"

"Great. This is quite a nice little event."

"Where are Susan and her husband?"

"They got involved at the antiques booth. I told them I'd just walk around and take in the sights. Who are your young friends?"

Alice introduced Sarah and Ashley to him, and then said to the girls, "This is Dr. Graves. He's a famous veterinarian who works at the Philadelphia Zoo and also treats exotic animals all over the world."

Mark laughed. "Not really famous."

"Do you treat whales?" asked Ashley.

"Sometimes."

"How about hippopotamuses?" asked Sarah.

He nodded, and the two girls tried to quiz him on every strange sort of animal they could think of.

"I think you girls get the idea," said Alice.

"That's cool," said Ashley. "You're just like Dr. Dolittle."

He smiled. "I've heard that one before."

"Hey, there's Jenny and Sissy," said Sarah suddenly, waving to their friends across the street. "We promised to hang with them today."

"I guess we'll see you later, Miss Howard," said Ashley. "Nice to meet you, Dr. Dolittle."

Alice was about to drop the remainder of her uneaten cotton candy in the trash receptacle when Mark stopped her. "Hey, you're not throwing that away, are you?"

She looked at him in surprise. "You want it?"

"Yeah, I haven't had cotton candy in years."

She shook her head and handed the candy over to him. "The first few bites taste good, but it gets awfully sweet after that."

He nodded as he stuffed a large wad into his mouth. Some got stuck in his beard and caused Alice to laugh. She pointed to her chin to clue him in.

"Have you seen much of the festival yet?" she asked.

"Not much, but I'd like to see more."

"I can walk with you for a bit if you like," she told him, "but I promised to go help my friend Vera at the silent auction booth pretty soon."

"Great, I'll enjoy your company while I can get it." He paused by a trashcan to drop off what was left of the cotton candy. "You're right. It did taste good at first."

She nodded and held up her sticky fingers. "And I need a place to wash off."

"Likewise. Where can we get a cup of good coffee?"

They stopped by the high school's food booth where they rinsed their hands and Mark ordered a latte and Alice got a cocoa. Then they walked up and down the street, pausing here and there to examine the various booths. As they walked, Alice was frequently stopped by friends, and more introductions were made.

"This is great," said Mark. "I'll probably know everyone in town before the day is half over."

"That's a distinct possibility," said Alice.

"Hello, Dr. Graves and Alice," said Clara Horn as she pushed her baby carriage up to them. "Do you want to see how your patient is doing?"

Mark nodded and peeked into the carriage. "Well, doesn't Daisy look pretty today."

Alice peered into the carriage and smiled. Daisy's black snout and dark beady eyes made an interesting contrast with the bright pink bonnet that Louise had knitted. The sweater seemed to fit her perfectly. "Your little Daisy looks very chic today, Clara."

"I thought about letting her walk through town just so that everyone could see her darling outfit," said Clara. "But her little legs are so short that I was afraid I might wear her out."

"That was a wise choice," said Mark. "She looks very comfortable in there."

Clara nodded. "I do let her get out and stroll for a spell. I know the exercise is good for her."

"That's right."

Clara reached over and took his hand, then spoke in a conspiring tone. "I heard that you might be moving to Acorn Hill, Dr. Graves. I've been telling everyone in town just how remarkable you are." Her face wrinkled into a smile. "I know Daisy would love to have her favorite doctor nearby."

He nodded. "Well, we'll see what happens."

Clara bid them good-bye and continued on her way.

"Word certainly gets around," he said.

"I'm sorry," said Alice. "My sisters told Aunt Ethel and she—"

"Not a problem." He chuckled. "That is precisely one of the things that charms me about a town like this. I'll never need to run an advertisement in the local paper."

"That's right. Just tell my aunt and by the end of the day everyone should know."

Just then his cell phone rang. "Excuse me." He paused to look at it, then said, "I better take this."

"I think I'll go check on Vera," said Alice, slightly relieved to get away.

He nodded and she turned to head over to the silent auction booth. She enjoyed Mark's company, but she was not sure that she would be comfortable spending the whole day with him. And, having to pause every two minutes to introduce him to someone was beginning to wear on her. She felt she needed a little break.

"Hello, Vera," she said as she entered the booth. "How's business?"

"Great," said Vera. "Do you need a number?"

"I've got one."

"So, is that handsome man you've been seen with the mysterious Dr. Graves?"

"I don't know why you'd think he was mysterious, Vera."

"Simply because I've never met him."

"I forgot. You were under the weather the last time he was here. I'll be sure to introduce you two before the day is over. Goodness knows, I've introduced him to half of Acorn Hill already."

"So, how's it going?" asked Vera in a lowered voice.

"The festival?" asked Alice innocently, although she knew exactly what Vera meant.

"No, silly. How's it going with the doctor?"

"All right, I guess."

"You guess?"

"I'm just not used to this." Alice glanced around. "It feels like everyone in town is staring at me and drawing conclusions. I'm sure I'll be doing damage control for the next couple of weeks."

Vera chuckled. "Well, just tell Aunt Ethel to spread the word that it's not that serious." Then she leaned over the table and peered at Alice. "If it's not, that is."

Alice waved her hand. "Oh, it's not, Vera. We're only friends."

"Hello, Vera and Alice," said Clarissa Cottrell as she bent over to sign up for a bidding number. "I thought I'd sneak away from the bakery long enough to place a couple of bids."

"Good for you," said Vera.

"Although I know I should wait until later since I'll probably just be bidding myself up."

Alice laughed. "I know what you mean, but remember it's all for a good cause."

"Right." Clarissa headed straight for the quilt.

"I'm bidding on that too," Alice whispered to Vera.

"Good luck," said Vera.

"Hello, ladies," said Mark as he came up to the booth.

"Hi, Mark," said Alice. "I'd like you to meet my very good friend Vera Humbert."

He shook her hand. "I've heard a lot about you. I even read about you in the newspaper last week."

"Goodness," said Vera. "They actually reported about that in Philadelphia?"

He shook his head. "Although, I wouldn't be surprised if they did run a human interest article on it. It's an unusual story. I read it in the *Acorn Nutshell*—online."

"The *Nutshell* is online?"

"That's right."

"Well, I'll have to tell my daughters. They're away at college, but I'm sure they'd like to read the local news from time to time, especially if they could do it online."

"This looks like an interesting booth," observed Mark.

"Here," said Vera as she handed him the secret notebook. "I'll give you a bidding number, and you can go in there and knock yourself out."

"Thanks." He signed the sheet and took a number from her. "I think I'll do that."

"We appreciate all this out-of-town money," teased Alice. "Do remember it's all for a good cause."

A few minutes later, Susan and her husband, Tom, appeared, and introductions were made. "Have you seen Mark?" asked Susan.

Alice pointed into the booth. "Right that way."

"You better get a number first," suggested Vera. "In case you want to place a bid on anything."

"And remember," said Alice with a grin, "it's for a good cause."

"We make a good team," said Vera.

"Well, of course," agreed Alice.

"Do you want to join us for lunch?" asked Mark when he finally emerged from the booth.

"No thanks," said Alice. "I'll stay here and help Vera."

"Okay, then shall I pick you up at the inn for dinner?"

"Yes, that would be fine."

"Around six then?"

"Great."

After Mark, Susan and Tom left, Vera turned to Alice with a frown. "You did not need to stay here to help me, Alice Howard. I am perfectly fine on my own."

"I know, Vera." Alice patted her arm. "I just wanted to. Okay?"

Vera's eyes lit up. "Okay then, because I am feeling

perfectly fine—never better. It's as if I have a whole new lease on life." She sighed happily. "I suppose you don't fully appreciate what you've got until something threatens to take it away."

"I'm sure you're right about that, Vera."

Chapter Twenty-Three

Alice helped Vera until her shift ended at two thirty, then the two of them slipped over to the Coffee Shop for a little break and a late lunch.

"What are you doing in here?" asked Hope as she handed them menus. "I thought you two would be at the Fall Festival all day."

"We thought we'd sneak away for a bit," said Alice. "It's pretty busy and noisy out there."

"Good," said Hope. "I plan to check out all the booths as soon as I clock out." She checked her watch. "Which should be in about twenty minutes. Is there anything good left?"

"Of course, although some things are a bit picked over," said Vera. "The silent auction tent will be running until five."

"Unfortunately, the bids over there are getting a little high," said Alice. "I was trying to get something myself and decided to lie low for a while. No sense in helping the price to go up."

"But it's for a good cause," teased Vera, mimicking what Alice had been telling folks all day.

They each ordered a cup of navy bean soup and shared a piece of blackberry pie, then lingered over a pot of Earl Grey tea.

"So, are you saying it's not getting a little bit serious with Mark?" asked Vera.

"How do you define 'a little bit serious'?"

"Well, you went to dinner with him once, spent some time with him today, and you're going out again tonight. Plus, the man wants to relocate his life to your hometown, Alice. I think I would define that as a little bit serious."

Alice shrugged. "I don't know."

"Well, there's nothing wrong with being a happy couple." Vera poured the last of the tea into Alice's cup. "Fred and I are a testament to that. Do you know how nice it was to have Fred around during my little poisoning spree?"

Alice laughed. "Don't call it that, Vera."

"Really, there's something to be said for having a good man by your side, Alice. You may be perfectly happy being single, especially now that you have your sisters at home, but what if the good Lord wanted something different for your life?"

"Goodness, I suppose I hadn't thought of it quite like

that, Vera. Of course, if I truly believed that God wanted me to, well, become more involved with Mark, then naturally, I'd do so. The problem is I'm just not sure that's really the case."

"Well, as long as you're open to the idea."

Alice glanced at the clock above the cash register. "Do you think we should head back? I'd really like to be the one to make the final bid on that quilt." She smiled. "*Since it is for a good cause.*"

"At the rate the bidding was going, I think you might need to take out an equity loan."

Alice left a tip on the table and the two of them headed back to the festival, stopping to visit with Jane at Sylvia's booth.

"How's business?" asked Vera.

"Great," said Jane. "Both my necklaces sold, and all but two of Alice's aprons went. Of course, one of those is already sold, but, honestly, I could've sold it a dozen times over. Next year, you better make them all like that, Alice."

Vera looked at the apron with the sold tag on it. "Very pretty." Then she picked up the other one. "This is nice too. I think I'll take it."

"Oh, I can make you one, Vera."

Vera's brows drew together. "Alice, have you forgotten that this is for a good cause?"

They both laughed, and Vera paid Jane for the apron.

"Sylvia's going to relieve me in a few minutes," said Jane, "so I can come by the silent auction and make some last-minute bids."

"That booth is going to be busy," said Alice.

Alice was right, that booth *was* busy. At a quarter to five it was swarming with last-minute bidders all hoping to secure their items with the highest bid. Alice noticed Susan and Tom hovering near an old butter churn, and she spied Mark moving through the crowd too. Just minutes before five Alice went to place her bid, but she stopped cold, stunned: The last bidder had jumped the bid by more than one hundred dollars.

Sadly, she put her pen back into her purse. That was just too dear for her part-time nurse's budget—even if it *was* for a good cause.

The bell rang and the bidding came to a close. Fred Humbert was running the show again, with Vera at his side, and together they went around and collected the bid papers. One by one, Fred announced the names of the highest bidders for each item. Susan and Tom got the butter churn. Hope had managed to get a set of pottery dishes, and Jane had placed the highest bid on the rice cooker that she wanted.

"But the big ticket item of the day is this beautiful

quilt," said Fred over the PA system. "And the highest bidder is Mark Graves."

Alice blinked in surprise. So Mark had been the bidder who upped the ante at the last minute.

"Maybe you can talk him out of it," whispered Jane with a twinkle in her eye.

Alice just shook her head as she watched Mark go up to collect the quilt.

As the crowd began dispersing, Mark came over to show it to her. "Did you see what I got?"

Alice smiled. "Yes, I've seen it before."

Jane gave Alice a gentle nudge with her elbow.

He smiled. "I suppose it seems odd for an old bachelor to buy something like this, but I was just so taken with it. Besides, as you told me, it's for a good cause, right?"

"Yes. It definitely is."

"Well, I guess we'll see you around six."

Alice nodded and waved good-bye.

"What do you think of that?" said Jane.

"What?"

"Mark's outbidding you for that quilt."

"I think it's nice that he got it."

Jane winked at her. "Maybe you'll get to share it with him someday."

"Jane!" Alice just shook her head. "I think I'll head for home now."

"I'm coming with you," said Jane. "Someone's got to make sure you pull yourself together for your date."

"It's not a date," said Alice in a lowered voice as they began walking toward home.

"The lady doth protest too much, methinks."

Somehow Alice managed to convince her younger sister that the clothes she was wearing would be perfectly suitable for dinner with Mark and his relatives. "Didn't you see how casually they were dressed?" she asked Jane. "They aren't going to change just to eat dinner."

Jane nodded. "Okay, you're probably right."

Fortunately, Alice *was* right. To her relief the dinner was an all-around casual affair at a family-style restaurant in Potterston. Susan and Tom were enjoyable to visit with, but Mark seemed unexpectedly quiet. Alice wondered if something was wrong. Something she had said? Had he learned that she had been disappointed not to win the quilt?

"Why so glum, bro?" asked Susan as dessert was served.

"You do seem a bit quiet tonight," said Tom. "Usually you're regaling us with some new animal tale."

Mark nodded solemnly. "I've just been mulling something over today."

"What's that?" asked Susan.

"I have a major decision to make."

Alice felt her throat go dry. Surely Mark was not referring to anything concerning her. She picked up her water glass and drained it with a gulp.

"I got a phone call from an old friend today. He's heading down to Brazil in a couple of weeks. He just got a grant to study endangered species on the Amazon and he has invited me to join him."

"How exciting," said Tom. "Sounds like it's right up your alley."

"And you've always loved the Amazon," said Susan. "So, what's the problem?"

"Well, I had also been considering retiring from my job at the zoo and starting a small animal practice in a place like Acorn Hill."

"Ah," said Susan. She glanced across the table at Alice, who was experiencing a strange mixture of disappointment and relief.

"How long will your friend's study be?" asked Alice.

"Six months," said Mark, his eyes looking directly into hers.

She sighed. "Goodness, six months isn't a very long

time. Perhaps you should consider going through with your retirement. That way you could go to help your friend with no strings attached. Then just see where the Lord leads you next."

"Yes, that makes a lot of sense." He smiled with what seemed like relief. "I've only been to the Amazon once, and only for a few days, but I was intrigued with the place. I've always dreamed of returning."

Alice nodded. "Then it seems you should go."

The four of them chatted more about South America, the Amazon and traveling in general as they drove Alice back to Acorn Hill. Then Mark got out to walk her up to the house. Pausing at the door, he took her hand.

"Alice, I haven't been completely honest with you."

She blinked. "What about?"

"Well, a couple of things." He looked down at the porch. "First of all, the main reason I feel conflicted about going to the Amazon is because of you—"

"Oh, Mark, you shouldn't—"

"Wait, Alice, I need to explain. I still have feelings for you, and I don't want to do the same thing I did forty years ago."

"This is completely different, Mark. I really believe you're absolutely right to go to the Amazon. I can see how excited you are about it, and I would feel horrible to think that I could have anything to do with your not going. And, really, six months is such a short time."

He smiled. "You are a wonderful person, Alice. I've always known that."

"Thank you. Now what was the other thing you weren't honest about?"

"Well, earlier today, when I signed up for the auction, I noticed a name a few spaces above mine. I wasn't trying to, but I do have a bit of a photographic memory. I saw Alice Howard with the number fifty-six next to it. I guess it sort of stuck in my mind."

"And?"

"Well, I saw the quilt and saw that number fifty-six had bid on it. Later on, I checked and saw that other bids were higher than yours and, well, I just couldn't resist." He released her hand. "Wait right here a minute." He dashed back to his SUV, opened the back and then returned with the quilt bundled up in his hands. "It's for you, Alice."

"Oh, Mark."

"I wanted you to have it."

She laughed. "I really wanted it too. But I can't take it from you."

He shook his head. "It wasn't for me."

"But—"

"No buts."

"Thank you."

Then, taking her hand in his, he leaned forward and kissed her on the cheek. "You're one in a million, Alice Howard." Then he released her hand and went down the stairs. "I'll be in touch."

Alice felt tears in her eyes as she waved good-bye. "Yes, and you take care, Dr. Graves." She watched as he got back into his SUV and drove away. But instead of feeling sad or disappointed, she only felt happy and relieved. She did not know what the long-term future held for either one of them, but she believed that what and where they were right now was exactly right—for both of them. And she would be praying for him daily.

"Alice!" exclaimed Jane when Alice came into the house holding the beautiful quilt in her arms. "Oh my goodness, does this mean you're getting married?"

Alice laughed at her younger sister and started to explain, but by then Louise and Cynthia had joined them.

"Let us start from the beginning," said Louise as she took Alice by the arm and led her to the kitchen. "Cynthia, put on the kettle," she commanded. "Jane, how about some of that pumpkin bread?"

It did not take long for Alice to set them all straight. "It's not that it's totally out of the realm of possibility," she said finally. "It's just that the timing isn't right for either one of us right now."

"No sense in rushing things," said Louise.

Cynthia frowned. "That's not what you say to me, Mother."

Louise just laughed. "That is because you are not getting any younger."

Cynthia looked at Alice. "And *she* is?"

Louise patted her daughter's hand. "It is all a matter of perspective, dear."

"Do we have time to read again tonight, Aunt Alice?" asked Cynthia eagerly.

"Sure, if you all want to," said Alice.

They moved their tea party to the den and Alice read.

February 19, 1927.

I turned seventeen today and I cannot believe how I feel so completely different from last year. Then I was hopeless and discouraged. Now I feel excited about life and I believe that God has a purpose for me. My studies are going well and my home life is more tolerable than before. Gladys is bigger than a house and mostly sits, but since I am willing to help out with her daily chores, she has become quite appreciative. She and I even talk sometimes when my father is out late. She told me about where she grew up and how her parents were poor and how she ran away only to find it difficult to earn her living as a seamstress. I feel a little sorry for her. I know that my father is not the easiest man to live with, but then it was her choice to marry him. It makes me realize, more than ever, how important it is to choose the right person to marry. I can see now that Adele Brooks would not be right for me. I want to marry a girl with more substance and understanding. I am praying to someday meet a wife who loves God with her whole heart, is generous toward those with less and who is pretty. I realize the part about pretty may be a little shallow on my part, but I figure a fellow has the right to dream.

"Good for Grandpa," said Cynthia. "And his dream came true, didn't it?"

"It sure did," said Louise. "Our mother was all that he described and more."

"She was beautiful," said Alice. "In every way." She looked down at the still-open journal. "The next entry is about Aunt Ethel's birth."

"Read it," said Jane.

April 2, 1927.

By the time I came home after working at the newspaper today, Gladys was the proud mother of a baby girl. My father had just left to take the doctor back home, and Mrs. Warner was still on hand to help out. She asked me if I wanted to see my little sister, and for the first time it occurred to me that Gladys's baby was actually my sister. I do not know why that had not sunk in before. So I told Mrs. Warner, "Yes, I'd like to see the baby," and within minutes she reappeared with what looked like a withered up prune baby, only very red. "Is that it?" I asked. First Mrs. Warner frowned at me, then she explained that this is how babies look when they are born. I hope she is right because in my opinion that is the homeliest baby I have ever seen—

Now Cynthia and Jane were both laughing so hard that Alice could barely finish, but somehow she managed.

I do not want to hurt Gladys's feelings, but I am curious about what she thinks of this prune baby. Still, I suppose a mother would love her baby no matter what. Just the same I have seen newborn foals and calves and pigs that are all much nicer to look at than my little sister who is to be named Ethel. Poor girl, not only is she homely, but her name is not much to speak of either.

"That's so hilarious," said Cynthia with enthusiasm. "Please read more."

After they all recovered from their laughter, Alice

read a few more very brief entries. They said little more than how much their father enjoyed his studies but remained busier than ever with farm work, his part-time job and preparing for exams. He also made note of how he was continually growing as a Christian, and finally Alice came to an entry that was more than a couple of sentences long.

June 11, 1927.

My father, Gladys and baby sister Ethel (who is really quite cute now) attended my graduation last night. It may be an assumption on my part, but I think they were proud of me. I graduated with top honors and delivered the valedictory speech to my class, and best of all, the principal of our school presented me with the Thornton Scholarship, which will pay for all of my college expenses. Afterwards, my father shook my hand and said that I was a "chip off the old block." Once again, I bit my tongue and simply thanked him. It is hard to forget that only a week ago he was dead set against my going to college at all.

"Ain't it enough that you been going to school for eleven long years already, boy?" he bellowed at me one evening after a particularly bad day of plowing in the north field. "I'm thinking it's about time you paid your dues to this farm, boy. Unless you think your fancy education is gonna make them

crops plant and harvest themselves." I tried to explain to him, once again, that farming was fine for him, but that I had no desire to spend my life toiling in the dirt. "I love books and learning," I told him. "Books don't put food on the table," he snapped back at me. Well, I was ready to give up then. To just turn around and walk outside and wait for him to cool off, but then Gladys spoke up.

"Now, George, you ain't being fair to Daniel. He worked hard to get this far with his education. Why shouldn't he have his chance to go on and make something of himself? Mr. Dolton already explained that it won't cost you one penny. Besides that, it might raise our standing in this community to have a college-educated son. People might treat our little Ethel with more respect if they knew her big brother was a scholar. Maybe Daniel will get himself some big fancy job like a lawyer or doctor or senator. Think about how you could go bragging around to all your friends about that. The good Lord only knows, but our Daniel here might even become rich and famous someday. You want to take that away from him? From us?"

To my utter surprise, my father seemed to consider his wife's line of reasoning, and during the course of the following week, he appeared to reach a genuine place of acceptance. Naturally, I consider this an honest-to-goodness miracle and I have thanked God numerous times for his mercy in this regard.

After the graduation ceremony, Mr. and Mrs. Dolton hosted a celebration party for me. Naturally, it was only a small affair with mostly church friends, a couple of school chums and my little family. All in all, it was an amazing day and gives me hope that God has even better things in store for me. More than ever I believe that as the Bible says, "all things are possible with God."

For God to take a poor farm boy from such a home as mine and present me with the chance to make something of my life is nothing short of miraculous. And, as I said in my graduation speech, no one knows what the future holds for any of us, but my goal is to be thankful and grateful for the opportunities that lie ahead, and to trust God with the challenges of tomorrow. For I know that my life is safe in his hands.

"Wow," said Jane. "That's a lot to wrap your brain around."

Alice nodded. "But that's just exactly how Father lived out his life."

"What a rich heritage," said Cynthia.

Louise nodded. "I must admit that I was concerned when we first began reading Father's journal. I felt alarmed to learn how troubled his youth had been. I had no idea that his family had been so, well, dysfunctional."

"But, you see," said Alice, "it's like Scripture says, God really does work things together for good for those who love the Lord and are called according to His purposes."

"I suspect that Father wouldn't have been the man he was if his life had been completely easy and normal," said Jane.

"And we wouldn't be who we are," said Alice.

"It is fascinating to see how we are all interconnected by family ties and history," said Louise. "It makes me see why it is important to understand these things better."

"But as Father would say," added Alice, "it's more important to understand that we're all part of a much bigger family. That way, despite whatever life brings our way, whether it seems to be good or bad, we'll always have a heavenly Father to take care of us."

"Amen," said Cynthia.

Alice closed the journal and smiled. "Now that's a promise you can take to bed with you."

Cream of Pumpkin Soup
SERVES EIGHT

4 cups pumpkin purée

2 tablespoons unsalted butter

1 medium onion, roughly diced

3 quarts chicken stock or low-
   sodium chicken broth

1 teaspoon salt

1 teaspoon ground coriander

½ teaspoon curry powder

½ teaspoon white pepper

3 cups milk or whipping cream
   (or combination of both)

⅓ cup walnut oil

To prepare pumpkin purée: Cut one small cooking pumpkin in half (four-pound pumpkin equals four cups purée) and remove seeds. Cover cut side of each pumpkin half with aluminum foil and place foil side up on a baking sheet. Bake at 350 degrees until very tender, around forty-five minutes to one hour. When pumpkin is cool enough to handle, scrape from peel and purée in blender, with juices, in batches.

Melt butter in a large saucepan over medium heat. Add the onion, stirring now and then, and cook until soft, around ten minutes. Add the pumpkin purée and continue to cook, stirring, for around fifteen minutes. Add the chicken stock, salt, coriander, curry and white pepper. Cover, increase heat to high and bring to a boil. Reduce heat to low and simmer fifteen minutes. Remove from heat, carefully pour into a food processor or blender, and purée until smooth. Combine purée, milk and walnut oil in saucepan. Cover, bring to a boil and cook two more minutes. Serve piping hot.

Winter Wonders

Chapter One

*L*ike a soft, downy comforter, winter had settled itself gently onto Acorn Hill. Alice Howard welcomed the slower pace of the quiet days and early evenings spent with a good book, the company of her sisters and a warm fire.

"I love January," she said to no one in particular as she laid another log on the crackling fire. "It's so calm and peaceful."

"Especially after the hustle and bustle of the holidays." Louise adjusted her glasses and started another row of knitting. She was working on an afghan in a soft shade of yellow.

"Oh, I don't know," said Jane as she refilled their teacups. "I've always found January to be rather dreary and tedious. Of course that might have been more true living in San Francisco than here. It always seemed the longest, grayest month to me. When I was in California I would sometimes gather up my seed catalogs and dream of summer and gardens, and I'd actually start counting off the days until spring would arrive."

"I used to feel that way too," admitted Alice, "but I suppose I've changed as I've grown older. I appreciate the quietness of winter more and more."

"As do I," said Louise. "Although my old bones do not always appreciate the cold weather."

Jane twisted a strand of her long dark hair and smiled. "Well, give me a few more years and I'll probably be right there with both of you."

"Father loved wintertime," said Alice. "He said it gave him time to think. Sometimes he'd spend hours and hours just working on his Sunday sermon."

"Speaking of sermons," said Jane, "did I mention that Kenneth is taking a couple of weeks to visit his parents in Boston?"

"Oh dear, are they ailing?" asked Alice.

"No, but Kenneth is concerned that they're getting too old to keep up their house. His mother has been talking about moving into a retirement home, and he wants to help them check out some places."

"He is such a good son," said Louise.

"Who's going to preach on Sunday?" asked Alice as Wendell jumped up and made himself comfortable in her lap. She stroked the tabby's thick winter coat.

"Henry Ley is going to cover for him," said Jane. "Henry's been working with a series of audiotapes that are supposed to help him control his stuttering."

"Well, it is a good time for him to try preaching. There should not be too many people at church," said Louise. "Have you noticed how the congregation has thinned out since the holidays?"

"That's just because some of the snowbirds have gone to Florida," said Alice.

"Florida," Jane sighed. "Now, wouldn't that be lovely."

"*Yoo-hoo*," called a familiar voice from the kitchen, "anybody home?"

"We're in the living room, Aunt Ethel," called Alice.

"Oh, you girls look so snug and warm on this cold winter's night," said Ethel, unbuttoning her coat and removing her faux fur hat.

"Let me take those for you," offered Jane.

"What brings you out?" asked Louise as she set her knitting project aside and picked up a teacup.

"Pure boredom," said Ethel. She flopped down next to Alice on the sofa.

"Boredom?" echoed Louise. "You know what I always tell my music students when they complain about being bored. Only boring people get bored."

"Oh, *please*," said Ethel in a slightly offended tone.

"I did not come over here to be lectured by my eldest niece."

Jane sat back down in the rocker and leaned forward with interest. "I think I know how you feel, Aunt Ethel. I was just telling these two that I never look forward to January. To be perfectly honest, I think it's a rather boring month too."

"It's not January so much..." Ethel eyed the plate of freshly made raisin scones on the coffee table.

"Help yourself," said Jane. "Tea?"

"Thank you." Ethel settled back into the sofa. "The reason I'm feeling bored has more to do with Lloyd Tynan than January."

Jane handed her aunt a cup of steaming orange pekoe tea. "What's up with Lloyd?"

"Lloyd has taken up bowling of all things."

"*Bowling?*" Louise's eyebrows rose as if Ethel had said that the mayor of their town had taken up skinny-dipping.

Ethel shook her head sadly. "He drives over to Potterston two nights a week."

"Two nights a week?" repeated Louise. "To bowl?"

"That's right. One night is for practicing and the other night is for the league."

"Lloyd is in a bowling league?" Jane giggled.

"That's right."

"Does he wear one of those shirts with his name embroidered on it?"

"It's baby blue, which is actually rather attractive with his eyes. He hasn't gotten his name on it yet, but I expect it's just a matter of time." Ethel looked as if she had bitten into a lemon.

Alice smiled. "I think it's nice that he's found a new hobby."

"But bowling?" She shook her head.

"It does seem a little odd," agreed Louise. "Lloyd does not seem to be the bowling type."

"And what exactly is the bowling type?" teased Jane. "Beer bellies, tattoos and bawdy jokes?"

"I don't know," said Ethel. "But, believe me, he seems to have really taken to the ridiculous sport. It's all Clark Barrett's fault."

"How's that?" asked Alice.

"One of the bowlers had to drop out of Clark's league for hip replacement surgery, so Clark invited Lloyd to join him one evening, 'just for fun,' he said. And that," Ethel snapped her fingers, "was that. Lloyd was hooked. Apparently he knocked down all those silly things—whatever they're called—all at the same time."

"They are called 'pins,'" said Jane, "and if he knocked them all down it was a strike. So does he wear the weird shoes and everything?"

"You better believe it. He even bought his own bowling ball. It's bright blue with a bag that matches." Ethel sighed. "I just never thought it would come to this."

"Come to what?" asked Louise.

"That he'd choose bowling over me."

"Oh, I'm sure that's not it," said Alice. "He probably just wanted to try something new. I remember Vera Humbert saying that she was on a bowling team in college. And she seemed to think it was lots of fun."

Ethel waved her hand. "Well, maybe it's fine for college kids. But at our age? Really."

"I think it's cute," said Jane.

"*Cute?*"

Jane nodded. "Yes. I can just imagine Lloyd in his new shoes and his baby-blue bowling shirt sending the ball spinning down the lane."

"Good grief!" Ethel scowled.

"In fact, I think it might be fun to go and watch him sometime."

"You can't be serious, Jane," Ethel said.

Jane frowned. "That does sound pretty weird. I must be more bored than I realized if I'm imagining that watching Lloyd bowl would be good entertainment."

Alice laughed. "Welcome to another Acorn Hill winter, Jane."

Jane looked somewhat perplexed now. "I don't remember feeling bored at all last year."

"That's because we were so busy getting the house fixed up," Alice reminded her.

Louise looked as though she was considering her boring-people speech again; fortunately she did not deliver it.

"Just think," said Alice, "now you have more time for your art and your jewelry and your cooking."

"That's true."

"Winter is a natural time to slow down and rest up," said Louise as she picked up her knitting again. "Even having no guests booked for the next couple of weeks is a blessing. I think this is God's way of giving us a much-needed break."

"I suppose." Jane sat back down but still did not look convinced.

"So why not just enjoy this little reprieve, Jane," said Alice as she petted the happily purring cat. "Life will get busy enough in time."

"Maybe." Jane wore a funny little smile now. "If it doesn't, maybe I will take up bowling too."

"It must be catching," mused Ethel.

Chapter Two

The following day, when Alice returned home from her shift at the hospital, she was surprised to spot an unfamiliar car parked in front of the inn. It looked to be an old Thunderbird, maybe from the sixties. A warm shade of beige, the sporty but dignified car appeared to be in mint condition. She resisted the urge to peek inside to see if its interior was equally perfect. Instead she quickened her pace, hoping to discover who the mystery visitor might be. She knew that no guests had booked rooms, but perhaps this visitor was here about something else.

She came through the front door to see a tall, white-haired man, in a hat and an overcoat, looking around as if he was lost.

"May I help you?" she asked as she removed her jacket.

"Is this a rest home?" he said with a twinkle in his eye as he peered at her nurse's uniform.

She smiled. "No. It's a bed-and-breakfast. I work part-time as a nurse at the hospital in Potterston."

"Oh." He nodded. "Well, I was told that there was an inn beside the old church. I knocked on the door, and then just let myself in."

"And no one is here?" Alice glanced around. "I'm sorry."

"I was hoping to get a room," he continued. "Dusk overtook me as I was passing through your quaint little town, and I don't really see that well after dark. I thought I'd just stop for the night."

"We have plenty of room," she assured him as she stepped behind the counter.

"Hello?" called Louise.

"Out in the foyer," said Alice. "We have a guest."

"Oh my," said Louise as she came in from the kitchen. "I was not expecting anyone, and I just stepped out to run some errands in town. Is Jane around?"

"Apparently not." Alice smiled at the man. "I'm sorry. We must seem terribly disorganized. It's not usually like this. It's just that we weren't expecting any guests this week."

"Oh, I don't want to be any trouble," he said.

"You're no trouble," said Alice as she offered him her hand. "I'm Alice Howard, and this is my sister Louise Smith."

"I'm Harold Branninger," he said and shook her hand.

"I can take it from here," said Louise, adjusting her glasses and picking up a pen. "Thank you, Alice."

"You're in good hands now," said Alice as she went upstairs.

"I can see that," said Harold.

Alice felt a mixture of disappointment and curiosity as she quickly showered and changed for dinner. She had been enjoying this little reprieve from guests, but now the man with the interesting car was going to change that. Only for one night, she reminded herself as she slipped into her comfortable loafers.

By the time Alice went downstairs, Jane had arrived home and was busy in the kitchen.

"I hear we have a guest," said Jane as she turned down the flame under a soup pot.

"His name is Harold," said Alice as she peeked in the pot to see what appeared to be New England clam chowder. "That smells delicious, Jane."

"I told Louise to invite him to join us for dinner," said Jane as she deftly slid two plump loaves of brown bread into the hot oven. "Since he's on his own and everything."

"That was good of you."

"Did you see his car?" asked Jane as she brushed off her hands on her white chef's apron.

Alice nodded. "Very nice."

"Yes, and in perfect condition. Did he say where he's from?"

"He didn't tell me. He did mention that he was just passing through."

"How old is he?" Jane asked this in a casual voice, but Alice could not help but wonder if her younger sister was interested.

Alice suppressed a smile. "Well, he's a tad older than you, Jane. I'm guessing late seventies."

"Oh." Jane nodded and then chuckled. "I was just curious, Alice."

Alice smiled now. "You have to feel a little sorry for any unattached male that shows up at a B and B run by three single women."

Jane laughed. "Oh sure, Alice, like we're all just desperately looking for husbands these days." She shook her head. "*Not.*"

Alice helped Jane set the table in the dining room, and before long the four of them were enjoying a supper of soup and bread.

"I feel like I landed in a fine feathered nest," said Harold after polishing off a second bowl of Jane's delicious chowder.

"I'm afraid that dinner wasn't very fancy tonight," said Jane.

He shook his head. "I've never been one for fancy foods. My late wife, Lily, always appreciated that I had fairly ordinary tastes." His face seemed to cloud over at the mention of his wife.

"How long has it been since you lost your wife?" asked Jane.

"Just a year now." He set down his spoon with a clink. "Sometimes it feels like a lifetime."

"What are you doing out on the road in the middle of winter?" asked Louise.

"I thought maybe a trip would help me to get past this...this...well, it's the anniversary of Lily's death this week. I thought that if I wasn't home...well, maybe it wouldn't be so hard."

"That makes perfect sense," said Alice as she began to clear the table.

"I should probably just sell my house and move to a condominium or something," he continued, "but it's hard to give up a lifetime of memories."

"Oh, just because you sell your house does not mean you lose those memories," said Louise gently. "I sold my house last year, and I really have not regretted it at all."

"But you've got this lovely place," said Harold. "Didn't you say it was your family home while growing up?"

Louise smiled. "That is true. I suppose that makes a big difference."

"I'm sure you'll figure out what's best for you to do,"

said Alice. "I've heard it's good to wait about a year before making any big decisions after losing a loved one."

"Well, it'll be a year tomorrow." He sighed.

"Where will you be headed tomorrow?" asked Louise.

He shrugged. "Wherever the road leads."

Alice thought that sounded awfully sad and lonely. "You are welcome to stay on here."

He seemed to brighten. "Now that you mention it, I think that might be a good idea." He glanced at the three sisters and smiled. "If that's all right with everyone, I mean. I don't want to intrude."

Louise waved her hand. "That would not be the case. We are a bed-and-breakfast. This is what we do."

"And we'd love to have you stay longer," agreed Jane. "Believe me, it's been pretty quiet around this old house."

"I noticed you have a piano," said Harold. "Playing has been a lifelong hobby for me."

"Louise is the musician in the family," said Alice. "I'm sure she'd be happy to share her piano with you."

"Of course," said Louise with a warm smile. "It would be a relief to have someone else providing the musical entertainment. What do you like to play?"

"Well, I've never been big on longhair music." He winked at Jane. "And I'm not talking about the Beatles. I always went more for old show tunes. You know like from the Rogers and Hammerstein musicals. Lively songs that make you want to kick up your heels."

One of Louise's eyebrows rose. Alice suspected that Harold's musical taste might pose a problem for her more conservative sister.

"Show tunes?" Louise did not seem enthusiastic.

Jane laughed as she picked up the nearly empty soup tureen. "I would love to hear some old show tunes, Harold. I suggest we have our dessert in the parlor and see what Louise's piano is capable of."

Alice decided that Louise's piano was capable of some very lively sounds as she carried a tray laden with dishes of cherry cobbler into the parlor. Harold was playing "It Might as Well Be Spring" from *State Fair*, and Louise was sitting in an armchair with a pained expression on her face. If Alice did not know better she might have thought that her older sister was suffering from a toothache. Fortunately, Harold could not see Louise's face from where he was seated at the piano.

Jane was right behind Alice with the tea tray. They both waited until Harold finished playing the tune before they set down their trays and applauded with enthusiasm.

"Oh, look what Jane has made," said Louise, obviously hoping to distract Harold from playing any more, "cherry cobbler."

It was not long before dessert was gone and Harold was back at Louise's piano hammering out the theme song from *Oklahoma*. Only now, Jane was singing along with him. She was, as usual, a little off-key, but what she lacked in musical ability she made up for in enthusiasm.

"Jane, how on earth did you know all the words to that song?" asked Alice when they finally finished with a rip-roaring end.

"We sang it in chorus when I was in junior high," she told them, "back when they actually let me participate in music, instead of just lip-syncing. Our teacher, Mrs. Harper, had us do a lot of show tunes." She grinned at Harold. "This is fun."

"Well, that's probably enough for one evening," said Harold.

Louise looked relieved as she picked up her teacup. "Now, tell us, Harold. Where are you from and how did you manage to stumble across Acorn Hill?"

"Until I retired about thirty years ago, I was a pilot in the air force," began Harold. "As a result, we lived all over the world: Germany, Korea, Japan, Spain. You name it and I've probably been there. After I retired, we settled down in Philadelphia. That's where my wife was from."

"My late husband and I made our home in Philadelphia too," said Louise.

He smiled and tipped his head. "Nice to meet you, neighbor."

Louise smiled.

"I grew up in Altoona," said Harold.

Louise nodded. "Penn State country."

"That's right. That's my alma mater."

"My late husband went to Penn State," said Louise. "His studies were briefly interrupted by the war, but he finally graduated in '49."

"I graduated in '49."

"You might have actually known Eliot," said Jane in amazement.

"*Eliot Smith?*" said Harold.

"That's right," said Louise. "You knew him?"

"Knew him?" Harold slapped his thigh and laughed. "He was a good buddy of mine. We were fraternity brothers. The old Alpha Phi boys."

Louise shook her head in wonder. "That's amazing!"

Harold looked at Louise more carefully. "So, you're the one who finally snatched up ol' Eliot. He must've been quite a bit older than you, Louise."

Alice thought she actually saw Louise blush as she fingered her pearls with a thoughtful expression. "Eliot was fifteen years my senior. He was seventy-five when he passed on."

Harold frowned. "I'm so sorry to hear about that...."

"It was a relentless case of cancer." Louise cleared her throat. "It has been about five years now."

Harold nodded. "Well, I only knew him during our college years, but he was a good man." Now Harold began playing the piano again, quietly, as if he was trying to remember something. "In fact, I still recall the time when Alpha Phi put on a show to raise money. Some of us seniors had just been to New York and had seen a new musical called *South Pacific* at the Majestic." He sighed. "Oh, what a time we had. Afterward, I purchased the sheet music for a couple of the songs and roped in some of the guys, including Eliot, to do a scene from the show. What a hoot that was. Eliot actually wore a grass skirt. You should've seen him." Harold was laughing hard now.

"No way!" cried Jane. "My brother-in-law, Eliot, in a grass skirt?"

"And coconuts!" Harold held his hands in the appropriate positions and laughed even harder.

Louise's blue eyes grew wide. "Indeed!"

"I'll bet I still have the photos somewhere," said Harold as he retrieved a handkerchief to wipe his eyes. "Oh my. Those were the days."

"It sounds like you had a lot of fun," said Alice.

"I can't get over the idea of Eliot in a grass skirt

and coconuts," said Jane. "I'd love to see those photos, Harold."

"*Humph.*" Louise stood up now, placing her empty teacup back on the tray. "Well, I find it a little hard to believe. Eliot was a fine musician, and I never once heard him playing or singing show tunes or anything frivolous."

Harold winked at Louise. "Well, you know what they say, Louise. Boys will be boys. And take it from me, Eliot liked to cut up now and then with the best of them. We all did. I realize you were still a little girl back then, but we were just fresh out of the service and a war that had been anything but frivolous. It was therapeutic for us to get a little silly sometimes." He smiled. "In fact, I still believe that."

"I think it's just what the doctor ordered," said Jane. "We all need to laugh more."

"It's certainly made me feel better," said Harold. Then he looked at his watch. "I must be keeping you ladies up. I will try not to wear out my welcome, and I will bid you good night. Thank you all for a most lovely evening."

"He's sweet," said Jane as soon as Harold was out of earshot.

"I think he's enjoying his visit," added Alice.

Louise shook her head. "Imagine that. Can you believe that he and Eliot were friends in college?"

"Why not?" asked Jane.

"Well, it is perfectly obvious that they were as different as night and day."

Jane poked her oldest sister. "I think Harold's taken quite a fancy to you, Louise."

"Well, that is just plain silly," said Louise as she gathered up her knitting. "Preposterous."

"I don't know," said Alice. "Jane may be right."

"Well," Louise just shook her head as she made her way to the door, "all I can say to that is *good night*."

Jane laughed. "Sleep well, Louie."

"Sweet dreams," called Alice.

"Do you think she'll dream about Harold?" asked Jane after Louise's footsteps could no longer be heard.

"Probably not." Alice balanced her tray of dishes as she flicked off the lamp by the piano.

"You're right. She'll probably have a nightmare about poor Eliot dressed up in a grass skirt and coconuts," said Jane with a giggle.

"Singing show tunes," added Alice.

"Poor Louise," said Jane. "Maybe I should take a mug of warm milk up to her."

Chapter Three

On her way to bed, Alice noticed a strip of light beneath Louise's door. She tapped lightly. "Louise?"

Louise opened the door. Her face was smeared with cold cream and her hair was partially rolled into sponge rollers. "Yes?"

"I'm sorry to bother you," said Alice. "I just wanted to make sure that Jane and I didn't hurt your feelings tonight."

"Sorry?" Louise frowned.

"Oh, we probably shouldn't have teased you about Harold. I guess we were just feeling a bit silly."

"Oh nonsense," said Louise, opening her door wider. "Come in here."

Alice stepped into Louise's room, pausing to admire the floral wallpaper. "This is really nice in here, Louise," she said. "I think I appreciate these flowers even more in the wintertime."

"It is cheery." Louise pointed to the chair by the

window. "Have a seat and tell me what is on your mind." Louise turned back to the mirror above her dresser and continued to roll her hair into the pink sponge rollers.

"You've started to roll your hair again?" asked Alice.

"Sometimes I just feel like doing it. Eliot always used to like how it looked after I had rolled it."

"Wasn't that strange about Harold knowing Eliot in college?"

Louise nodded. "It took me a bit by surprise, but then he is about Eliot's age, or rather the age Eliot would be now. Eliot would have turned eighty last fall. Goodness, that sounds old."

"It's not that far off, you know," said Alice as she ran her fingers over the green velvet chair. "Not when you consider how time seems to fly faster the older we get."

"That is true," Louise turned and looked at Alice, "but I do not always feel that old on the inside." She shook her head. "I have to admit, Alice, I did come up here tonight with my feathers slightly ruffled. With the talk of Eliot and Harold, and what you and Jane said, well, I suppose I was feeling a little like a schoolgirl. Then I looked in the mirror and saw this old silver-haired woman. It was so odd. I just stared and stared." She smiled sheepishly. "Then I got out the cold cream and the sponge rollers, as if I really thought I could keep the years at bay."

"You're a lovely looking woman for your age," insisted Alice, "and I do think that Harold was taking notice."

Louise waved her hand. "Well, just for the record, I am not interested in Harold Branninger."

Alice studied her sister for a moment. "Then why are you going to the effort? I mean with the cold cream and curlers?"

Louise sat down on the edge of her bed, her hands resting loosely in her lap. "I think it was the talk about Eliot in his college days." She reached over and picked up the silver-framed wedding photo from her bedside table and traced her finger over the image of Eliot. "He has been gone five years, but goodness, I still miss him dearly."

Alice nodded.

"I still think of him as he was when we met— a distinguished-looking man in his late thirties. Oh, I was so smitten by him, Alice. Sometimes I still feel the thrill of it."

She set down the photo and laughed. "Is that silly?"

Alice shook her head. "Not at all. I think it's sweet."

"For that reason, I firmly believe that Eliot Smith was, and will always remain, the only man for me. Does that make sense?"

"Perfect sense, Louise." Alice sighed. "Please, forgive Jane and me for teasing you about Harold tonight. I promise not to do that again."

Louise smiled. "Well, as long as I am being completely honest with you, and just between you and me, I will admit that I did find the old gentleman's attentions to be flattering."

Alice laughed. "Well, why not?"

"Although he is an atrocious pianist. I wanted to tell him to stop playing and singing before the neighborhood dogs started howling, but I managed to control myself."

"You did."

"But I am sure you will understand if I must excuse myself early tomorrow night. I mean, should Harold decide to entertain us again."

"I won't even question it."

"Thank you, Alice."

Alice said good night and tiptoed down the darkened hallway to her room. She was thankful that she had taken a moment to clear things up with her sister, and she would be sure to let Jane know that they must stop teasing Louise about Harold.

In her room, Alice picked up the letter she had received earlier that week from Mark Graves, her college beau with whom she had recently renewed acquaintance.

Mark had posted a letter from Brazil where he was enjoying a stint on the Amazon. Traveling by boat with a biological research group, Mark was the veterinarian for the project, and he was having the time of his life. Even so, he had taken time out to write Alice once a week. She cherished his letters and kept them bundled up in a shoebox. Mark's stories were entertaining and interesting—even his hair-raising tale in the latest letter of how they had been invited to what turned out to be a horrible cockfight. Naturally Mark and his fellow animal-loving researchers were completely outraged by the brutal scene. They were in a foreign country where cockfights were legal, but before they slipped away into the night Mark and his colleagues managed to free several of the fighting cocks. Alice thought that was brave, if slightly foolhardy. But she understood and respected Mark's love for animals. Under the same circumstances, she might even have done the same. It was odd that he was working in places where animals were treated with such cruelty. She knew that it was hard on him to witness the brutality of events like bullfights and cockfights.

Alice put the letter in the box along with the others. She said her prayers before she went to bed, and, as usual, she prayed for Mark's safety and good health as he continued his Amazon tour. She also prayed for their guest,

Harold Branninger. She prayed that God would help Harold to get over the loss of his wife and be able to move on with his life.

"Help us to encourage Harold," she added. "Help him to find peace and comfort in our little inn. Amen."

Chapter Four

Alice was always glad when her part-time work-week ended and she could stay at home with her sisters and be more involved with the comings and goings at their bed-and-breakfast. She was always equally glad when the weekend was past and it was time to return to her job at the hospital. She liked the sense of purpose and balance that this routine brought to her life. As she went downstairs and smelled the fragrance of Jane's vanilla Belgian waffles, she felt thankful that it was her day off and that she could enjoy a leisurely breakfast.

"Need some help?" she offered as she pushed open the swinging door in time to spy Jane removing a golden, crusty waffle from the iron.

"Morning," said Jane. "Sure, would you warm up that maple syrup?"

Alice removed the metal lid and put the glass syrup container into the microwave, watching it carefully lest it get too hot. Then she set it on the kitchen table and began to make a pot of tea.

"Any big plans for today?" asked Jane as she poured more batter into the waffle iron.

"Not really. I thought I might go to town to see if Viola's gotten in any new mysteries."

"Good luck," said Jane as she took a sip from her large mug of coffee. "Last time I was in her shop, she was on her high horse again about my reading 'trashy novels.'" Jane shook her head. "I was buying Oprah's latest book-club book, which is *not* trashy."

Alice laughed. "Viola just wants us to expand our minds. You should hear her taking me to task for reading mysteries."

"Makes you wonder how that woman stays in business."

"Supply and demand," said Alice. "She owns the only bookstore in town."

"Well, some of us know how to get our books online." Jane checked on the waffle but decided it was not ready.

"Our guest isn't up yet?"

"I think I heard him shuffling around a few minutes ago," said Jane.

"I, *uh*, I talked to Louise last night," began Alice, unsure how much to tell Jane. She decided on a condensed version, simply saying that Louise did not appreciate their teasing.

"She should lighten up a little," said Jane.

"Well..." Alice paused. "The reason it bothers her is that she really did love Eliot and she still misses him."

"Well, *I* don't want to make her feel bad." Jane checked the waffle again. "Maybe I should lighten up—on her."

Before long Louise and Harold came downstairs, and they were all seated in the dining room again.

"I haven't had waffles in years." Harold smacked his lips. "These look fantastic."

"*Yoo-hoo*," called a female voice from the kitchen.

"That's Aunt Ethel," said Jane to Harold. "She lives next door and pops in now and then."

"We're in the dining room," called Alice.

"Oh, it smells divine in here," said Ethel, peering at the large platter of crisp, golden waffles. "I am completely out of coffee at my house," she continued, "and I wondered if I could beg a cup from my favorite nieces."

"Why don't you pull up a chair and join us," said Jane.

Ethel smiled. "Well, I must say these waffles look awfully tempting. Don't mind if I do."

Alice went to the kitchen to get another place setting. By the time she returned, introductions had been made.

"Harold went to college with Eliot," said Jane.

"Our Eliot?" said Ethel.

Louise nodded.

"Well, isn't that something." Ethel smiled at Harold. "What brings you to Acorn Hill?"

"I needed to get away for a while," he told her.

"It's the one-year anniversary of his wife's death," said Jane. "He thought a road trip might help him to deal with it."

"That's right," said Harold. "As it turns out, I was right. Your lovely nieces here have proven good medicine for me."

"You should've heard him playing the piano last night," said Jane.

"I am surprised you did not," added Louise wryly.

Jane tossed a warning glance at her sister. "We had the best time singing old show tunes. Harold knows them all."

"I love old show tunes," said Ethel. "I'm so sorry I missed that."

"We're going to do it again," said Jane. "At least I think we are. How about it, Harold? Are you up for another sing-along tonight?"

He shrugged and glanced at Louise. "Well, if everyone is—"

"Of course we are," said Jane. "Let's plan on seven

thirty. We'll have dessert in the parlor again. Aunt Ethel, you are invited too."

"Well, thank you," said Ethel.

"Why don't you bring Lloyd," suggested Alice. "I haven't seen him since the last church board meeting."

"*Humph*." Ethel frowned. "You won't be seeing Lloyd Tynan tonight."

"Bowling night?" Jane asked.

"Our mayor has recently taken up a new hobby," Alice explained to Harold.

"No, it's not bowling night tonight," said Ethel. "Lloyd is heading for Philadelphia for a mayoral conference."

"Well, you can't fault him for that, Auntie," said Alice.

"It's not just that," said Ethel in a wounded voice. "He never seems to have time for me these days."

"He's just busy," said Alice.

"Too busy for me," said Ethel as she helped herself to another waffle.

"I find that hard to believe," said Harold.

Ethel stopped with her forked waffle in midair halfway between the platter and her plate. "Pardon?"

"I find it hard to believe that a man with any sense would be too busy for someone like you."

Ethel sat up a little straighter as she dropped the waffle onto her plate. "Well, thank you." She reached up and patted her red-tinted hair and smiled at the guest. "That's very kind of you."

Harold smiled. "When I left home yesterday, I never dreamed that I would find myself sitting here in the company of so many lovely women."

"Oh, do go on," said Jane with a teasing smile.

"No, I'm serious," said Harold. "Yesterday, I felt so down and blue that I wasn't even sure I could go on. So I packed my bag and just got in my car and started driving, hardly paying any attention to where I went. Then I ended up in this quaint little town named Acorn Hill and this lovely inn"— he shook his head—"and I feel better than I've felt in ages."

Alice smiled. "Well, we're glad you came."

"That's right," agreed Jane. "And you're welcome to stay as long as you like."

"That is true," said Louise. "We do not have another room booked for almost two weeks."

Harold picked up his coffee cup. "Well, I may just take you up on that."

By the time Alice and Jane started clearing the table, Ethel had heard several of Harold's flying stories from the war.

"Goodness," said Ethel. "That was awfully brave of you."

He waved his hand. "It's what we had to do back then."

"So, do you have any plans today?" asked Jane as she refilled his coffee cup.

"I'm not sure what there is to do around here," he said. "I thought I'd get in my car and check out the local area."

"Is that your lovely car parked out front?" asked Ethel.

"That's my baby," said Harold.

"Oh, I just love T-birds," said Ethel with a coquettish smile.

"Well, I'll have to take you for a spin sometime."

"I'm heading out to Potterston," announced Louise as she stood up. "I have to pick up some new sheet music for my students. Does anyone need anything while I am out?"

"Potterston?" said Harold. "Is that nearby?"

"Yes," said Ethel and she proceeded to give him directions.

Alice went into the kitchen to help Jane clean up.

"Looks like Harold's charming Aunt Ethel," said Jane as she wiped off the waffle iron.

"Oh, that just seems to be his way," said Alice as she rinsed the plates and loaded them in the dishwasher. "He's perfectly harmless, I'm sure."

"Well, Aunt Ethel is sure eating it up."

"Probably makes her feel better since Lloyd's a little distracted."

"Yes, maybe having Harold around will be good for Aunt Ethel."

"And he sure seems to be enjoying himself." Alice put the last plate in and closed the door just as the phone began to ring. "I'll get that," she told Jane.

"Hello, Cynthia," said Alice as she recognized her niece's voice. "Louise just stepped out, but—"

"That's okay," said Cynthia quickly. "I can talk to you about this."

"What I can I do for you?"

"I have a problem that I thought you ladies might be able to help me with."

"Sure," said Alice. "What is it?"

"Well, I'm the editor for a children's book being written by a woman, a kind of celebrity writer. That means she's not a writer at all but has a big name that the publisher thinks would look great on the cover of a children's book."

"Oh, and that's a problem?"

"Yeah." Cynthia groaned. "I've been working with her for months but getting absolutely nowhere. Now the book's deadline is only a week away, but we can't get any solid work done. She gets so distracted all the time by her other projects. I was wondering if I could bring her to Grace Chapel Inn for a week. So that we could work without interruption."

"Oh, that's a wonderful idea," said Alice. "We only have one guest right now, so we have plenty of room."

"Oh, I'm so glad, Aunt Alice. The publisher will cover the bill for everything—even the extra meals. We would want to eat all our meals at the inn, if that's okay. Quite frankly I'd have been willing to sleep on the floor just to make this work out."

"Don't worry, providing the meals will be fine and you won't need to sleep on the floor, dear."

"I just knew that my family could help me."

"So, when do you plan to arrive, dear?"

"I'm going to see if she can leave tomorrow," said Cynthia. "Believe me, we don't have a moment to lose."

"Tomorrow's just fine. By the way, who is this woman?"

"Have you heard of Victoria Martin?"

"You mean Victoria Martin, the home and garden expert?"

"That's the one."

"Of course, dear, everyone's heard of Victoria Martin. That's who you're bringing here?"

Alice could see Jane mouthing the words now, with a look of horror on her face: *Victoria Martin's coming here?*

Alice nodded at her sister. "And when do you expect to arrive?"

"Maybe around dinnertime. Do you think Jane will mind?"

Alice made a funny face at Jane. "No, you know Jane never minds having extra guests for dinner."

Now Jane was furiously shaking her head and making a slashing signal across her throat.

"Thanks so much, Aunt Alice. I can't wait to see all of you again."

"We look forward to seeing you too, dear. And Victoria too."

Alice had barely hung up the phone before Jane exploded. "No way, she cannot bring Victoria Martin here, Alice. What on earth can she be thinking?"

"Hold on, Jane. Let me explain."

Jane was still firmly shaking her head. "Do you know who Victoria Martin is, Alice?"

"Of course. Everyone knows."

"She's the Domestic Diva, the Garden Goddess, the Queen of Design." Jane dramatically pulled on her hair. "She can't come *here*."

"Why not?"

"Look at this place," said Jane, indicating her kitchen.

"It looks great, Jane. I love the way you redecorated it last year and—"

"But to someone like Victoria Martin it'll look provincial and amateurish and—"

"You're making too much of this, Jane." Alice put her

hand on her younger sister's shoulder. "Now, take a deep breath and tell yourself, Victoria Martin is just an ordinary woman like me. She puts on her trousers one leg at a time too." Alice giggled at the thought of Victoria Martin putting on trousers.

"You don't get it, Alice." Jane shook her head and sank down into a chair. "This is my world. I mean cooking and gardening and decorating. It's something I take great pride and pleasure in doing."

"You're very good at it, Jane."

"Not compared to Victoria Martin."

"We should never compare ourselves—"

"How can I help it? That woman does it *all*. She has her TV shows and home care products and cookbooks and—"

"What difference does that make?" Alice felt confused now. Why should Jane care so much about someone like Victoria Martin?

Jane shook her head. "I don't know. I guess it's just really, really intimidating."

Alice sat down beside Jane. "I thought you'd love the idea. You have nothing to be intimidated by, Jane. You are a fantastic cook. Your garden is amazing. Your artistic talent at decorating is incredible. Why should you of all people be intimidated?"

Jane looked into Alice's eyes. "Really?"

Alice nodded. "I think Victoria Martin might actually learn a trick or two from you, Jane."

Now Jane laughed. "Be that as it may, I have a lot to do."

"And here's a little perk," said Alice. "Cynthia said the publisher will cover everything on the bill. Extra meals and whatever. I'm sure Louise will agree that it won't hurt our monthly finances at all."

"No, I suppose it won't. When did Cynthia say they were coming?"

"Tomorrow evening, in time for dinner."

Jane gasped. "*Oh my word!*"

Alice gently patted her on the back. "Now remember, just take deep breaths, relax and tell yourself this is no big deal."

"Sure, I can tell myself that, Alice. It's just that I won't believe me."

Chapter Five

"Do you remember those old White Tornado commercials from the sixties?" asked Alice as she and Louise sipped hot cocoa out on the front porch. Fortunately for them, it was a relatively mild day, crisp and bright, with not a cloud in the sky.

Louise pulled her woolen scarf up around her neck and nodded. "I think so. It was for some housecleaning product."

"Yes." Alice wrapped the red-and-black plaid blanket more snugly over her knees. "Well, that's what's going on inside our house right now."

"Is that why you met me out here?" asked Louise.

"Exactly. I had to take a break from it, and I wanted to tell you about Cynthia's plans before you went in."

"Well, it's a bit chilly, but the cocoa is a nice touch."

"Jane is into the spring cleaning a little early," said Alice.

"What's wrong with the poor girl?" asked Louise.

Alice laughed. "It's Victoria Martin."

"Victoria Martin? The author Cynthia is bringing here?" Louise frowned. "That name sounds familiar, but I'm not quite with you. Who are we talking about?"

"The Domestic Goddess of Home and Garden television." Alice made room for Wendell to jump into her lap, smoothing his coat as he settled himself into the warm woolen blanket.

Louise nodded. "Oh yes. Now I remember. Wasn't she involved in some sort of copyright problem on one of her cookbooks?"

"Yes, but she was cleared."

"That's right, but tell me, what does Victoria Martin have to do with Jane and the White Tornado?"

"Well, our baby sister is convinced that Victoria's visit is for a white-glove test, rather than to work with Cynthia on a children's book."

Louise smiled. "You know, Cynthia told me ages ago that she was working with some celebrity on a children's book."

"Apparently, it's still not written. The due date is next week, and Cynthia is getting nervous."

"I can imagine." Louise shook her head. "Poor Cynthia. She told me that her job could be hanging on the success of this silly book. Did she tell you the woman can't even write?"

"She mentioned something along that line."

"So Jane is in a dither because she thinks Victoria Martin will criticize our housekeeping, and Cynthia is in a dither because her job may be on the line. Good heavens. What is next?"

"Here comes Harold," said Alice, and she waved as the Thunderbird pulled up in front of the house.

"Oh, I almost forgot about our music man," said Louise. "I wonder what he has been up to today."

"Hello," called Alice as Harold came up the porch steps. "Would you care for some hot cocoa?"

"That sounds delightful," said Harold as he joined them on the porch. "And is that real whipped cream?"

"Jane wouldn't settle for imitation," said Alice.

Harold sighed. "Ah, the country life."

"Well, we are not exactly country folks," said Louise, "but I suppose we seem a bit slow compared to Philadelphia."

"It's a pace I could get used to."

"So, what have you been doing with yourself today, Harold?" asked Alice. She was trying to think of a casual way to explain the frantic cleaning spree that was taking place behind the closed front door.

"I've had a marvelous day." Harold took a sip of cocoa and grinned. "I even turned out to be rather lucky."

"Lucky?" Louise frowned. "What do you mean?"

"At the track."

"The track?" repeated Alice.

"What kind of track?"

"The racetrack," said Harold.

"*Racetrack?*" Louise looked surprised. "I had no idea we had horse racing around here."

"Not horses," said Harold. "Dogs. There's a dog track just outside of Potterston."

"Dogs?" Alice was puzzled.

"Greyhounds, to be specific. I picked a winner today."

"My goodness," said Louise. Suddenly Alice remembered a story that Mark had told her during his last visit to Acorn Hill. "Isn't that cruel for the dogs?" she asked Harold.

"Oh no, the dogs love it. You should see them go."

"Chasing a mechanical rabbit?" queried Louise.

"That's right. But, of course, they never catch it."

"Is that really like fun, Harold?" Louise reached for one of the sugar cookies that Alice had brought out along with the cocoa.

"What do you consider to be fun, Louise?" asked Harold. "I'm curious."

"Fun?" She closed her eyes as if to consider this. "Fun is a classical concert in the park on a soft spring evening. Fun is seeing the children's eyes light up when they put on one of their little performances at church. Fun is a trip to the seashore on a warm summer day or hot cocoa on the porch on a sunny winter day." She sighed.

"Well, those things are nice," said Harold, "but they're not exactly what I would describe as *fun*."

Louise nodded. "I guess, like beauty, fun is in the eyes of the beholder. What is fun to me would probably be completely boring to you."

"And what's fun to me would probably be scandalous to you."

Her eyebrow lifted. "Scandalous? Please, tell us you're not involved in anything illegal or immoral or illicit."

"No, no, nothing quite that exciting. I do enjoy betting at the track now and then. And I used to play poker with my buddies every Saturday night, but most of them are long gone now." He sadly shook his head. "I may be old, ladies, but I'm not dead."

"Certainly not," said Louise.

"A friend of mine is a veterinarian," said Alice. "He told me a very sad story about a racing dog. A family adopted a greyhound that had been rescued—"

"Rescued?" repeated Louise. "What do you mean?"

"Well, Mark said that when the greyhounds get hurt, which often happens, or if they're past their prime, they are put down."

"Put down? As in killed?" asked Louise.

"Yes," Alice nodded solemnly, "and they're not always killed in a humane way. It's really awful."

"Oh, I don't think that could be true," said Harold. "Greyhound racing is a legal sport. The authorities wouldn't allow people to be cruel to dogs just for the sake of the sport."

"You wouldn't think so," said Alice, "but what if no one is paying any attention?"

"But why would they kill the dogs?" asked Harold. "They are beautiful animals, and the way they run is something to behold. Not only that, but they're very valuable. Now tell me, Alice, why would someone kill a valuable dog?"

"Probably because it is not valuable once it has been injured," offered Louise. "Why would they waste money feeding a dog that cannot run?"

"Exactly," said Alice. "Mark said that once the dogs can't race anymore, they are worthless to their owners. There are some places where people have set up greyhound adoption groups to save the dogs from being killed."

"I wonder if such a thing exists in Potterston," ventured Louise.

"I don't know," said Alice, "but I'm sure it wouldn't be hard to find out."

Harold laughed. "I think you're creating a tempest in a teapot, ladies. I'm sure the dogs are well cared for. Really, you should come to the track with me and see for yourself. It was obvious that the owner of Copper King, the dog I bet on, loved the animal. I'll bet you that Copper is chowing down on a T-bone as we speak."

"But what happens when Copper can't run?" asked Alice.

Harold scratched his head. "I don't know the answer to that, but I'm betting that you're going to find out. When you do, you can let me know."

"And if I discover any inhumane treatment?"

"You prove to me that those dogs are mistreated, and I give you my word that I won't step onto a dog track again. But, if you ask me, those dogs were having the time of their lives down there. They are born and bred to run, Alice."

"That may be true. My worry is what happens to the animals when they can't run."

Alice's concern for racing dogs took her somewhat by surprise. She had not given these poor animals much thought before today, other than when she had heard Mark's story. She decided that she would look into the Potterston track first thing next week. In the meantime,

there was work to be done in preparation for the visit of
Queen Victoria, Jane's name for their expected guest. It
seemed that, at least in Jane's mind, this white-gloved
perfectionist woman must surely rule.

Chapter Six

"Oh, do sing another one, Harold," insisted Ethel. "How about something from *The Sound of Music*? Do you know any of those songs? I just loved that movie. I still remember the night that my husband Bob and I went to the theater in Potterston to see it. It was the middle of summer and—"

"If you will excuse me," Louise stifled a yawn, "I think perhaps I will call it a night."

Harold winked at her. "My music scaring you off again?"

She forced a believable smile. "No, no, really, I am just tired. If I am going to be of any help to Jane tomorrow, I better turn in."

"In that case, I bid you *adieu*." Harold began to play the good-bye song from *The Sound of Music*. "So long, farewell, *auf Wiedersehen*, good night," they all sang, waving to Louise as she made her exit.

Alice wished she could join her older sister, but she

feared it might appear rude to have both of them leaving at once. She was more than a little worn out from all the cleaning that had gone on. She did not know if Jane would ever be satisfied. In fact, Jane had made a long list of tasks that had to be completed by the following afternoon. Alice noticed that Jane had even included "dust canning jars on back porch" on the list.

"Oh, Harold," gushed Ethel as they finished another song. "You are so talented. I don't know when I've ever had so much fun."

Jane was laughing too. "Yes, I'm so thankful that you're here, Harold. I think I needed this break tonight."

"Probably helps to get your mind off that silly Victoria Martin," said Ethel. "*Tsk-tsk*. I don't know why you're getting yourself all worked up about her in the first place, Jane."

"Because everything she does is so absolutely perfect," said Jane, as if that explained it.

"Oh, Jane," said Ethel. "She has dozens of staff people who do everything for her. She probably just sits around eating bonbons most of the time and telling everyone else what to do." She grinned. "*Hmmm*, actually, that doesn't sound like a bad life to me."

"You and Victoria will probably get along famously," said Jane dryly.

Ethel's eyes twinkled. "I'm sure we will. Just as long as she doesn't come over to my house. Good gracious, I'd die a thousand deaths if Victoria Martin looked into one of my closets."

"See!" Jane pointed at her aunt. "That's just what I'm talking about."

"Which room are you putting her in?" asked Ethel.

"Well, Louise thought I should put her in the Symphony Room."

"Of course," said Ethel. "That's her favorite, because she chose the decor."

"I was thinking the Garden Room might be more fitting since Victoria is as well known for her gardening as for anything else."

"I think the Garden Room is perfect," said Alice.

"I must say I'm enjoying my Sunset Room," said Harold.

"Thanks," said Jane. "I did that one and the Garden Room."

"It reminds me of a brief stint in Italy. So sunny and warm-looking."

Jane was beaming now. "That's what I was going for. Sort of southern France, or maybe even Tuscany."

"Well, you did a wonderful job with it." Harold smiled. "That's one of the things I really like about your inn. It's not fussy. I stayed in a few B and Bs with Lily. She loved those places, but I found them to be a bit uncomfortable with all their lace curtains and breakable objects and antique furniture everywhere."

"We wanted this to feel more comfortable," said Alice, "but it wasn't easy agreeing on things."

"It's plain to see that you three sisters really have a knack for it."

Alice hoped that Victoria Martin would see it that way, for Jane's sake. She hoped that Victoria would be kind and gracious. Jane seemed to be putting such stock in her visit.

"That's a great idea," said Jane suddenly. "Don't you think so, Alice?"

Alice blinked and looked at her sister. "I'm sorry, I must've been daydreaming."

"Aunt Ethel has just suggested that we host a sing-along night."

"Isn't that what this is?" asked Alice.

"No, something on a grander scale," said Ethel. "We could invite a few friends. I know that Lloyd would probably enjoy a musical night. If we can tear him away from his bowling ball, that is."

Jane laughed. "We can make it on a night when Lloyd's not bowling. How about a week from tomorrow, on Saturday? After Victoria Martin's departure. Is that okay with you, Harold?"

Harold nodded.

"We could dress up," said Ethel suddenly, "like characters from our favorite musical movies. Maybe I'll come as Eliza in *My Fair Lady*. I have a big purple hat a bit like the one that Audrey Hepburn wore."

"That's a great idea," said Jane. "Oh, this party will be just the thing to break up the winter doldrums for everyone."

"Doldrums?" repeated Harold. "I'd say that life here is anything but dull." Then he broke out into another song.

Alice slipped out of the room on the pretext of removing their empty dessert dishes, but what she really wanted was to get away from the music. She liked show tunes, but she had a bit of a headache—probably from all the cleaning products that she had been using all day. She slipped on her jacket and went into the unheated sunroom. Even that place had made Jane's hit list. Everything in there had been vacuumed and dusted, and all the pillow coverings from the wicker furniture had been removed to be laundered. As a result, the room looked stark and bare. That would all change by the next day. Alice had overheard Jane on the phone with the local florist, Craig Tracy, ordering plants suitable for the cooler temperatures of the sunroom.

Alice sighed as she leaned back in the loveseat. She only hoped this did not turn out to be much ado about nothing. Just then Wendell hopped into her lap. He rubbed the side of his head against her hand in a way that she had always found comforting. She gave him a little scratch under his chin and wondered if he, too, was feeling displaced by all this busyness.

She looked out the window and up to the sky where a sliver of pale moon was just making its appearance. She knew it was selfish, but she resented all this hustle and bustle that had intruded onto her winter quiet. First Harold and his music. Now Victoria Martin. Yet she knew that people like Harold and Victoria had needs too. And perhaps their needs could best be met at a place like Grace Chapel Inn.

"Help me to be more gracious and generous," she prayed as she cuddled Wendell. "Help me to keep an open heart as well as an open home, and give me a good attitude as I help my sister Jane tomorrow. I know that the best way to show Your love to anyone is by being a good servant. Please, show me how I can better serve those around me, putting their needs above my own. Amen."

Alice looked up at the dark sky again. It never ceased to amaze her how refreshed she always felt after praying. She knew there was not anything special about her words or the way she prayed them. Perhaps it was just making contact, but then, of course, God was always nearby.

Chapter Seven

*D*id anyone wash the front windows yet?" Jane asked Alice.

"Vera is working on it."

Jane pushed a damp strand of dark hair away from her eyes. "I know I'm a terrible slave driver," she admitted as she continued kneading a lump of dough. "I really appreciate you calling out the troops to help today."

"No problem," said Alice, sneaking a freshly made chocolate from a sheet of waxed paper. "Everyone was excited to help out. There hasn't been a celebrity of this caliber in Acorn Hill since FDR's campaign stop in the thirties."

"And you can remember *that*?"

Alice grinned. "Very funny. I remember Mother and Father talking about it."

"*Yoo-hoo*," called Ethel. "Craig Tracy is here with more flowers."

"Tell him to bring them out to the back porch," said Jane.

"*Tsk-tsk*. Goodness knows why you need so many flowers," Ethel said. "Don't you think it's a bit extravagant?"

"Actually, Craig and I have an agreement. He happened to have more blooms than he needed this week, and I promised to repay him out of my garden next summer."

"Well, that was smart of you, Jane." Ethel patted her on the back. "I always did think you took after me."

Jane smiled patiently and then returned to her dough.

"Hey, Jane," called Craig from the laundry room, holding up a bunch of pale purple freesia and peach-colored roses. "Whaddya think of these?"

Jane nodded. "Gorgeous."

Craig set the blooms in a galvanized bucket and came into the kitchen. "Smells good in here."

"Help yourself to"—Jane shrugged—"whatever. There are truffles there and some ginger biscotti by the stove, and Alice just made a fresh pot of coffee."

"Sit down, Craig," said Alice, "and I'll get you a cup."

"This place is really hopping," said Craig as he picked out a chocolate.

"Thanks to Alice," said Jane, giving the dough a final whop. "She called out the troops."

"Well, they look like happy troopers," said Craig. "It seems we can always count on the ladies at the inn to bring some excitement to this little town."

"Really?" Jane did not look convinced.

"Seriously. This place used to be pretty dull before the inn got going. Seems like there's been something happening ever since."

Alice poured herself a cup of tea. "You don't miss the old quietness, Craig?"

He laughed. "Hardly."

"You young people," said Alice in a good-natured tone.

"It's good for business," said Craig as he snagged another truffle.

"Good for business?" Alice pulled up a stool across from him. "I thought Jane said you were doing some kind of swap on the flowers."

He grinned. "There's more than one kind of business."

"I told Craig that he could do all the floral arrangements and that we'd put his business card in a couple of conspicuous spots."

"*Ah*," said Alice, "and if Ms. Victoria is impressed, maybe she'll recommend Wild Things on the air?"

Jane nodded. "Who knows? Maybe she'll invite Craig to be on her show."

"Well, I seriously doubt that, but I still think this is

kind of fun. I hope I get to meet the domestic diva before she skips town."

"Don't worry," said Jane. "We'll be needing some fresh flowers by the end of the week."

He gave her a thumbs-up. "I'm your man, Jane."

"Did I hear that someone's looking for a plumber?" called a voice from the back porch.

"Come on in, Fred," called Alice. "The faucet in the bedroom that Victoria Martin will be using has just the tiniest drip."

"Can't have that," said Fred as he eyed Jane's truffles.

"Help yourself," said Jane.

"Why, thank you very much." He picked one up and popped it into his mouth. "*Mm-mm*. I figured it would be worth the trip."

"There will be more when you're finished," said Jane.

"Well, I'll get right on it then," said Fred. "According to Vera, this Victoria gal, whoever she is, might go flipping crazy over something like a dripping faucet."

"It's possible," said Craig. "I've heard stories."

"Oh, you guys," said Jane as she carefully laid a tea towel over her just-shaped loaves. "You make her sound like a monster. Good grief, she can't help it if she's a perfectionist."

"And you would know," teased Craig.

"I am not a perfectionist," claimed Jane.

Alice chuckled. "Well, what do you call a person who wants everything to be *just right*?"

"*Just right* is not necessarily perfection." Jane frowned. "Is it?"

"I plead the Fifth," said Craig. "I guess I had better get to work."

"Did you get the vases, Alice?"

"They're sparkling clean and right by the laundry sink," said Alice.

Jane picked up her list now, carefully checking things off. "Oh, Alice, I completely forgot something."

"What is it?"

"Could you run into town and get me some sheet spray?"

Alice frowned. "Sheet spray?"

"Yes. I told Sylvia about it last fall and she just started carrying it."

"What is sheet spray?"

"Well, that's not what it's really called, but it's a scented spray that you mist onto sheets to make them smell nice."

Alice nodded, although she really did not think it seemed terribly important.

"Get lavender," said Jane.

"Lavender," repeated Alice. "Sheet spray. Anything else?"

"Well, now that you mention it. I thought I was going to have time to go to the store for a few last-minute items, but looking at the clock now... Oh, Alice, would you mind terribly?"

"Are you sure you want *me* to go, Jane? The last time I went shopping for you, I didn't do too well. Remember, I got the wrong kind of tomatoes and the wrong cheese."

"Give me a minute," said Jane, grabbing a pen. "I'll go over my list and be very, very specific so that there's no way you won't know what I mean."

"All right," agreed Alice. "I'm just not very experienced with all these gourmet foods."

Jane laughed. "These are hardly gourmet, Alice." She handed her the list. "Thanks, so much. I really appreciate it."

Actually, Alice welcomed the opportunity to get out of the house. It was feeling more and more like Grand Central Station. Her visions of a quiet weekend during a quiet month had completely vanished.

"Need a ride?" asked Harold when he and Alice nearly collided on the front porch.

"It looks like you're just coming in," said Alice as she hung Jane's big canvas shopping bag over her arm.

"Well, just momentarily," he told her. "I need a sweater under my overcoat. It's a bit nippy out here."

"Well, thanks anyway," said Alice, "but I think I will enjoy walking to town. I could use the fresh air and exercise."

He nodded. "Jane assured me that everything will settle down and get back to normal inside the inn by this evening."

"I hope you don't feel put out," said Alice. "Really, this isn't how things are usually around here."

"Oh, I know. Having this Victoria person coming to the inn is a pretty big deal."

"So, where are you off to today?" asked Alice.

Harold took on a sheepish look. "Oh, I thought, well, maybe I'd go see the races. I might poke around and check out the conditions you were worried about."

Alice nodded, though unconvinced. "So, you're not going to bet or anything?"

He grinned. "Well, now I wouldn't go that far, little lady. I guess I'll just have to sniff around and see how it goes." He brightened. "Hey, would you like to come with me? You could see for yourself."

She actually considered the offer but then shook her head. "Sorry, there's just too much to do at the inn today."

"I figured."

"But you can tell me what you discover. Maybe I can go some other time."

"Right." He tipped his hat, and Alice wished him a nice day.

It bothered her that Harold was going off to the dog track again. It was not that she had anything against people watching races and sporting events, but after their conversation, she had hoped that he might see dog racing differently. She promised herself that she would look into this more closely after the weekend. There was no sense in rushing to judgment about something one knows nothing about. Maybe Harold was right. Maybe those dogs did love to race. Maybe their owners did treat them with kindness and respect. Anyway, she decided as she entered the fabric store that she did not have time to deal with those issues anytime soon.

"Hello, Alice," said Sylvia. "How goes it at the inn?"

"It's buzzing like a beehive," said Alice.

"So how'd you escape?"

"I'm the errand girl today."

"Aha." Sylvia grinned. "So, what can I do for you?"

"I need some sheet spray."

Sylvia frowned. "*Sheet spray?*"

Alice nodded. "It's used to make the bedding smell nice."

"Oh, you must be talking about our new linen pot-pourri spritzer."

"That sounds right. Jane said to get lavender."

Soon Sylvia had wrapped and bagged a glass jar of lavender spray. Alice was surprised at the cost but figured a little bit must go a long way. "Thank you, Sylvia," she said.

"I'm hoping to at least catch a glimpse of her," said Sylvia.

It took Alice a moment to figure out what Sylvia meant. "Oh right. You mean Victoria Martin."

Sylvia nodded. "I'd love to have her visit my shop. She's an excellent seamstress, you know. I even sell her books here."

"I could mention that to Cynthia."

Sylvia winked at her. "Thanks, Alice."

Everyone seemed to want a piece of Victoria Martin. Alice began to feel sorry for the woman. What *would* it be like to have everyone grasping for your attention wherever you went? Would you ever get a moment's peace? How would you know whether someone was just being friendly, or if he was opportunistic? It could be confusing, not to mention demanding. Well, if Alice had thought that she had suffered a setback with this interruption of her quiet January, she wondered how it would feel to step into Victoria Martin's shoes, as expensive as they must be, for just a day or two. Fortunately for Alice, that would never happen. Alice reminded herself to count her blessings as she started down Acorn Avenue toward the library, where she wanted to drop off a book. As she passed Time for Tea, she waved at its owner, Wilhelm Wood, who signaled her to come in.

"Hi, Wilhelm," said Alice, opening the door.

"Thanks for stopping, Alice. I have something for the inn." He smiled. "Do you have time?"

"Of course."

As Alice entered, classical music wafted toward her over the crowded shelves of ceramic teapots, fragile-looking cups and boxes and boxes of teas.

She breathed in a deep breath. "Oh, Wilhelm, as usual, it smells so delightful in here."

"I recently created a new brew and I think it's magnificent," he told her as he led her to the counter in back of the shop. "It's a black tea with a secret mix of spices. Very warming and perfect for winter." He handed her a small brown package. "I'm calling it Wilhelm's Winter Spice."

"How much?" asked Alice as she extracted her wallet from her bag.

"Complimentary," said Wilhelm with a smile.

"Really?" Alice nodded. "How thoughtful."

"I, uh, I was hoping that Victoria Martin might get to sample it." He smiled. "Perhaps she might appreciate the fine blend of tea and spices and—"

"And want to know where in the world we got it?"

He folded his hands together and nodded. "One can only hope."

"Do you have a business card?" asked Alice, wondering if she had somehow turned into Acorn Hill's personal ambassador to Victoria Martin.

"I most certainly do." He handed her several. "Thank you, Alice."

"You're welcome. Thank you for the tea."

She dropped off her library book, then turned onto Berry Lane and walked toward the General Store. It was slow going because she was stopped by a number of friends and neighbors, all eager to hear more about the celebrity who was coming to town. It was not until Florence Simpson accosted her, however, that Alice felt herself getting irritated—and nervous for Cynthia's sake. She tried to explain to Florence that Victoria was coming to Acorn Hill for some *uninterrupted* quiet time in order to finish her children's book with Cynthia.

"It's not a social occasion," Alice assured Florence.

"Well, I should've known you would want to keep her to yourselves," said Florence in an offended tone.

"It's not that," said Alice. "It's just that Cynthia is facing a deadline and she needs to keep Victoria focused."

"That's not what I heard from your aunt. Ethel

told me that there's going to be some big wingding at the inn."

Alice frowned. "A wingding?"

"Yes, and I heard that not only is Victoria Martin there, but also a renowned musician who has been performing nightly."

"Harold?" Alice shook her head. "I'm sorry, Florence, but Harold is just a nice gentleman who likes to play show tunes on the piano." Now Alice bit her lip. She knew that a sing-along night was in the works, but it was not up to her to invite people. If Jane and Ethel wanted to invite Florence Simpson, then that would be their decision. "Maybe you should ask Aunt Ethel to tell you more about Harold," said Alice, hoping that this might end the conversation.

"Don't worry," snapped Florence. "I intend to."

Alice controlled herself from rolling her eyes as she entered the store and headed for the produce section. Now if only she could manage to pick out some decent salad vegetables and make it to the checkout without further ado. No wonder Jane had asked Alice to come to town.

Chapter Eight

"They should be here by now," said Louise for what must have been the fifth time.

"It's still early," said Alice as she glanced around the dining room. Everything looked perfect. At least it did to Alice. She was not so sure if Jane would agree. It was amazing how Jane could walk into a room, any room, and find something that needed tweaking. Whether it was a picture that was just slightly crooked, or a rose that had slipped just a millimeter, or a curtain not quite hanging straight, Jane would notice.

"Did you ask Cynthia when they would arrive?" asked Louise.

"Actually, I didn't. She said they'd be here in time for dinner."

"But she did not give a specific time? Like six o'clock? Or six thirty?"

"Don't worry, Louise," called Jane from the kitchen. "I didn't fix anything that will be ruined—at least if they get here within the hour."

"Well, it is almost seven," said Louise. "And I have tried Cynthia's cell phone, but I keep getting her message service. I am worried."

"Maybe you should pray for her," suggested Alice. "That usually works better than worrying."

"Maybe I should," Louise said as she paced into the living room.

Alice looked around the dining room and wondered when she had ever seen it looking lovelier. The soft green walls seemed to glow in the candlelight of the pale lavender tapers. Jane had chosen pale lavender as an accent color in this room. Inspired by the freesias, Alice guessed. They would be using the fine china tonight, and Jane had talked Ethel into polishing the silver, even though Ethel was not invited for dinner on Victoria Martin's first night at the inn.

"I'm sorry, Aunt Ethel," Jane had said firmly, "but I think it's important that we keep this dinner small on her first evening with us. Don't worry, we'll make sure that you come over while she's here."

"Well," said Ethel in a stiff voice as she polished a spoon, "if you think that's best."

"I do," said Jane. "Just for tonight, Auntie. Then we'll see how it goes."

Alice said another silent prayer for the safe travel of

Cynthia and Victoria, and before she reached "amen," the doorbell was ringing and she could hear Louise's voice greeting them in the foyer.

Although Alice had never considered herself the type to be starstruck, she suddenly began to feel very nervous. She looked down at her dark brown wool jumper, smoothing the front with her hands. Jane had said that no one had to dress up for the occasion, but Alice knew that she expected something beyond her usual weekend uniform of jeans and sweaters.

"Have they arrived?" asked Jane, suddenly emerging from the kitchen with her apron still on.

"Yes," said Alice.

"Does everything still look okay in here?" Jane glanced nervously around the dining room, pausing to adjust a folded linen napkin. "I think those candles still have a few hours left in them. Thank goodness I got the dripless kind."

Alice patted her sister on the back and smiled. "Everything's perfect, Jane. Really. We should all just try to relax and enjoy this evening."

Jane nodded. "You're right, Alice. As usual, you are absolutely right." She turned. "I'll be in the kitchen if anyone needs me."

"You don't want to come out here and meet her?"

Jane turned back and frowned. "Should I?"

"Of course. You're not just the cook, Jane."

"Should I take off my apron?"

Alice shrugged.

Jane hurried to remove her apron, gave it a toss into the kitchen and came out to join Alice.

"Here they are," said Louise as she led Victoria and Cynthia into the foyer. "My two sisters, Alice and Jane Howard. Co-owners with me of Grace Chapel Inn."

"It's a lovely place you have here," said Victoria as she handed Louise her fur-trimmed coat and Cynthia kissed her aunts.

"Do you need help with your bags?" asked Alice.

"They're in the trunk," said Cynthia with an expression that Alice could not decipher.

"Why don't Alice and I get them," offered Jane. "Louise can show you to your rooms."

Cynthia looked relieved as she handed over the keys. "Thanks, Aunt Jane."

"Cynthia looks a little frazzled," said Alice as they went out toward the sidewalk. "She must be worn out from work."

"Or from Victoria."

"She still has a whole week with her." Alice shook her head.

"Wow, is this Cynthia's car?" asked Jane when they spotted the silver Mercedes parked behind Harold's car.

"Maybe it's a rental or something," said Alice as she waited for Jane to open the trunk.

"My word!" exclaimed Jane when she saw the trunk stuffed with a very expensive set of Louis Vuitton luggage. "Is this *all* Victoria's?"

"Well, it doesn't look like Cynthia's."

Together they tugged and pulled until all the luggage, including one small dark suitcase, was out on the street. Then, taking two trips each, they hauled it up to the front porch. Fortunately, Cynthia met them there. "Need some help?" she offered.

"Thanks," said Jane. "You didn't tell us you guys were moving here for good."

"Yeah," said Cynthia. "That's what I thought too."

"Cool wheels," said Jane.

"The car belongs to my boss, and she threatened to fire me if I put a single scratch on it. She said she was only joking, but I'm not so sure. It was so nerve-racking to drive through traffic with Victoria's constant yammering about how she cannot afford to be taking time away from her businesses right now."

Alice patted her niece on the shoulder. "It's okay, Cynthia, you're with family now. We'll help you through this."

"That's right," said Jane as she opened the door. "This is what family is for."

"Everything looks great," said Cynthia. "Did you go to much trouble?"

"It was nothing," said Jane as she winked at Alice and they all made their way up the stairs.

"It's a little small." Victoria's voice was coming from the direction of the Garden Room, their best bedroom.

"I am sorry," said Louise. "It is the largest one in the house."

"Then I guess it'll have to do."

"Here are your bags," said Jane from the hallway.

"Put them right there," said Victoria, pointing to a space by the closet. "If they'll all fit." She shook her head. "I always overpack, but you never know what the weather might be, or what you might need to dress for. Samantha told me that Acorn Hill doesn't have much in the way of shopping."

"Samantha?" asked Louise.

"Isn't that your daughter's name?"

"You mean Cynthia." Louise frowned slightly.

"Cynthia, Samantha..." Victoria shrugged.

"Dinner is ready whenever you are," said Jane as she set the last bag on the chair by the closet.

"Yes, dinner," said Victoria. "I am starving. Saman... uh...Cynthia told me that the inn normally doesn't serve dinner, so I guess our meal will be simple."

"Oh, you will be pleasantly surprised," said Louise.

"That's right," added Alice. "Jane was a well-known chef in San Francisco."

"San Francisco?" Victoria's eyes lit up. "Oh, I just adore that town. Tell me, Jean, where was it that you cooked in the city by the bay?"

"It's Jane. Have you ever heard of the Blue Fish Grille?"

Victoria thought for a bit, then said, "No. I've never heard of it."

"Oh."

"Never mind," said Victoria. "I'm sure that whatever you threw together for us will be perfectly fine. And as I said, I'm famished. I haven't eaten since an early lunch. Just give me a few minutes to freshen up. I assume we're not dressing for dinner." Then she laughed.

"Whenever you're ready," said Jane as the three sisters exited what had once been their parents' bedroom.

"'I assume we're not dressing for dinner,'" Jane imitated Victoria as soon as they were halfway down the stairs.

"*Jane.*" Louise scowled.

"Well, really," said Jane.

"I know," said Louise, "but for Cynthia's sake, we must be polite."

"But, of course, dear sister," said Jane in a sweet

voice. "I shall be nothing but polite—at least while Queen Victoria is within earshot."

"From the sound of things, I'm guessing your special guest has arrived?" Harold said as he emerged from the parlor where he had been holed up since six. Fortunately he had found a good book to read.

"She's here," said Alice.

"The *queen* will be down shortly," said Jane in a dramatic formal voice.

"Now, Jane." Louise shook her finger at her.

"Sorry." Jane made a face. "It's time for the kitchen help to get back to the scullery."

"May I help you?" offered Alice.

"That would be perfectly delightful," said Jane in her formal voice again. She offered Alice her arm, and the two glided toward the kitchen, noses in the air.

Alice tried to cheer up Jane as she filled the soup tureen.

"You've done a beautiful job with everything, Jane."

Jane rolled her eyes as she filled the breadbasket. "And all for *what*?"

"Because you love Cynthia."

Jane almost smiled. "Well..."

"And perhaps you wanted to impress Victoria Martin."

Jane sighed. "You're right."

"Some people don't want to be impressed."

Jane stopped her work on the salad plates, her hand in midair, holding a curly white strand of something Alice could not identify. Jane stared at Alice as if she had said something quite profound. "What do you mean?"

"There are some people who don't want to be impressed by *anyone*."

"I've never considered that," said Jane, "but I think you're right. So, how did you get so smart, Alice?"

Alice smiled. "From experience. There's an administrator at the hospital who is always finding fault with everyone. Honestly, I think that even if she heard that one of the nurses brought someone back from the dead, she'd probably just shrug and act as if it were an everyday occurrence."

Jane laughed. "Maybe those kinds of people are afraid their importance will diminish if someone else is good at something."

"Exactly," said Alice as she set the soup ladle in the tureen. "I'm sure they must have a self-image problem. It's sad, really, because if they could only learn how to lift others up, they would probably feel a lot better about themselves too."

Jane shook her head. "Sometimes I think you're a genius, Alice."

Alice laughed. "I can assure you that I'm not."

"Well, you're awfully wise."

"It must be a God thing."

Jane put the last touch on the final salad, then went across the room and hugged her sister. "Oh, Alice, what would I do without you?"

"Serve dinner by yourself?"

"I can hear them coming into the dining room," said Jane. Then she put on a brave face as she picked up a tray of perfectly arranged salad plates and nodded toward the swinging door. "Okay, let's do this thing, Sis."

"I'm right behind you," said Alice as she balanced the steaming tureen and followed.

Chapter Nine

Jane had gone all out for dinner. Her menu included tomato bisque that was so creamy it seemed to caress the tongue, followed by salads that were not only true works of art but also delicious. Next was crown roast of pork with roasted pear and walnut dressing. Alice could not remember when she had seen such a meal before.

"I always put a dollop of crème fraîche on my tomato bisque," said Victoria.

"I used to do that too, but I've been trying to cut down on fats," said Jane. "If you'd like some..."

Victoria waved her hand. "No, no, don't trouble yourself."

Louise and Cynthia kept the conversation going during the salad course. Alice noticed that Victoria seemed to pick at her salad, but her plate was clean when it came time for the next course.

"The salad was divine," said Cynthia. "I'll have to remember how you did this so I can try it at home."

"It's quite simple," said Victoria. "I'm sure you'll have no problem."

Cynthia attempted to laugh. "Even 'simple' tests my culinary skills. Right, Aunt Jane?"

"You were getting pretty good in the kitchen last time you were here."

"Well, that's only because you were coaching me."

Victoria laughed loudly. "That reminds me of my cooking show. Sometimes I get these people to come on, celebrity types, you know. And, of course, they've assured me that they are *experts* at some particular recipe. Well, the camera begins to roll, and it's not long before we can all see that they don't know the first thing about cooking. Oh, my goodness, it can turn into such a scene. And then at the end of the show I have to take a bite and actually act as if I like it." She laughed again. "I always keep a napkin handy, just in case."

Everyone laughed politely, and to Alice's relief, Harold began to question Victoria about her various projects. Thankfully, this kept the conversation moving smoothly until Jane brought out the entrée.

"Crown roast of pork," said Victoria with a look that was hard to read. "Well, I haven't had *this* for a while." She looked around the table now, as if she were searching for something. "Many people think they should serve Merlot with this dish, but I always prefer a nice light Pinot Noir, just barely chilled."

"I'm sorry, Victoria," said Jane, "but we generally don't serve wine at meals."

Victoria's eyebrows rose as if this were remarkable.

"Our father was the pastor of the church next door," Alice explained quickly. "He always felt that it was important not to set a bad example for his congregation."

"I see." Victoria took a sip of ice water.

"But I do agree with you," said Jane. "If I was serving this in the restaurant, I'd recommend a nice Pinot Noir."

"You would actually serve crown roast in your restaurant?" Victoria looked skeptical.

"Well, probably not, but if I did..." Jane handed Victoria her plate with a stiff smile.

Alice was not sure what this conversation was really about, but she recognized that a sparring match was going on and she felt sorry for Jane. She wished that Victoria would say something nice. Perhaps it would have been better if the sisters had served a bit of wine with dinner. In cases like this, it might actually be helpful—or not. Who could be sure? Alice said a silent prayer that dinner would move along smoothly without Jane's feathers getting too ruffled.

"Have you ever tried a bit of rosemary with this

recipe?" Victoria pursed her lips together as if she had bitten into something slightly offensive.

"I like to use thyme and marjoram," said Jane, "but rosemary would be interesting too."

Victoria nodded. "Yes. It would probably be preferable to marjoram."

Jane did not say anything.

"I think it's wonderful," said Cynthia. "It melts in your mouth."

"It's delicious, Jane," offered Harold. "Don't know when I've had a meal half this good. Of course, my late wife, Lily, was never terribly comfortable in the kitchen."

"Now, I just don't understand that," said Victoria. "All it takes is a little practice, a good recipe book, and anyone can manage to cook. The problem is most people simply don't even try. I've often told my staff that I could probably teach a monkey to cook. Really, cooking is not that difficult."

"It is for me," said Alice. "I would never attempt to make a meal like this. When my father was alive I did all the cooking for us, but I always served very simple fare. Jane's the one who can really do miracles in the kitchen."

"That's right," said Louise. "Wait until you taste Jane's chocolate truffles. The town is just crazy about them."

"I created a special truffle," said Victoria. "It became so popular that we began selling it on my website."

"You can sell truffles on a website?" said Alice.

"Of course, you can sell anything on a website," said Victoria. "Have you ever looked at mine?"

Alice shook her head. "I'm not very computer savvy."

Victoria shook her finger at Alice. "Not good. There's no excuse for not using a computer these days. Back in the old days, when computers first came out and were so difficult to use, I could understand. Now all you do is turn them on and click the mouse. It couldn't be easier. And my website is simple enough to remember, it's my name. Someone tried to steal it early on in the game, thinking he could sell it back to me and make a lot of money. I finally had to have my attorney threaten to take him to court before I got it back."

At last it was time for dessert. Alice helped Jane clear the table. "Would you like me to put on the teakettle?" she offered.

"It's already hot," said Jane. "And the decaf is ready to go too. Just turn the pot on."

"You're so organized." Alice watched as Jane carefully placed raspberry chocolate tarts on dainty dishes and topped them with a small dollop of whipped cream, then added mint sprigs along with a few fresh raspberries.

"Where do you find fresh raspberries this time of year?" asked Alice.

"They grow them in hothouses," said Jane. "And they're not cheap. Don't tell, but I also used some frozen raspberries in the filling."

"I'm sure no one will notice," said Alice as she poured hot water into a fine china teapot.

"Don't be so sure."

Everyone seemed suitably impressed as Jane distributed the desserts. Well, almost everyone. It was hard to tell what Victoria was thinking. Alice thought she looked bored, or maybe just tired. Jane had told her that Victoria was about the same age as Alice but that she had probably undergone plastic surgery to make her look younger. There was, however, a certain look around her eyes that suggested she might actually be closer to Louise's age. Of course, Alice would not mention this to anyone.

"I grow raspberries at my home in New Hampshire. I just love eating them fresh, right off the vine. They're so sweet and juicy in the summer." She picked up a raspberry with her fingers and shook her head. "These hothouse berries, well, they just don't quite cut it, do they, Jane?"

"I guess not," said Jane in a deflated voice.

"How many homes do you have?" asked Harold.

"How many homes?" echoed Victoria as if she had been asked a difficult math question. "Well, there's the one in New Hampshire. It's my main home, but I also have a home in North Carolina and one in Maui and another in Malibu and one in British Columbia." She paused as if to think. "And, oh yes, there's the villa in Tuscany."

"Tuscany?" said Harold, then he launched into one of his exciting World War II stories that managed to keep everyone amused and engaged until the last sips of coffee and tea were taken.

"That was a fantastic dinner, Aunt Jane," said Cynthia. "Let me help you clean up."

"That's all right, Cynthia," said Alice quickly. "I plan to help Jane. You've already had a long day of—"

"No, no." Cynthia tossed Alice a warning look. "I insist. You must let me help. I love being in Aunt Jane's kitchen."

Victoria glanced over at Jane. "Before my visit is over, you must let me see your kitchen, Jane. You know I am something of an expert in kitchen design. I expect I might be able to give you a tip or two."

"Oh, that's all right," said Jane. "I wouldn't expect you to—"

"It's no trouble, Jane. I would be glad to help."

Jane nodded as she began gathering up plates. "Well, thank you, Victoria."

"Don't even mention it." Victoria patted her lips with a napkin.

"Perhaps you'd like to join us in the parlor," offered Harold. "The ladies and I have been enjoying a bit of music in the evenings."

"Music?" Victoria looked somewhat interested. "What kind of music?"

"Actually," said Louise quickly, "you may have your choice. Harold likes to play show tunes," she cleared her throat, "and I play classical."

Victoria nodded. "Well, I'm in the mood for a bit of classical myself."

Alice released a sigh of relief as Louise, Harold and Victoria exited from the dining room. "I'm glad that's over," she whispered to Cynthia.

Cynthia nodded as she helped clear the last things from the table. "I feel so bad for Aunt Jane. I don't know what makes that woman so rude, but I've been putting up with it since this morning, and if you guys hadn't let me help out in the kitchen, I might've thrown myself down on the floor and kicked and screamed."

"Oh, that might be going to extremes, Cynthia." Alice smiled as she pushed open the swinging door. "In any case, we're always happy to get good kitchen help."

"You can say that again," said Jane as she ran water into the deep sink.

Cynthia went over and gently rubbed her aunt's back

"I'm so sorry about Victoria, Aunt Jane. She can really be wicked sometimes."

"Is she ever nice?" asked Alice.

"Oh yes," said Cynthia. "She's nice whenever she's on camera, or when she's trying to sell something to some bigwig exec, or whenever she wants to get her way. Believe me, she can be very, very nice."

Alice shook her head and began transferring the leftovers from their formal dishes into storage containers.

"Are you crying, Aunt Jane?" asked Cynthia.

Alice turned around to look at her younger sister. "Jane?"

Jane wiped her eyes. "Yes, as a matter of fact, I am crying. I know it's stupid, but I can't help myself."

"Poor Jane," said Alice as she came over and patted her back.

"Your sympathy will only make it worse." Jane grabbed a tissue and swiped at her tears.

"Did she really get to you that much?" Cynthia looked very concerned now. "Maybe I made a mistake bringing her here. Oh, I'm sorry, Aunt Jane."

"No, no," said Jane. "It's not that, not completely anyway. I mean I might be just tired or maybe disappointed. I guess I'd just hoped that she'd appreciate *something. Anything!*" Jane sobbed even harder now. "It's—it's silly, I know.

I feel like a baby carrying on like—like this. But I just want—wanted her to—to like me." Jane took more tissues and blew her nose.

"Oh, Aunt Jane," said Cynthia in a soothing voice. "I don't think Victoria likes *anyone*. Well, other than her pair of Dobermans. She seems to like them well enough. Their names are Rob and Roy. Believe me, it was all I could do to talk her into not bringing them with her this week. They're like her bodyguards, you know."

"Seriously?" Alice tried to imagine Victoria with a pair of big, aggressive dogs.

"Yes. She talks about them as if they're her children."

"Does she have children?" asked Alice.

"No, she's never been married."

"Oh."

"I'm sorry," said Jane as she began to recover. "I really didn't mean to fall apart like this. It's so unlike me."

"I know it is, dear," said Alice, "and I have just the remedy for you."

"What?"

Alice pointed toward the back staircase. "I want you to go up there and get ready while I draw you a hot bath. You will sit there and soak until you are ready for bed. Then you will get into bed and just read or whatever until you fall asleep."

"But, Alice." Jane waved her hands around the messy kitchen. "What about this?"

"You don't worry one bit about this," said Cynthia. "I will take care of it."

"I'll be back down to help you," Alice assured her, "as soon as we get Jane taken care of."

"But—"

"No buts," said Alice.

"That's right," agreed Cynthia. "And you're outnumbered so don't even think about arguing."

Jane held up her hands in mock surrender. "You win."

Alice followed Jane up the stairs, then went into Jane's bathroom and began filling the claw-foot tub with water. Next, she generously poured some lavender-scented bath oil into the flowing water. She found a couple of candles to light and turned Jane's radio on to a station that played the soft jazz that she knew Jane liked.

"There you go," said Alice as Jane stepped into the bathroom, now wrapped in her terry robe. "Enjoy."

Jane looked around and actually smiled. "You'd make a good lady-in-waiting."

Alice laughed. "Well thanks, I guess." Alice stepped toward the door and then paused. "Really, Jane, don't think about what happened tonight. As Cynthia said, that's just the kind of person Victoria is. It's no reflection on you. Honestly, I was impressed with your dinner tonight. You amaze me. I'll bet that Victoria couldn't possibly pull off something like that dinner without the help of all her dozens of assistants."

Jane dipped her hand into the tub to test the temperature and nodded. "You know, Alice, you might just be right."

Alice reached into her pocket. "I brought these up, just in case." She set two wrapped truffles on the shelf next to the tub.

Jane sighed. "When all else fails, go for the chocolate. Thanks, Alice."

Chapter Ten

"How's it going?" said Ethel as she sat down at the kitchen table with a cup of coffee. She reminded Alice a little of Buffy, a small rusty-colored terrier that they had had as children. He used to sit on the kitchen floor as he waited eagerly for a doggy treat, tail wagging back and forth with anticipation. Alice could almost imagine Ethel's tail wagging as she waited for a tasty morsel.

"It's going okay," said Alice, looking toward Jane.

"Come on," urged Ethel. "A little more description, please."

"We had a lovely dinner last night. Jane made crown roast and—"

"I don't want to hear about the menu," said Ethel. "Tell me about *Victoria*. What's she really like?"

Jane turned around from the counter by the oven where she had been quietly stirring a bowl of some kind of yellow, lumpy batter. Alice had not asked Jane what she was concocting because she sensed that her younger sister, despite the bath and early bedtime, might still be feeling a little fragile.

"You'll have to get to know her for yourself," said Jane.

"Alice, could you get me a package of blueberries from the freezer?"

"Sure." Alice went for the blueberries.

"How do you suggest I do that?" asked Ethel.

"Why don't you join us for breakfast," offered Jane.

Alice set the blueberries next to Jane.

"Well, I haven't had breakfast yet," said Ethel. "I noticed the light on in your kitchen and decided to pop over to see if everything was all right."

Jane smiled. "I decided to get up early and get a head start on things." She glanced at Alice. "By the way, you and Cynthia did a great job on the kitchen last night."

"Thanks," said Alice. "We thought just in case Victoria comes looking..."

"Well, I'm not going to worry about that," said Jane. "I realized last night that it's foolish to try to appear perfect for Victoria or anyone else for that matter."

"Really?"

"Yes. It occurred to me that I should be more interested in pleasing God and myself than some snooty—" Jane stopped herself. "Sorry, I meant to control my tongue today."

"So she is snooty," declared Ethel in an I-knew-that tone of voice.

Jane shrugged. "You'll have to see for yourself. But, as I was saying, I decided that I need to focus more on pleasing God and myself. Everything I did yesterday was doing neither. So today I got up early, took a nice run and a long hot shower and came down here to putter around in my kitchen. And I decided to make blueberry muffins, with frozen blueberries, which I know won't measure up to some people's high standards, but they suit me just fine." She tossed the loosely frozen blueberries into the batter and gave it a stir.

"I love your blueberry muffins," said Alice.

"I do too," said Ethel, almost as if she were afraid to criticize her niece.

"So do I." Jane nodded. "And I am making plain old sausage and bacon and eggs to go with it. And if someone doesn't like it, well, she can just make her own breakfast or go see what's cooking at the Coffee Shop."

Alice giggled.

"I think your breakfast menu sounds perfectly fine, Jane. Besides, I've never known you to make 'just plain' anything."

Of course, Alice was right. Jane's breakfast *was* fit for a king, or even for someone who thought she was a queen.

Alice sensed that Ethel was disappointed, because there was little small talk going on. Victoria was consumed with reading a small pile of e-mail that Cynthia had printed out for her, and Harold seemed intrigued by the newspaper.

"Well, we're off to work now," said Cynthia as she set down her empty coffee cup. "Unless you need help—"

"No," said Alice. "You two go work in the library. Remember that's what you came here for. May I bring you anything? Like coffee or tea?"

"I'd like some tea," said Victoria, "at around ten o'clock. And perhaps a little something to go with it?" She glanced at Jane.

"Of course," said Jane. "No problem."

"And I'd like a black tea," said Victoria. "If that's possible. I usually drink green tea in the afternoon, but I enjoy black tea up until lunchtime."

Jane nodded.

"Thank you." Victoria gathered her papers and stood.

"Have a good day, ladies," said Harold, pouring himself another cup of coffee.

"She doesn't seem like she's all that bad," said Ethel when she and the three sisters were back in the kitchen. "Oh, a bit presumptuous, I suppose, but she's not horrible. Did you notice that she looks much older in person than she does on television?"

"That's because they use makeup and lights to make you look good," said Jane as she set the remaining muffins in her covered pastry dish.

Ethel patted her hair. "I'd like to get my hands on some of that cosmetic help."

Louise chuckled. "So, how is it going with Lloyd? Did he make it back from the mayoral conference yet?"

"He was supposed to get back last night," said Ethel. "Although I haven't heard a word from him. *Humph*. He specifically mentioned that he wanted to be in church today to see how Pastor Ley handles things with Pastor Kenneth away."

"*Church!*" said Alice. "With all that's been going on around here, I almost forgot that it was Sunday today. Not only that, but we forgot to invite Victoria to attend this morning's service."

Jane laughed. "Honestly, Alice, do you think she'd actually go?"

"Probably not. But we should at least invite her and make her feel welcome."

"They may just want to work all day," suggested Jane.

"Well," said Ethel. "They can at least take an hour off for the Lord's day."

"Not everyone sees it that way, Aunt," said Louise.

"I'll deliver their tea tray a little before ten so that

I can remind them it's Sunday," said Alice. "And then I'll invite them to church."

"You're a braver woman than I," said Jane as she rinsed off a platter.

"Did you invite Harold to church?" asked Alice.

"I did," said Jane. "And he told me that he might come."

"Good for him," said Louise. "Now, I must excuse myself. I planned to practice at the organ, as well as warm up the sanctuary."

"Are you going to turn the furnace up?" asked Alice.

"Yes," said Louise. "It may only be one hour, but I am tired of freezing during the service. If anyone has a problem with it, I will just tell him that I will cover the additional expense."

"That's good of you," said Alice.

"No, it is mostly selfish," admitted Louise. "I can hardly play the organ when my hands are so cold and stiff."

"Maybe you should get some of those fingerless gloves, Louie," teased Jane.

"Certainly," said Louise. "And perhaps a silk top hat to go with them as well?"

"Happy practicing," called Alice as Louise bundled into her warm coat.

Alice tapped on the closed door to the library at a

quarter before ten. "Excuse me," she said as she opened the door.

"Is it ten already?" said Victoria as she removed her reading glasses.

Cynthia peered up from her laptop and looked relieved.

"It's a little before ten," admitted Alice, "but I wanted to let you know that you're both welcome to attend church with us this morning. I forgot to mention that at breakfast."

Victoria looked slightly surprised. "Church?"

"Yes, we always go to church," said Cynthia. "But if you'd rather work—"

"How long does it take?" asked Victoria.

"It's only about an hour," said Alice. "Our father always felt that a short service was more meaningful than one that dragged out for hours."

"Your father sounds like he was a sensible man." Victoria turned to Cynthia. "I suppose you'd like to go to church?"

Cynthia shrugged. "Well..."

"So, we shall go." Victoria looked down at her gray wool slacks and cashmere sweater set. "Does this mean we need to change our clothes?"

"No, not at all," said Alice. "You look perfectly fine. Lots of women wear slacks."

"What about my jeans?" asked Cynthia hopefully.

"I don't mind a bit," said Alice, "and I'm sure God doesn't either."

"What about my mother?"

"I guess that's between you two."

"Thanks for the tea, Alice," said Cynthia. "And tell Aunt Jane those scones look delicious."

"She just made them," said Alice. "They're still warm."

Victoria was already reaching for one.

"They're especially tasty," said Alice, hesitating to watch Victoria take a bite. In that moment, Alice saw Victoria's eyes flutter ever so slightly as if to say, "My these are good." Of course, her lips remained still.

Alice went out and closed the door behind her, before she hurried back to the kitchen to tell Jane.

"But she didn't say anything?" said Jane in a weary voice.

"She didn't say anything with her *mouth*, but if you had seen the look in her eyes..." Alice tried to imitate it, which only made Jane laugh.

"Alice." Jane giggled. "You look like a love-struck teenager."

"Thanks," said Alice. "Speaking of teenagers, or almost teenagers, I need to get to church early to talk to some of my ANGELs about next Wednesday's meeting."

"See you there," called Jane.

Alice found several of her ANGELs and explained to them that they were going to do a baking project instead of what they had previously planned. "It's for the Mead family," Alice told the girls in a lowered voice. "Mrs. Mead will be getting home from surgery tomorrow, and I thought it would be nice to fix them a basket of baked goods."

"Sounds great to me," said Ashley. "Do we need to bring anything?"

"That's exactly why I wanted to tell you," said Alice as she handed the girls little slips of paper, each with one of the ingredients written on it. Alice had learned long ago that the girls became even more enthusiastic about helping others when they contributed something to the projects. She always took care not to ask for any expensive items from households that were struggling. Just the same, she allowed everyone to help.

"See you on Wednesday, Miss Howard," said Sissy.

"Hey, Miss Howard," said Jenny suddenly. "Why don't you ask Victoria Martin to come help us on Wednesday night? My mom says she always watches her on TV and that she's a really good cook."

"Yeah," agreed Sissy. "Maybe she could teach us how to make something really special."

Alice forced a smile to her lips. "Well, I'm not sure

if she'll be able to do that or not, but I'll make sure that I mention it to her."

Alice went over to their regular pew and was surprised to see Ethel sitting there with Harold. Alice slipped in beside her and whispered, "Where's Lloyd?"

Ethel's eyebrows rose slightly. "I wouldn't have the vaguest."

"Oh."

Alice glanced over to where Louise was quietly playing on the organ to see that her sister was casting curious looks in their direction, as if to ask what Ethel was up to. Alice shrugged to indicate that *she* had not the vaguest. It reminded her of when they had been girls, sending secret messages back and forth, and she had to control herself from giggling as Pastor Ley made his way up to the platform.

Overall, the service went smoothly. Pastor Ley really did seem to be making improvement in his speech, although he did get stuck at one point, but then he took a big breath and smiled and just went on. The content of the sermon was uplifting, so Alice felt she was being completely honest when she said, "Pastor Ley, I believe that's the best sermon I've ever heard you deliver."

He grinned broadly as he shook her hand. "Thanks, Alice. Th—That means a lot coming from you."

His wife Patsy was beaming too. "Wasn't it wonderful!"

Alice nodded.

"I'm so glad, especially since we've got a couple of guests today," continued Patsy. Then, taking Alice's hand and stepping away from where Pastor Ley was greeting church members by the door, she lowered her voice. "Do you think you could possibly introduce me?" Patsy was looking at Victoria Martin now. Alice had noticed Victoria and Cynthia slipping into the church a few minutes late. They had quietly taken seats in the back but were now surrounded by several women in the congregation who were chattering away like magpies.

"I think we could manage that," said Alice. "If you can be patient."

Patsy nodded and stepped even farther away from her husband, who was now greeting Lloyd Tynan. "But, tell me, Alice, what is going on between Ethel and Lloyd these days?"

Alice glanced at Lloyd and noticed a slightly troubled expression creasing his usually smooth brow. "I'm not sure," she admitted.

"Well, Ethel certainly seems taken by your new guest."

"She does, doesn't she?" Alice watched as her aunt linked her arm into Harold's and they walked down the aisle toward the door. Ethel was gazing up into his face as if he had lit up the moon.

"Well, perhaps she's just trying to make him feel at home," offered Patsy.

"Perhaps," said Alice, but somehow she did not think so.

"Hello, Alice," said Lloyd as he made his way from Pastor Ley over to where she was standing. "Nice sermon today."

"It was, wasn't it?" She noticed Lloyd's glance moving in Ethel's direction. "How was your mayoral convention?"

"Oh, it wasn't really a convention. More of a conference," Lloyd hesitated, then asked, "Do you happen to know who the gentleman over there is?"

"Why, yes, he's staying at the inn. His name is Harold Branninger, and can you believe that he came upon our inn by accident, but he went to college with Louise's husband Eliot?"

"Really?" Lloyd peered at Harold with open curiosity. "That must make him fairly old? Eighty, you think?"

Alice shrugged. "I suppose. Although he looks younger."

"Hmmm."

Alice felt sorry for Lloyd and hoped that Ethel was not carrying on like this on his account. "How's your bowling been going, Lloyd?" she asked to change the subject.

He turned and smiled. "It's been going pretty well.

Who would've thought that old Lloyd Tynan would know how to throw a bowling ball?"

"Sounds like you're having fun."

"Oh, I am..." Then the sound of Ethel's overly loud laughter seemed to interrupt Lloyd's thoughts. He glanced to where the couple was now chatting with Pastor Ley.

"Harold was a World War Two pilot," Ethel said loudly. "Oh my, the stories this man can tell. We'll have to have you over to hear him play the piano sometime. He's just marvelous."

Lloyd seemed to bristle, then he adjusted his bowtie, nodded to Alice and made a quick exit. Alice watched the mayor going out the door. Was he hurt? Angry? Embarrassed? It was hard to know with Lloyd. Being the perennial diplomat, he was a master at keeping his feelings under control. She was ashamed of her aunt's behavior and planned to have a chat with her about it. In the meantime, she wanted to introduce Patsy to Victoria Martin.

Oh, to have life return to its quiet January normalcy, she thought as she went over to speak to Victoria. *Wouldn't that be grand?*

Chapter Eleven

Alice waited until the middle of the afternoon before she went over and tapped on Ethel's door. "Alice!" said Ethel as if it were a surprise to see her niece at her door. "I was just making a pot of tea. Will you join me?"

Alice smiled. "Yes, that sounds nice."

Ethel peered out the door as she let Alice in. "It's been so overcast today, I wonder if it's going to snow."

"The weatherman hasn't predicted snow," said Alice as she removed her coat and scarf, "but it sure is cold out."

"Come sit by my fire and take the chill off."

Alice made herself comfortable in the rocker by the fireplace. She prayed silently for the right words to say to her aunt.

"Here you go, dear," said Ethel as she handed Alice a cup of tea. "It's a new blend."

"From Wilhelm?" asked Alice.

Her aunt nodded and sat down. "He said it's his

secret recipe, Wilhelm's Winter Spice, I believe he calls it. I haven't tried it myself yet."

"Oh, this must be what he gave me to share with Victoria. I haven't tried it either, but I did brew a pot for Victoria and Cynthia before church this morning." Alice took a sip, and then nearly sputtered when she tasted it. "Oh!"

"Oh!" echoed her aunt. "Why would Craig get excited over this tea?"

Alice took a sniff of it. "It smells okay."

"But it tastes awful." Ethel made a face.

Alice took another careful sip, but it was so strong that she regretted giving the tea a second chance."

"I can't believe you actually gave it another try, dear." Ethel was standing up now. "Let's throw this stuff out and make a fresh pot."

A wave of apprehension swept over Alice as she followed her aunt into the little kitchen. "Oh dear."

"What's wrong?"

"I served that tea to Victoria and Cynthia."

Ethel chuckled. "Well, now Victoria will have something legitimate to complain about."

"Oh, how awful." Alice sat down at a kitchen stool and watched as her aunt poured the dark brown brew down the sink.

"Did Victoria say anything about it?"

"No, I went straight to church afterward. Oh, poor Cynthia, she must think I'm nuts."

"Oh pish-posh. Just tell her it's Wilhelm's fault."

Alice picked up the brown packet of tea that was still on the counter. "I wonder what he put in here?"

"His secret recipe, of course."

Before long, Ethel had brewed a fresh pot of sweet-smelling Earl Grey, and they were seated comfortably by the fireplace again.

"So, what brings you to my little house?" asked Ethel as she put her feet up on the needlework footstool.

"I spoke to Lloyd at church today," she began, "and he seemed a little disturbed."

"Disturbed?"

"Seeing you on Harold's arm."

"Oh, *that*." Ethel waved her hand. "I was just having a little fun."

"A little fun?" Alice studied her aunt.

"Oh, why not?"

"Well, Lloyd seemed a bit troubled by it."

"Oh, I don't think he really cares one way or another," said Ethel a bit sadly.

"What makes you think that?"

"Well, he's so caught up in his own little world these

days." Ethel sighed. "The truth is I fear that Lloyd has grown weary of me."

"Just because he took up bowling?"

Ethel looked truly sad. "But he never even invited me to go along."

"Would you go?"

"Probably not, but he could've at least asked."

Alice took a slow sip of tea as she considered this. "Aunt Ethel?"

"Yes?"

"Do you really care for Lloyd?"

"Of course."

"You two seem to have a fairly committed relationship." Alice sighed. "I was concerned when I talked to Lloyd. I thought you should know he looked unhappy."

"Oh, I'm not stupid, Alice. I *know* what you're saying." Ethel leaned forward now. "You don't approve of my flirting with Harold."

"Are you trying to make Lloyd jealous, Auntie?"

Ethel shrugged. "No, I know from experience that ploy doesn't work in real life, not the way it does in the movies. Although I was watching an old film the other night, and a little bit of jealousy did seem to solve all the heroine's problems."

Alice frowned. "But you really wouldn't resort to something like that, would you?"

"No, not on purpose anyway. I suppose I was simply enjoying Harold's attention. It's nice that someone around here appreciates me."

"Do you feel that Lloyd doesn't appreciate you anymore?"

Ethel set her cup down and stood up. She began pacing back and forth across her pastel-colored braided rug, rubbing her chin with each step. Then finally she stopped and turned to face Alice. "He seems to have forgotten all about me, Alice. He seems to like his old bowling ball more than he likes me."

"Oh, Auntie, I don't think that's true."

"We used to do *everything* together. Now I scarcely see him at all. The truth is I'm not like you and your sisters, Alice. You three seem to get along just fine on your own, but I'm all alone and I need a man in my life."

"But then why are you treating Lloyd like this, Aunt Ethel?"

Ethel frowned. "Like what?"

"Oh, you know what I mean. You said yourself that you were flirting with Harold after church today."

"I was simply introducing him to my friends," said Ethel.

"But you completely ignored poor Lloyd," said Alice. "How do you think that made him feel?"

Ethel sat back down and thought about what Alice had said.

"And what about poor Harold?" added Alice. "Is it fair to toy with his affections?"

Ethel waved her hand in a dismissive way. "Oh, that Harold, he's not taking me seriously for a single second."

"Maybe not, but still..."

"You do have me concerned about my dear Lloyd now. I hope I haven't hurt him. Goodness, I wonder how I can make this up to him."

"I'm sure you'll think of something."

Ethel nodded. "I suppose there's no rush."

"Aunt Ethel!"

"Oh, don't worry, I won't use Harold to bother Lloyd anymore, but I might just wait a bit and see what Lloyd plans to do about this whole bowling thing."

Alice finished her tea and stood. "Thanks for the tea. I should probably get back and start helping Jane with dinner."

"Oh, certainly, she's not bending over backward to impress Queen Victoria again, is she?"

"No. I think she's planning a simple meal. Just the same, I should go help."

"Well, tell her that I said tea and toast should be

sufficient. That woman could stand to take off a few pounds, if you ask me."

Ethel's comments about tea got Alice worried again. What had Wilhelm put in that tea anyway?

She decided to dash into town to his shop before she went home. She knew that Wilhelm's, unlike many of the local businesses, was open in the afternoon on Sundays. The bell tinkled merrily as she entered.

"Hello?" she called.

"Coming," said Wilhelm. He poked his head out of the backroom and, using his hand to fan the air, he held up a wooden pipe. "Just enjoying a little smoke back here. Be right out, Alice."

He came out smiling.

"I didn't know that you smoked a pipe, Wilhelm."

"Oh, I try to keep it a secret. Mostly so Mother won't find out. She does not approve of tobacco of any kind. I have to hide my pipe and tobacco from her. You won't tell her, will you?"

Alice laughed. "Of course not."

"So, what brings you here today?" He rubbed his hands together. "Let me guess. I'll bet you'd like to get some more of my special blend tea."

"Well..." She cleared her throat. "That's what I wanted to talk to you about."

"What?" He frowned. "Is something wrong?" He slapped his hand over his mouth. "Don't tell me—did Victoria Martin hate it?"

"Well, I'm not really sure. You see, I served it to her this morning. Then I left and went to church."

He looked relieved. "Oh, then what's the problem?"

"Well...I hadn't tried your tea yet, but I was just at Aunt Ethel's, and she made us a pot."

He nodded expectantly, as if he was anticipating high praise. "And?"

"And, well, it wasn't very good."

If she had slapped him across the face, he could not have looked more surprised and crushed. "You didn't like it?"

She shook her head.

He scratched his slightly balding head. "How about Ethel? Did she like it?"

Alice shook her head again. "I hate being the bearer of bad news."

"I just don't understand it. Mother and I both think it's fantastic. We were almost through our first batch in a week. That's why I had her make the second batch just last Friday."

"Your mother made the second batch?" Wilhelm's mother was known in town as something of a scatterbrain.

She tended shop for Wilhelm occasionally, but often when she did, something would go wrong.

"Do you think she messed up the recipe?" he asked.

"Have you had any of the tea from the new batch yourself?"

"No, she had it all packaged and ready for sale by the time I got back from my errands."

"And what my aunt purchased was from that batch?"

"It must have been."

"Do you have any left?"

"Of course." He held up a brown package. "It's right here." He opened up the package marked 'Wilhelm's Winter Spice' and took a whiff. "Oh no!"

Obviously, her nose had not been sensitive enough to detect the problem, but Wilhelm's was.

"Oh, this is terrible."

"I know. You should brew up a pot and taste it yourself."

"I don't have to," said Wilhelm. "I can tell it would be horrendous." He shook his head sadly. "Well, that explains it."

"Explains what?"

"Why my tobacco tin, the one that looks just like a tea tin in order to camouflage it, was nearly empty today."

"Your mother put *tobacco* in your special tea?"

He took another sniff and made a face. "Apparently so."

"Oh, that's awful."

"I know. It was my favorite pipe tobacco too. Just the same it would be nasty in the tea." He peered into her eyes. "Oh, I'm so sorry, Alice. I cannot believe that I sent that over for"—he slapped his hand to his brow dramatically—"for *Victoria Martin!*"

"Oh, it could be worse, Wilhelm."

"I don't see how."

"Well, she didn't die from it."

"Good grief, do you think a person could die from ingesting tobacco?"

"Well, she didn't eat the leaves. Many men chew tobacco and," she made a face, "extract the juices. I suppose it couldn't be too harmful. Besides, I saw her in church and she was perfectly fine."

"*Victoria Martin went to church?*"

"She did."

He seemed to think this was as confusing as the tea catastrophe. "Oh my, maybe it was the tea."

Alice laughed. "I doubt it, but if that's the case maybe I should serve it to all our guests."

"Good heavens, no," said Wilhelm. "I hate to ask, but I'm sure I won't sleep a wink tonight if I don't." He took a deep breath. "Did you give her my card yet?"

Alice grimaced. "I, *uh*, I actually set it on the tea tray."

Wilhelm let out a low groan. "I am history."

She patted him on the shoulder. "Maybe she didn't see it, Wilhelm. They were busy working, you know. Maybe tea spilled on it."

He stood up straight and looked her in the eyes. "You must find out, Alice. I'll never be able to show my face in town again."

She smiled. Wilhelm could be so theatrical at times. "All right. I'll try to find out what happened."

"Will you call me, Alice?" He put his hands together as if he were pleading. "Please, as soon as you know?"

She nodded. "Yes. I'll get right back to you."

"Thank you." He picked up a package of tea that he knew Alice liked. "Here, you must take this for your troubles, Alice."

"Oh, you don't have—"

"I insist. I am so embarrassed. And, sometime, when we've recovered from this shock, you must try the real special blend." He shook his head. "It's really excellent, unlike"—he held the package of tobacco tea at arm's length as if it were poison—"this horrible stuff." Then he threw it into the trash.

Poor Wilhelm, thought Alice, as she hurried toward home. She felt a bit sorry for Cynthia and Victoria too. Had they actually drunk that foul-tasting brew?

Chapter Twelve

By the time Alice got home, Jane was already working on dinner. "Sorry I'm so late," said Alice as she hung up her coat and reached for an apron.

"It's okay." Jane handed her some potatoes and a peeler.

"You won't believe what I just found out," she began and then told Jane the whole tea story until they were both laughing so hard they had tears coming down their faces.

"*Stop it!*" said Jane, holding her sides. "You keep this up, Alice, and I'm going to banish you from my kitchen."

"I'm sorry," Alice wiped her eyes, "but has Cynthia mentioned anything about the tea? Good grief, she probably thought we were trying to poison them."

"She never said a single word about it," said Jane. "Although, as I recall, she was having coffee. She brought the tea tray back in here this afternoon, and I made them some fresh green tea, along with a plate of ginger biscotti." Jane thought for a moment. "The teapot was nearly empty when I poured it into the sink and rinsed it out."

"*Nearly empty?*" Alice shook her head. "That can't be." Then she went over to the tea cupboard and took out the brown package of Wilhelm's Winter Spice. She opened it and held it out for her sister to sniff.

"Yuck!" Jane pulled her head back. "I can tell there's something wrong with that."

Alice nodded. "I'm afraid you're right. But why would they drink it?"

"Maybe Cynthia realized it was bad and poured it into the potted fern." Jane frowned. "Although, I hope not. That plant was just starting to look good."

It was not until dinner that the mystery of the tea was solved. After a bit of small talk about their work on the book, and Victoria's assessment of the service at Grace Chapel, or more specifically, the "preacher with the funny way of talking," Alice managed to bring up the tea.

"I wanted to say something about this morning's tea," she began, wondering just how a person said something like this.

"Oh yes," said Victoria suddenly. "I told Cynthia to remind me to say something about that."

Alice flushed. "I—"

"That was the *best* tea," said Victoria. "*Really.* I even kept the business card for the shop, which is something I almost never do. As you might imagine, I am handed cards every time I turn around. Anyway, I told Cynthia that we simply must pay this place a special visit. I'd like to buy several pounds of that tea if possible."

Alice was so shocked she was speechless. She hoped her mouth was not hanging open.

"*Uh*, it's a special blend," said Jane quickly. "Wilhelm Wood, the proprietor of Time for Tea, used a secret recipe. It's called Wilhelm's Winter Spice."

Louise's eyebrows lifted as she looked from Jane to Alice. They had shared the story with her just shortly before dinner.

"I told Victoria that we could visit Time for Tea tomorrow," said Cynthia innocently. "I think we should be due for a walk around the town by then."

"Oh yes," said Louise. "Victoria might enjoy our quaint little town."

"Now that I've sampled this special tea, I *am* interested," said Victoria. "I sometimes find items that I can carry on my website in little hole-in-the-wall places just like this."

Alice could not wait for dinner to end so she could call Wilhelm. She made sure that Victoria and Cynthia were well out of earshot, off listening to Harold playing show tunes, before she picked up the phone and called Wilhelm at home.

It took several repetitions before Wilhelm understood what she was telling him. Even then he sounded skeptical. Meanwhile, Jane and Louise were cleaning up the kitchen but were also listening, barely suppressing laughter and making it even more difficult for Alice to get her message across.

"I am not putting you on, Wilhelm. Victoria said she loves your special blend tea."

"The tea with the tobacco?"

"Yes. Wilhelm's Winter Spice, and it is *the tea with the tobacco*."

"And this is *the* Victoria Martin, famed cuisine chef, expert in all areas of house and garden and food and wine?"

"Yes. I know it sounds crazy, but that's what she said. I even have witnesses." Alice glanced at her sisters, who were now laughing aloud. "Well, they might not be the most reliable witnesses."

Jane grabbed the phone from Alice. "Listen, Wilhelm, this is Jane. What Alice is saying is true. Victoria thinks your stinky tobacco tea is the bee's knees. Not only that, but she plans to pay you a visit tomorrow." Jane rolled her eyes at whatever the poor man was saying on the other end.

"Calm down, Wilhelm," she told him. "Now, listen to me. Take a deep breath and just listen, okay?" She winked at Alice. "Do you have any more of that tobacco?" She paused. "Good, good. Now, your mother probably doesn't know exactly how she mixed it, but you might ask her." Another pause. "Yes, we still have our package of tea, and I'm guessing Aunt Ethel has hers, since she probably plans to return it for a full refund."

Louise and Alice listened as Jane and Wilhelm discussed the process of figuring out what went into that tea and being prepared to make more. "Of course, you do realize that you'll have to tell her about the secret ingredient.... That's okay, Wilhelm, I know you do. But, hey, you know what they say you should do when life gives you lemons." She laughed and hung up, and then turned to her sisters. "In a very stiff voice, Wilhelm just informed me that my little adage couldn't possibly apply to tobacco and tea."

When the sisters had recovered, they took dessert and tea (a nice decaffeinated jasmine) into the parlor.

"Are you really up for Harold's music tonight?" Jane asked Louise before they entered the room.

"After hearing about the tobacco tea?" Louise grinned. "I think I am up for almost anything."

Harold was just winding down a song as the sisters came in.

"That sounded great," said Jane as she began pouring tea.

"Time for a break," said Harold as he pushed himself away from the piano. "And this looks worthy of breaking for."

"Oh, it's only crème caramel," said Jane.

The room got quiet as they all enjoyed their custards. Alice sneaked a peek at Victoria, who seemed happy to eat every last bit.

"You know," said Victoria as she picked up her teacup and leaned back into the easy chair, "custard was one of the first things I learned to cook." She sighed as if enjoying a good memory. "It was my grandmother who taught me how to make it. Oh, it wasn't sophisticated like this. My grandmother didn't know a thing about French cuisine. Her recipe was a simple farm one. Steamed milk and farm-fresh eggs." She sighed again. "It always makes me happy just remembering."

Alice cleared her throat. "That reminds me of something, Victoria."

Victoria snapped back to attention, and Alice almost regretted interrupting her little reverie. "What's that?"

"Well, I lead a church group of girls. They're called

the ANGELs." She chuckled. "Not that they are, mind you. The purpose of the group is to help others, and this week we are going to be doing some baking for a family. The mother is recovering from surgery. And, well, the girls asked me if you'd be interested in joining us." Alice smiled. "I realize that's a lot to ask. I told them it probably wouldn't work out."

"How old are these girls?" asked Victoria.

"They're preteens," said Alice. "It's a rather lively age, but they're sweet."

"Preteens?" Victoria seemed to be chewing on this. "And this activity is when?"

"Wednesday night." Alice blinked. "In the church basement."

"Oh, why don't you just do it here, Alice," suggested Jane. "My kitchen is much better than the one in the church basement."

"And warmer too," added Louise.

"Yes," agreed Victoria. "And much more photogenic, I'm sure."

"Photogenic?" said Alice, confused.

"Yes." Victoria turned to Cynthia. "You were saying that we need to get some photographs of me doing something with children. I think this is the perfect opportunity."

Cynthia's eyes lit up. "I think you are right. Would it be okay, Aunt Alice?"

"Well, I guess so. I'm sure the girls would be thrilled."

"We'd have to get their parents to sign release forms," said Cynthia as she pulled out her notebook and jotted something down, "but that should be no problem."

"Then it's settled," said Victoria, obviously pleased with herself, "Wednesday night in Jane's kitchen."

"Right," said Alice, wondering what she had gotten herself into. What had she been thinking, having Victoria and the ANGELs and a photographer—all here in Jane's kitchen? Who knew what could go wrong? She looked at Jane as if searching for backup or a way out, but Jane just smiled at her as if they did things like cook with Victoria Martin every day of the week.

After Victoria had turned in, Cynthia was told the tobacco tea story. They all agreed that Wilhelm was the person to inform her of the secret ingredient if she truly wanted to buy some of his special brew.

"Maybe Victoria is a secret smoker and the tea satisfies her nicotine craving," Jane suggested.

"Or maybe she has absolutely no sense of taste," Cynthia said.

"Maybe she chews," Jane said, warming to the topic.

"*Jane, stop!*" Louise commanded.

Somehow they managed to suppress their giggles as they all tiptoed off to their various bedrooms.

Chapter Thirteen

Alice was thankful to return to the peaceful routine of work on Monday. *It's funny*, she thought as she drove toward Potterston, *going to work today feels more relaxing than being at home.*

Despite a busy morning, Alice did not forget her commitment to check out the dog-racing track during her lunch hour. She had asked about the track at the hospital, but no one knew much about it since it had only recently opened. Though tempted to relax and put her feet up in the nurses' lounge, instead she bundled up into her heavy wool coat, scarf and gloves, and drove to the address she had found in the phone book. She was not sure what to expect. Still, she felt the need to go—to see this place for herself.

There were no races going on, and the parking lot and stands were almost empty. But there were a number of people and some dogs milling about. She parked on the edge of the lot and tried to look as inconspicuous as possible as she approached what looked like an entrance to the racetrack. She felt certain that someone would stop her, but she managed to walk right through the gate along with several other people. As she entered, what she saw alarmed her. She noticed things like muzzles and tight collars, and a dog with a bad limp that was being picked up and *shoved* into a box, even though he was yelping in pain.

Once inside, she noticed more and more things that seemed to flag that all was not well in the world of racing dogs. Oh, some owners seemed genuinely to care about their dogs, but in an area where people were working with their dogs, some people yelled at the animals. One man kicked his. Alice bit her lip and looked away. She continued walking to an area where trucks were parked, not far from the starting gates. Then, turning a corner, she saw a scene that completely horrified her, one that would stay with her for a long, long time. There, stretched out on the frozen grass, were two lifeless dogs. One was a soft golden brown, the other was white with a few chocolate brown spots. Her hand flew to her mouth in revulsion. Just then a large, bearded man appeared with a bright blue plastic tarp.

"Whaddya think you're doing over here?" he demanded.

She just stood there, speechlessly staring at the two dogs.

The man seemed to soften a little. "Look, lady, I

know this don't look good, but both these dogs needed to be put down. It was the humane thing to do, you know."

She shook her head and stepped backward without speaking.

"Let me tell you, lady, there are some folks who wouldn't handle it like this. Some folks would just—" He scowled. "Look, I don't even know why I'm bothering with you. These were *my* dogs, okay? I have a right to do what I want with them. And they weren't no good for anything. *You get it?*" Then he cursed and turned away. Throwing the tarp over them, he began to wrap them up as if they were nothing more than rubbish.

Alice cried tears of outrage as she hurried back to her car. She wished she could wash her hands, although she had touched nothing at the track. She looked at her watch. She still had a half hour before her lunch break would end. She started her engine, and feeling her hands shaking, she drove away from the track and parked at a nearby convenience store. There she took out a pad of paper and furiously began to pen a letter to the editor. Okay, it might not be much, but it was a start. People needed to know about these brutalities. She started her letter with the heading: *Run for Your Life!* Then proceeded to write down what she had just witnessed.

By the time she finished and got back to the hospital,

her lunch break was over, but Alice had no appetite anyway. On her next break, she called Carlene Moss at the *Acorn Nutshell*. It was only a small-town paper, but Alice thought that perhaps Carlene would have some ideas about dealing with this deplorable situation. Maybe she would even write an article about it. She quickly explained what had happened and what she had seen.

"You know, I've heard rumors of these things before," said Carlene, "but I'm sorry to say, I have never actually looked into it."

"Well, I wrote what I think could be a letter to the editor. Is it too late to get it in this week's edition?"

"Can you fax it to me?"

"Sure," said Alice. She could use the fax machine in the nurses' station.

"You get it to me today, and it'll come out on Wednesday," said Carlene.

"Wednesday," said Alice. "That's the same day of the next race. I wonder if I could possibly garner enough interest to get people to come out and stage some kind of a protest."

"I don't know," said Carlene. "Maybe you should wait and let me run a bigger story on it next week."

"Those poor dogs can't wait," said Alice with emotion. "You should have seen them."

"That makes me so mad," said Carlene. "Well, I'm with you, Alice. You go ahead and invite the locals to stage a protest. I might even come myself, if I can get away."

"Right," said Alice. Then she hung up and wrote a few more lines challenging the good people of Acorn Hill to join with her "to take a stand together against the inhumane treatment and cruelty to dogs at the Potterston racetrack." Then she faxed her letter to the number that Carlene had given her.

Although this action was just a beginning, it did make Alice feel a little bit better. At least she was doing *something*. Now, if only she could get those images of the poor dogs out of her head. She really did not want to have nightmares about her experience.

By the time she finished what turned out to be a demanding shift, she had pushed the greyhound dilemma to the back of her mind. Her hospital work required her full attention. It was not until after she had gone home and cleaned up for dinner that she had time to revisit what had transpired during her lunch hour. Seeing Harold enjoying a congenial visit with Victoria in the living room brought the issue back to her. It was just before dinner, but she could not help herself. "Harold," she said. "I thought you might be interested to know that I visited the racetrack today."

Victoria's eyes widened. "Are you joking, Alice? You don't seem like the track type."

"The racetrack's not open on Mondays," said Harold.

"Maybe not to the general public," said Alice as she sat down in the chair across from them. "But the trainers are there, I guess to prepare the dogs for the next race."

"You're speaking of dog racing?" Victoria's voice was flat.

Alice nodded. "Greyhounds."

"I know what breed of dogs they use to race," said Victoria. "I deplore the practice. In fact, I belong to an organization that campaigns against the sport." She laughed in a sarcastic tone. "If you can call it a sport, that is."

"Wait a minute," said Harold. "I happen to enjoy dog races. I've never seen a single cruel act."

"Well, of course not," snorted Victoria, "they wouldn't show their dark side in public."

"Well, I saw some things today that were not meant for the public," said Alice.

"It's time for dinner," called Louise from the dining room.

Alice now realized this was not the time to discuss such a distasteful issue. As they walked to the dining room, she changed the topic to the weather. "I heard there's a slight chance of snow later this week," she said as everyone took seats at the table.

"Oh, I would love to see some snow," said Jane as she set the soup tureen on the table.

It was Louise's turn to say the blessing. Having guests joining them for dinner was not the norm at Grace Chapel Inn, and Alice had noticed how Victoria had originally seemed to bristle just slightly at their family ritual. Now she appeared to have settled into the routine and simply bowed her head with the rest of them.

"We walked around town a bit today," said Cynthia as the soup was served.

"Oh?" Alice looked up from her bowl, a naughty smile playing on her lips. "Did you visit Time for Tea?"

Cynthia ducked her head to hide her reaction, but Victoria responded, "We did visit the little tea shop. I found Wilhelm Wood to be a perfect dear. I asked him to make me up a special batch of his new signature tea."

"Signature tea?" Louise's eyebrow lifted.

"Yes." Victoria nodded. "I told him I would have it tested for possible inclusion in the Victoria Line."

Jane's eyes were sparkling when she asked, "And was Wilhelm happy about that?"

"In fact, he seemed somewhat taken aback. He's a very dignified fellow," said Victoria, "which I can certainly appreciate. I was grateful he didn't become giddy the way some people do."

"Giddy...," repeated Louise while giving Jane a warning look. "No, I am sure that Wilhelm controlled his... joy at the news."

Alice and her sisters, of course, knew why he had seemed so controlled. How embarrassing it would be for Wilhelm, a man who loved fine tea, to have his name attached to this "signature" tea that was really just a horrible and foul-tasting mistake. Alice wondered if he had revealed the secret ingredient yet. It did not seem as if he had.

Harold could tell something was going on, but he knew better than to ask about it in front of Victoria. Soon the subject changed to the other shops in town. It seemed that Victoria had approved of both Craig Tracy's flower shop and Sylvia Songer's fabric shop.

"I found several pieces of vintage cloth at Sylvia's Buttons," said Victoria. "I don't think the owner had any idea as to the value because I got them for a song." Victoria laughed.

"Oh, Sylvia knows the old pieces are valuable," said Jane, "but there aren't many people in Acorn Hill who can afford such things. I'm sure she was honored to have you in her shop."

"It's funny, isn't it?" said Victoria. "That happens to me all the time. People *give* me merchandise or *reduce* the price on items, and I, of all people, could certainly afford to pay more." She laughed again. "I'm not complaining, mind you."

"How's the book coming?" asked Alice, once again eager to change the subject since she thought she noticed faint sparks flashing in Jane's eyes.

"Oh, don't ask," said Victoria.

Cynthia shook her head. "It's not coming too well." She glanced at Victoria. "*We* keep changing our minds."

"And it's due the end of the week?" asked Jane.

"Something like that," said Cynthia.

Alice felt sorry for her niece. Not only did she look completely discouraged, but she also had dark circles under her eyes. "Is there anything we can do to help?" she asked.

Cynthia shook her head. "You are doing plenty. We're the ones who need to get our act together."

"Perhaps we should start earlier tomorrow," offered Victoria. "I have no problem working before breakfast."

"Yes, that might be a good idea," agreed Cynthia. "In that case, I may turn in early tonight. Also, I need to go over today's notes to see if I can figure something out."

"Goodness," said Louise. "I had no idea that writing a children's book was so challenging."

Cynthia laughed. "That's what most people think. You have no idea how many people come to me—people who have never published a single word—and tell me that they think they will write a children's book. They think it should be easy."

"Why is it so difficult?" asked Alice.

"Well, you're writing a complete story with a beginning, a middle, and an end. You need a strong character, a good plot, and it has to be about something children care about. And you have to do all this in a minimum of words. It's very tricky."

"And then you have to consider the art," said Jane.

"Yes." Cynthia nodded enthusiastically. "You must write each spread—that's like how the book looks when it's open in your lap—as a specific scene that lends itself to illustration. Also, you want each spread to be different. Believe me, it's not all that easy."

"I have to agree with her," said Victoria. "I came here thinking it would be a snap." She sighed. "Unfortunately it's turning out to be quite overwhelming."

Cynthia reached over and patted Victoria's hand. "Don't worry, we're going to nail this thing by the end of the week."

"I certainly hope so." Victoria looked surprisingly serious just then. "I really despise failing at *anything*."

"I know how you feel," said Cynthia.

Poor Cynthia, thought Alice, *has much more at stake with this book than Victoria.* "I will be praying for you both," she said. "I will make it the top of my prayer list for each day."

Victoria looked stunned. "You pray every single day?"

Alice smiled. "Actually, I pray off and on throughout the day." She shrugged. "It's very comforting, really, just talking to God."

"Talking to God?" Victoria looked unconvinced. "Does He listen?"

Alice laughed. "I believe He does. My prayers are always answered."

Now Victoria looked quite skeptical. "Always? That's hard to believe."

"Always," said Alice in a firm voice. "Of course, I don't always like His answers. Sometimes He says 'no,' but many times He goes beyond what I could imagine."

"I can vouch for that," said Jane. "I wasn't much into prayer before I moved back home. That's been steadily changing."

"Interesting," said Harold. It was almost the first word he had spoken during the meal. Perhaps it was hard getting a word in edgewise with five chatty ladies at the table. "My wife became a firm believer in prayer during the last few years of her life."

"That must have been a comfort to her," said Louise.

"Oh, it was." He nodded thoughtfully. "And, oddly enough, it was a comfort to me too. I guess that was because in some ways she seemed much more at peace with her situation than I was. Of course, everything changed once she was gone."

"I have discovered," said Louise, "that things like prayer and faith must be worked out on an individual basis."

"I agree," said Jane. "Even though our father was a pastor, each of his three daughters had to come to her belief in an individual way."

"And at an individual time," added Alice.

"That's because God is infinitely creative," said Jane. "He didn't make any of us alike."

"That's true enough," said Harold. "Once again, you ladies have given me something—well, besides this lovely dinner—to chew on."

Chapter Fourteen

hile Cynthia and Victoria worked, Louise was at a book club meeting, and Jane was attending Sylvia's quilting class. Alice sat at the dining room table making protest signs. Harold came upon her sitting there with pieces of poster board and felt pens spread out across the table.

"You're really taking this seriously?" he said as he looked over her shoulder.

She nodded as she carefully filled in the block letter with a black felt pen.

"STOP CRUELTY TO INNOCENT DOGS," read Harold. "*Hmmm*."

"Well, it's not the snappiest line," said Alice, "but it's the best I can do at the moment."

"Why are you making so many of them?" he asked.

"Because I expect to be joined by others," she explained without looking up. "I said I'd bring the signs."

"Have you ever done anything like this before?"

"Well, no, but there's a first time for everything." Alice felt unsure now. Maybe this was a crazy idea after all. She had not had the opportunity to describe to Harold what she had seen at the track on Monday. Taking a break from her sign making, she stood up and looked the old man in the eye. "I never told you about the scene at the racetrack, Harold, about what I saw on Monday during my lunch break."

"Well, no, you didn't say much about it."

"I saw two dead dogs, Harold."

His brow creased slightly. "How did they die?"

"I don't know for sure, but it didn't look good."

He shook his head. "I'm sure it didn't. But perhaps these dogs needed to be put down for a good reason."

"That's what their owner said."

"So?"

"Well, that wasn't all. Trainers were yelling at their dogs and hitting them."

He nodded. "I don't know much about training animals, but that doesn't sound too terrible to me."

"And the dogs are kept in these tiny boxes." She held up her hands to show the dimensions.

He nodded again. "How do you know the dogs don't like it in there?"

"Because one poor dog was yelping as he was stuffed into his." Alice sighed in frustration. It seemed obvious that Harold was not sympathetic to her cause. He went into the kitchen and returned with a cup of coffee.

"I'm not saying you're wrong, Alice," he said in a kind voice. "I don't agree with cruelty to animals either. But it's possible that you're overreacting."

She considered this, then finally said, "It's possible, Harold, but I really don't think I am."

"Well, I wish you the best tomorrow." He winked at her. "Maybe I'll head out to the track myself."

She started to feel hopeful but then realized he would probably be up in the stands cheering for whichever dog he had bet on.

The next morning, Alice stopped by the Coffee Shop to pick up the new edition of the *Acorn Nutshell* on her way to work.

"Eager to read the local news, Alice?" called Hope from behind the counter.

Alice smiled. "Actually, I wrote a letter to the editor. I'm hoping it made it in here today."

Hope filled Ronald Simpson's coffee cup. "I'll have to read it when I have time." She rolled her eyes as Chuck Parker waved his cup at her. "Which might not be until next March."

"Sooner than that, I hope," called Alice as she went back outside.

Alice opened the paper when she got into her car. There at the top of the "Editor's Mailbag" was her letter, with the heading in large type: RUN FOR YOUR LIFE! She was embarrassed as she read what she had written so hastily and with such passion. Of course, it was true, but it did not sound like her. She wondered what her friends and neighbors would think; however, she had little time to worry about that now. She started the car and drove to the hospital, which she found was busier than usual with several unscheduled surgeries and three nurses out with the flu. As a result, she worked right through her lunch break and it was two thirty before she was reminded of her plans for the day.

"I thought you were taking off early today," said her supervisor.

Alice looked at her watch. "I guess I lost track of the time."

"Well, things seem to have finally settled down, and I noticed you missed your lunch break. Feel free to leave whenever you need to, Alice."

"Thanks." Within minutes she was bundled up, in her car and nervously driving toward the racetrack. Her heart pounded as her car neared the track. She had never done anything like this in her entire life and was not sure she could do it now. She could tell by the parking lot that there had to be a good-sized crowd expected. That was encouraging: Perhaps the presence of her and her friends would make these people think twice about what they had previously considered "innocent fun."

In her letter in the *Nutshell*, she had invited interested parties to meet her at the main entrance. She had also spoken individually with several people, including her sisters and her best friend Vera Humbert. All had promised, a few somewhat reluctantly, to arrive around three when the final segment of races would be run.

When Alice reached the main entrance, laden with her cumbersome pile of homemade signs, she saw not a single soul that she recognized. She paced back and forth for a bit, searching the faces in the crowd and silently praying that God would show her what to do next. And finally, sticking the other signs back in her trunk, she selected one that read, "DOG ABUSE IS NOT A SPORT."

Then, holding it up in front of her, she planted herself next to the front entrance and waited.

She could feel her blood pressure rise as the first group of people approached. It consisted of three middle-aged men and a younger woman. At first they looked at her curiously, perhaps feeling sorry for the old woman in the heavy wool coat. Upon reading the sign, however, their countenances changed, and one of the men made a rude and unrepeatable comment.

"Get a life," snapped the young woman as she pulled her fur coat more tightly around her and strutted past.

Next came two men, probably in their thirties. Bracing herself, she held up her sign so that they could easily read it.

"Aw, come on," said one. "Give us a break."

"Yeah, you 'PITA PETA' people need to lighten up."

On it went. Feeling that she was doing her duty, Alice persevered, but the temperature was dropping steadily, and despite her hat, gloves and scarf, she was getting very cold. Then a few snowflakes began to fly. Finally, she decided that everyone who was coming to the races was already inside, and ready to give it up, she started to leave. Just then people started drifting back out. Torn between wanting to be warm—not to mention ending what was probably the most unusual thing she had ever attempted—and feeling her responsibility to make a statement, she decided to remain a bit longer. Perhaps Vera would come after all. Or maybe her sisters. She glanced at the clock above the entrance. It was just a little past four now. Certainly she could give this protest more than an hour of her time. Besides, she noticed, people were coming out in greater numbers now. It seemed that they, too, were getting cold.

What Alice had not counted on was that many of

these people were not only cold and grumpy (after losing their bets, she suspected), but also had been imbibing. What had started out as a handful of rude remarks and jibes was quickly becoming more personal and threatening.

Dear God, she prayed silently as a group of angry spectators clustered around her, *help me through this*.

"Stay out of what you don't understand!" yelled an angry man with alcohol on his breath.

"Go home, old woman!" This came from a man only inches from her face.

Alice simply closed her eyes and held up her sign, praying all the while. The voices continued their assault, but the specific words became blurred in her ears as she silently repeated Psalm 23 in her head.

A bright flash of light caused her to open her eyes. Standing in front of her, snapping pictures, was a young man. He had his camera focused on her and the angry crowd, which had grown surprisingly large. Toward the back of the crowd was Carlene. Then Alice heard, "Break it up! Break it up!" and saw police moving toward her. She was not sure whether to be thankful or frightened.

"Alice!" called Harold, waving frantically from the sidelines. "You need some help?"

She never had a chance to answer.

"What's going on here, ma'am?" demanded an officer.

"I was protesting," she began.

"Did you know this is private property?" he asked her.

"Well, no."

"The owner of the property has made a complaint," he told her. "We have to take you in."

"You're going to arrest me?"

"That's right."

Now she was feeling slightly faint. She searched through the dispersing crowd, hunting for Harold or Carlene. Finally she spotted them. Both were trying to press their way through.

"Excuse me," called Harold, waving to the police. "I'm with the lady."

"Let him through," yelled an officer.

"Let me through!" yelled Carlene. "I'm the press."

Soon both Carlene and Harold were standing nearby, and Alice felt slightly better, though decidedly light-headed. She hoped she was not about to faint.

"May I escort the lady home?" offered Harold in his most charming manner.

"Sorry," said the officer. "She's going downtown."

"Downtown?" repeated Carlene. "You mean you're arresting her?"

"That's right," said the officer. He looked from

Harold to Carlene. "Are you people involved in this protest too?"

Harold shook his head.

"I'm a reporter," said Carlene.

"Do you really need to arrest her?" asked Harold. "I can vouch that this woman is interested only in peaceful protest."

"Has nothing to do with it." The officer turned his attention back to Alice now. "You want to come quietly, little lady?"

She nodded and handed him her sign. "Are you going to handcuff me?" she asked in a voice that was barely audible.

"Nah, I don't think that'll be necessary." Now he actually smiled at her. "Just come along, okay?"

She nodded again and began walking with the policemen toward their cars. She was surprised to see the blue lights flashing, amazed that they had gone to all this trouble on account of her and her protest. When they reached the car, the officer introduced himself to her as Sergeant Crane, and then wrote down her full name, address, Social Security number and birth date in his little book.

"I'll let your sisters know, Alice," called Harold from nearby.

"Don't worry, Alice," called Carlene. "They won't be able to hold you for long."

Snowflakes were flying faster now, and Alice watched them numbly as she rode in the backseat of the squad car— like a criminal. They were now passing the hospital where she had worked for years as a respected head nurse. There was Ron White scraping snow off the windows of his old dented pickup. She started to wave but then thought better of it. With a sinking heart, she watched the snowflakes zipping past the side window as the car continued toward town. Oh, what had she gotten herself into?

It was getting dusky when they reached the police station in downtown Potterston. They did not park in front as she had expected, but went down a narrow alley where they took her into a side door that appeared to be close to the city jail.

"Are you going to lock me up?" she asked as she glanced at the security gates in the hallway that she felt certain led to the jail. She wondered what it would be like in one of those cells, and whether or not she would have to spend the night.

"We'll see," said Sergeant Crane.

First, he filled out some preliminary paperwork, and then took her to where a stern-looking woman took her photograph and copies of her fingerprints. Alice did not know when she had felt so foolish and humiliated. She considered trying to explain her dilemma to the tight-lipped woman but decided it was probably not worth the effort. After what seemed like an hour, Sergeant Crane finally led her to his office.

"Alice," called Harold from the waiting area.

"He your husband?" asked the sergeant.

"No, just a friend."

"Do you want him to join us?"

"Could he?" asked Alice hopefully. She and Harold might not see everything eye-to-eye, but he was certainly better than no one right now.

"Sure." Sergeant Crane called out to Harold. "Care to join us?"

Alice was surprised at how comforting it was to have Harold sitting next to her in Sergeant Crane's little office.

Harold reached over and squeezed her gloved hand as the sergeant turned on his computer and waited for the screen to warm up. "Don't worry," said the sergeant. "I'm sure we'll have you out of here in no time."

"Did you call my sisters yet?" she asked Harold with some uncertainty. She was not sure how eager she was to have them knowing her whereabouts.

"I haven't had a chance yet. Do you want me to do that now?"

"*Nooo*," she said slowly, "maybe not yet. I know Jane will be busy with dinner and—"

"Okay," interrupted the sergeant. "I need to ask a few more questions and run this through the computer."

So, for what seemed like a long time, she answered questions and waited while the sergeant went to attend to some other, obviously more pressing, matter.

Alice looked at her watch. "Goodness, it's six thirty," she said. She turned to Harold. "Perhaps you'd better call my sisters now. They may be worried."

"Right." He nodded. "There's a pay phone in the lobby."

He had just left when Alice realized that tonight was the ANGELs meeting and that the girls had planned to meet at the inn for their baking project, the project that Victoria was planning to participate in. *Good grief,* she thought, *could things get any worse?*

Soon Harold returned. "You're right, they were worried. I spoke with Louise."

"What did she say?"

"As you can imagine she was quite stunned by the news." He smiled.

Alice *could* imagine.

"I told her that if all went well, we'd have you home in no time."

She shook her head, swallowing against the lump now forming in her throat. "I don't know about that." A tear trickled down her cheek.

Harold pulled a clean white handkerchief from his pocket and handed it to her."Oh, come now, Alice. This isn't so bad, really."

"I know." She nodded and wiped her eyes. "It's just...I feel so...so stupid. I don't know why I decided to take on this thing. I mean, it seemed right at the time. But, really, this is just so unlike me."

He patted her hand. "Well, I've got a little confession to make, Alice."

She looked up at him in surprise.

"I decided to come out to the track early today. Just to look around, you know. After the things you'd said, well, I was curious." He cleared his throat. "I wandered over to the area where the trucks all park and they keep the dogs, back where the public isn't really supposed to be." He shook his head. "Well."

"Did you see something?"

He nodded sadly. "I saw a couple of things that made me realize this wasn't the kind of sport I want to support. I waited around for you until almost three o'clock, but I was so cold by then that I went into the concessions and got some coffee. Then, I met an old friend from my days in the service and we got to talking. Well, by the time I came back outside, there you were getting mobbed by the crazies."

Just then the sergeant came back. "Sorry to keep you, Miss Howard."

"That's all right." She forced a tiny smile to her lips.

"Well, let me run this now and see if you're wanted in any other states." He chuckled. "Not that we think you are. Your record is as clean as a whistle, Miss Howard. And I have good news. I called the track owner and he agreed not to press charges. However, you may not step on the property again."

Alice gave a smile and waited patiently. It was half past seven by the time she was released. She took a moment to phone home, concerned about what might be going on in Jane's kitchen with her ANGELs and Victoria Martin.

"Don't worry," Jane assured her. "Everything is under control."

"You sound a little stressed," said Alice.

Jane laughed. "You should talk, sister."

"What a day!" said Alice.

"You're telling me." Jane sighed. "We'll have a lot to talk about when you get here."

"Please, give my girls my apologies."

"Don't worry. We already did. They think you're a local hero now for saving the dogs."

"I didn't save anything," said Alice with disappointment.

"Watch out with that!" Jane suddenly yelped.

"Is everything okay?" asked Alice.

"Ashley's got her pigtail stuck in my Cuisinart," said Jane quickly. "Gotta go!"

Chapter Fifteen

I have to pick up my car," Alice told Harold as they pulled away from the police station. Fortunately, it had stopped snowing, at least for the moment.

"No problem," said Harold as he turned up his heater. "I don't recall seeing any security gates at the racetrack. We should be able to go right in and get your car." He glanced at her as they stopped at the red light. "Are you sure you're able to drive? You've had quite an afternoon."

"I should get it tonight," she said. "Just in case the snow is worse tomorrow."

"Do you work tomorrow?" he asked as he pulled into the parking lot at the track.

"My part-time workweek ended today," she told him. "Thank goodness. I usually work a half-day on Thursday, but I decided to take some vacation hours tomorrow."

He parked next to her car, then got out and helped her to scrape off the snow. "I'll follow you home," he said.

"Oh, I forgot," she said suddenly. "You don't like to drive after dark."

His grin showed up in his headlights. "Well, I figure if you can stand up to the racing fans and get yourself arrested and nearly thrown in jail, I should be able to drive back to Acorn Hill."

"We'll take it slowly," she promised. "The roads will be slick."

Alice kept a vigilant eye on the pair of headlights that followed her. She also prayed that God would get them both home safely as well as watch over whatever might be going on in Jane's kitchen.

By the time she parked her car in front of the inn, she felt as if she had been through a war. The little digital clock in her car said it was eight thirty, and she knew that was about the time when the ANGELs would normally be cleaning up. But nothing felt normal about this day.

"How are you doing?" she asked Harold as she waited for him to climb out of his car.

"Not too bad," he said as he walked over to her. "You know what?"

"What?" she asked as they walked up the front walk, their feet making crunching noises in the freshly fallen snow.

"Driving in the snow and the dark reminded me of back when I was flying reconnaissance during the war."

"Really?" She turned and peered at his face in the porch light.

He was beaming. "Yes, I actually found it invigorating and exciting."

She opened the door to the sounds of many voices. "My girls group is here tonight," she warned him. "You may want to make yourself scarce."

"Not on your life," he said as he removed his overcoat. "I'm just starting to like all this craziness."

"Miss Howard!" shrieked Ashley, who had heard the front door open and had come to investigate. "They let you out of jail."

Soon all her ANGELs were in the front hall clustered around her, hugging her and acting as if she had just survived a life-threatening experience.

"Did they really lock you up?" asked Jenny with wide eyes.

"Did you ride in a police car?" asked Sissy.

"Did you need a lawyer?" asked Linda.

"Slow down," said Alice as she quickly filled them in on the most basic details. "Now, I want to know what you girls have been up to. Last I heard, it sounded as if things were out of control in my sister's kitchen."

Alice pushed open the swinging doors and frowned. "This doesn't look good," she said to no one in particular.

"It's not our fault, Miss Howard," claimed Sissy. "It's Miss Martin who kept messing things up."

"*Miss Martin?*" Alice looked skeptically at her less-than-angelic ANGELs.

"That's the truth," said Jane as she emerged from the laundry room.

"Honestly," said Ashley as she twirled a pigtail that was coated with something like batter. "She's the messiest cook we've ever seen. She spilled flour and sugar all over the counters when she was measuring. Then she let three eggs roll off the counter and smash on the floor."

"Well, she is used to lots of helpers to measure and clean up," said Jane, unable to hide the satisfaction in her voice even as she made excuses for Victoria.

"Miss Martin isn't a very good baker," said Jenny in a quiet voice. "None of her things turned out right."

"Where is Miss Martin?" asked Alice with concern.

"She went to bed with a headache," said Ashley. "My mom does that a lot too, especially when I have friends over."

"Did we get any baking done for the Meads?" asked Alice.

"Oh yeah," said Jenny.

The girls pulled Alice over to the counter where a number of interesting items were cooling, taking time to point out which things they had helped to create.

"And there's still some things in the oven," said Sissy with pride.

Alice glanced at Jane, certain that any successes were a result of her sister's generous help. "Did you all tell Ms. Howard thank you?"

"Thank you, Ms. Howard," they all chanted.

To Alice's relief, the parents began to arrive to pick up their girls. Once the house had quieted down, Alice asked Harold if he was as hungry as she was.

"You two just sit down right here," said Jane, pointing to the kitchen table. "You tell me what happened at the racetrack while I warm up your dinners."

"Don't start without me," called Louise as she hurried into the kitchen. "I want to hear every word."

Alice and Harold recapped the story. Alice filled in the facts and Harold added the drama, and by the time they finished their late supper, Alice's story was told.

"My goodness," said Louise.

"We wanted to come," said Jane. "But then I heard that Victoria had arranged for a camera crew to be in my kitchen." She shook her head. "Well, I felt I had to get things in order."

Louise laughed as she waved her arm around the incredibly messy kitchen. "As if that mattered, Jane."

Jane rolled her eyes.

"I would have come," said Louise, "but it had started to snow over here, and you know how I hate driving on snow."

"Vera called," said Jane, "and said they had an emergency meeting at the school because of an outbreak of lice."

"*Ugh*," said Louise.

"Some of the ANGELs go to Vera's school," said Alice.

"Yes," said Jane, "but Vera said the outbreak was limited to the lower grades."

"Thank goodness," sighed Louise. "Just the thought makes me feel itchy."

Harold laughed. "Life never seems to slow down for you ladies." He stood up and saluted them. "Good night all."

"Was Cynthia down here for the baking project?" asked Alice.

"No, thank goodness," said Louise. "The poor girl was in her room trying to make heads or tails of what she and Victoria worked on today. It does not sound as if the book is coming along too well."

"And the week's almost over," said Alice.

"Just halfway," said Jane.

"Feels to me as though it should be over," said Louise in a weary voice.

Then they all said good night and went quietly up the stairs to their rooms, with hopes of enjoying a long winter's nap.

Chapter Sixteen

I heard about your little adventure yesterday," said Victoria when Alice came into the dining room for breakfast.

Alice forced a smile as she poured herself a cup of tea. "Yes, it was a rather startling day."

"Is that Alice?" called Jane as she emerged from the kitchen with a platter of tempting cheese blintzes.

"Sorry," said Alice, "I didn't mean to sleep so late."

Jane set the platter next to a bowl of shiny golden peaches that Alice knew Jane had canned herself last summer. "That's not it," said Jane. "I've just been dying to tell you what I discovered last night."

"Last night?" Alice felt confused.

"Yes." Jane sat down and poured herself a cup of coffee. "I couldn't sleep, and I decided to do some research online about greyhound racing."

"Everyone's getting into the act," said Harold as he lowered his newspaper.

"Well, maybe it's about time," said Jane. "The things I read and saw about the mistreatment of greyhounds made me absolutely sick. I even printed a few things out for you to read, Alice. Although I'd suggest you have your breakfast first."

"I wish you'd have let me know that you were staging a protest yesterday," said Victoria. "I might've been able to help you."

"Really?" Alice peered over her teacup at Victoria.

"Well, I'm sure Cynthia wouldn't have allowed me to attend it since we haven't made too much progress on the book yet." Victoria scowled. "But I might've been able to get you some publicity."

Alice frowned. "I'm not sure that would've helped much. I'm afraid I didn't make much of an impact standing there all by myself and holding up my one little sign."

"You made enough of an impact to get yourself arrested," said Jane. "That's nothing to sneeze at."

Alice smiled. "I guess not. To be honest, if I'd known that I was going to end up being fingerprinted at the Potterston police station, I might've reconsidered the whole thing from the start."

"I think you just went about it all wrong," said Victoria as she pushed away her now empty plate.

"I'm sure I did," agreed Alice, not eager to be lectured

by this woman who apparently considered herself to be an expert on all things—all things other than baking projects with giggling preteen girls. The thought made Alice smile.

"What you failed to do was plan," continued Victoria without noticing Alice's reaction. "You know what they say you should do when you fail to plan."

"Plan to fail," offered Alice automatically. This was something a certain hospital administrator liked to say repeatedly at work, not to Alice, of course, but she used that line on many of the more inexperienced nurses and aides.

"That's right," said Victoria. She glanced over at Cynthia now. "How firm is our book deadline, Cynthia?"

Cynthia's eyes widened. "It's pretty firm, Victoria."

"What if I spoke to Edward," said Victoria in a suddenly sweet voice. "What if I pleaded and begged him to give us just a few more days?"

"Why would you do that?" Cynthia's expression was a mix of confusion and exasperation.

"So that I could help your aunt with her greyhound protest."

Cynthia glanced at Alice. "Do you want help, Aunt Alice?"

Alice was at a loss for words. The truth was she

wanted to put this whole thing far, far behind her. "I—
uh—I'm not sure."

"Oh, it's perfectly understandable that you should
feel discouraged, Alice," said Victoria. "You meant well,
but it went wrong."

"What are you suggesting, Victoria?" asked Jane.

"I think Alice should let me contact my friends
and my connections, and we should all help her to stage
another protest. A protest during which no one gets
arrested, but which gets national press coverage."

"National press coverage?" repeated Alice, her
interest now growing.

"Of course." Victoria sat up straighter. "Whenever
you attach the name of Victoria Martin to a cause, you
can be assured of national press coverage. Now what
days do they have races?"

"The next race days are Friday and Saturday,"
offered Harold.

"Well, Friday is too soon, but Saturday might work,"
said Victoria. "If I get on the phone this morning and
get the wheels rolling."

"You'd do all that for me?" asked Alice in a meek
voice.

Victoria cleared her throat. "Nothing personal,
Alice, but I'd do *all that* for the dogs."

Alice nodded, feeling embarrassed. "Of course, that's what I meant."

Victoria smiled now. "Then it's settled?"

"Well, wait a minute," said Cynthia. "Nothing is settled until you get Mr. Wentworth to agree to delaying our deadline."

Victoria smiled. "No problem. Just leave Edward to me."

As usual, Victoria was right. By mid-morning her short phone call to the publisher had secured them five additional days to finish the book.

"Oh, Aunt Alice," said Cynthia as she told her mother and aunts the news. "I don't know whether to thank you or to scream."

"I'm sorry," said Alice.

"I'm with Cynthia," said Louise. "I do not know whether we should be happy or go pull our hair out. Do you realize that your greyhound protest means we must put up with Victoria Martin for five more days?"

"Hey," said Jane. "I'm the one who should be complaining the most."

"I'm sorry, Jane." Alice wondered what she could do to make it up to them.

"It's okay, Alice," said Jane. "After reading up on those poor dogs last night, I can see why you're concerned. I plan to help with the protest for sure."

"I want to help too," said Louise.

"I still have signs," said Alice hopefully.

"Maybe we can liven them up," offered Jane.

"Of course," said Alice. "You're the artist."

"Actually, I was thinking more about using some of the photos I found on the website. I could print them out on the printer. Maybe blow some of them up."

"If you don't mind, I'll stay home and work," said Cynthia. "Maybe I'll get more done without Victoria."

"That's fine, dear. I'll call Vera and a few others and make sure we get a good showing," said Alice.

"Maybe I should pack a picnic lunch and some hot beverages," suggested Jane.

"Do the dogs race in weather like this?" asked Louise. "We've got an inch of snow on the ground."

"According to what I read last night, they do," said Jane. "I read one story about how owners make their dogs run in such low temperatures that they get frostbitten feet and are killed because of it. They also suffer from heat strokes when it's hot out. It can be a cruel sport."

"Even Harold is starting to agree with us," said Alice as she relayed his experience at the track yesterday.

"Well, Alice," said Louise. "It looks like you've really started something here."

"I didn't start it," said Alice.

"But you're starting to get it noticed," said Louise. "And that's what counts."

Before the day was over, Alice had enlisted all kinds of support for her cause, from Carlene, who had been talking to everyone in town, to Vera, who had her fifth graders write letters and make posters and was considering a "field trip" to help with the protest. Even Alice's ANGELs were on board.

"My mom said she'll take a load of us in her van," said Ashley Moore when she called Alice that evening. "Just tell us when and where."

It was settled. Saturday at noon, the protesters would converge on public property, the sides of the street that led to the racetrack. The first race would not begin until one, but this would give them a chance to target the dog owners.

"I realize that not all greyhound owners are cruel to their dogs," said Alice at dinner, "but I think the good ones should take some responsibility here too."

"That's right," said Victoria. "If responsible owners know of cases of mistreatment, they should be required to report them." Then she went on to tell about all the contacts she had made and who would be attending the protest.

Suddenly Alice felt bad for Jane. She had made a perfectly lovely meal, but it seemed that talk of greyhounds was taking over and casting a negative light on everything. Alice decided to try to change the subject. "Did you manage to get any good photos last night, Victoria?" she asked.

Victoria's laughter had an edge of sarcasm to it. "Well, that remains to be seen." She exhaled loudly. "I suppose you heard what a fiasco that became, Alice."

"I heard it got a little crazy."

"I occasionally have children on my television show," said Victoria, "but it's always within a very calm and controlled environment. And, of course, we're never broadcasting live. We can always go back and edit our tapes and delete anything that doesn't work."

Alice chuckled. "Sometimes I wish life was like that."

"I'm with you," agreed Jane.

"Your girls, Alice, are a lively bunch, but I haven't the foggiest idea why you call them angels," said Victoria. "If you ask me, they are really a bunch of little devils."

Alice smiled. "Actually, ANGELs is an acronym."

"For what?" asked Victoria.

"Sorry, but you'd have to be an ANGEL to know that. Speaking of ANGELs," continued Alice, "they'll be joining us at the racetrack on Saturday."

"I suppose it wouldn't hurt to have some children present," said Victoria.

"Speaking of children," said Cynthia, "do you think

we could spend a couple of hours on the book this evening, Victoria?"

Victoria shrugged. "If you think it's necessary."

Cynthia looked like she was a pot that was close to boiling over. "I think so," she said in a tight voice.

As promised, Alice had been praying for the pair of them on a daily basis. She had been asking God to give them some sort of divine inspiration that would not only rescue Cynthia's job, but also lead to a wonderful book for children. Now she had a feeling she was asking for a real miracle.

Chapter Seventeen

*O*h my," said Jane on Friday morning as she and Alice fixed breakfast. "With all that's been going on with the dog-racing protest, I have completely forgotten about our sing-along tomorrow night."

"Oh dear," said Alice. "I'm afraid I did too. That'll be an awfully busy day. Have you already invited people?"

"Yes. To be honest, I wish we could postpone it to when Victoria is gone, but Cynthia is looking forward to it."

"Victoria still rubbing you wrong?"

Jane shrugged. "It's hard not to let that woman get to me."

"It's nice how she's helping with the protest."

"I suppose so, although I suspect it's mostly self-serving."

"You don't think she cares about the dogs?"

"Maybe, but I doubt that she would involve herself

if she didn't think it would improve her public image. Cynthia said that's why she's doing the children's book."

Alice finished squeezing the oranges that Jane had set out for juice. "Well, just the same, maybe it's good for Victoria."

"You mean to humanize her?"

Alice chuckled as she remembered how humble and human the protest had made her feel. "It couldn't hurt."

"I don't know," said Jane as she flipped a pancake. "With all her cameras and media people clustering around, she might just enjoy all the attention."

"Those cameras and media people will be good for the dogs."

Jane smiled. "As usual, you're probably right."

"Oh, Jane," said Alice. "I wish you wouldn't say that all the time." Then she described, in more detail, some of the things she had experienced on Wednesday.

"Good grief," said Jane as she piled the pancakes on the already warmed plate. "That must've been awful."

"It was one of my worst moments," said Alice. "Believe me, I was questioning myself even more than the police were. If Harold hadn't shown up when he did, I'm sure I would've just crumbled and sobbed."

"Poor Alice," said Jane as she patted her sister's back.

"You know what helped me to get through it, Jane?"

Alice now lowered her voice because she thought she heard someone in the dining room. "I thought about all the Bible heroes who had been persecuted for doing the right thing. I thought if they could endure what they went through, surely I could put up with a little discomfort and humiliation for those poor, helpless animals. Of course, compared to those of the Bible heroes, my cause was fairly insignificant."

"Well, I'm proud of you," said Jane.

After breakfast, Alice took time to write Mark Graves a letter. She knew that he would enjoy hearing about her effort—even if somewhat haphazard and ill-planned—in staging her first animal-protection protest. For Mark's sake, she took a more humorous approach as she described her detention at the police station. Then she decided to leave her letter unfinished until after Saturday's event. No one could know how that would turn out.

Since Jane insisted on carrying on with her sing-along party, and Louise planned to spend the morning getting groceries and running errands, Alice rolled up her sleeves and recruited herself as Jane's number-one KP person. "At your service," she told Jane with a mock salute.

Jane's plan was to prepare everything ahead of time. "Just in case we don't get back when we expect," said Jane.

"Oh, I think we should easily be back here by mid-afternoon," Alice assured her.

"Yes, but last time you thought you'd be back in time for ANGELs," Jane reminded her.

"Don't worry, I'm sure we won't end up in jail," said Alice, inwardly shuddering at the thought of a second arrest within the same week. If the police took her in again, they would probably lock her up.

"Well, I'd just rather have everything ready," said Jane.

"I think that's smart," agreed Alice. "I hope you'll feel free to leave the protest early if necessary."

"Yes, I might do that."

"*Yoo-hoo*," called Ethel from the back porch as she let herself in.

"Hey, Aunt Ethel," said Jane. "Did you come over to see our jailbird in person?"

"I heard all about it," said Ethel. "Our Alice is the talk of the town." Now she peered at Alice as if she thought the experience might have changed something about her. "Are you okay, Alice?"

Alice laughed. "Of course I'm okay. I'll admit it did shake me up some. I was just telling Jane if Harold hadn't been there to bail me out—"

"He had to *bail* you out?"

"Well, not literally. He was just there to lend moral

support, which I badly needed at the time." Alice paused. "Speaking of Harold?"

Ethel smiled. "Don't trouble yourself, Alice. Lloyd and I are working it all out."

"Good."

"In fact, I think I almost have him talked into escorting me to Jane's little party tomorrow night." She looked at Jane now. "It's still on, isn't it? I heard that half the town is planning some kind of march at the Potterston racetrack Saturday."

"At least half," said Jane, "but the party is still on."

"Oh good." Ethel clapped her hands. "I'm already working on outfits for Lloyd and me."

"What are they?" asked Jane.

"Top secret," said Ethel. "Need any help in here, girls?"

Soon Ethel was working with them and it did not take too long before Jane convinced her aunt to do her civic duty and attend the protest with them.

"I suppose I could go," said Ethel. "Lloyd was considering it, although he was a bit concerned about taking a political position on something like this."

"A political position?" asked Alice.

"Well, you know," said Ethel. "He was telling me that this whole animal-rights thing is very divisive among constituents."

"In Acorn Hill?" Alice was skeptical.

"Don't you remember the flap over Clara Horn's pig?"

Alice laughed. "That hardly seemed an animal-rights issue. Besides, I'd think the citizens of Acorn Hill would appreciate their mayor taking a stand against this kind of outrageous animal abuse."

"Yes, you're probably right, dear."

Just then, Cynthia burst through the swinging door. "It's useless," she said as she shook her head and helped herself to a gingersnap still warm from the oven. "That woman is totally insane."

"What's wrong now?" asked Jane as she wiped her hands on her apron and poured Cynthia a cup of coffee.

"She just doesn't get it," said Cynthia as she sank into a kitchen chair. "We were almost getting somewhere today. We decided to create this character, a little beaver that, of course, she wants to call Bucky."

"That's cute," said Ethel.

Cynthia frowned at her great aunt. "Cute, maybe, but not very original."

"Oh."

"But anyway, we're really starting to cook on this Bucky Beaver when Victoria suddenly suggests that we turn him into an otter. So, I'm trying to work with her, and I agree, but when I suggest we should consider another name, she won't budge. 'No,' she tells me in her I'm-the-boss tone, 'this is going to be Bucky Otter.'" Cynthia shook her head. "Bucky Otter!"

Jane and Alice laughed, but Ethel seemed to think that Bucky Otter was just fine.

"Can't she call him Oliver or Oscar?" suggested Jane.

"I'm afraid if I suggest a new name, she might change the animal on me. And we already started researching otters, which are really sort of cute."

"Maybe you could change his name later," said Alice. "Sometimes people do that when they have babies at the hospital. One day they're calling the baby Hortense after someone's great-grandmother, and the next day they've changed it to Hannah."

"That's not a bad idea, Aunt Alice," said Cynthia. "I could wait until the proof stage to suggest it."

"What's your story about?" asked Ethel.

Cynthia rolled her eyes. "Good question. The book is supposed to have to do with conservation, from an animal's perspective. At least that's where we are right now. I can't believe it's taken us nearly a week to get that far."

"That sounds like it has potential," said Alice hopefully.

"Maybe," said Cynthia. "Mind if I take some of these gingersnaps along with our morning tea?"

"Not at all," said Jane.

Jane fixed an appealing tea tray, complete with a little bouquet of flowers just delivered from Wild Things, and sent Cynthia back to her challenging task.

"Good luck with Bucky Otter," called Jane.

They heard Cynthia groan as she went through the swinging door.

"Poor Cynthia," said Alice.

"That's right," said Jane, "and the next time I start feeling sorry for myself for having to cook for that woman, I need to remember that at least I don't have to spend the whole day working on a book with her."

"Whatever they're paying Cynthia is probably not nearly enough."

"I still don't know what's wrong with Bucky Beaver," said Ethel.

Chapter Eighteen

What are you going to dress up as?" Jane asked Alice, as the two of them were finishing some of the party preparations Friday afternoon.

"Dress up?" repeated Alice as she put the large mixing bowl away.

"You know, for the party. Everyone is supposed to come as a favorite character from a musical."

"Oh, I guess I forgot. I can't even think of a musical offhand."

"Well, just remember back to when you were a kid and some musical that you really loved."

"The only one that comes to mind is *The Wizard of Oz.*"

"No!" said Jane as she closed the dishwasher. "You can't do that one."

Alice laughed. "I wasn't planning on it. It's just the only one I can think of at the moment."

"Sorry." Jane smiled. "It's just that I want to come as Dorothy. I already have the outfit. I did it once at the restaurant for Halloween. I even have these great ruby slippers."

"Oh, you'll be a perfect Dorothy," said Alice.

Jane studied Alice. "You could be another character from *The Wizard of Oz*."

"Which one?"

"How about Glinda?" offered Jane. "She was fair like you and very lovely."

Alice laughed. "Somehow I just don't see myself in a sparkling gown."

Jane considered this. "Well, how about the Scarecrow then?"

"The Scarecrow?" Alice nodded. "That wouldn't be too bad."

"I could lend you my overalls."

Alice waved her hand. "They would never fit."

"Don't be so sure, they're big on me."

"Well, we could try. After all, the scarecrow was supposed to be stuffed with straw, so maybe I can stuff myself into your overalls."

"We're all done in here for now," said Jane. "Want to traipse over to Sylvia's and see if we can find anything to inspire us?"

"Let's," said Alice, "I've been dying to put on my boots and try out that snow."

The two sisters acted like schoolgirls as they threw snowballs and laughed and joked on their way to town. Stopping at the Coffee Shop for hot cocoa, they were immediately questioned by Hope and several others about the upcoming protest.

"Is it really true that Victoria Martin is going to be at the racetrack?" asked Betsy Long.

"I already told her that's what your aunt told me just this morning," said Hope, teasing her friend, "but she just won't believe *me*."

"It's not that," said Betsy. "Ethel doesn't always get her facts straight."

Jane nodded. "She is a dear, but I'd have to agree with you."

"Hope is right on the money," said Alice. "Victoria Martin is planning to make an appearance."

"So, do you think we'll get to meet her if we go?" asked Betsy. "I mean that might give us some added incentive."

"We can't promise anything," said Alice. "Really, I think it's best that you come out of support for the cause. Those poor dogs need someone to defend them."

"Right," said Betsy. "I know that, but I just think it would be thrilling to meet Victoria Martin too. I always try to watch her show whenever I'm not working."

"Speaking of which," hinted Hope.

"Oh yeah, I better go," said Betsy as she glanced at the clock. "This was supposed to be a break. See you all on Saturday."

"I hope people aren't disappointed," said Jane in a quiet voice once the two of them were settled into a corner booth.

"In what?"

"In Victoria. I mean, she can be a little rude sometimes."

"A bit abrupt," added Alice as she sipped her cocoa.

"It'll be sad if she hurts anyone's feelings."

"Well..." Alice sighed. "I guess we can't control that."

"Hey," called Carlene from the front of the coffee shop. "There you are."

They both looked up.

"You, Alice Howard," said Carlene as she came their way. "The woman of the hour."

"Oh, I don't know—"

"Don't act modest, Alice. What you did Wednesday was one of the bravest things I've ever witnessed...from a local anyway."

Alice shrugged. "I just did what I felt I should. Really, it wasn't much. To be perfectly honest, it was pretty embarrassing down at the jail."

"Mind if I join you girls?"

"Not at all," said Jane, scooting over to make room.

Carlene laid a large envelope on the table. "I just thought you might like to see these photos." She opened it up and slid out several black and white shots of Alice being surrounded by the angry racing fans.

"Oh my," said Alice, as she suddenly remembered how overwhelming it had really been.

"Wow!" said Jane. "I didn't realize that they'd really surrounded you like that." She pointed to a particularly angry man. "Look at that guy. It looks like he's about to hit you."

Alice felt a shudder go through her.

"These are good, Carlene," said Jane. "What are you going to do with them?"

"I wrote a story for our paper, but then I decided to make it available to the AP, and it's actually getting picked up by some papers around the state. Of course, I'm making mention of the next protest and how your friend Victoria Martin will be on hand to make a statement."

"Our friend?" Alice frowned. "I wouldn't go that far."

"Your guest, whatever. I don't think it really matters. The point is, people are paying attention. The event on Saturday promises to be a big deal." She grinned. "All because of you, Alice."

"Well..." Alice shrugged again.

"My sister is so modest," said Jane. "I'd probably be signing autographs for everyone."

"I won't take any more of your time," said Carlene, standing. "I just thought you might like to know. Make sure you get a copy of the *Philadelphia Inquirer* tomorrow, Alice."

"Thanks, Carlene." Alice waved, then shook her head. "Goodness, it just keeps getting bigger."

"Does that make you uncomfortable?"

"Well, sort of, actually."

"Then just remember, it's for the dogs."

Alice brightened. "Yes, you're absolutely right, Jane. It's for the dogs."

"In fact, we could even say that we're going to the dogs."

Alice grinned.

"Speaking of going, we'd better head over to Sylvia's now."

They spent a pleasant hour visiting with Sylvia and picking out a few things for Alice's scarecrow costume. Alice was content to let Jane take the lead in this since all things creative seemed to come under Jane's jurisdiction.

"Are you sure you have time for this?" she asked as they walked through the snow toward home. "I know you've got a lot on your plate right now, Jane."

"This will be simple really," Jane assured her. "Mostly just sewing on a few patches and making your burlap head cover-up. Unless you'd rather just wear makeup."

"I think it'd be fun to look as much like the original scarecrow as possible," said Alice.

"Good." Jane smiled. "I was hoping you'd get into the spirit of things."

"What's Louise going to dress as?" asked Alice.

"I'm not sure," said Jane, "but if she's willing, I'd love to talk her into being Glinda, the good witch. There are still some old prom dresses in the attic that could be worked into something suitable."

"Well, if anyone can talk Louise into this, it would be you."

"I don't know, Alice." Jane winked at her. "Lately, it seems like you've become the sister with the power of persuasion."

"How's that?"

"Well, look at what you've got going for everyone on Saturday."

Alice shook her head. It was ironic that she of all people should be the one to get something like this rolling. Really, who would have guessed?

Chapter Nineteen

After Jane and Alice returned to the inn that afternoon, they turned their attention to costumes for Saturday's party. "I feel silly," complained Louise as Jane adjusted the inserts she had fashioned to make the old prom dress fit. "You look lovely," said Alice. "That color suits you, Louise."

Jane had set up her sewing station in the kitchen so that she could keep an eye on her various baking projects for the party.

"I can't believe I agreed to do this," said Louise.

"You make a perfect Glinda," said Alice. "Even your hair is the right color."

"Was Glinda's hair silver?" asked Louise.

"Well," Alice said, "it was light."

"I have a blond wig for you to wear," Jane mumbled through the pins in her mouth.

"I do not want to wear a wig," said Louise. "That is going too far."

"Why do *you* have a blonde wig, Jane?" asked Alice as she turned a page of the *Inquirer.*

Jane laughed. "Oh, I don't know. I was going through a phase."

"Hey, look at this," said Alice suddenly. She held up the newspaper so that they could see the black and white photo of her being mobbed by the angry racing fans. Louise adjusted her glasses and leaned forward to see.

"Oh my word!" she exclaimed.

"Wow," said Jane, "you really are a celebrity now."

"Not a very flattering photo," said Louise.

"Well, no."

"It's dramatic," said Jane as she returned to her pinning, "and that's what gets people's attention."

"I'm not sure I like this heading," said Alice. "*Animal Rights Activist Protests in Potterston.* I'm not really an animal rights activist. I don't belong to any organizations."

"Maybe they'll start recruiting you now," suggested Jane.

Then Alice read the article aloud to them. It was generally positive. "I wouldn't have minded if they'd left out my arrest," she said as she folded the paper and looked back at her sisters.

"That adds to the sympathy factor," said Jane as

she placed the last pin and stepped back to admire her work. "You almost don't notice the inserts on the sides."

"I told you I would not fit into this old dress," said Louise.

"It wasn't that far off," Jane reminded her. "Not bad for, what, fifty years ago."

"Not quite." Louise stood straighter.

"What's going on in here?" said a familiar, but not necessarily welcome, voice. Alice turned in time to see Victoria coming through the swinging doors with Cynthia following her.

"We're doing a fitting," said Alice quickly. She stood up and attempted to send Cynthia a signal that this was not the best time to bring Victoria into the kitchen. She felt bad, since her job was to keep anyone from entering the kitchen during the fitting.

"Let's see," said Victoria, pushing past Alice.

Alice turned and saw her older sister's eyes flash with anger.

"Why in the world are you dressed like that, Louise?" demanded Victoria as if she had a right to know.

Louise scowled. "It is supposed to be my costume for the party tomorrow night. But I am not sure that I am—"

"Come on, Louise," pleaded Jane. "You said you'd do this." She turned to Victoria and Cynthia. "We wanted it to be a surprise, but we're doing *The Wizard of Oz*. I'm coming as Dorothy. Alice is the Scarecrow. And we want Louise to be Glinda."

"Which is perfectly ridiculous," said Louise.

"*Hmmm.*" Victoria nodded as she walked closer and seemed to study the dress. "You should put some glitter on the skirt," she suggested.

"Yes," said Jane, "that's my plan."

"*Oz?*" said Victoria with interest. "That's one of my favorite movies."

"What are you planning to dress as, Victoria?" asked Jane.

"I haven't had a chance to really consider it." Victoria shook her head. "It's a shame because I have some wonderful costumes at home, but none that are from musicals."

"I remember watching your Halloween show last year," said Jane. "You wore a pretty convincing witch costume."

Victoria nodded, then suddenly looked at Jane as if she had just struck gold. "That's it!" she exclaimed. "I could be the Wicked Witch of the West."

Jane grinned. "Oh, Victoria, that would be perfect. Would you like to join our cast for Oz?"

"Yes." Victoria nodded. "I'll call my assistant right

this minute and have him ship the costume to me overnight."

"Now *I'm* feeling left out," said Cynthia sadly. "Everyone has a part in Oz except me. Maybe I could dress up like Toto."

"No," said Jane. "I already have a little stuffed Toto to carry in my wicker basket."

"Well, there's still the Tin Man," said Victoria. "Although that might be difficult to pull off this late in the game."

"And the Cowardly Lion," offered Alice.

"You'd make a cute lion," said Jane. "I have some brown sweats that would probably work okay. I could make you a tail and trim the hood with yellow yarn like a lion's mane."

"Do you really have time for that, Aunt Jane?" asked Cynthia hopefully.

"I do as long as you all agree to one thing."

"What's that?" asked Cynthia.

"We all have to sing 'We're Off to See the Wizard' together."

Although her sisters protested that they would all go off-key if Jane sang, they finally agreed, and Victoria and Cynthia went back to work on their children's book.

"Cynthia said that the book is getting steadily worse," said Louise after the two went back to the library.

"Well, maybe delaying the deadline was a good idea after all," said Jane. "Now, turn around, Louise. I want to see if it's hanging straight."

Jane chuckled as her sister turned slowly around.

Louise frowned when she faced Jane. "Are you laughing at me?"

"No, no." Jane emphatically shook her head.

"Well, what then?" Louise looked unconvinced.

"Victoria," sputtered Jane. "Playing the Wicked Witch of the West. It's priceless!"

"I thought that would amuse you," said Alice.

"It is rather fitting," Louise said.

"Talk about typecasting," said Jane. "She won't even have to act to carry it off."

Later in the afternoon, Alice came up with an idea to help Jane. She decided to invite her ANGELs to serve at the party. "I thought they could dress up like Munchkins," said Alice.

"Oh, that'd be so adorable," said Jane, "and the extra help would be great."

Alice called up Ashley Moore and explained her idea, then asked her to call the others.

"Sure, Miss Howard," said Ashley eagerly. "I think that sounds like fun."

"Do the best you can with the costumes," Alice told her. "Do you even know what a Munchkin is?"

"Of course," said Ashley. "Everyone's seen *The Wizard of Oz*. We have the movie. I saw it, like, a zillion times when I was a little kid. I know all the songs by heart."

Alice smiled. "Good. Maybe you'll want to sing for us."

"Do you think we could sing the Munchkin song?" asked Ashley eagerly.

"I don't see why not. You talk to the other girls about it."

"Cool."

Alice was about to hang up when Ashley asked about the protest on Saturday.

"Yes, it's still on."

"Good, we're planning on coming. Hey, my mom showed me your article in the newspaper, Miss Howard. That was so cool."

Alice laughed. "Cool?"

"Yeah, it's like you're famous now."

After Alice hung up she wondered if this would be her fifteen minutes of fame. Not that she had ever wanted to be famous, but it was not so bad either.

Chapter Twenty

As Alice walked toward the stairway, she heard a sound coming from the hall. She turned to see Harold standing in the shadows with a package in his arms.

"Pssst," he said with his forefinger over his lips.

"What is it?" she whispered.

"Can you meet me in the parlor?"

She nodded and then looked over her shoulder as if she was worried that someone was listening. Of course she had no idea why she should care. Just the same, she tiptoed as she followed Harold into the parlor. Once in the parlor, he closed the door and set his package on a chair. "I need some help," he told her.

"Doing what?"

He sat down and began opening his package. "I wanted to keep this as a surprise until tomorrow night," he said. "I had Sylvia Songer help me with a costume, but she didn't have time to hem the pants. Do you know how to sew, Alice?"

She smiled. "I do."

He sighed in relief as he pulled out a pair of red and white striped pants and handed them to her.

"Wow," she said as she held up the satiny trousers. "These are bright."

He grinned. "I know. Wait until you see the whole outfit."

"So, who are you coming as?" She could see another garment in the bag that was royal blue. "Uncle Sam?"

"Close. *Yankee Doodle Dandy*. It's my favorite musical."

"It looks like Sylvia already pinned them up," said Alice as she examined the bottoms of the trousers. "This shouldn't take very long."

"Do you mind?" He looked hopeful. "I expect to pay you."

She waved her hand at him. "No, you don't need to do that." Then she got an idea. "Do you know how to sew at all, Harold?"

He shook his head. "I can't even thread a needle."

"Well, instead of just hemming these, I'm going to give you a little sewing lesson. How does that sound?"

He nodded. "That sounds great. I often wished that I'd had Lily give me a little instruction before she passed away, but she got so weak from her treatments."

"If you're going to be a bachelor, you should learn at

least how to sew on a button and a few other tricks," Alice told him.

"I'd like that."

"Let me get my sewing basket."

"I'll be right here."

It was not long before Harold's Uncle Sam trousers were hemmed: one leg by Alice and the other by Harold. She even taught him how to sew on a button.

"Why, this is easy as pie," said Harold as he tied off the last knot.

"Have you ever made a pie?"

He grinned sheepishly. "Well, no. I'm even worse in the kitchen."

"What do you do for food when you're home?" she asked.

"Frozen dinners mostly."

She made a face and said, "I have another idea."

He smiled. "I think I like it already."

After a brief conversation with Jane, it was agreed that Harold would perform KP duty for dinner that night. This actually worked out well, since Alice was able to use the time to create more posters for the protest the next day. She just hoped it would not hurt the quality of the food—Jane was having a hard enough time with Victoria's negative commentary on her meals without actually having something wrong with the dinner.

"Everything okay in here?" asked Alice shortly before dinnertime.

"It's great," said Jane. "Harold is a natural."

"Oh, I don't know about that, but it is sort of fun. Plus, Jane lets me have samples. That in itself is a good incentive to work."

"Harold has practically made the cobbler single-handedly."

"I wouldn't say that." He laughed. "Of course, if it turns out well, I expect to take all the credit."

"And if it doesn't?" Jane pointed a wooden spoon at him with a threatening look in her eye.

He nodded. "I'll take the blame."

Jane laughed. "Glad we got that clear."

"Actually, you can blame anything you like on me," he offered, "although I don't know why you'd need to do that. As far as I'm concerned, your cooking is flawless."

"Well, thank you."

As Alice set the table in the dining room, she listened to the happy banter between Harold and Jane in the kitchen. Not for the first time, she sincerely thanked God for Grace Chapel Inn and the way it had ministered to the needs of the guests—as well as the sisters—over the past year. It was really quite amazing, beyond what any of them had hoped or dreamed.

"Is that dinner I smell?" asked Cynthia as she stuck her head into the dining room.

"It is." Alice smiled at her niece. "Are you done for the day?"

"I think so." Cynthia stepped in and looked around approvingly. "This room is always so pretty in the evening, with the candlelight, crystal and china. May I help with anything?"

"You can fill the water glasses," said Alice as she folded a napkin precisely.

Soon Cynthia returned with the water pitcher. "Victoria went to her room to freshen up," she said as she filled a glass. "I think she just needed a break from me. I know that I need one from her."

"Well, as you said, maybe it'll help to have her gone for a while tomorrow," said Alice. "It will give you some time to yourself."

Cynthia nodded. "I just wish I had something that was worthwhile to work on."

"How's Bucky Otter doing?"

Cynthia groaned. "He no longer exists. Now we have Rocky Robin."

"Well, at least that has something of a ring to it."

"I guess, but now I can't get Victoria off the

early-bird-gets-the-worm theme."

"Oh."

"I'm already starting to imagine what it's going to feel like to go job hunting next week."

Alice patted Cynthia on the back. "Oh, don't give up yet."

She sighed. "It's hopeless, Aunt Alice. There is no way I am going to pull a book out of all the garbled notes that we've accumulated this past week. I could more easily pull a rabbit from my hat."

"Well, I'm praying for you both," said Alice. "I believe God is going to help you come up with something."

"Thanks, Aunt Alice. I really hope you're right."

Soon they were all seated around the dinner table. Tonight was Alice's turn to say grace.

"Dear heavenly Father, we thank You for all Your gracious blessings on our lives, and we thank You for the food that's been so lovingly prepared by Jane and Harold. We ask that You bless it to our use. Amen."

"Amen."

Victoria looked slightly startled. "Did I hear you say that Harold helped to fix dinner?"

Alice smiled. "That's right. He was having a cooking lesson with Jane."

"A little bachelor home ec," said Jane. "And he did

very well. I'd give him an A plus."

"He also had a little sewing lesson today," added Alice. "I'd give him an A plus in that too."

He winked at Victoria. "I think they're just trying to make me take care of myself so that they can send me on my way."

She smiled at him. "Oh, I don't see how that can be, Harold. It seems to me everyone is enjoying your company." She glanced over at Alice now. "Although, if it were I, I'd still want to keep you a helpless bachelor."

He frowned. "Why's that?"

"So you'll be more in need of a woman's abilities."

Alice wondered if Victoria was actually flirting with Harold. However, Harold seemed to like it.

Finally it was time for Harold's creation. He went into the kitchen with Jane and emerged with a large peach cobbler that looked just as if Jane had made it. Of course, Alice knew from experience that Jane had probably stood over him each step of the way, making sure he was doing everything just right.

"Looks delicious," said Louise.

"You know what they say," said Harold as he began to serve it onto dessert plates. "The proof of the pudding is in the eating."

He put a generous dollop of whipped cream on each

one, and Jane came out with coffee and tea.

"This is excellent," said Victoria. Suddenly the room got unexpectedly quiet. It was the first compliment she had given at any meal.

Jane stared at Victoria with a slight frown but said nothing.

Louise nodded. "It is very good. Harold makes it nearly as well as Jane."

Jane gave Louise a half smile.

Before long the dessert plates were empty, and Alice was helping Jane to clear the table. Everyone else had retired to the parlor to listen to Louise play the piano. They had agreed to classical music tonight since they all knew that tomorrow night would be nothing but show tunes.

"That woman!" said Jane as she set a stack of dishes in the sink.

"Don't let her get to you," said Alice.

"How can I not?"

"Just remember that Victoria would feel threatened if she actually admitted that you were an excellent cook, Jane. You know that has to be it."

"I suppose you're right, but it's still irritating."

"I know."

"Just when I think I've got a handle on it and I'm not

going to let that woman get under my skin, she gets me."

Alice laughed. "Maybe God is trying to teach you something."

"What?"

"That you must do what you do to please Him, not Victoria Martin."

"I know. I know."

Alice filled the kettle with fresh water and put it on the stove.

"So," said Jane. "Did you see Victoria flirting with Harold tonight?"

"Do you think she really was?"

"I do." Jane nodded. "How funny would that be?"

"He must be nearly twenty years older than she," said Alice as she turned on the flame.

"He's such a sweet old guy." Jane frowned. "In fact, I think he's way too good for someone like Victoria. Too bad Louise isn't attracted to him."

"I'm glad Louise didn't hear that."

"You're right. Please, don't tell her."

Chapter Twenty-One

$\mathcal{A}$lice got up early on Saturday morning so that she could walk with Vera. Because of their hectic schedules, they had only walked once earlier in the week. She was surprised to see Victoria when she came down the stairs to the second floor.

"You're up early, Victoria."

"As you are." Victoria looked at her. "Do you jog like your sister Jane?"

Alice laughed. "No, but I do try to walk three times a week."

"Really?" said Victoria. "So do I. Unfortunately I haven't managed to do that this week." She patted her ample hips. "That and your sister's rich food are playing havoc with my figure."

As badly as Alice wanted to just slip out the door and hurry over to Vera's, she knew the proper thing to do would be to invite Victoria. "Would you like to join us?" she asked meekly.

"Us?"

"Yes, I walk with my friend Vera."

"Do you think Vera would mind if I came?"

"No, I'm sure she'd love to meet you."

"Well, just let me go and change my shoes," said Victoria.

Alice went downstairs to wait. She considered calling Vera to warn her but did not want to risk being overheard by Victoria.

"All ready," said Victoria as she came down the stairs in a fancy pair of athletic shoes.

It was cold and crisp outside, but the snow from Thursday was nearly gone.

"I hope we get snow again soon," said Alice.

Victoria looked up at the clear morning sky. "Well, fortunately, I don't think that's going to happen today. I would not enjoy protesting at the dog races during a blizzard."

"No, I don't think I would either."

"Now, who is this friend Vera?"

"She teaches fifth grade," said Alice. "Her husband Fred runs the local hardware store."

"Must be nice," said Victoria.

"To run a hardware store? Or teach?" Alice felt confused.

"Neither," said Victoria. "Well, and both, I mean it must be nice to live such an ordinary life."

"Oh." Alice wondered how Vera would feel about that kind of description of her life.

"Sometimes I wonder what my life would be like if I hadn't become so well known and successful. Now I can hardly go anywhere or do anything without everyone knowing me by name. It's really a hardship, you know."

"I really wouldn't know," said Alice. "Although some of my ANGELs feel certain that I must be a celebrity now that I've had my picture in the *Inquirer*."

Victoria made a noise that sounded similar to laughter. "Oh, there are plenty of benefits to my life," continued Victoria. "All my homes and my travels and being treated with respect wherever I go, but still...sometimes one wonders."

"This is Vera's house," said Alice, waving at Vera in her kitchen window.

Alice introduced the two women, quickly explaining to Vera that Victoria had decided at the last minute to join them. "I assured her you wouldn't mind," she said.

"Not at all," said Vera with a cheerful smile. "Not everyone can say they've walked with Victoria Martin."

Victoria sniffed. "Yes, I was just saying to Alice how fortunate you both are to be able to live such simple lives."

Vera's brows lifted slightly. "Simple?" she repeated.

Victoria waved a cashmere-gloved hand at her. "Oh, it's not a bad thing. I mean that you get to go about your daily tasks and chores without constantly being recognized by the public."

"Oh." Vera nodded as if she understood, but Alice suspected she was only being polite. It was fortunate that she and Vera had both decided to do only a short walk. Thirty minutes would be more than enough time if the conversation continued like this.

"Are we walking too fast for you?" asked Vera.

"No, not at all. I actually go much faster than this when I'm with Rob and Roy."

"Rob and Roy?" echoed Vera.

"Oh, those are my dogs," said Victoria. "My babies."

"I see."

"A pair of beautiful Doberman pinschers," said Victoria. "Oh, how I miss the boys."

"Victoria is going to the protest with us today," said Alice.

"So I've heard," said Vera. "Should be quite an event."

"Yes," agreed Victoria. "Certainly it will be much better attended than poor Alice's last effort."

"Well, at least Alice got the wheels rolling," said Vera generously. "I would've gone myself, but we had, uh, other pressing matters to attend to at my school."

"That's right," said Victoria. "Alice says you are a teacher. How nice."

"I'm not sure that I'd call it nice," said Vera, "but I do find it fulfilling. I must say I love the children."

"I'm writing a children's book," said Victoria.

"Really?" said Vera with interest, although Alice knew good and well that this was old news to Vera. "How's it coming?"

Victoria frowned. "Not too well, I'm afraid. My editor and I just can't seem to see eye-to-eye."

"Have you written other books for children?" asked Vera.

"Well, no, but I have written cookbooks and decorating books and even one on gardening."

"Do you know much about children?" asked Vera.

"As much as anyone, I suppose."

Vera nodded. "Do you have children or grandchildren?"

"Oh no." Victoria shook her head. "I never had time for that."

"I see."

"I don't think that matters so much. My publisher has full confidence in my ability to carry this off."

"Right." Vera looked amused now. "Have you read many children's books?"

"Well, no. There's been no reason to."

"Maybe it would help if you read some," suggested Vera.

"You know, that's not a bad idea," said Victoria. "I wonder where I could get some."

"I have quite a few picture books still," said Vera. "They're too young for my fifth graders, but I'm saving them for my grandchildren."

"You have grandchildren?" asked Victoria.

"Not yet. But I have two grown daughters and I expect it's only a matter of time. Although I'm in no hurry."

"Perhaps you could pick out some of the better books and lend them to me," said Victoria.

"Sure." Vera wore an expression that Alice could not read, but she seemed perplexed about something.

"How's Fred?" asked Alice.

"Okay," said Vera. "Although he's worried that the new snow shovels haven't arrived yet. He's sure that we're going to have the big snow any day now, and every year he gets at least a dozen people coming in to replace their snow shovels." Vera chuckled. "Now, if they weren't such tightwads and bought the sturdy metal ones in the first place, they wouldn't have to replace them so often. But then those plastic ones are temptingly cheap."

"Why does your husband carry cheap plastic snow shovels?" asked Victoria.

"Because that's what some people want," said Vera. "Of course, he always has the good ones too."

The threesome got quiet as they did the return loop back toward Vera's house. Vera seemed to be concentrating hard on something.

"Do you and Fred have your costumes for tonight?" asked Alice as Vera's house came within sight.

"We do," said Vera. "I'm coming as Molly Brown and Fred is coming—now don't laugh—as Moses."

"Moses?" said Victoria. "*The Ten Commandments* was not a musical."

"I know." Vera shook her head. "I've tried and tried to tell him, but he just won't listen. The truth is Fred hates musicals."

"But why Moses?" asked Alice.

"*The Ten Commandments* is his favorite movie," said Vera as they reached her front yard. "Besides, it was easy. He's just wearing his bathrobe over his clothes with a stick-on beard." Her brow furrowed slightly as she glanced up at her house, and that was when Alice knew exactly what was bothering her good friend. Vera was a busy full-time schoolteacher and was not overly fond of domesticities. She was probably not eager to have Victoria Martin walking through her house and seeing how "ordinary" people lived. Alice knew for a fact that what little cleaning was done at the Humberts was usually done on Saturdays.

"Why don't you go through your picture books and drop them by the inn later today," suggested Alice.

"That's a good idea," said Vera, looking considerably relieved. "I'll do that on my way to the protest rally. Did I tell you that several of my fifth graders asked to go with me? I think it's important that they're taking an interest in something like this."

"Well," said Victoria, pausing as if to catch her breath. "What kind of children don't love and care about dogs?"

"That's true," said Vera.

"See you later," said Alice.

"Nice meeting you," called Victoria as they turned around and began heading back to the inn.

"Are you getting winded?" asked Alice, slowing down a bit. She would feel horrible if Victoria Martin keeled over from a heart attack.

"I'm all right," Victoria said, huffing slightly.

Alice slowed it down a bit more.

"Your friend seems nice," said Victoria. "Although I don't know how she can stand the color of her house. I think it is absolutely hideous."

Alice had never been crazy about the mustard yellow, but she would never dream of mentioning this to Vera. "The color is a common one for old homes in this part of the country. But it wasn't something Vera chose. Fred used that paint because of a mix-up at the hardware store a few years back. Apparently a customer had ordered the wrong paint number and when he saw the color, he was very upset and wanted something else."

"*Oops.*"

"Fred had already mixed about twenty gallons of it. The original color was a bright canary yellow, but Fred managed to tone it down to a more traditional shade."

"It was the customer's mistake," said Victoria as they reached the walk. "He should've made him pay for it."

"Fred's not like that."

"Amazing that man can stay in business."

"He put the paint on sale, but by the end of the summer it was still sitting there. Fred knew his own house needed painting, so finally he just decided to use it himself."

"Good grief," said Victoria. "I wouldn't paint my house that color if someone offered me millions to do it."

By now they were at the front door, and Alice was greatly relieved. "Excuse me," she told Victoria. "I'm going to run up and take a shower now."

"See you at breakfast," said Victoria as she flopped herself down on the bench in the foyer. "I hope we didn't wear you out," called Alice.

"Not," she gave a little gasp, "at all."

Chapter Twenty-Two

When Alice came to breakfast, only Jane and Louise were still there. "Where's everyone?" she asked as she sat down and poured herself a cup of tea.

"Harold went to town for something," said Louise, "and Victoria went to her room looking somewhat fatigued."

"Oh dear," said Alice. "She walked with Vera and me, and I'm afraid we went too fast. I hope she's okay."

"I'm sure she's fine. Cynthia didn't even seem to mind. She's getting caught up on her e-mail."

"Quiche?" offered Jane as she handed the pie plate to Alice. "I figured we'd better fortify ourselves this morning," said Jane. "It's going to be a long day."

"It's cold out there," said Alice. "Don't forget to put on your long johns."

"Hey, that's not a bad idea," said Jane.

"I don't own long johns," said Louise.

"I've got some you can borrow," offered Alice.

Louise poured herself another cup of coffee and sighed. "I'll be glad when things settle down and we can get back to an ordinary routine."

"What is ordinary?" asked Jane.

"According to Victoria, we are," said Alice.

"*Yoo-hoo*," called Ethel from the kitchen, "anyone home?"

"In the dining room," called Jane.

"Oh, I thought you'd be done with breakfast by now."

"We're just enjoying a bit of leisure while we can," said Jane. "Make yourself at home."

"Thank you." Ethel removed her jacket, poured herself a cup of coffee and sat down next to Alice. "I thought you'd all be glad to know that everything is just fine between Lloyd and me."

"That's good," said Alice.

"So, Lloyd's not going to be coming around here and challenging Harold to a duel or anything?" teased Jane.

"No, of course not." Ethel chuckled. "Although Lloyd is not overly fond of our Harold. He wants to know exactly how long he plans to stay."

"I was wondering that myself," said Louise.

"Oh, he's just lonely," said Jane.

"Even so, I'm sure he's not planning on taking up residency in the inn," said Ethel.

"Well, he at least has to stay until our little party," said Jane. "After all, he's our main entertainment."

"I suppose," said Ethel. "I'll just have to make sure to keep him and Lloyd safely apart tonight."

"Really, Auntie," said Jane. "I can't imagine that Lloyd would have any hard feelings toward our sweet Harold."

Ethel patted her hair. "Lloyd Tynan, it seems, is a very possessive man when it comes to me."

"So how's his bowling coming?"

"Oh, I think he may be getting bored with it. He told me that he really dislikes coming home smelling like an ash tray every bowling night. It seems there is a bar right next to their lanes and the smoke drifts over."

"Sounds lovely," said Louise.

"So, I'm hoping he'll give it up before long."

"Did you get your costume yet?" asked Jane.

Ethel smiled. "Actually, I'm still working on both our costumes."

"Both?"

"Lloyd and I are coming together."

"As what?" asked Louise.

"Oh, I can't tell," said Ethel coyly. "It's supposed to be a surprise."

"Speaking of Lloyd," began Alice, "did he make up his mind yet?"

"His mind?"

"About coming to the protest today."

"Oh, that." Ethel made a face. "Now, it's not that I don't like dogs, because I do, in their place, which isn't in my house. But, growing up on a farm and then marrying a farmer, well, I just don't go in for all this animal-rights business. The next thing you know we'll all be eating soy burgers and wearing pleather." She grinned. "I read that in one of my magazines."

"This isn't exactly about animal rights," said Alice. "It's more about preventing the cruel and inhumane treatment of racing dogs. You should see some of the photos that Jane's found on the Internet."

"Yes," said Jane. "It's really appalling."

"Be that as it may, Lloyd and I have both decided it's for the best to avoid the protest today. I told him that I would tell you and that you'd all understand. You do, don't you?"

"Well," said Alice as she picked up her plate, "I think if you knew more about this, you'd—"

"You have to look at my photos, Aunt Ethel," said Jane as she got up.

Even from the kitchen, Alice could hear her aunt still talking to Louise. "It's not that I don't care," she told her. "It's just that I think all these claims of dog abuse are a little overblown."

"Oh, but I don't think—"

"We all know that Alice is a very sensitive person," said Ethel. "She can barely even kill a spider. I've seen her trap one in a mason jar and then let it loose in the garden. We can't all be like that."

Louise said something in response, but Alice could not hear her as she turned on the sink faucet and began rinsing plates and loading them into the dishwasher. It was odd, thought Alice, that her own aunt was taking an opposing position, but someone like Victoria Martin was supportive. Then, Ethel often held opinions that differed from Alice and her sisters. *No need to obsess over it*, she told herself as she closed the door to the dishwasher.

"Oh my word!" said Ethel, loud enough to be heard over the water running in the sink.

Alice turned off the faucet, dried her hands and hurried out to the dining room to see what the problem was. Without saying anything, she simply stood in the doorway and watched. Jane had spread her posters with the blown-up photos from the Internet across the dining room table in a most dramatic fashion.

"*Oh dear!*" Ethel looked horrified, her hand clasped

over her mouth, as she looked from poster to poster of suffering and deceased greyhound dogs.

"Goodness," said Louise sadly. "They look even more pitiful when the photos are enlarged."

Ethel shook her head. "*Tsk-tsk.* I had no idea."

"See," said Jane, pointing her finger with conviction. "It's a lot more serious than most people assume."

"I can see I was wrong," said Ethel.

Alice slipped back into the kitchen to finish cleaning up. She knew there was no need for her to say anything. The photos were shocking, even to Alice, who had seen most of them before.

Finally Ethel came into the kitchen and patted Alice on the back. "Don't you worry, dear," she told her. "I'm going to go call Lloyd the minute I get home. I expect we'll both be there today."

"Thanks," said Alice with a grateful smile.

"I really didn't believe it was that bad."

"Most people don't."

"I want to bring Lloyd over here to see Jane's photos too."

Alice nodded as she wiped down the kitchen table.

"If he feels as passionate about this as I do now,

he may even want to say a few words at the rally today. Would that be okay, Alice?"

"Of course. I was hoping he would."

"Oh good." Ethel clapped her hands. "What a day this is going to be."

Chapter Twenty-Three

"Whom shall I ride with today?" asked Victoria as they were preparing to leave for the protest.

"Oh right," said Louise, "Cynthia is staying home to work. Well, you are certainly welcome to ride with Jane and me. We do not plan to stay as long as Alice, so we are taking separate cars."

"Or you could ride with me," Alice offered, although she seriously doubted that Victoria Martin would want to ride in her little Toyota.

"Perhaps you would rather take the Mercedes and simply follow us," suggested Jane. "If you would be more comfortable."

Victoria looked slightly surprised. "Oh, I don't drive."

"Really? How do you get around?" asked Louise.

Victoria smiled, perhaps a bit smugly. "Oh, I have drivers, of course."

"Of course," said Jane as she filled a thermos with coffee.

"I'm ready," said Alice as she slipped on her warm-est gloves. "I'll go ahead since I have the signs."

"I think I'll go with Alice," announced Victoria.

Alice nodded. "I apologize for my humble wheels. My car isn't fancy, Victoria."

Victoria waved her hand dismissively. "As long as it's mechanically sound and won't run out of gas, I promise not to complain."

Jane winked at Alice.

"Well, I think I can guarantee that much." Alice opened the front door.

"I do believe it's gotten colder out," said Victoria as they stepped out to the porch.

"I'm glad the heater works well," said Alice as they walked over to where her car was parked. "I hope you're dressed warmly, Victoria."

"I'm wearing my silk long underwear," she said, "as well as a lot of layers."

"Good for you."

"This isn't so bad," said Victoria as she surveyed the interior of Alice's car. "I'm sure it's very economical for you."

Alice nodded and started the ignition. "And dependable."

Soon they were on their way, with Alice praying a

silent prayer for the day ahead. She only partially listened as Victoria rambled about how many cars she owned.

"Of course, there's the Land Rover in New Hampshire." She laughed. "And I nearly forgot about the Jaguar in Malibu. It's a convertible."

"That's a lot of vehicles for someone who doesn't even drive," commented Alice.

"Isn't it. But just because I don't drive doesn't mean I don't need to get around. Normally I like to get around in style."

Once again, Alice felt like apologizing for her car, but she did not.

"I think the media people plan to start showing up around one," said Victoria. "That's what my publicist told me."

Alice nodded. "Do you think there will be a lot?" She did not want this to turn into some crazy circus event.

"It's hard to say. It depends on what else is going on in the area. So far I haven't heard of anything too sensational—no bombings, plane crashes or violent crimes."

"Thank goodness," said Alice.

"I'd considered asking my assistant to drive down and bring Rob and Roy. I thought it would be awfully clever to have my dogs protesting the abuse of dogs. Don't you think?"

"I'm sure the media people would've liked that, but would your dogs have liked the crowds and noise?"

"Probably not. They're very protective of me and don't always know exactly who is friend or foe. I'm sure they're better off at home."

"Have you always had dogs?"

"Not always. There was a period of about ten or fifteen years, back when I was getting my career off the ground when I had neither the time nor energy for pets. Nor family or children either for that matter. Probably one of the reasons I've never married." She turned to peer at Alice. "Have you ever been married?"

"No. I had a romance in college that had promise, but it didn't work out."

"Oh yes," said Victoria quickly. "The same thing happened to me."

"Really?" Alice waited to see if Victoria wanted to say more.

"Yes. His name was George Harding. He was handsome, athletic, intelligent. Oh my, he was really something." Victoria leaned back and sighed.

"What happened?"

"I don't usually tell people this, but you seem like a trustworthy person, Alice," said Victoria.

"Your secrets are safe with me," Alice assured her.

"Well, I was only nineteen at the time, but believe me, I was completely smitten by this man. I could see myself cooking and cleaning for him, doing his laundry and darning his socks. I imagined us living in a little cottage with pale blue shutters and a white picket fence, maybe by the sea. I would grow beautiful roses and we would have had lots of children. I imagined perhaps four or five. Oh yes, and a cat and a dog too. It was going to be a perfect life."

"And?"

Victoria sighed. "Oh, George enjoyed my company for about a year. Then Margaret Spencer came along."

"Margaret Spencer?"

"Only the most gorgeous woman in the college. She took campus by storm as a freshman. Oh my, she had a thick mane of blond curls, long legs, sparkling blue eyes and a smile that was truly captivating. All the boys were just crazy for Maggie Spencer."

"And did George fall for her too?"

"Not only did he fall for her, but he married her as soon as he graduated. They were the toast of the campus that year. Their pictures are on every other page of the yearbook."

"Oh."

"Yes." Victoria shook her head. "I was heartbroken.

Devastated. The remainder of my college experience passed by in a bit of a foggy blur. I actually started drinking quite heavily during my junior year. How I ever managed to graduate with a home economics degree is still something of a mystery to me, but I do have the certificate to prove it. It hangs on the wall in my office."

Alice chuckled. "Look at you now, Victoria, and what you have made of your life. It's really quite spectacular, don't you think?"

"I suppose."

Alice felt sorry for Victoria. It seemed obvious that despite her multiple homes, expensive cars, and highly visible, profitable career, this woman was not happy.

"I know I'm not like you, Victoria," began Alice, "but I have found a certain satisfaction in my unmarried life."

"Really?" Victoria sounded skeptical.

"Yes. I like knowing that I can pretty much come and go as I please. Of course, I check in with my sisters now that they live at home, but I've always enjoyed the simplicity of making my own choices. I can spend my time doing what I like, even if that means doing nothing at all. I like being able to read in bed until midnight, or making peanut butter on toast for breakfast. You know, little things like that."

"I suppose."

"And even though my college sweetheart is still sort of in the picture—"

"What?" said Victoria. "Don't tell me you're still dating the man you loved in college?"

"Well, not exactly." Alice smiled. "We hadn't seen each other in nearly forty years, and then last fall he unexpectedly popped back into my life."

"Really?"

"Yes. I was shocked at first, but then we spent some time together, getting reacquainted and filling in the blank spaces. It was actually nice. I discovered that we'd both grown and changed over the years."

"But hadn't he married?"

"To my surprise, he hadn't. His career is very demanding, and apparently he just never had the time or the inclination."

"How remarkable. So, do you think that you'll get married?"

"Well, the subject did come up. To be honest, I had mixed emotions about it. Then Mark was offered the opportunity of a lifetime. He's an exotic animal vet, you see, and he was invited to work with a research team in the Amazon."

"How extraordinary."

"Yes. That's where he is right now."

"Well, I never would've guessed that you would have such an exciting love life, Alice."

"Oh, I wouldn't go that far."

"I had fancies about a meeting with George a few years back..."

Alice waited.

"My alma mater was having a forty-year reunion for the decade of the 1960s. That's when George and I both attended. Well, I knew there was a good chance that George wouldn't be there, but I'd seen a show on television about people who met their lost loves at reunions..." She laughed. "I thought, well, maybe that was going to happen to me."

"I've heard stories like that too," admitted Alice.

"So, I spent about eight months dieting, faithfully working out with my personal trainer, and I even got some rather minor plastic surgery done." She glanced quickly at Alice. "I'm trusting you not to repeat this."

Alice nodded. "You can trust me, Victoria."

"Yes, I believe I can. So, I had my hair done just right and basically looked better than I'd looked in years, possibly even better than in college, although the years do have a way of catching up with us. But for my age, I was looking good. In fact, I still watch tapes of my television shows during that time just to remind myself of how good I can look when I really put my mind to it."

"And how did it go?"

"Well, I got to campus with my usual entourage. Naturally, there were some local media people there doing spots on the returning college graduates who'd been successful."

Alice could just imagine a sleek and perfectly coifed Victoria emerging from an expensive limo with cameras flashing.

"It was really fun. I had people I couldn't even remember coming up to me and saying how much they'd liked me back in our college days." She laughed sadly. "Naturally, I hadn't the slightest clue who they were. But finally, just before dinner, I managed to ask someone about George Harding. I did it in a very nonchalant manner, as if I'd barely known him."

"You must've been nervous."

"A bit, but to be perfectly honest, I thought there was a pretty good chance that George would be bald and wrinkled with a potbelly that hung over his belt. That's how most of the other men were looking. Anyway, I was completely prepared to simply smile at him, say hello and just strut away. You know, show him just what he'd missed out on by not marrying me."

Alice chuckled. "So what happened?"

"It turned out he was there. My friend pointed him out across the room. And, as fate would have it, he still looked darn good. His hair was silver at the temples, but he was still handsome and athletic-looking. Standing next to him was his wife Maggie. No one had to tell me that it was she. And here is what seems completely unfair. That woman looked as if she'd barely aged at all. Still a gorgeous blond with long legs and a smile that flashed clear across the room."

"Oh." Alice felt even more sorry for Victoria now. "Did you talk to George at all?"

"Just barely, but when Maggie discovered who I was, well, she would hardly leave my side. It seems she is one of my biggest fans. She regularly watches all my shows and has every one of my books. Not only that, but she assured me that she ran her household in exactly the way I prescribed."

"Didn't that make you feel good?" asked Alice. They were nearing the racetrack now and she wanted to bring this tale to a graceful ending.

"I suppose it should have, but all I could think of was how it should've been *me* taking care of George with such perfection. Here she was doing it, using my advice and know-how."

Alice put on her signal to turn toward the track. "That must have felt unfair."

Victoria nodded. "I'll say. It's like I'd been doing all the work, but Maggie was getting all the benefits."

Alice was parking her car now. Carlene had secured permission for them to park in a nearby parking lot of a business that was not open on Saturdays. "No need to take chances," she had advised Alice.

"That's quite a story, Victoria," said Alice as they climbed out of the car. She started unloading her signs.

"Here, let me help you with those," offered Victoria in a slightly gruff voice. She took a small stack of signs under her arm.

"Thanks," said Alice as she closed the trunk.

"Now," said Victoria. "If you ever repeat that story, I'll have my attorneys all over you like freckles on an Irishman."

Alice started. "I would never."

Victoria nodded, then smiled. "I know. I was just checking."

Chapter Twenty-Four

Alice knew that today's protest was not about her, but she had to admit to herself that she felt a small twinge of dismay when Victoria captured all the limelight. It started with the few locals who had gathered along the street. As soon as they recognized Victoria Martin, they began to cluster around her, asking for autographs. Alice wondered if they had come here to protest or to get a glimpse of daytime television's domestic diva.

They had barely taken care of the autographs and introductions, as well as a few photographs with local housewives posing next to the Queen of Cuisine, before the first media van came roaring down the street toward them.

"Where's the fire?" said Victoria dryly. The crowd around her all laughed.

"It's beginning," said Alice.

"Bring it on," said Victoria as she picked up a sign

and held it high. Others followed her example and within moments, the small crowd organized itself into an impressive protest group.

"Save the dogs!" a couple of teenagers began chanting as they marched up and down the street.

Soon, more protesters arrived, lining the streets with signs and enthusiasm, and more media vans began to show up. Alice spotted Louise and Jane walking toward them and thought that perhaps it was time to join her sisters. After all, Victoria seemed to have things under control with her fans and newscasters clamoring for her attention.

"Don't leave me," hissed Victoria into Alice's ear.

"Oh." Alice was surprised. "You want me to stay with you?"

"Yes." Victoria nodded vigorously. "I need someone I can count on by my side."

"Okay." Alice just waved to her sisters, who had wisely brought folding chairs that they were now setting up farther on down the street.

"What is it that first drew your interest to this cause?" demanded a pretty brunette reporter as she shoved the microphone up close to Victoria's face.

"I've always been a dog lover," said Victoria just as cool and calm as you please. "I was appalled to learn of the inhumane treatment of greyhound racing dogs. I have friends in my home state who have founded a group that works to protect and adopt unwanted racing dogs."

"But what brought you to Potterston, Pennsylvania?" continued the woman. "Why have you suddenly become interested in this particular racing track?"

"I'm staying at a local inn," said Victoria. Now she winked at Alice. "It's located in the charming town of Acorn Hill."

"And how did you learn of the troubles over here in Potterston?"

Now Victoria put her arm around Alice's shoulder and pulled her into the shot. "My friend and innkeeper Alice Howard brought the issue to my attention when she first protested at this track just this week."

Now the microphone was thrust into Alice's face. "Are you the woman who was arrested after nearly being mobbed this week?"

"Oh, I wasn't—"

"That's right," said Victoria, pulling the microphone back to her. "Poor Alice was simply attempting to make a statement against the cruelty to dogs when racing patrons got angry and unruly."

"And then she was arrested?" said the woman.

"That's right. Naturally, she was released the same evening."

"What good do you think this protest will do?" asked another reporter.

"It will raise the level of public awareness," said Victoria. "When the good people of Potterston realize what kind of ugly business is going on at the racetrack, I'm sure they will want to do their part to help the poor dogs and maybe even get this place shut down."

"Do you really think the racetrack can be shut down?" asked the woman.

"Actually, I can't speak about the legalities of such things," said Victoria, "but I will say this." She paused to look intently at both of the cameras. "The senseless slaughter of young greyhounds, simply because their owners no longer consider them to be profitable, is a stain on our society."

So it went for the next hour. New media groups appeared and Victoria continued making her speeches. Alice recognized that Victoria was the perfect spokeswoman for this event. Even though Alice grew weary of the crowd's constantly pressing closer to get a peek at Victoria Martin, she never left her side and truly appreciated her participation.

Some of the racing fans jeered as they drove toward

the track, but nothing got out of hand. Lloyd had taken on the role of unofficial event organizer, using his bullhorn to remind people that this was a peaceful rally and warning all protesters to stay clear of the street.

"There will be no blocking of traffic," he announced in a stern voice.

"Would you like some refreshments?" asked Jane after she had pushed her way through the small throng still clustered around Victoria. At that moment there were no camera interviews taking place, and Alice could tell that Victoria was getting weary.

"That would be lovely," said Victoria in a tired voice.

Then to Alice's surprise, Jane took Victoria by the arm and said, "Come with me." Jane pushed her way through the surprised onlookers and Alice followed.

"You two sit down," said Jane when they reached the section where Louise, Jane, and even Harold were comfortably arranged with chairs, picnic basket and, of course, their signs posted so all could see.

Soon Alice and Victoria were seated side by side. Jane put a red plaid blanket over their laps as Louise handed them each a steaming cup of cocoa.

"My, this is good," said Victoria after only one sip. "Do I taste a bit of cinnamon in here?"

Jane answered as she handed them sandwiches. "Yes, I find it gives an extra warmth to the cocoa."

Victoria nodded.

The sandwiches were simply egg salad, but made with, as always, the usual Jane flair. Alice was definitely enjoying hers.

"*Hmmm,*" said Victoria. "These are good. Do I detect a bit of nutmeg?"

Jane nodded, looking slightly stunned by this unexpected praise.

"I'll have to try that myself," said Victoria.

Alice smiled. After all the beautiful meals Jane had carefully prepared, this was the first compliment Victoria had ever given to Jane's culinary skills.

Across the street, the ANGELs were marching and singing the "Bingo" song now. They had started with "Who Let the Dogs Out?" Then they moved on to other dog tunes, like "How Much Is That Doggy in the Window?" Alice wondered just how many canine tunes they had in their repertoire.

"How are you two holding up?" asked Harold.

"Very well, thanks," said Victoria between bites.

"It looked as if you were in the midst of a media frenzy about ten minutes ago," said Louise as she sipped her coffee.

"It's impressive how much coverage we're getting," said Jane as she opened a tin of sugar cookies and offered them around.

"That's all thanks to Victoria," said Alice as she took a cookie.

Victoria waved her hand. "You can thank my publicist."

"Hello," called Ethel as she came over to join them. "My, this is quite an event, Alice. You can be proud."

Alice nodded to Victoria. "She's the main reason for the crowd."

"Well, they care about the dogs, too, we hope," said Jane as she offered Ethel a cookie.

"Lloyd is doing a great job keeping the crowd in line," said Alice. "I'm glad you decided to come."

"Well, after seeing those photos," Ethel shook her head, "we couldn't not come."

"Lloyd wondered if this might be a good time to give a little speech," said Ethel. "Now that the news people are gone."

"I think that would be perfect," said Alice.

"By all means," agreed Victoria.

Lloyd got on his bullhorn again and called everyone to attention. Then he gave an encouraging little pep talk. Ever the diplomat, he gave credit to Victoria, inviting her to stand as the crowd applauded. Then to everyone's surprise, Lloyd walked over and handed Victoria a giant brass key tied with a red ribbon. "Although we are in Potterston right now, on behalf of the citizens of Acorn Hill, we want to present you with this humble gift. It is the key to our town and the key to our hearts. We have all enjoyed your stay with us, and we hope that you'll come to visit us often."

"Well, thank you," said Victoria. "I'm honored. I have thoroughly enjoyed your charming little town as well as the hospitality at Grace Chapel Inn. Thank you very much."

Another local media van came down the street. Victoria took a refill on the cocoa, and then she and Alice made it back to the corner where they had been standing. As before, Victoria gave an eloquent interview. As she was finishing, another van appeared, this one from one of the major network stations in Philadelphia.

The plan had been for the protest to last for about an hour or so, just long enough to make a real statement. It was getting ever colder, and some people had been there for a long time. The crowd slowly began to thin out. It was nearly two o'clock when the last media van, from another big station in Philadelphia, began packing up. Jane and Louise had gone home already, as had most of the citizens of Acorn Hill. Only a few stragglers remained, and it appeared that they were about ready to call it a day too.

"Should we go now?" asked Alice.

Victoria glanced around to see that only a couple of teenagers remained, probably from Potterston since Alice did not recognize them. "Yes. I think we've completed our business here."

Chapter Twenty-Five

As they were starting for Alice's car, a red pickup truck came speeding toward them from the direction of the racetrack. As the pickup turned onto the street, something fell from its bed, making a loud whack as it hit the ground.

"My goodness," said Victoria. "What on earth?"

"It's a dog crate," said Alice.

The truck continued down the road, despite the efforts of two boys who waved for the truck to stop.

Alice heard a yelping sound and began to run toward the crate. Soon she, Victoria and the boys were kneeling next to it. "It sounds as if he's hurt," said Alice as the whimpering continued.

"Let's get him out of there," commanded Victoria.

Soon they had the box opened and Victoria was examining the buff-colored greyhound. "It looks like he's injured his hind leg," she said finally, stroking the dog's sleek coat.

"He's cold," said Alice, removing her coat to cover him.

"Let's get him into the car."

"Want some help?" offered one of the boys.

"Thanks," said Alice. "It's just over here."

The taller boy easily lifted the lightweight dog and carried him over to her car, waiting while she opened the door and spread a blanket on the back seat. Then the boy gently slid in the dog. The other boy had gathered up what remained of the protest signs and carried them over to her car. "Thanks," said Alice as she opened the trunk and he put them in. "Thanks to both of you."

"No problem," said the taller one. "This is, like, a real rescue."

Alice nodded. "We better see about getting this dog to the vet," she told them.

"Good luck," called the shorter boy.

Victoria had gotten into the backseat with the injured dog. "Poor thing," she was saying in a soothing voice.

"Everything okay back there?" asked Alice as she leaned over to peer inside.

"Here's your coat back," said Victoria as she wrapped the still shivering dog in the blanket. He yelped in pain as she tucked it around him. "It's okay, boy," she said soothingly, and then asked Alice, "Do you know where the closest vet is?"

"I think I do," said Alice. "I just hope he's open."

"I've got my cell phone," said Victoria. She reached for her purse and began digging around to find it. "Here." She handed it to Alice. "Why don't you call?"

Alice frowned. "I don't know how to use one of those things."

Victoria laughed and took the cell phone back. First she got information and then she handed the phone to Alice. "I don't know the name of the clinic."

Alice asked for the phone number and waited until she was connected. Fortunately, the vet was in and Alice quickly explained their situation and said they would be right over. She handed the phone back to Victoria and, closing the back door, went around to the driver's side. That is when she saw the red pickup just pulling up beside her.

"Hey, have you seen my dog, lady?" demanded a man who appeared to be in his thirties. He had on a black leather jacket and an angry expression. Then he peered in the window and spotted Victoria and the dog in the backseat.

"The dog crate fell off your truck," Alice told him.

"I know." The man scowled. "I noticed that when I got to the gas station."

Now Victoria got out of the car. "What's the problem?" she asked.

"This is the owner of the dog," said Alice.

"Well, did you know that your dog is injured?" countered Victoria.

"Oh, he's probably just fine." The man leaned over and looked in the car. "Come on, Zipper, let's go now."

The dog let out a painful yelp.

"See," said Victoria. "He needs to be treated."

"Well, that's my business," snapped the man. "Gimme my dog."

"Not so fast," said Victoria, stepping in front of the man. "First I need to ask you whether you intend to have him treated or not."

"Look, lady, this dog is my property. I own him and can do whatever I see fit to him."

"Not according to the law."

"Outta my way, lady."

"Not until I know exactly what you plan to do with him," said Victoria without batting an eyelash.

Just then another pickup truck pulled up. "What's the problem, Jack?" called the man from the other truck.

"These old broads have kidnapped my dog," yelled Jack.

"That's not true," said Alice. "The dog was injured when his crate fell off the truck. We were about to get him some medical attention."

"He's my dog," said Jack. "I'll be the one to see to his needs."

Victoria stood up even straighter now, looking Jack directly in the eyes. "The dog's been injured. He is most likely lame. Tell me the truth, Jack, what do you really intend to do with him?"

"Listen, lady, he's my dog and my business, and even if I do plan to put him down, it's got nothing to do with you and your tree-hugging, animal-loving, fanatical friends. So just mind your own business."

Alice had noticed the other man in the pickup using his cell phone. Now she saw a pair of patrol cars slowly turning off the highway and coming down the road that led to the track.

"Look, Jack," said Victoria, not backing down for a minute. "How much would you like for your dog? I can afford to pay good money."

He looked tempted for a moment but then suddenly changed his mind. "He's not for sale, lady."

"Why not?" she pleaded. "He's of no use to you once he's lame."

"It's the principle."

"But you're only going to kill him," she said. "Why not let me take him and find him a good home?"

"Because I said no." He made a fist. "Give me back my dog."

"I will not," said Victoria. She climbed into the car. "Let's go, Alice."

Alice followed Victoria's orders and got inside. "Victoria," she said, "the police are coming. This could get messy."

"I am not going to give this poor dog back to that animal," she seethed. "He will only kill it. Maybe even brutally now that I've made him mad."

"But what about the police?"

"They will understand."

Alice opened her door and got out of the car as the officer approached.

"Mind if I ask you ladies some questions?" said the policeman.

Alice nodded, as did Victoria, who remained in the back seat.

"Hey, aren't you the woman we arrested a few days ago?" asked the officer. "Hey, Sarge," he called over his shoulder. "You better get over here and see this."

Alice now saw Sergeant Crane coming their way. She wished that the parking lot would open and swallow her up. "Hello," she said weakly.

"What's going on today, Miss Howard?" he asked with what seemed like genuine interest.

"Well," she began. Then slowly, searching for the right words, she told him about their dog rescue, assuring him that they most certainly were not dognappers.

"But then I came back," said Jack. "And now they won't give me my dog."

"Is that true?" asked Sergeant Crane.

"My friend wants to buy the dog," said Alice.

"The dog is *not* for sale!" yelled Jack.

"Settle down," said Sergeant Crane.

"The dog is injured and we know that it's common practice to kill dogs that can no longer run."

"It's none of your business," said Jack.

"It's wrong," said Alice. "Please, why can't you just sell us the dog? As my friend says, she can well afford it. You just name the price."

Jack was looking tempted, but his friend gave him an elbow and a dark scowl. "You gonna let these females tell you how to live your life?" demanded his friend.

"That's right," said Jack. "The dog's not for sale. I want him back."

Sergeant Crane looked at Alice. "Sounds like the dog's not for sale."

Alice felt seriously close to tears. "But why not?" she

pleaded with Jack. "You know that you don't really want him."

Jack folded his arms across his chest and just looked away.

"I'm sorry," said Sergeant Crane. "Your friend is going to have to turn over that dog."

Alice leaned over and motioned through the window to Victoria to come out. Victoria just sat there shaking her head. Then Alice started to open the door but discovered it was locked. Of course, her keys were inside, already in the ignition. "Victoria!" she called, tapping on the window. "Unlock the doors."

Again, Victoria just shook her head and continued petting the dog.

"Oh dear." Alice looked up at Sergeant Crane. "I don't know what to do."

"May I have your permission to enter your car, Miss Howard?" asked Sergeant Crane.

Alice frowned. "Are you going to break a window?"

"No." He laughed. "We have easier ways."

"Okay."

"I'll be right back," he told her.

Now Alice pounded even harder on the window. "Please, Victoria," she yelled. "You've got to let him take his dog. Open the door."

Victoria was totally ignoring her. Despite Alice's pity for the dog, she was getting irritated at Victoria. What possible good did she think this was going to do?

Soon, Sergeant Crane returned with a long flat metal strip that he used to unlock Alice's car. Then he leaned in to speak to Victoria. "Do you want to hand over that dog, ma'am? Or do I need to take you in?"

"I refuse to surrender this poor animal to an owner who will most likely kill him before the night is over." She narrowed her eyes. "There are laws protecting animals, you know."

The sergeant scratched his head. "That's true enough, but you are breaking the law by not returning this man's dog to him."

"That's right," said Victoria. "I have offered to pay him for the dog, and to take the dog in for medical attention."

"I know. I know." Sergeant Crane stood up and motioned to the other officer. "I need some backup here."

Soon the two policemen had managed to extract a very stubborn Victoria Martin from the backseat of Alice's car. Alice was thankful the media were not around to get this. It would have surely made the news across the country.

The younger officer put her in handcuffs, recited her rights to her and then led her off to one of the patrol cars.

"I'll meet you at the station," called Alice, hoping that she was not about to be arrested too, perhaps as an accomplice.

"Now," said Sergeant Crane, turning his attention back to Alice. "As for you. How do you keep managing to get yourself into these situations?"

"We were simply having a peaceful protest," Alice told him. "If the crate hadn't fallen from the—"

"Yes, yes." Sergeant Crane frowned. "Well, the truth is, I'm an animal lover myself. Your friend is right. Animals do have a few rights too. I'm going to order this dog into protective custody until we can sort this thing out."

Now Jack let out with a string of cuss words and kicked the tire on his truck. "You people!" he burst out.

"Watch it, buddy!" said the sergeant.

Soon Sergeant Crane had collected the information he needed from an angry Jack and gave Alice instructions to take the dog to the vet. "Now, don't let me down," he told her as she opened the door to her car.

"I won't," she assured him, glancing nervously to where Jack was still standing nearby. "By the way," she said loud enough for Jack to hear. "I don't know if you knew it or not, but the woman you just arrested is a celebrity."

"A celebrity?" Sergeant Crane looked surprised, and it seemed that she had captured Jack's interest as well.

"Yes. Victoria Martin. She has a television show and knows all sorts of important people. Anyway, I'm sure there will be media coverage when they find out. Also, her lawyers will probably be coming soon."

He nodded. "Thanks for the heads up."

"A celebrity?" repeated Jack.

Alice nodded. "Yes. She probably would've paid dearly for that dog."

The man cussed angrily, then got into his truck and drove off.

"See you at the station?" said Sergeant Crane.

"I'll be there as soon as I drop Zipper off."

Chapter Twenty-Six

*A*lice felt slightly better to be entering the police station through the main entrance this time. "I'm here for Victoria Martin," she told the receptionist.

"*The* Victoria Martin?" asked the woman.

"That's right."

"Here?"

"Yes."

The woman nervously looked over her shoulder. "Is she doing one of her shows here or something?"

"Not exactly." Alice smiled. "She's been arrested."

The receptionist's eyes grew large. "Victoria Martin has been arrested?"

Alice nodded. "Sergeant Crane said that I could join her."

The receptionist shrugged. "Sure, fine. No one ever tells me anything around here."

"Thank you," said Alice as she went back to the office that she had visited just a few days before. She spied

Victoria sitting in exactly the same chair that Alice had occupied on Wednesday. She was sitting slightly slumped over, still wearing her coat, with what looked like a cup of black coffee in her hands. It was her expression that stopped Alice. The poor woman looked as if she had lost her last friend, or someone had killed her dog.

"Victoria," said Alice.

Victoria sat a bit straighter. "Alice. I'm so glad you're here."

"Good news," said Alice as she pulled a chair up next to Victoria. "The sergeant let me take the dog. He's in protective custody."

Victoria brightened now. "Really?"

"Yes. I just dropped him at the vet."

"Oh, I'm so relieved."

"Have you called your attorney yet?"

"Yes, but I had to leave a message. He'll be checking his pager, I hope."

"Well, if this is anything like when I was in here, I'm sure they'll be releasing you soon."

"Do you think so?"

"Of course. I'm sure you don't have any prior convictions." Alice laughed.

"Don't be too sure."

Alice's eyes grew wider. "You do?"

"Just a couple of crazy things in college, during my drinking days, you know. Oh, and a minor scrap with a neighbor over a tree that he was trying to cut down— I could've sworn it was on my property. But those are in different states."

"Oh."

Unfortunately for Victoria, her previous record did, indeed, show up. But Sergeant Crane was no fool. Instead of putting her in jail, he let her out on bail. Alice wrote a check for the required amount, since Victoria only had her American Express card with her. Despite Victoria's pleading, the Potterston Police Station did not take American Express.

"Don't leave home without it," she muttered as the two of them went out to find Alice's car. "Ha!"

"Hey, lady!" yelled a man from the other side of the street.

"Oh no," said Victoria."It's that horrible man again. That crazy dog owner who got me into this mess."

"It's okay," said Alice. "We're right in front of the police station." Alice waved to an officer who was just coming out of the building. "He can't do anything to us here."

"I just want to talk to you," said the man as he jogged across the street.

"What do you want?" asked Victoria in the most imperious tone Alice had ever heard.

"Look, lady, I'm sorry about what happened at the track. You see, I've had a bad day—a bad month. My wife left me with three little kids a few weeks ago. I have a regular job, but dog racing helps to pay the bills, you know. And, believe it or not, Zipper was one of my favorite dogs, but he got disqualified at the track today."

"And what has this to do with me?" she demanded.

"Well, if you're still interested," he shrugged, "and you probably aren't, but I'd be willing to sell him."

"And what makes you think I want him now?" she demanded.

He shook his head now. "Fine. I figured as much." Then he started to walk away.

"Wait!" called Alice. "I might be interested."

He turned hopefully.

"I don't have a lot of money, but I—"

"Never mind." Victoria laid her hand on Alice's shoulder. "I want to buy the dog after all."

The man came back and looked at her. "Serious?"

She nodded solemnly. "Although things would've gone much simpler if we'd taken care of this *before* I was arrested."

"Yeah, it was pretty stupid on my part." He looked down at the ground. "Sorry 'bout that."

"All right," said Victoria in a firm voice. "I will purchase your dog from you, but only if you will march right back into the police station with me and tell them that you are not pressing charges."

"Fair enough."

Back they went to the police station. Fortunately, Sergeant Crane was not too busy and actually seemed rather pleased that they had reached an agreement. "It's refreshing to see citizens working out their problems outside of the court system," he told them as they finally finished the paperwork and returned the bail check to Alice.

Alice wrote Jack a generous check, for which Victoria would reimburse her later. After that, they stopped by the vet's.

"It's just a sprain," the vet assured them as Victoria paid the bill. Fortunately, the vet did take American Express. "But it's bad enough that you can be sure he'll never race again. Is that a problem?"

"Goodness, no," said Victoria. "I do not intend to race him." She smiled as she stroked the dog's smooth nose. "Although when he's better he'll probably enjoy giving Rob and Roy a run for their money. Rather, *my* money."

The vet looked slightly confused, although he nodded as if he understood. Alice suspected he thought he was dealing with a couple of batty old ladies.

Alice carried the still slightly sedated Zipper to her car and gently laid him in the backseat again. The dog licked her hand as if to say thanks as she put the blanket over him. "Now just rest there," she told him.

"Oh my," said Victoria as they were finally driving back toward Acorn Hill. "What a day."

Alice sighed. "I'll say."

"Something odd happened," said Victoria.

"Only *one* thing?"

"Well, one thing in particular. It happened when I was sitting in your backseat with Zipper. I experienced the most realistic flashback."

"What do you mean?"

Then Victoria launched into a story from her childhood. Her mother had died when she was nine years old and her father took her to her maternal grandparents to live. "It was only supposed to be a temporary thing," she said. "Just until my father got relocated and found work. After a while, I realized that he would never come back for me."

"I'm sorry," said Alice.

"My grandparents were good people, but they were rather cool and distant. They were quite a change from my parents, who had enjoyed lively music and friends and tended to laugh a lot. And although my grandparents weren't well off, they still seemed very formal and proper, at least to me. As a result, I suppose I felt like I was something of a burden to them so I tried to remain quiet and stay out of their way.

"Anyway, the event I just remembered happened on a Saturday. I was walking down an alley near my grandparents' home when I saw a boy from school. I knew that he was a bully, and I started to turn around and go the other way. Then I heard this pitiful yelping sound, and I could see that this boy had a puppy. I went a little closer and saw that he'd tied a rope around the puppy's neck, and he was swinging the poor little dog around and around as if he were a toy. Well, it was as if all the frustration and rage that I'd been keeping inside of me since my mother's death just burst to the surface, and like a wild girl I began screaming at him and beating on him with my fists until he dropped the poor dog and ran. Then I scooped up the limp puppy and, sobbing, I removed the rope and just held him to me and petted his coat. I still remember the silky feeling of his soft black fur. I started walking home, and by the time I got there, the puppy had come back to life."

"Oh my, what a brave and wonderful thing to have done," said Alice. "Did your grandparents let you keep him?"

"Well, I assumed they wouldn't allow me to have a pet. So I kept the puppy hidden in my room all weekend, sneaking him food when no one was looking. But by Sunday night, my grandfather discovered my secret. To my surprise, after I told him the story, my grandfather let me keep the pup. My grandmother, bless her heart, knit him a little blue sweater. That was when I began to see my grandparents in a whole new light."

"That's a great story," said Alice.

"I'd almost forgotten it," admitted Victoria. "Until I was sitting back there with Zipper. It's as if all those old protective feelings just came rushing back at me and I knew there was no way I was letting him go back with that Jack person."

"I don't think Jack was really so bad," said Alice. "As he said, he was having a bad week."

"But I'm sure he planned to dispose of his dog."

Alice nodded sadly. "You're probably right."

Chapter Twenty-Seven

*W*hat took you two so long?" asked Jane when Alice came through the front door. "It's almost six o'clock."

Alice paused, holding the door open, until Victoria entered carrying the wounded dog. "What on earth?" said Jane.

"This is Zipper," said Alice. "Victoria's new adoptee."

"Don't tell me you guys performed a rescue after we left." Jane reached over and patted the dog's head.

"Sort of," said Alice.

"Here," offered Jane, outstretching her arms. "You want me to help you with him?"

"Thanks," said Victoria as she handed the dog over to Jane. "Do you think it's okay if I keep him in my room? I'll gladly pay if anything gets damaged."

Jane glanced at Alice and she just shrugged.

"Sure," said Jane. "Why not."

"What's this?" asked Louise as she emerged from the

dining room and spied Zipper. "Wendell just shot past me like a streak."

"This is Zipper," said Jane. "Victoria's new pet. Wendell will be okay when he gets used to him...I hope."

Jane and Victoria went upstairs with the dog, and Alice explained to Louise what had happened. "I'm sorry I didn't call," said Alice, "but everything happened so fast."

"Well, you better grab yourself a bite to eat. We ate early in order to get ready for the party. I shall take a tray up to Victoria."

"Thanks," said Alice. "It's been quite a day."

After a quick dinner, Alice went up to her room and took a shower, then sat down and put her feet up for a bit. She woke up to a knocking on her door.

"Alice?" called Jane.

"Come in," said Alice groggily, glancing at her clock to discover it was already seven.

"Are you okay?" asked Jane as she came into the room.

"Look at you!" Alice stood up and went over to examine Jane's costume. "You look just like Dorothy."

Jane laughed and held out her basket for Alice to see. "And Toto too."

"I must've fallen asleep. I'll get into my costume and be right down."

"Yes," said Jane with a bright smile. "You're missing

the fun. Several people are already here and the costumes are wonderful."

It did not take Alice long to get into her scarecrow costume, humming "If I Only Had a Brain," as she dressed. She wished she could remember all the words to that tune, but maybe Jane could help her. Finally she went downstairs, where happy strains of music were pouring out of the parlor.

"Hi, Miss Howard," said Ashley as she came out of the dining room with a tray of canapés.

"How did you know it was me?" demanded Alice with some disappointment.

"Mrs. Smith, I mean Glinda the Good Witch, said you were the Scarecrow."

"And I know you are a Munchkin," said Alice.

Ashley did a mock curtsey. "Yes, and all of us Munchkins are going to do our song after more people get here." Then she lowered her voice. "You should see Mr. Tracy."

"What's he dressed like?"

"He's Willy Wonka," giggled Ashley.

"Who is Willy Wonka?" asked Alice.

"You know, Miss Howard, *Willy Wonka and the Chocolate Factory.*"

Alice nodded. It sounded vaguely familiar.

"He looks just like him too." Ashley grinned. "And his pockets are full of candy."

"Come in. Come in." Alice heard what sounded like Louise's voice, only at a slightly higher pitch, behind her. Surprised, Alice turned just in time to see her older, and normally reserved, sister wearing a long, blond curly wig and a sparkling blue gown. She gave a good imitation of Billie Burke's bubbling laugh as she waved a glittery wand at what appeared to be Lloyd and Ethel now entering the foyer.

"Aunt Ethel," said Louise. "Don't you look stunning."

"Why, thank you, Louise," laughed Ethel. "Or should I call you Glinda?"

"Hello," said Alice as she attempted a loose-jointed scarecrow-like bow.

"Alice?"

She did a little soft-shoe step and pointed her forefinger to her slightly cocked head. "Scarecrow to you," she said, then studied the pair. Lloyd wore tails, complete with white tie, top hat and cane. Ethel had on a golden satin gown and what appeared to be high-heeled tap shoes. "Who are you two supposed to be?" asked Alice. "You look very glamorous."

Ethel did a little tap step and held out her hand for Lloyd. "Your turn, Fred." Poor Lloyd was not quite as adept as his partner.

"Fred Astaire and Ginger Rogers?" ventured Louise.

"That's right," said Ethel as she gave her full skirt a swirl. "From *Swing Time*. Of course, I was probably still in diapers when that film came out."

"Of course," said Louise, winking at Alice.

"And look at you!" said Louise as someone came toward them from the dining room.

"Good evening, ladies and gentleman," said Harold as he tipped his stars-and-stripes hat.

"*Yankee Doodle Dandy*," said Alice, responding to the group's questioning look. Of course, she had had a heads-up on this one, or she would have been guessing with them.

"If you are in here, who is that playing piano?" asked Louise.

He grinned. "My backup, Patsy Ley."

"I didn't know Patsy could play so well," said Louise.

"Hidden talents," said Harold.

"What a great costume!" said Lloyd as he stepped up and took a better look at Harold's outfit. "Now, something like that would sure come in handy for my July Fourth speech."

"Perhaps we can work out a deal," offered Harold.

As if they were old friends, Harold and Lloyd continued to chat amicably as Alice went off to help in the kitchen.

"Actually I don't need help," said Jane. "Your Munchkins seem to have things under control." She took Alice's arm. "I think we should join the others."

They picked up Louise and Cynthia on their way to the parlor, and waiting for a pause in the music, they made their entrance singing "We're Off to See the Wizard." Jane and Cynthia did most of the singing since Alice and Louise could not remember all of the words, but when they finished everyone in the room clapped loudly and demanded an encore.

Then, to the surprise of Alice and Jane, Louise and Cynthia did a wonderful rendition of "Over the Rainbow" that brought tears to Alice's eyes. Even though it was getting a bit stuffy beneath her scratchy burlap mask, she was thankful that it hid her tears.

It was not long before the party was in full swing and, despite the demands of a busy day, Alice found that she was having a wonderful time.

"Where's the Wicked Witch of the West?" asked Louise when it was getting close to eight. "You know, her costume arrived this afternoon. I put it in her room."

"Maybe a tornado dumped a house on her," said Alice as she waved at Wilhelm Wood. "Look at Wilhelm," she said to Louise, nodding toward the door where Wilhelm was wearing a tweed suit with vest and bow tie. He even had the perfect pipe to go with it.

"Who is he supposed to be? Sherlock Holmes?" asked Louise. "I don't recall any Sherlock Holmes musicals, do you?"

"No." Alice chuckled. "He and Sylvia coordinated their outfits. She is coming as Eliza Doolittle from *My Fair Lady* and Wilhelm is supposed to be Henry Higgins, the stuffy fellow who tries to turn her into a lady."

"He looks so dignified in that old-fashioned suit."

"Oh, there's Sylvia now," said Alice, waving again.

"Oh my," said Louise. "Just look at her."

Heads turned when Sylvia entered the parlor and took Wilhelm's arm. No longer the shy and unassuming seamstress, Sylvia was bedecked in a beautiful lavender gown and matching hat.

"You look lovely," said Jane as she greeted her friend.

"Just like Eliza," said Sylvia with a smile.

Harold was back at the piano again, and Wilhelm was trying to get everyone's attention. "Miss Eliza Doolittle and I have a little number we'd like to perform." He cleared his throat and motioned to Sylvia, who was still talking with Alice and Jane.

Sylvia turned around and grinned at Wilhelm, and then sang out, "Just you wait 'enry 'iggins, just you wait." Everyone laughed, and before long she was joining him in singing "The Rain in Spain."

The evening went on with their friends and neighbors showing up in all sorts of getups and taking turns performing songs. Even elderly Clara Horn came dressed up like Miss Piggy. "In honor of my pet pig Daisy," she told everyone. "It was my granddaughter's idea."

Some of their guests sang quite expertly, while others were off-key and missed a few of the words, but it seemed that everyone was having a good time. The Munchkins were a huge hit when they sang. Craig Tracy gave all the girls candy and followed their performance with a number of his own, the "Oompa-Loompa" song.

"We should recruit him for the church choir," said Louise.

Jane nodded as she passed the platter of cheese puffs. "I'll mention it to him."

"And now for a little song and dance," announced Harold as Ethel and Lloyd took the floor. Lloyd only stepped on Ethel's feet a couple of times, and between the two of them, they were on key about half the time, but it was hard to beat their unbridled enthusiasm. They both bowed gracefully when their song, "A Fine Romance," was over. Naturally, the crowd clapped and cheered.

"Who knew that our mayor could sing and dance?" called out Fred Humbert.

"It hasn't been easy on my poor toes," said Ethel

as she dramatically daubed her forehead with a handkerchief. "We only had a few evenings to practice, mind you."

"Yes," teased Lloyd, "and I thought Ethel would never learn the foxtrot."

"Oh pish posh," said Ethel.

Next Harold sang "Give My Regards to Broadway." As he finished, the crowd's attention turned toward the doorway as someone in black burst into the room making a wild cackling sort of laugh.

With her tall, pointed hat and her face painted green, Victoria made a spectacular entrance. She rushed over to where Jane was chatting with Craig Tracy and pointed a finger in her face. "I'll get you, Dorothy," she shrieked, "and your little dog too!"

"Oh dear," said Alice in her best dramatic voice, "it's the Wicked Witch of the West! Whatever shall we do?"

The room was quiet, as if the guests were expecting more.

"I'll take care of her," said Louise as she went over to where Jane was pretending to cower from Victoria. "I shall use my good magic on her," and Louise waved her wand over Victoria's pointed black hat. "From now on you shall be a good witch and only use your magic to help others."

"Oh," cried Victoria dramatically, "I think I'm melting." Then she pretended to be shrinking as she cried, "I'm melting, I'm melting."

The room erupted into a loud clapping and cheering, and Harold started playing another show tune.

"That was great," said Jane, patting Victoria on the back.

"My, yes," agreed Louise. "What an entrance. You must have taken acting lessons."

"I used to enjoy drama," said Victoria, pausing to rub her nose. "But I must admit that this green makeup is a bit irritating. Do you mind if I remove it?"

"No, not at all," said Alice, "and I'll take off this mask. It makes it impossible for me to enjoy Jane's delectable treats."

Alice and Victoria retreated to the downstairs bathroom to alter their appearances. "How's Zipper?" asked Alice as she handed Victoria another tissue.

"He's sleeping soundly, poor guy." Victoria got the last of the green off and tossed the soiled tissue into the trash. "I think today wore him out."

"I took a nap too," admitted Alice. "If Jane hadn't awakened me, I'd probably still be snoozing."

"As would I," said Victoria as she adjusted her hat. "It was only the sounds of music and laughter that roused me."

"Sorry about that," said Alice as they went back out to join the party.

"Oh," said Victoria, "I was looking forward to this. It's really fun."

Alice smiled at her. "For the Wicked Witch of the West, you're being awfully congenial."

Victoria laughed. "I'm usually accused of being quite witchy, you know. I guess you and your sisters must have worn me down a bit this past week."

"I hear there is something in the water here in Acorn Hill," joked Alice. "It makes us all act a little nicer."

"Speaking of water..." Victoria leaned in and spoke in a quiet voice. "Before my entrance, I saw Wilhelm and he confessed something to me."

Alice's eyes grew wide. "About his tea?"

Victoria nodded.

"About his secret ingredient?"

Victoria laughed. "That tea did have a nice *smoky* quality to it."

"Poor Wilhelm," said Alice, "he felt perfectly horrible about the mistake."

"I don't know if it was such a mistake," said Victoria. "He's going to work on substituting other ingredients that would produce a similar flavor. He could be on to something." Victoria held her hands up as if she were about to cast a spell. "It might be perfectly magical." Then she flitted off to visit with the other guests.

The party lasted later than Alice and her sisters had expected. It was past midnight before the remaining guests, the lively Fred and Ginger, made their exit.

"Oh my," said Jane, sinking into a chair and putting her ruby slippers on a footstool. "I am completely exhausted."

Louise removed her glittery crown and wig and sighed. "And I am ready to retire my crown for good."

"That was a great party," said Cynthia as she sank down onto the sofa. "You guys really know how to live."

Alice laughed and flopped down beside her.

"Did the Wicked Witch of the West already turn in?" asked Louise, glancing over her shoulder.

Cynthia nodded. "Yes, I warned her that I wanted to get an early start in the morning. I figured we could get a couple of hours in before church."

"And Harold called it a night too," said Alice. "I hope he didn't overtax himself."

"He looked as though he was having the time of his life," said Louise. "He was the hit of the party."

"I think Victoria's entrance was quite a hit too," said Alice. "Did you see the look on Aunt Ethel's face when she first came into the room?"

Cynthia nodded. "I thought poor Patsy Ley was going to faint."

"Talk about your drama queens," said Jane.

"She was a good sport," said Alice.

"Yes, she was," agreed Louise, "but I am not. My feet are aching from these pumps, and I am going to call it a night. I promise to rise early and help clean up in the morning."

"Yes," agreed Alice. "Let's *all* hit the hay."

Jane laughed. "Are you trying to make a joke, Scarecrow?"

Alice put on her Scarecrow voice. "Well, I would if I only had a brain."

"Oh, not again," said Jane groaning. "It's too late."

After turning off all the lights, the four of them went up the stairs softly humming "We're Off to See the Wizard."

Chapter Twenty-Eight

*A*lice awoke feeling strangely refreshed the next morning. She got up early and tiptoed downstairs and began picking up from last night's party. The house was quiet and still, and Alice was reminded of a time when it had nearly always been like this. When only she and Father lived there, the two of them would rattle around in this big old house. Would she return to those days if she could? Probably not, she thought as she threw another plastic punch cup into her trash bag. Living with her sisters and running the inn had become a wonderful way of life for her, and she did not want to give it up for anything.

"Alice." Jane had on her pale gray sweats and her hair tied back in a messy ponytail. "How long have you been up?"

"Longer than you," teased Alice. "It looks like you just crawled out of bed."

Jane gave a stretch. "I did."

"There's coffee in the kitchen."

"You're a saint."

Alice just shook her head. "If only sainthood came so easily."

"It looks like you've just about got everything cleaned up."

"I figured I should, since I wasn't much use in getting things ready yesterday."

"Oh, there really wasn't that much," said Jane. "Especially after we'd gotten most of the food and stuff prepared ahead of time."

Alice picked up a few more things and then joined her sister in the kitchen.

"I put the teakettle on," said Jane as she sliced up a long loaf of French bread. "I think it's almost hot."

"Making French toast?" asked Alice when she noticed the eggs and cream nearby.

Jane nodded. "I thought I'd keep it simple."

"Sounds good to me."

"Hello," said Louise as she came into the kitchen. "It looks like the Brownies have already been here."

Alice laughed. "Do you remember when Mother used to say that after we'd try to surprise her by doing something?"

Louise nodded as she poured herself a cup of coffee. "And we would play right along."

All three sisters worked together to fix breakfast, and it was not long before the table was set and the others were joining them.

"How's the dog, Victoria?" asked Jane as she set a large bowl of homemade applesauce on the table.

"Zipper is doing fine," said Victoria as she poured herself a cup of coffee. "He ate the scraps that you gave me and even made an attempt to stand up on his own, but I think the leg still hurts too much. I carried him outside so that he could relieve himself."

"That's one lucky dog," said Harold as he set down the newspaper. Of course, everyone had heard the story by this time.

"I'll say," said Victoria. "If Alice and I had left just a couple minutes sooner, poor Zipper would probably be history now."

"There is a pet supply store in Potterston," said Alice. "It doesn't open until after noon on Sundays, but you could find some things for Zipper there."

"That's a good idea," said Victoria. "Perhaps Cynthia will let me take a little break and drive me over there."

Cynthia just shrugged. "Probably won't make a difference anyway."

"Is someone feeling discouraged?" asked Victoria in a slightly placating tone.

Cynthia held up her hands. "It just seems like we keep taking two steps forward and one step back. We only have three more days until our deadline."

Victoria frowned now. "Is that all?"

"That's all."

"Did you see the children's books that Vera dropped off?" asked Alice hopefully.

"I glanced at a few of them yesterday."

"Any inspirations?" asked Cynthia.

Victoria shook her head. "Not really."

Then Alice thought of something. "Of course, I don't really know much about publishing, but I do recall reading something once about the art of writing."

"Yes?" said Cynthia eagerly.

"Aren't writers supposed to write about what they know?"

Cynthia rolled her eyes. "Yes. That's usually the best route."

"Well, it just hit me that Victoria has a really wonderful animal story that actually happened to her as a little girl. Remember what you told me yesterday, Victoria?"

Now Victoria's eyes lit up. "Do you think?"

Alice nodded. "It was a lovely story."

"What?" demanded Cynthia. "What is it? Tell me, Victoria."

Victoria smiled. "Now, just hold your horses, Cynthia. I'm sure that the whole table isn't interested in my childhood memory."

"*Au contraire*," said Jane as she sat back down at the table. "I'm interested."

"As am I," said Louise.

"I'd love to hear it," agreed Harold.

Now Victoria clasped her hands together as she looked around the table at her captive audience. "Well, then." Once again, Victoria related the story. This time she gave more details, and sensing that her listeners were interested, she added drama. Finally, she ended it by telling of her grandmother's knitting the little blue sweater.

Cynthia's face lit up. "I think we may have something here."

"Really?" Victoria seemed hopeful.

"Really." Cynthia pushed away her unfinished breakfast plate. "If you'll excuse me, I'd like to go start putting that in my computer. Just the bare bones, mind you. We'll flesh it out."

"Wonderful," said Victoria with a satisfied sigh.

"That's a great story," said Jane as she refilled Victoria's coffee cup.

"I thought so too," said Alice.

"I wonder," said Victoria. "Do you think there might be some way of tying Zipper's story into it?"

Jane frowned. "I'm no expert," she said, "but I think the story would have more impact if it was about rescuing one dog."

"Perhaps you could have a special section in the back of the book," suggested Alice, "making mention of how you rescued Zipper and that reminded you of when you were a little girl."

"That's an excellent idea," said Louise. "Maybe someone should be taking notes for Cynthia."

They sat around the dining room table, with Alice taking notes, as they did a little brainstorming for Victoria's book. Even Harold had a few ideas.

"Oh, this is really good," said Victoria as she stood up and reached for Alice's notes. "I can't wait to tell Cynthia our ideas."

Cynthia and Victoria became deeply involved in their efforts. Alice noticed that they were even later than the previous week in coming to church. Once again, they slipped into a rear pew, and to Alice's surprise, Victoria was treated less as a celebrity when the service was over.

"Looks like the locals are getting used to seeing her around," said Jane, nodding over to where only Patsy Ley was politely conversing with Victoria. Then Alice and Jane went over to ask how the book was progressing.

"It's amazing," said Cynthia. "Everything is just falling into place. I love Aunt Alice's idea about including something about the greyhound rescue in the back."

"Yes," said Victoria enthusiastically. "Cynthia has even suggested doing a photo shoot with me and my dogs."

"That would be a nice touch," said Jane.

"Speaking of dogs," said Alice, "would you like me to pick up some things for Zipper this afternoon? I thought it might be helpful since it seems like you and Cynthia have finally gotten on track."

"That'd be great," said Cynthia. "It really does feel like we're making progress. In fact, it was going so well that I was even tempted to skip church this morning. Then I remembered how you'd been praying that we'd come up with something, and I thought it would be ungrateful to bail out on God like that."

Alice laughed. "I don't think God would think you were bailing out on Him. Still, I'm glad you both came."

Then Victoria rattled off the things she thought that Zipper might need from the pet store.

"I'll head right over," said Alice as she buttoned up her coat.

"Need any company?" offered Jane.

They stopped at the inn to pick up Alice's car, but since it was not quite noon, they decided to drop by the Coffee Shop. As they were about to enter, Alice heard someone calling her name. She turned to see Carlene Moss hurrying down the street toward them.

"Have you got a minute, Alice?" she called out breathlessly.

"Of course."

"I thought you might enjoy hearing the latest news," Carlene said.

"What's that?"

"Well, remember there were a number of high school kids at your demonstration yesterday?"

"Yes, but it wasn't really my demonstration," said Alice.

Carlene smiled. "Yes, I know, but anyway it seems that some of the protesters from yesterday's march are going to organize a greyhound adoption group. I had a message on my voice mail this morning asking if I would cover the story in the *Acorn Nutshell* this week. Apparently there were two teenage boys who helped you and Victoria with that greyhound yesterday, and they were so impressed with your saving that dog that they want to do more of the same."

"That's fantastic!" Alice clapped her hands with enthusiasm.

Carlene nodded. "Not only that, but a dog owner called. He wanted to go on record that there were many caring dog owners and that they were all in favor of regulations to protect the dogs. Anyway, I'd like to get some quotes from you and from Victoria, and maybe a photo of the dog. Do you think you could call me later today or tomorrow?"

"Of course. You know that I'd be happy to do anything to help this cause."

Carlene patted Alice on the back. "You've already done a lot, Alice. You got the ball rolling and that's a lot more than anyone else was doing."

"How nice that the local teens want to join the cause," said Jane. "I'll bet they can really generate enthusiasm."

"Thanks for telling us," said Alice. "I'll pass the information along to Victoria."

"Be in touch," said Carlene as she headed across the street.

"Isn't that wonderful," said Alice as she pushed open the door to the Coffee Shop.

"It's great." Jane sniffed the air. "*Hmmm*. I haven't had a slice of blackberry pie in ages."

Alice laughed. "Do you really think we should? After all, we had French toast for breakfast."

"That was breakfast," said Jane with a grin. "It's lunchtime now."

"So it is," said Alice as they sat down at the counter.

"Hey, you two," said Hope. "That was quite a party last night."

"I liked your Mary Poppins outfit," said Alice. "Very clever."

"And your rendition of 'A Spoonful of Sugar' wasn't bad either," added Jane.

"I think you should have a party like that at least once a year," said Hope as she set two water glasses in front of them.

"We'd have to talk Harold into coming back," said Jane.

"I overheard him telling Viola Reed that he was considering buying a place and moving here permanently," Hope told them.

"Wouldn't that be nice," said Alice.

"We're both having pie," said Jane with a slightly guilty expression.

"Blackberry?" asked Hope.

Alice and Jane both nodded.

"À la mode?"

They exchanged glances, and then nodded again.

"Some things never change," said Hope with a grin.

Chapter Twenty-Nine

*V*ictoria's book was finished by Monday afternoon. In celebration, Jane fixed a special dinner.

"It's completely edited and on its way," announced Cynthia at dinner. "My boss will have it on his desk tomorrow."

"Signed, sealed and delivered," said Victoria.

"Congratulations to you both," said Harold, holding up his water glass in a toast. "Here's to its becoming a classic."

Everyone else raised their glass with him.

"And to touching the hearts of children," added Alice.

"And to selling a million copies," said Jane.

As they were sitting around the table after dinner, Harold also announced that he, like Cynthia and Victoria, would be checking out the next day.

"It's been a delightful time," he told them, "but I fear I've overstayed my welcome."

Naturally, they all protested that this was not true.

"Oh, I'm sure Louise will be happy to have her piano all to herself." He winked at her.

Louise shook her head. "The truth is I have begun to develop an appreciation for music other than the classics. Just seeing what a good time everyone had on Saturday night reminded me that sometimes we need a change of pace."

"Here, here," said Jane.

"We've heard a rumor," Alice said to Harold. "Is it true that you're thinking of moving to Acorn Hill?"

He laughed. "Well, I don't know. I'll have to go home and see how I like it there. You ladies have all given me hope that there is life beyond what I've been living. I'll see how it goes in Philadelphia, and if I don't like it there, well, you just never know. One thing you can count on," he smiled at all of them, "I do plan to come back to visit."

"Oh good," said Jane. "Our friends are already making plans for next year's show-tunes party. Sylvia said that she's had several people in her shop talking about what kinds of costumes they'd like her to help them with for next year."

"That reminds me," said Harold. "I wanted to leave my costume for your mayor. He thought perhaps he could use it for the Fourth of July."

Jane laughed. "I can just see Lloyd wearing something like that."

"Maybe Aunt Ethel will want to have one made to match," said Alice.

"Speaking of Lloyd and Aunt Ethel," said Louise, "have you heard the latest?"

"Oh dear," said Alice. "What's wrong now?"

"Nothing's wrong," said Louise. "After Saturday's party, Aunt Ethel talked Lloyd into giving up bowling."

"Really?" Jane looked disappointed. "I thought it was sort of cool that he'd turned into a bowler."

"Well, apparently he has not been doing too well at it," continued Louise, "and Aunt Ethel has convinced him that the two of them should take tap-dancing lessons together."

"Tap-dancing lessons," repeated Victoria. "How interesting."

"Where will they do that?" asked Alice.

"I believe that the Potterston senior center offers a class."

"Fred and Ginger," said Jane. "Now if Aunt Ethel could only learn how to carry a tune."

"*Whoa*, is that ever the pot calling the kettle black, Aunt Jane," said Cynthia.

They all laughed as Alice and Jane began to clear away the dishes.

Chapter Thirty

"It is nice and quiet around here," said Alice as she and her two sisters sat in the sunroom and watched the snowflakes falling from the pewter-colored sky. It was Alice's first day off since their three guests had left.

Jane took a sip of cocoa and sighed. "Yes, it is rather nice, after all."

"Oh?" Louise's brow lifted slightly. "Did I hear my youngest sister admitting that she sometimes enjoys a little peace and quiet?"

Jane smiled. "I suppose so."

"It was sort of fun having all that activity too," said Alice. Wendell purred as she ran her hand down his thick winter coat. "Still, I do enjoy a little bit of winter quiet."

Louise sighed. "Especially on days like this."

"It looks like there's almost two inches of snow now," said Jane as she refilled their cocoa cups.

"And two more expected before nightfall," said Alice.

"Cynthia called this morning," said Louise. "She said that the publisher loves Victoria's book."

"That's wonderful," said Alice. "Did she say how their trip home went? Was the dog okay?"

"Sounded like it went fine," said Louise.

"He seemed like a sweet dog," said Jane, "but I'll bet he'll be a handful once he starts feeling better."

"Well, Victoria has lots of space for dogs who like to run," said Alice. "Not only that, but she told me she had a professional trainer work with her other dogs and she plans to get him for Zipper as well."

"Imagine," said Jane. "Having that much money."

"Money doesn't buy happiness, Jane," said Louise.

"If I were in Victoria's shoes," said Jane, "I'm sure that I would be happy as a clam."

"Don't be so sure," said Alice. "Victoria's life hasn't been nearly as charmed as she lets people believe."

"What?" said Jane with curiosity. "Did she tell you something?"

Alice just shook her head. "I'm only saying that things aren't always what they seem. It's possible that someone like Victoria would like to trade places with someone like you, Jane."

Jane waved her hand. "Oh yeah, sure."

"Are you saying that you do not have a good life?" asked Louise.

"No, not at all," said Jane as she took another piece of banana nut bread from the plate and pulled up the red plaid throw more snugly around her legs. "I love my life."

Alice smiled and leaned back in her chair contentedly. "So do I."

Louise nodded. "It is nice, isn't it?"

They sat quietly for a while, just soaking in the silence and the pristine white beauty of the snow blanketing all around the sunroom. Alice watched as the bare branches of the maple tree became dusted with a coating of white.

"Oh my goodness," said Louise, reaching into her skirt pocket. "I almost forgot, Jane. There was a card for you in the mail today. I did not mean to snoop, but it looks as if it is from Victoria."

"You're kidding," said Jane as she eagerly reached for the envelope. "Victoria actually wrote something to me?" She examined the exterior of the pale green envelope with suspicion. "Maybe it's a recipe for the *proper* way to prepare a crown roast."

Louise and Alice waited as she carefully tore open the envelope and extracted a pretty note card with a pressed flower on the front.

"What does it say?" Louise demanded finally.

"Yes," said Alice as she tried to read Jane's expression, "don't keep us in suspense."

"Shall I read it aloud?"

"Please," urged Alice.

"Okay." Jane looked as if she was suppressing a smile.

Dear Jane,

I wanted to take a moment from my busy schedule to thank you for being such an exemplary hostess and chef during my stay at your family's inn. Although I may not have mentioned it, I found your cooking to be some of the finest I have had the pleasure to enjoy. You see, I have learned over the years to be sparing in my compliments in the areas of cooking and homemaking because I am so often accosted by people who hope to be invited to make an appearance on my show. But I do not fear that will be the case with you.

Jane stopped reading and giggled.

"*And?*" queried Louise. "Is that all?"

"Not quite."

Louise and Alice both watched their younger sister, waiting for her to continue.

Jane continued in a Victoria-like voice.

And because I feel so comfortable with you and your sisters and in your lovely inn, I am certain that I shall be making it one of my regular getaway spots in the future.

Louise's eyebrow arched. "Seriously?"

"That's what it says," said Jane. "And it is signed, 'Fondly, Victoria.'"

"Oh my," said Alice, "how do you feel about her visiting again?"

Jane replaced the note card in its envelope. "Well, I should have known that God wasn't finished with me yet."

"Oh, *Jane*," said Louise.

Alice laughed. "I think we can all be very thankful that God is never finished with any of us."

"More cocoa?" offered Jane with a small smile.

"Thanks," said Alice.

Louise sighed. "I just love the quiet wonders of a snowy, winter day."

Tomato Bisque
SERVES SIX

3 tablespoons butter

1 medium onion, coarsely chopped

2 tablespoons all-purpose flour

2 cups water

4 pounds tomatoes, peeled,
   seeded and cut into pieces

2 tablespoons light brown sugar

6 whole cloves

1 teaspoon salt

Freshly ground black pepper

1 cup light cream or whipping cream

Over medium heat, melt the butter in a large saucepan. Add the onion and stir until onion is tender. Sprinkle in flour and continue stirring until mixture foams. Stir in water and bring to a boil. Measure out ¾ cup of the tomato pieces and set aside for later. Add the remaining tomato pieces to the boiling mixture. Stir in the brown sugar and cloves. Reduce the heat and simmer, uncovered, for thirty minutes.

Transfer to a sieve and pass the mixture through. Return to the saucepan and stir in the remaining ¾ cup of tomato pieces. Blend in the salt, pepper and cream. Place over medium heat and warm gently, but do not boil. Serve immediately.

About the Author

*M*elody Carlson is the award-winning author of more than 200 books for women, teens, and children. She has two grown sons and a granddaughter and lives in central Oregon with her husband and chocolate lab.

Tales from Grace Chapel Inn

Once you visit the charming village of Acorn Hill, you'll never want to leave. Here, the three Howard sisters reunite after their father's death and turn the family home into a bed-and-breakfast. They rekindle old memories, rediscover the bonds of sisterhood, revel in the blessings of friendship and meet many fascinating guests along the way.